D0950054

Dedicated, with gratitude and respect, to the memory of the great many doctors, mental health nurses and health-care assistants who lost their lives to Covid-19.

You only tell the truth when you're
wearing a mask.

BOB DYLAN

I was on my way to scrounge some tobacco from Lucy, who I sometimes call L-Plate, and is probably the poshest person I've ever met – who doesn't like anyone touching her and thinks the world is flat – when I heard it all kicking off in the little room next to the canteen. The room with the yellow wallpaper and the settee. The 'music' room, because there's some dusty bongos on a shelf and a guitar with four strings.

I could still smell that watery curry Eileen had done for lunch.

I'd eaten it all, don't get me wrong. Two plates full, because I've always had a big appetite and you eat what's put in front of you, but the whiff of it an hour or so afterwards was making me feel slightly sick. Yeah, I remember that. Mind you, lots of things make me feel a bit green around the gills these days and it's not like this place ever smells particularly lovely, let's be honest.

So … I was bowling down the corridor, trying not to think about the smell and gasping for a fag, when I heard all the shouting.

Swearing and screaming, stuff being chucked about, all that.

This was a Wednesday afternoon, two days before they found the body.

The sound really echoes in here, so I didn't think too much about it to begin with. It's not like I haven't seen people lose it before, so I thought it might just be a row that sounded a lot worse than it was and it wasn't until I actually got to the doorway and saw how full-on things were that I knew I was going to have to do something about it. That I needed to step in.

I'm an idiot. *Three* days before they found the body. Three ...

It was a proper scrum in there. A couple of people were watching – one bloke I don't know very well was actually clapping, like he thought it was some kind of special entertainment that had been laid on – but everyone else was grabbing and grunting, lurching around the room and knocking furniture over. Watching from the doorway, I couldn't really tell who was doing the fighting and who was trying to stop the people who were doing the fighting. It was too late to work out what had started it, but I guessed it didn't really matter by then and had probably never mattered much to begin with.

It doesn't take much round here.

Half a dozen of them tangled up, scratching or pulling hair and calling each other all sorts. A *mêlée*, that's the word, right? French, for a bunch of bad-tempered twats making idiots of themselves.

Wrestling and cursing, spitting threats.

The Waiter, he was there, and the Somali woman who likes touching people's feet was getting properly stuck in, which was amazing as she's about five foot nothing and skinny as a stick. Ilias was throwing his considerable weight about as was Lauren, while Donna and Big Gay Bob wriggled and squealed. And The Thing was there, obviously ... he was right in the thick of it, kicking a chair over then trying to swing a punch at Kevin, who was backed up against a wall, while somebody else whose face I couldn't see beneath their hoodie was hanging on to The Thing's arm for dear life.

I mean, Christ on a bike.

I wasn't remotely surprised that none of the people who get paid to sort out stuff like this were in much of a hurry. They've seen it all before, that's the truth. What I'm saying is, I couldn't just hang about waiting for one of that lot to get their arse in gear and put a stop to it. Besides, I'd broken up plenty of rucks in my time, so it wasn't a big deal. I've been trained for it, haven't I?

Bloody hell, Al . . . get a grip. Getting the facts straight is important, right? Something else I've been trained for.

The *first* body. The first of the bodies.

It was obvious pretty quickly after I'd steamed in that I wasn't really making a lot of difference, that I wasn't going to be able to do much physically. To be fair though, I didn't have my equipment – baton, pepper spray, taser, what have you – so I wasn't going to give myself a hard time about it. In the end, the only thing I could do was climb on to one of the few chairs that was still the right way up, take a breath and scream louder than anyone else until I had their attention.

Well, most of them at least, though a few were still muttering.

'I'm going to give you one chance to break this up before things get serious, all right?' I left a little pause then, for what I'd said to sink in, because I've always thought that's effective. Makes them think a bit. 'So, do yourselves a favour and stop playing silly buggers.' A good hard look after that, at each and every one of them. 'Do you understand what I'm saying? I'm not messing around, here. This is a public order offence and I am a police officer . . .'

And I have to say, that did the trick, though watching some of them put the furniture back where it belonged while the others drifted back out into the corridor, I can't say I felt particularly proud of myself. Like, I wasn't exactly happy about it. I knew even then that, later on, crying myself to sleep, I'd be thinking about why they'd done what I wanted.

Not because I'd made anyone see sense or frightened them.

Not because I had any kind of authority.

Truth was, they just couldn't be bothered fighting any more because they were all too busy laughing.

PART ONE

SUDDEN OR SUSPICIOUS

ONE

In the interests of getting the key information across as efficiently as possible, as well as jazzing the story up a tad, I've decided to pretend this is a job interview. I think I can still remember what one of those is like. So, imagine that I'm dressed up to the nines, selling myself to you in pursuit of some once-in-a-lifetime career opportunity, and not just mooching about in a nuthouse, wearing tracksuit bottoms and slippers, like some saddo. Right, *nuthouse*. Probably not the most politically correct terminology, I accept that, even though it's what the people in here call it.

So . . .

Acute. Psychiatric. Ward.

That better? Can we crack on? Last thing I want to do is offend anyone's delicate sensibilities.

My name is Alice Frances Armitage. Al, sometimes. I am thirty-one years old. Average height, average weight – though I'm a bit skinnier than usual right this minute – average . . .

everything. I'm a dirty-blonde, curly-haired northerner –
Huddersfield, if you're interested – something of a gobshite
if my mother is to be believed, and up until several months
ago I was a detective constable in north London with one of
the Metropolitan Police's homicide units.

To all intents and purposes, I still am.

By which I mean it's something of a moot point.

By which I mean it's . . . complicated.

The Met were very understanding about the PTSD. I
mean, they have to be, considering it's more or less an occupational hazard, but they were a little less sympathetic once
the drink and drugs kicked in, despite the fact that they only
kicked in at all because of the aforementioned trauma. See
how tricky this is? The so-called 'psychosis' is a little harder
to pin down in terms of the chronology. It's all a bit . . .
chicken and egg. No, I'm not daft enough to think the wine
and the weed did a lot to help matters, but I'm positive that
most of the strange stuff in my head was/is trauma-related
and it's far too easy to put what happened down to external
and self-inflicted influences.

In a nutshell, you can't blame it all on Merlot and skunk.

Very easy for the Met though, obviously, because that
was when the sympathy and understanding went out of the
window and a period of paid compassionate leave became
something very different. I'm fighting it, of course, and my
Federation rep thinks I've got an excellent chance of re-
instatement once I'm out of here. Not to mention a strong
case for unfair dismissal and a claim for loss of earnings that
he's bang up for chasing.

So, let The Thing and the rest of them take the piss
all they like. I might not have my warrant card to hand

at the moment, but, as far as I'm concerned, I am still a police officer.

I think I'll knock the job-interview angle on the head now. I can't really be bothered keeping it up, besides which I'm not sure the drink and drugs stuff would be going down too well in an interview anyway and the work experience does come to something of an abrupt halt.

So, Miss Armitage, what happened in January? You don't appear to have worked at all after that ...

Yeah, there are some things I would definitely be leaving out, like the whole assault thing, and, to be fair, *Detained under Sections 2 and 3 of the Mental Health Act, 1983* doesn't tend to look awfully good on a CV.

Actually, limited job opportunities aside, there's all sorts of stuff that gets a bit more complicated once you've been sectioned, certainly after a 'three'. Everything changes, basically. You can choose not to tell people and I mean most people do, for obvious reasons, but it's all there on your records. Your time in the bin, every nasty little detail laid bare at the click of a mouse. Insurance for a start: that's a bloody nightmare afterwards and travelling anywhere is a whole lot more hassle. There are some places that really don't want you popping over for a holiday, America for one, which is pretty bloody ironic really, considering who they used to have running the place.

It's the way things work, I get that, but still.

You're struggling with shit, so you get help – whether you asked for it or not – you recover, to one degree or another, then you have loads more shit to deal with once you're back in the real world. It's no wonder so many people end up in places like this time and time again.

There's no stigma when you're all in the same boat.

Anyway, that's probably as much as you need to know for now. That's the what-do-you-call-it, the *context*. There's plenty more to come, obviously, and even though I've mentioned a few characters already, there's loads you still need to know about each of them and about everything that happened. I'll try not to leave anything important out, but a lot of it will depend on how I'm doing on a particular day and whether the most recent meds have kicked in or are just starting to wear off.

You'll have to bear with me, is what I'm saying.

Difficult to believe, some of it, I can promise you that, but not once you know what it's like in here. Certainly not when you're dealing with it every minute. When you know the people and what they're capable of on a bad day, it's really not surprising at all. To be honest, what's surprising is that stuff like this doesn't happen more often.

I remember talking to The Thing about it one morning at the meds hatch and that's pretty much what we were saying. You take a bunch of people who are all going through the worst time in their life, who are prone to mood swings like you wouldn't believe and are all capable of kicking off at a moment's notice. Who see and hear things that aren't real. Who are paranoid or delusional or more often both, and are seriously unpredictable even when they're drugged off their tits. Who are *angry* or *jumpy* or *nervy* or any of the other seven dwarves of lunacy that knock around in here twenty-four hours a day. You take those people and lock them all up together and it's like you're asking for trouble, wouldn't you say?

A good day is when something awful *doesn't* happen.

A murder isn't really anything to write home about in a place like this, not when you think about it. It's almost inevitable, I reckon, like the noise and the smell. You ask me, a murder's par for the course.

Even two of them.

TWO

I know they found Kevin's body on the Saturday because it was the day after my tribunal and that was definitely the day before. Official stuff like that never happens on a weekend, because the doctors and therapists aren't around then and certainly not any solicitors. They're strictly Monday to Friday, nine to five, which is a bit odd, considering that the weekends are probably the most difficult time around here and you'd think a few *more* staff might be a good idea. Saturdays and Sundays are when reality – or as close to it as some people in here ever get – tends to hit home. When the patients realise what they're missing, when they get even more bored than usual, which often means trouble.

The Weekend Wobble, that's what Marcus calls it.

Again, in the interests of accuracy, I should say it was actually my second tribunal. I'd already been through one when I was first brought into the unit on a Section Two. That's when they can keep you for up to twenty-eight days,

12

when theoretically you're there to be assessed, and obviously I wasn't remotely happy about the situation, so I applied for a tribunal as soon as I could. Why wouldn't you, right? No joy that time, though, and a fortnight later, after a couple of unsavoury incidents which aren't really relevant, my Section Two became a Section Three.

A 'three' is a treatment order that means they can keep you for up to six months, because they think you're a risk to yourself or others, so you won't be very surprised to hear I got another tribunal application in before you could say 'anti-psychotic'. Trust me, I was knocking on the door of the nurses' office before they'd finished the admission paperwork.

Whatever else happens in here, you should never forget you have *rights*.

My mum and dad wanted to come down for this one, to support me, they said, but I knocked that idea on the head straight away because they'd made no secret of the fact they thought this was where I should be. That it was *all for the best*. To be honest, apart from the solicitor – who I'd spoken to for all of ten minutes – I didn't really have *anyone* fighting my corner, but you certainly don't want your own nearest and dearest agreeing with the people who are trying to keep you locked up.

I might not be well, I'll grant you that, but I'm not mental.

So, it was the usual suspects: a table and two rows of plastic chairs in the MDR (Multi-Discipline Room) at the end of the main corridor.

Marcus the ward manager and one of the other nurses.

Dr Bakshi, the consultant psych, and one of her juniors, whose name I forgot straight away.

A so-called lay person – a middle-aged bloke who smiled a lot, but was probably just some busybody with nothing better to do – and a judge who looked like she'd sucked a lemon or had the rough end of a pineapple shoved up her arse. Or both.

Me and my solicitor, Simon.

To begin with, I thought it was going pretty well. There was a lot of positive-looking nodding when I made my statement, at any rate. I told them I'd been there six weeks already, which was longer than anyone else except Lauren. Actually, I think Ilias *might* have been there a bit longer than me … I've got a vague memory of him being around the night I was admitted, but those first few days are a bit of a blur.

It doesn't matter …

I told them I thought I was doing well, that the meds were really working and that I wasn't thinking any of the ridiculous things I'd been thinking when I first arrived. I told them I felt like I was *me* again. Marcus and the other nurse said that was very encouraging to hear and told the judge I was responding well to treatment. That sounded good at the time, but looking back of course, what it really meant was: so *more* treatment is definitely a good idea.

You live and learn, right?

Even then, I still felt like I was in with a chance, until they read out an email from Andy. I'll have a lot more to say about him later on, but all you need to know for the moment is that Andy's the bloke I'd been in a relationship with until six weeks earlier, when I'd smashed him over the head with a wine bottle.

He was worried about me, that was the gist of his email. He wanted the doctors and the judge to know how very concerned he was, following a phone conversation with me a few nights before, when I had allegedly told him I still suspected he was not who he said he was. When I got hysterical and said that I wouldn't hesitate to hurt him if I needed to defend myself against him or any of the others.

She still believes all that rubbish, he said, the conspiracy stuff.

She threatened me.

There was a bit of shouting after that was read out, I can tell you. Crying and shouting and I might have kicked my chair over. While the judge was telling me to calm down, I was telling *her* that Andy was full of it, that I'd never said any such thing and that he was gaslighting me like he always did. Making it all up because of what had happened the last time I'd seen him.

The bottle, all that.

Anyway, to cut a long tribunal short, I walked out after that and it wasn't until about twenty minutes later that Simon found me and told me the decision. They would send it in writing within a few days, he said, along with information about when I could apply again, but I'd already decided that I wouldn't bother. Nobody enjoys repeatedly banging their head against a wall, do they? Well, except Graham, who likes it so much that he has a permanent dent in his forehead and they have to keep repainting his favourite bit of wall to get the blood off.

That afternoon, after the tribunal, when I'd calmed down a bit and had some lunch, I was sitting with Ilias in the music room. I was wearing my headphones even though I wasn't actually listening to anything. Sometimes I am, but if I'm honest, most of the time the cable just runs into my pocket. It's a good way to avoid having to talk to people.

Ilias waved because he had something to say so I sighed and took the headphones off. Waited.

'I'm glad you're staying,' he said.

'*I'm* fucking not,' I said.

Someone started shouting a few rooms down, something about money they'd had stolen. Ilias and I listened for a minute, then lost interest.

'Do you want to play chess?'

I told him I didn't, same as I always do. I've never seen Ilias play chess and I'm not convinced he knows how. I've never even seen a chess set in here, although there are some jigsaws in a cupboard.

'What day is it?' Ilias asked.

'Friday,' I said.

'It's Saturday tomorrow.' No flies on Ilias. 'Saturday, then Sunday.' Just a nasty rash on his neck. 'Saturdays are rubbish, aren't they?'

I couldn't disagree with him, though the truth is I was never a big fan of the weekend in any case. All that pressure to relax and enjoy yourself. That was if you *had* a weekend. Criminals don't tend to take the weekend off, the opposite if anything, so working as a copper never really gave me much time to go to car-boot sales or pop to the garden centre anyway. One of the things I liked about the job.

'Boring. Saturdays are so *boring*.'

Like I said before . . .

'They last so much longer than all the other days and nothing interesting ever happens.' Ilias looked sad. 'I don't mean like fights or whatever, because they're boring, too. I mean, something really interesting.'

Remember what I said about memory? What I might and

might not have done? I can't swear to it, but I really hope that, just before Ilias broke wind as noisily as ever before wandering away to see if anyone else fancied playing chess, I said, 'Careful what you wish for.'

THREE

The alarm goes off in this place a couple of times a week, more if it's a full moon, so it's not like it's that big a deal. Yeah, the nurses snap to it fast enough, but the patients don't rush around panicking or anything like that. Mostly you just carry on chatting shit – albeit a bit louder – or eating your tea or whatever until it stops. But this time there was a scream first, so it was pretty obvious something bad had happened.

Debbie, the nurse who found the body, has got quite a gob on her.

This was the Saturday night, just before eleven o'clock, and most people were already in bed. I was sitting with Shaun and The Thing in the canteen – which in a pointless attempt to sound a bit more upmarket is officially called the *dining room* – just letting the last meal of the day go down a bit and talking about nothing.

Music probably, or telly. Bitching about the fact that Lauren never lets anyone else get hold of the TV remote.

When we walked out into the hall, we could see Debbie running from the corridor where the men's bedrooms are, so that's when I knew it was her who had done the screaming and most likely her that had sounded the alarm. All the staff have personal alarms attached to their belts and, if they press them, it makes the big alarm go off all over the unit. I remember a patient getting hold of one once and hiding it, then pressing it when he was bored and causing mayhem for days.

Anyway, Debbie looked seriously upset.

The three of us stood and watched as George and Femi came tearing out of the nurses' station, and even though Debbie was trying to be professional and keeping her voice down when she spoke to them, once the alarm had stopped we all heard her say Kevin's name and the look on the other nurses' faces told us everything we needed to know.

'Fuck,' Shaun said. 'Oh, Christ, oh fuck.' He started scratching hard at his neck and chest, so I took hold of his arm and told him it was going to be all right.

'Maybe the Thing got him,' The Thing said.

I stepped away from them and moved as close as I could to where the nurses were huddled so as to try and hear a bit more, but George looked at me and shook his head. Then they all hurried back down the men's corridor, presumably heading for Kevin's room to take a look at what Debbie had found. A few minutes later, Debbie and Femi came back, grim-faced, and shortly after that George began herding those who had been in the other rooms on the men's corridor towards the lobby. Most of them stumbled along peacefully enough, bleary-eyed, one or two clutching their duvets around them. A few were shouting about being woken up and demanding to know what was going on.

'You can't make me leave my room.'

19

'I'm sorry, but—'

'It's my room.'

'There's been an incident—'

'I don't care.'

Once the bedrooms had been emptied – well, apart from Kevin's, because that poor soul wasn't going anywhere for the time being – George stood guard at the entrance to the corridor to make sure that nobody went back. He just stared and raised one of his big hands whenever anyone looked like they were about to. Under normal circumstances, that would probably have been Marcus's job as ward manager, but he doesn't work nights. I wondered if anyone had called him, if he was on his way in, but I don't remember seeing him until the next day.

'Where are we going to sleep?' Ilias asked. 'I'm tired.'

'We will get it all sorted out,' Femi said.

It was easier said than done, of course. With eight or nine blokes to find rooms for and no spare places on the female corridor – even as a temporary measure – it took some doing. Drugged up and sleepy as most of them were, nobody was very happy about the situation. Ilias and The Thing immediately volunteered to take the two 'seclusion' rooms and planted themselves outside the doors to make damn sure they got them. There happened to be a couple of empty rooms on the ward directly opposite this one and a few more on the floor below, though nobody was particularly keen on that, because by all accounts there's some hardcore head-cases down there. There wasn't much choice in the end and, except for a couple of the Informals who were collected by ambulance and taken to a nearby hospital, all the male patients were bedded down again by the time the police arrived.

That was the worst bit for me, the real kick in the teeth.

Shunted out of the way, like I was useless.

Like I was the same as the rest of them.

Even though it was the men's corridor where the 'incident' had taken place, the nurses made it clear straight away that they wanted all the female patients who weren't in bed already to return to their rooms.

I was wide awake, buzzing with it, but not being anything like ready for bed wasn't the most annoying thing. I marched straight up to Femi like she didn't know the rules. 'We don't have to be in bed until midnight.'

'I know,' she said. 'But this is not . . . normal. We need everyone in their rooms so that the police can do their job when they get here.'

'That's the point,' I said. 'I can help.' My fingers were itching to wrap themselves around a warrant card that wasn't there. 'I know how this works.'

Femi just nodded, flashed a thin smile, then placed a hand in the small of my back and pushed. I pushed back, but only because I was pissed off. I knew it was a waste of time, because I could already see Lauren and Donna and a few of the others who had been woken up by all the commotion drifting back towards their rooms.

'It's not fair,' I said.

'We have a protocol,' Femi said.

'When someone dies, you mean?'

Femi said nothing, just made sure I was moving in the right direction.

'Kevin is dead, isn't he?'

For obvious reasons, women are not allowed on the men's corridor and vice versa. For some of the same reasons they're not awfully keen on anyone going into anyone else's bedroom. I mean, privacy is important to everyone, I get that. That doesn't mean certain stuff doesn't happen between patients, because trust me, it certainly does. In plain sight, quite often, because I've seen them at it.

A quick hand-job in the corner of the music room.

A fumble in the bushes when patients are allowed outside.

Still, isn't it nice to know they have rules that are meant to prevent such terrible things?

I reckoned, though, that with everything that was happening on the ward that evening, and with coppers causing chaos all over the show, the staff would probably be way too busy to worry about an innocent spot of bedroom-hopping. So, half an hour after I'd been safely tucked up, I knocked quietly on a couple of doors and brought L-Plate and Donna back to my room to see what they made of it all.

'He killed himself, didn't he.' Donna wasn't asking a question.

'Most obvious explanation,' L-Plate said. She was sitting on the end of my bed brushing her hair, wearing expensive pyjamas with embroidered stars on them that her parents had brought her from home. 'I don't think he's been awfully happy lately.'

L-Plate's lovely, but even if you discount the heroin and the flat-Earth stuff, she's not the sharpest tool in the box. 'How many people in here are happy?' I asked.

'Well, yeah . . . but even less happy than usual.'

'Topped himself,' Donna said. 'Course he has.'

'How's he done that, then?' I stared around my room, a replica of the other nineteen on the ward. A single bed and a grimy window behind a rip-proof curtain. A chair made deliberately heavy so nobody can throw it. A wardrobe with three shelves and nothing you can hang anything from.

Least of all yourself.

'You want to do it bad enough, you find a way,' Donna said.

Donna, the Walker, who was here because she's threatened to do it countless times, who *has* been doing it for several years in one of the slowest and cruellest ways possible. I looked at her, perched on the chair that probably weighed three times what she did. Wrists that a baby could wrap its hands around and a collarbone knitting-needle-thin beneath her ratty pink dressing gown. 'Not sure I buy it,' I said.

Killing yourself in here is actually incredibly difficult and you won't be surprised to hear that's because it's supposed to be. If you're deemed to be at risk, then they tend to keep an eye on you, like *all the time*. Plus, you're permanently denied anything you might be able to hurt yourself with, and even when you first come in, when you're getting the measure of the place and the staff are getting the measure of *you*, they take away anything they class as risky.

That first night, once I'd stopped wailing and trying to kick whichever nurse was daft enough to get close, they took away all sorts.

My trainers (laces, right?).

My belt (OK).

Nail scissors (fair enough).

Tweezers (annoying).

A bra with under-wiring (taking the piss).

They confiscate your phone, too, and God knows how anyone is supposed to kill themselves with a Samsung. Maybe they're worried you might choke yourself with it, or call a hitman to come and do the job for you, but to be fair, unless there's some specific reason not to, they do give it back within a couple of days.

I mean, thank Christ, right?

If I wasn't allowed my phone, I think I might actually *want* to kill myself.

'So, what do you think happened, Al?' L-Plate asked.

I didn't tell her what I thought because, to be honest, I was scared as much as anything. I was excited, don't get me wrong, all those professional instincts starting to kick in, but I was ... wary. Right then, with a body cooling just yards away, it was no more than a feeling and I try to steer clear of those, with good reason. Eighteen months before, I'd had a feeling that the crack-head who'd invited us in to his flat on the Mile End Road was harmless. If it hadn't been for that, there wouldn't have been any PTSD or any need for the variety of things I poured and snorted and popped into my body to numb that pain. I would not have ended up thinking that the people I loved most in the world were trying to kill me or that strangers could read my mind. I would not have hurt anyone.

Looking at L-Plate, I could feel myself starting to shake a little. I tried to smile and shoved my hands beneath my thighs so she wouldn't see.

I said, 'I really don't know.'

It was a feeling that put me in here.

FOUR

Fleet Ward (home to yours truly for the time being) is located directly opposite Effra Ward, one of four acute psychiatric wards in the notably knackered and unattractive Shackleton Unit – the dedicated Mental Health Facility at Hendon Community Hospital. Fleet – don't ask me, the names are something to do with lost rivers of London – is a mixed ward that can take up to twenty-one patients at a push, but usually holds somewhere between fifteen to eighteen. Normally, there's more or less a fifty-fifty split between men and women, and around the same when it comes to the voluntary patients – the 'Informals' – and those who had no say-so in the matter.

Those of us who were dragged here, kicking and screaming.

Or were tricked into it.

Or don't even remember.

I don't tend to hang around much with the voluntary lot,

because there doesn't seem any point trying to get to know them. Most of the time, they're only in for a few days and some of them are only here at all because they're homeless and fancy a bed for a couple of nights and four meals a day. 'Revolving door' patients, that's what the nurses call them. In, out, then back in again, when they get fed up with cardboard mattresses and getting pissed on by arseholes in the middle of the night. When it all gets too much or there's a cold snap.

Fair play to them, they're probably every bit as messed up as the rest of us, but as far as the business with Kevin and everything that happened afterwards goes, they're not that important.

So, for now I'll stick to talking about those who were around at the time and, in most cases, still are. The strangest of the strangers who, ironically, stop me going mad. My fellow Fleet Ward Fuck-Ups. My best friends and, every now and again, worst enemies. My tribe ... my family.

This wild and wet-brained gang of giddy kippers I knock about with.

The *sectioned* ...

So, to coin a poncey phrase ... allow me to introduce the ladies and gentlemen of the chorus.

Blokes to begin with, I think, because there's a fair few to remember.

KEVIN. Well ... dead, obviously, but it doesn't seem right or kind that's *all* he is, or all you ever know about him. He was ten years younger than me and he supported West Ham, which was a shame, but there you go. He had 'issues', of course, and you can take it as read that everyone I'm going to describe has plenty, so I won't use that stupid word again. Kevin's were all about his parents, I think, but he never went into details. He was one of the friendliest in here. Too friendly sometimes, if I'm honest, meaning that certain people took advantage and he didn't really stand up for himself enough, which you've got to in this place. I think he was a skinhead before he came in and I remember how much he smiled when he showed me his tattoos. He had a lovely smile. I never found out how he ended up on Fleet Ward, what went on before he was sectioned, but I do know there'd been a lot of drugs, probably still were . . . well, you'll see.

He was fit, too, I don't mind telling you that.

GRAHAM, aka The Waiter. I should point out that nearly all these nicknames are ones I've come up with myself and most of the people concerned don't even know about them. I've always been rubbish at putting names with faces, so they helped me remember who was who early on, and now sometimes I use real names and sometimes the ones I've made up, depending on my mood or my memory, or how drugged up I am, which tends to affect both those things. This one isn't the most inspired nickname, I'm well aware of that, but it works. Graham doesn't bring people meals or carry drinks or anything like that. He's the *waiter* because he waits, simple as that. All the bloody time, *waiting*. You always know where Graham is, because once he's had his breakfast he'll be standing at the meds hatch, waiting for it to open. As soon as he's taken his meds, he'll be outside the dining room waiting for them to start dishing up lunch. Then back to the meds hatch, then the dining room, then the meds hatch again, same daft routine every day. You get used to seeing him, just standing there staring into space, always the first in line even if it's half an hour early. Once, when it had started to get on my tits a bit, I marched up to the meds hatch (which wasn't due to open for like an *hour*) and asked him what the hell he was standing there for, what the point was. He looked at me like I was an idiot and said, 'I don't like queuing.'

Graham is probably pushing fifty and always wears Fleet Ward's limited edition and stylish pale-blue pyjamas. He is very tall and very thin; a bit ... spidery. His face never changes much and he's not exactly chatty. In fact, that might have been one of the longest conversations I've ever had with him.

ILIAS, aka The Grand Master. The chess thing, right? Greek, I think, or maybe Turkish. Ilias is early thirties, I'm guessing ... dark and squat and properly hairy. I know that, because he's fond of walking about with his shirt off, and sometimes his pants, no matter how often the staff tell him it's not really appropriate. He can lose his temper at the slightest thing and when that happens it's like he really hates you, but ten minutes later he's crying and hugging you and, frankly, that can wind you up a bit. I'm talking about *massive* mood-swings, when you don't know whether you're coming or going. I'm no expert, but my guess is that he's a proper schizo; I mean like bipolar to the max. He certainly comes out with the weirdest shit of anyone here, just out of nowhere. Stuff that can make you fall about one minute, then something else that makes you feel like you need to stand under a hot shower for a while. I say that, but basically he's a big, stupid puppy most of the time and, if anyone was to ask, I'd still tell them Ilias was my mate and that I think he's probably harmless. Obviously, nobody in here is completely harmless, I mean tell that to Kevin, but you know what I'm saying, right?

He's harmless *enough*.

ROBERT, aka Big Gay Bob. Robert, who's, I don't know . . . forty? . . . isn't particularly big – he's actually a bit on the short side, and a lot on the bald side – and I have no evidence whatsoever that he is even remotely gay, but sometimes it's how things go. What everyone around here does know is that Bob talks about the women he's slept with constantly. I promise you, he's got shagging on the brain, and if you find yourself in a conversation with him – and he does like a chat – it'll end up on your brain, too. I swear, you could be talking to him about anything – football, steam engines, the fucking Holocaust – and he'd find some way to crowbar in a story about the things he once got up to with some 'pneumatic blonde' in a hotel room in Brighton or the 'foxy redhead' he got seriously fruity with in a pub car park in Leeds. I don't want you to think he's sleazy though, because he's really not. It's more comical than anything, actually, a bit . . . *Carry-On.* All that happened was that one of the women – maybe it was Lauren – pointed out that constantly banging on about your success with the opposite sex is a clear sign that you're actually preoccupied with your own. A closet-case or whatever. So, that was when the nickname first got thrown about for a laugh and it stuck. It's all a bit of fun and the truth is that Bob seems to like it, plays up to it even, as if he's secretly thrilled to have an . . . identity, you know?

And the truth is that, actually, he *is* rather camp.

*

SHAUN, aka The Sheep. Yeah, he's Welsh, so shoot me for being predictable, but it's actually a boss nickname because he's a ... follower, you know? Shaun's one of the younger ones and he's just a bit lost, I think, but the fact is he'll do pretty much anything anyone tells him to and believes whatever you say to him. Literally, anything. I'm secretly a multi-millionaire. I was on *Love Island*. You name it. Who knows if he was that gullible before whatever happened to him happened, but something's got messed up in his head and now it's like he's a blank page or just something that other people can twist and mould into whatever suits them.

The other thing you should know is that Shaun can be a bit needy. Almost every day, he'll come up to you more than once and point to some tiny blemish on his chin – a spot or whatever – and ask, 'Am I going to die, am I going to die, am I going to die?' Once he's been reassured that he's not likely to pop off any time soon he's right as ninepence, but half an hour later, he'll be panic-stricken and asking you again. I mean, my mum's a bit of a hypochondriac, but that's ridiculous.

He's not daft though, I really don't mean that, and he's probably the person I've had the nicest conversations with ... the most *normal* conversations. He's pretty bloody lovely as a matter of fact, but he was very angry for a while after what happened to Kevin. They were close, those two, I might as well tell you that. I'd thought they were just mates, until one lunchtime when I saw Shaun with his hand on Kevin's cock under the table in the dining room, so I suppose it's understandable that he was a bit upset. He hasn't stopped being upset, actually. He still cries, a lot.

*

TONY, aka The Thing. Now, the thing you need to remember about The Thing is that *he* isn't actually the Thing. He's just *called* The Thing because the Thing is the thing he's obsessed with. The Thing is what scares him to death twenty-four hours a day. The Thing is . . . his thing. You also need to bear in mind that Tony is what a lot of people would think of as seriously scary himself. He's a massive bloke from Croydon who looks like Anthony Joshua, if Anthony let himself go a bit. I'm telling you, he's built like a brick shithouse, but just the mention of the Thing . . . seriously, just one malicious whisper of the name . . . is enough to reduce him to a gibbering wreck. Screaming, trying to climb out of the nearest window, the full works. So . . . the Thing – according to the World of Tony – is an evil entity of some sort that, for reasons none of us can or particularly want to understand, is trying to kill him and – here's the crucial bit – has the special power to transform itself into anything it wants. Anything or anyone. The Thing could be me, then the next day it might be one of the staff. Or a dog, or a daddy-long-legs, or a pair of shoes. The Thing is a hugely powerful and endlessly cunning shape-shifter.

My ex-flatmate Sophie came in to visit me one day and found herself alone with Tony in the music room for a few minutes. To this day, I don't know what he said to upset her so much, but a few days later she sent him a postcard which read: *Dear Tony, it was lovely to meet you. Oh, and by the way, I have transformed myself into this postcard. Have a nice day. Lots of love, the Thing x*

Tony did not leave his room for almost a week afterwards.

FIVE

I can't say it was the most restful night's sleep I've ever had. I was far too excited by what was likely to be happening on the other side of the ward, though to be fair it probably had more to do with the fact that I'd set an alarm on my phone to wake me up every half an hour. I wanted to see what was going on.

Why wouldn't I?

I didn't want to miss anything.

The first time I crept out, Femi ushered me back to bed as soon as she saw me. I didn't make a fuss, just told her I needed the toilet on the way and, after lurking in the bog until I thought she'd probably got bored, I managed to sneak another few minutes before she collared me again.

Eyes like a hawk and ears like a bat, that one.

The corridor that Kevin's room was on had been cordoned off with crime-scene tape. Just seeing that familiar ribbon of blue and white plastic was a proper buzz. Made the butterflies start to flutter a little, you know? Kevin's room was at the far end, so I couldn't hear anything that was actually being said or see much beyond the odd figure wandering in and out of the bedroom in question, but that didn't matter. I knew what was going on, obviously. I knew what stage they were at.

A Homicide Assessment Team. Just a couple of officers, probably, there to examine the scene and try to establish whether or not a sudden death was actually a suspicious one. There to decide if they needed to bring in detectives, CSIs, all the rest of it.

There was a local uniform standing just in front of the cordon and I picked my moment to try and grab a few words. Femi had gone back to the nurses' station and from where I was standing I could see her and George drinking tea and talking to Debbie. Femi laid a hand on Debbie's shoulder as she was still clearly upset at finding the body. When I was sure they wouldn't see me, I darted across to see what I could get out of the uniform. Like a bloody ninja, I was.

'Oh,' he said. The poor lad had obviously been told that all the patients were safely tucked up out of the way and clearly hadn't got the foggiest what to do, confronted with me. He actually jumped a little and began looking around for help.

'What do you reckon?' I asked. 'The HAT team going to call it?'

'Sorry?'

'It's OK,' I said. 'I'm Job.'

He looked at me: nodding up at him, all business, in a ratty dressing gown and slippers. He said, 'Yeah, course you are,' then began waving over my head to try and attract the attention of someone in the nurses' station.

I could happily have slapped him, but I knew I wouldn't be doing myself any favours and I guessed I didn't have long.

I saw an officer stepping out of Kevin's room, so I raised a hand and shouted past the uniform.

'Tell Brian Holloway that Al says hello.'

My DCI. One of the decent ones. A good mate, as well.

The officer at the far end of the corridor glanced my way, ignored me, then stepped back into Kevin's bedroom. I don't really know what I was expecting, because Hendon isn't my team's area anyway, so I wasn't likely to know any of this lot and there was next to no chance they would know any of mine. It was annoying, all the same.

I turned back to the uniform. 'Holloway's my guvnor,' I said. 'We've worked a lot of cases together.'

Now, the bloke had his arms spread and his size tens firmly planted, like he was expecting me to bolt past him at any moment. He still hadn't got a clue what to do with me, that much was obvious, but before I could make things any harder for him Femi and George arrived to save his bacon, giving it 'Come on, Alice' and 'Back to bed, there's a good girl . . .'

I couldn't help but smile at the look of relief on the wood-entop's face as I trotted back towards my bedroom like a *very* good girl. I wasn't that bothered, because I already knew how things were going to pan out. The next steps on the investigation's *critical path*.

I'd taken those steps myself plenty of times.

They'd be bringing in the big guns soon enough, and I'd be there when they did.

Maybe being stuck in here's thrown my timing off a little, because an hour or so later – I'd decided to leave it a bit longer, in case Femi and the rest were keeping an eye out – when I snuck out of my bedroom again, things had moved a lot faster than I'd reckoned on. The most irritating thing was that I'd missed them taking Kevin's body away and that's not because I'm ghoulish or anything, but because that's a moment that counts for something as a copper. Should do, anyway. It's about paying the proper respect, besides which, as someone who'd cared about the victim – and I'd already decided that's what Kevin was – I had no way of knowing when or if any of us would get the chance to say a proper goodbye.

I'd wanted to be there when they carried that body bag out.

By now, the forensic bods were busy doing their thing, coming and going with toolkits and evidence bags, decked out in their plastic bodysuits and bootees, same as the detectives. It was easy to tell who was who though, because, as usual, the detectives were mostly standing around and nattering, looking uneasy, waiting for the CSIs to finish. I'd found a spot just inside the doorway of the dining room where I knew I couldn't be seen directly by anyone in the nurses' station and I watched one of the CSIs on their way out. I guessed all the emergency vehicles were parked outside the main entrance. I watched him – I think it was a him – signal to the nurses' station, then wait at the airlock for one of the staff to open up. A minute later, Malaika – one of the healthcare assistants – came running towards him brandishing the keys.

'Sorry,' she said.

'No rush,' the CSI said.

Not for poor bloody Kevin, at any rate.

For the half a minute or so the CSI was standing inside the airlock waiting to be let out the other side, it was like something out of a science-fiction film. I imagined he was an astronaut about to step into the blackness of space or on to the platform of an orbiting station, and not just that grim brown lobby and the stinky lift down to the car park. I remember thinking it would be fun to tell people that, wondering who would get the biggest kick out of it. I could probably convince Shaun that I *had* seen an astronaut, of course.

I was also wondering exactly what that CSI was carrying away in his Styrofoam evidence box; what they'd found in Kevin's bedroom. A weapon, maybe? Was there a lot of blood? Debbie had certainly screamed like she'd stumbled across something horrific, and, trust me, it takes a lot to give a mental-health nurse the heebie-jeebies.

A knife would have made sense, I decided. Easy enough to pinch one from the kitchen or even bring one in from the outside. Yes, they're supposed to search you if you've been out, but on the rare occasions they bother to pat anyone down, it's always a bit ... sloppy.

They're more hands-on at the average airport.

When I looked away from the airlock, I could see that one of the detectives was standing near the men's toilet staring at me, so even though I knew I wouldn't be given very long I wandered out into plain view, shoved my hands into the pockets of my dressing gown and stepped across to have a word.

'Who's the SIO?' I asked.

'Excuse me?' He had his hood down, so I could see the confusion. He was forty-something, with a shaved head and glasses. Like a football hooligan trying to look clever.

'Only, you can tell whoever's running the show that I'm around if they want a word.'

'I'll pass it on,' he said.

It was hard to tell if he was taking the piss or not, but I decided to give him the benefit of the doubt. 'I've got intel, make sure you tell them that.'

'Good to know.'

'*Inside* intel.'

'Right.'

I nodded and he nodded back. I said, 'You know where I am, yeah?'

Sadly, it quickly became clear that Femi and George knew where I was, too. They loomed behind the detective who immediately stood aside when he clocked what was going on.

'Alice,' Femi said. 'What do you think you're doing?'

I shook my head and pressed my wrists together, like I was waiting to be cuffed. I glanced at the cop to see if he appreciated the joke, but he didn't seem to find it any funnier than Femi and George did.

George began guiding me back towards my own corridor. He said, 'This is getting silly, now, pet. You do know we are dealing with a very serious situation.'

'Of course I know. Why do you think I'm out here?' I looked back at the cop who was watching them lead me away. I shook my head, like, *Isn't this ridiculous?* Like, *They just don't get it.*

When we were outside my bedroom door, George said, 'If we catch you out of your room again, we're going to have a problem. You understand?'

I knew he was talking about changing the status of my obs. At that time I was on hourly observation, like most of the others, but he could easily change it to fifteen-minute intermittent obs if he thought I was playing up, or *within eyesight observation*, or even the dreaded *within arm's length,*

37

which would mean someone being in my bedroom with me. Nobody in their right mind wanted to be on WAL.

I told him I understood perfectly and leaned across to give Femi a hug.

'She'll be good,' Femi said. 'Won't you?'

Half an hour later, when I opened my bedroom door again, Femi was sitting outside, smiling at me. Half an hour after that, she was still there and, this time, she didn't even bother looking up from her magazine. I told her she was an ugly bitch and slammed my door and shouted for a while, but I knew she wasn't going anywhere.

I didn't sleep much for the rest of the night, but I didn't try and leave my room again.

It wasn't a big deal, because I'd seen what I needed to. I'd put a word in where it mattered, I'd made myself known. I kicked off the duvet and lay awake thinking about Kevin and my ex-partner Johnno and about knives twisting in bellies. I closed my eyes and tried to imagine what it would feel like to *be* the knife. Sliding and turning, hard and sharp and wet.

I knew that, by the morning, Kevin's bedroom would be sealed off and that the staff would be doing their best to get things back to normal. Ilias, Lauren and the rest of the gang would be mooching around, curious, but none the wiser. I knew that the crime-scene tape would have been taken down and any crucial evidence logged and locked away. I knew that the homicide team would be gone.

It was cool, though. It was all good.

Because I knew they'd be back.

SIX

Say what you like about Fleet Ward – and trust me, I've got plenty to say on the subject – but it puts most other places to shame when it comes to the variety of its breakfast menu. Just a picturesque fifteen-second totter from dining room to meds hatch gives all customers the option to start their day with a cheeky benzodiazepine after tucking into their Frosties. Or, you might prefer an artisanal Selective Serotonin Reuptake Inhibitor – which perfectly complements lighter 'fayre' such as fruit or pastries (currently unavailable) – or even, for those with a somewhat more unusual perspective, a custom-crafted anti-psychotic, designed to follow a full English that's guaranteed to put hair on your chest and take ten years off your life-expectancy.

There's even a mixture of 'desserts' for a few select occupants with more complicated demands. Uppers, downers, mood-stabilisers . . . whatever the customer requires or their consultant prescribes. Take it from someone who knows, if you're not overly bothered about décor or service, this is the place to be. Reservations are not required, but it's always busy, and if happy pills and botulism are what you're into, the Fleet caters for all tastes and conditions.

It helps if you're bonkers, obvs.

That Sunday morning, the day after they'd found Kevin's body, I breakfasted like a champion on scrambled eggs, which would soon be followed by olanzapine and some tasty sodium valproate. While Eileen and one of her less than chatty assistants cleared the dirty cups and plates away, I sat in the dining room with Ilias (bacon sandwich and risperidone), Lauren (sausage, egg, beans, lorazepam and clozapine), Shaun (toast and sertraline) and Donna (Greek yoghurt brought in by a visitor – unopened – and lamotrigine).

'That was gorgeous.' Lauren dropped a meaty hand on to Eileen's arm as she passed. 'Best ever.'

Eileen smiled and said, 'Glad to hear it.'

Lauren took this as a cue and began to sing a song in praise of her breakfast, but it was mercifully short and then she just sat looking grumpy, because she hadn't been able to come up with anything that rhymed with sausage.

'Where's Kevin?' Ilias asked.

Everyone stared at him.

'Oh, yeah,' Ilias said.

Donna pushed her uneaten yoghurt away. 'It feels weird, doesn't it?'

'Takes a while to sink in,' I said.

'I still think he killed himself.' Donna was stretching in her chair, getting ready for a few hours' walking. 'It's so sad.'

'You're wrong,' I said.

'You don't know any better than the rest of us,' Lauren said.

'Oh, I think I do. I've already talked to one of the detectives.'

'Bollocks,' Lauren said.

Shaun had begun to cry. He put his hands over his face.

'It's OK to be upset,' I said. 'You need to get it out.'

Lauren grinned. 'He's always getting it out. Under the table, usually. Or was that Kevin?'

I shook my head and nodded towards Shaun. 'Seriously? You reckon it's all right to make stupid jokes like that when his friend's been murdered?'

'Who's been murdered?' Ilias said.

'You're full of shit,' Lauren said. 'Piss off.'

When Shaun stopped sobbing and took his hands away, he left one finger pressed to his chin. He leaned towards me, wide-eyed.

'Am I going to die? Am I going to die? Am I going to die . . . ?'

I assured him that he was going to be fine and he nodded, grateful. He plastered on a smile and I watched him get up and walk slowly towards the door where Malaika was standing ready to wrap an arm around his shoulder.

'Come on, darling,' she said.

People were getting up from the other tables, lurking. We watched Graham dabbing gently at the corners of his mouth with a paper napkin before standing up and heading out, ready to take his place at the meds hatch. The Thing walked across and stood by our table for a minute or so swishing his kilt around.

Did I mention that Tony wears a kilt?

I probably should have done, considering that he's about as

Scottish as I am, but I suppose it's just not one of the things I find remotely strange any more.

I've got used to all sorts of weirdness.

'I need to go and pack,' Tony said.

'Course you do,' Lauren said.

Something else I forgot. Tony spends at least a couple of hours every day standing by the airlock with his coat on and his bags packed, waiting for his relatives from America to come and collect him. I'd been there several days before one of the nurses told me that Tony doesn't have any relatives in America. I'm not convinced he has any relatives anywhere, because nobody comes to visit. That may be his choice, of course, because he can never be sure he isn't sitting there passing the time of day with the Thing.

When Tony had gone, Ilias said, 'Does anyone want to play chess?'

'Oh for fuck's sake,' Lauren said.

I shook my head.

'Come on,' Ilias said. 'Sundays are so boring.'

'Not boring any more.' Lauren sat back and sniffed. Jerked a thumb in my direction. 'Not now Juliet Bravo over here reckons there's been a . . . murder.'

She rolled the Rs, showing off, and Donna laughed, which was annoying. I resisted the temptation to point out she was doing *Taggart* and not *Juliet Bravo*. 'I don't reckon anything,' I said. 'There were homicide detectives here all night. A full forensic team. I told you, I've talked to them. I'm actually going to be helping with the investigation.'

Lauren began to sing again, changing the words to that old song by Sophie Ellis-Something-or-other. 'It's murder on the Fleet Ward . . . like to burn this fucking place right down . . .'

'Is that true?' Donna asked, when Lauren had finished. 'You helping?'

'It makes sense, when you think about it,' I said. 'To make use of a professional on the inside.'

'Can I be your what-do-you-call-it?' Ilias asked. 'Sidekick.'

Lauren laughed, hissing through her manky teeth like someone had let the bad air out of her. I looked at one of the egg-streaked forks that Eileen hadn't taken away yet and thought about pushing it into Lauren's fat face.

'I'll see how it goes,' I said. 'I'll have a word with the DCI.'

Lauren was still laughing when Marcus came over to sit with us. He's not normally here on a Sunday, but obviously this was no ordinary weekend. He asked how everyone was feeling and said he hoped that we weren't too shaken up by what had happened the night before.

'I'm used to it,' I said. 'I was just telling this lot that the Murder Squad were all over this place while they were all asleep.'

'Now, hang on, Alice—'

'There were detectives here though, weren't there?'

'Please don't talk about murder. It's not helpful.'

'Tell them.'

'Yes, there were detectives here. And by all accounts, you were being very naughty.'

'Just doing my job,' I said.

Marcus shook his head, then said what he'd come across to say. 'I wanted to let you know that unfortunately there won't be any classes tomorrow, because the occupational therapist won't be coming in.'

'That's not on,' Lauren said.

'Doesn't bother me,' Ilias said.

'What about doing my drawing?' Donna's pale-blue eyes filled immediately with tears. They're probably no bigger than anyone else's, but because the rest of her face is so thin they always seem enormous, like she's E.T., or one of those sad-looking kids in the paintings. 'When's she coming back?'

Marcus shrugged. 'I can't say. You know how it goes.'

We knew well enough, even if most of them didn't actually understand the reasons. The ward psychologist had gone on maternity leave before I arrived and had never come back. There were two fewer beds than when I first came in, one less nurse and more agency staff.

All about money, same as usual. The allocation of resources.

'Same bullshit in the Met,' I said.

'It's less than satisfactory, but what can we do?' Marcus stood up. 'As it happens, we would have needed to suspend tomorrow's classes anyway, because the police have said they will be coming back. They will need to talk to everyone. Staff and patients.'

It was an effort not to punch the air or shout something.

I *was* thinking about Kevin, of course I was – about that body bag being unzipped on a slab somewhere and what those who loved him would be going through – but there's no point pretending that I wasn't as stupidly excited as I'd been since the night they frogmarched me in here. That morning dose of olanzapine was already starting to kick in and take some of the edges off, but even so, I suddenly felt as alive, as much like myself, as I could remember feeling in a long time.

'Statements, right?' I was trying not to shout. 'They need to take our statements.'

'I believe so,' Marcus said.

'Find out where everyone was, what they were doing when the body was discovered. *Before* it was discovered.' I was nodding and looking round the table, at Ilias and Donna, then finally at Lauren. I let my eyes settle on hers: piggy and puffed-up. I let what I'd said hang for just long enough.

'So we'd better get our stories straight.'

SEVEN

'Hello, ladies!'

It's what major-league tossers say, isn't it? Blokes out on the sniff, stinking of Paco Rabanne and coming on to any group of women in a bar or wherever, on the off-chance there might just be one who's thirsty/short-sighted/desperate enough to let some stubbly bellend buy her a drink. It might well be the kind of thing Andy's taken to saying, now he's single again. To be honest, it might be the kind of cheesy crap my ex always trotted out. We weren't really together long enough for me to get to know him all that well. Oh, I certainly found out enough, though, and before you say anything, I don't need reminding that he probably thinks exactly the same thing. That he's well shot of a mentalist like me, that he had a narrow escape and was lucky he discovered what I was really like when he did.

Fractured skull notwithstanding.

What *am* I really like, though? Well, that's the $64,000 question . . .

Was I me when I was making an honest living, doing my best to catch rapists and killers? Or was I only the real me once I became 'unwell' and started to see just how evil so-called innocent people can be? What the ordinary punters we think of as *good* and *kind* are actually capable of? The dark desires and the secret schemes and the deals they make with the devil (figuratively speaking; I was never that far gone) . . .

It's a tricky one, you can't deny that, surely.

Are you . . . *you* when you're stone cold sober or does the real you only come out to play after you've had a few? Maybe you should think about that for a while before you judge me, or anyone else who's sitting where I am for that matter. All I'm saying.

Talking of which . . . hello, ladies!

To be fair, I think most of this lot would let you buy them a drink, and I dare say one or two would happily shag you if there was a bag of crisps thrown in, but you need to bear in mind that a lack of self-esteem is a major issue in here.

So, take a bow, my bitches.

LUCY, aka L-Plate. I reckon her parents probably own most of Sussex or something, because she talks like she's one of the royal family and they're always bringing her in fancy food and gorgeous clothes, but for all that, she's actually dead nice. We have a real laugh, me and L-Plate, though she can lose it a bit if you stand too close to her and she does *not* like being touched. Gets properly freaked out about it. I saw her spit at George once, when he tried to put his arm round her. Same as a lot of people, I don't know if L was messed up before the drugs, or if the drugs messed her up, but either way ... I know why kids from *my* neck of the woods end up on the hard stuff, but I've never really understood posh people and heroin. Like, I've got a polo pony and a house that has a maze in the garden, so what am I missing? Oh yeah, a decent smack habit.

Only the finest China White though, and needles from Cartier, natch.

I already mentioned the flat-Earth thing, but that's pretty tame compared with some of the theories L-Plate trots out. The coronavirus 5G thing and 9/11 was an inside job and the moon isn't real and the Beatles never existed and do not get her started on the vapour trails that planes leave. Depending on what mood she's in, either the government's trying to control the weather or they're spraying us all with something that's going to turn us into zombies. Look, I know I've come out with some strange stuff in my time, but this is proper nutter level, and it's even funnier when she's doing it in this cut-glass accent and looks like something out of *Vogue*. From a distance, I should add, because when you get close (as close as she'll let anyone) you can see that she's got iffy skin and teeth like that bloke out of the Pogues. She's not got a bad bone in her, though, that's the most important thing, and you'll never hear her slagging anyone off. When L-Plate's not ranting like some loopy duchess, she'd give you the shirt off her back, and believe me, any one of her cast-offs would be well worth having, because if you stuck it on eBay you could probably pay your mortgage for a few months.

DONNA, aka The Walker. The fact that Donna makes L-Plate (who's got a figure I would kill for) look a bit on the chunky side tells you all you need to know, really. Well, it doesn't, of course. It doesn't tell you *why*. If I knew what was actually going on in anyone's head, I'd be the one with the Mercedes and the office at the end of the corridor. The truth is, I can only tell you about the oddballs I'm holed up with based on what they do and which meds they're on. What they come out with.

Donna doesn't actually come out with anything that you wouldn't hear at the average bus stop or post-office queue, but you only need to look at her to see what's wrong. What the wrongness has done to her, at any rate. You only need to watch her taking an eternity to cut a carrot into twenty pieces, push it around her plate for a while, then spend the next couple of hours walking furiously up and down the corridor to burn off the calories she hasn't taken in. She wears a tracksuit all the time, like she's in training for something.

She's not the only patient who says she shouldn't actually be here, but (not counting yours truly) Donna's probably the only one who really shouldn't. By rights, she should be in a proper eating-disorder clinic, but apparently they can't find anywhere that's got room for her. Ilias says it's ridiculous, because it's not like she takes up a lot of space.

She told me once she was from the south-west somewhere, but I can't remember the name of the place. She's got an accent, but it's very soft like the rest of her. Her personality, I'm talking about. Her body's all angles and pointy bits. She's a gentle soul, wouldn't say boo to a goose and never raises her voice, but it's like she's on the verge of tears all the time, so you have to tread a bit carefully with her. First time my dad saw her, he said she was like a ghost and I know what he was on about. She floats around the place like she's haunting it, though I think he just meant that you could virtually see through her.

So, yeah, Donna walks. Morning, noon and night, wearing out the lino, and she won't stop, even when she's having a conversation. If you want to talk to her about anything, then you'd best be prepared for a half-marathon, which is ironic really, as I've never met anyone in more need of half a Marathon . . . and several Mars bars. Yeah, I know they're called Snickers now, but the joke wouldn't work, would it?

JAMILAH, aka The Foot Woman. Fifty-something, if I had to hazard a guess. A petite Somali woman, with the most beautiful grey hair which – when she takes her headscarf off – comes down to her waist. Jammy (I'm not sure she loves it when I call her that) is another one who doesn't have much to say for herself, though there is one topic about which she's unusually vocal. She probably doesn't suggest it quite as often as Ilias suggests playing chess or Shaun asks if he's going to die, but there isn't a day goes by without her offering to give me – or anyone else in the same room – a pedicure. There's nothing threatening or creepy about it, I don't want you to think that, because the truth is she's always extremely polite.

'Would you like a pedicure, Alice?' Softly-spoken, a thick accent. 'No? OK, then . . .'

First thing in the morning, she's all set to go to work, keen as mustard to get at your trotters. Same if you're eating, or, even stranger, after a tap-tap on your bedroom door in the middle of the night.

Now, I've no idea if this is something she's done professionally, if it's part of a past life she's clinging on to, but I doubt it, somehow. I know I'm a fine one to talk about clinging to anything, but my relationship with the Job is very different, all right? There's some serious unfinished business. So, with Jamilah, I can only presume it's something ... sexual. I mean some people have a thing about feet, don't they? Granted, she doesn't look like she'd find anything sexually arousing, not even sex, but this is probably the last place you should judge any book by its cover, so I'm keeping an open mind.

I do know that I'm not queuing up for her services any time soon.

I don't know exactly what a pedicure involves, but I've had mates who've done it and I know there's a certain amount of ... shaping involved and trimming. I know things get removed. I mean, I'm guessing she had as much gear taken off her when she came in as the rest of us, but some people are sneakier than others, so is it really worth taking the risk?

I'm not letting anyone in here come at my feet with tools.

LAUREN, aka The Singer. From Kent or Essex ... that neck of the woods, and I almost went with another nickname entirely, because a couple of nights after I got here she marched into my room, asked if she could use my bathroom and proceeded to piss all over the floor. I mean *everywhere*, and not just in my bathroom, either. Everybody else's too as it turned out, like she was marking her territory. So I nearly went with Cat-Woman, but even though the piss-spraying is marginally more unpleasant than her tuneless wailing it happens a bit less often, and trust me, she's nothing like those sexy women in the Batman films, so The Singer it is.

Lauren could be anywhere between thirty and fifty, and actually looks a bit like Adele (before she started living on fresh air and kale and lost all that weight) but sadly labours under the tragic misapprehension that she also sounds like her. I must say, though, sometimes the singing can be quite funny. This is her third time on section, and I have to admit that I did laugh a few days after I came in, when I found her in the toilets, serenading herself in the mirror.

'I'm once, twice ... three times a loony ...'

But ...

You know how prisons have a 'Daddy' or whatever? Someone who everyone's a bit wary of and who more or less runs the place? Well, Lauren's the Daddy on Fleet Ward. Nobody messes with Lauren, not Ilias, not Tony ... nobody. Even George and Marcus give her a wide berth when she's got one on her and she's on a WAL more often than she isn't.

She's just ... bad.

Some people are, right? I met plenty of them when I was working, nicked my fair share, so there was something about her I clocked straight away that I definitely did not like the look of. It's not drugs, I'm fairly sure of that, so I can only think it's some kind of bog-standard disorder. Serious ADHD or a skewed personality thing. Who knows, maybe she can't help herself. Maybe she skulks back to her bedroom every night and weeps into her pillow, hugs a teddy bear or whatever, but the fact is that, out here during the day, she can be a dreadful cow. Like all bullies she wants a reaction and she usually gets one from most people. Tears or fawning, a daily shouting match.

I try not to get involved and steer clear of her, but it's hard.

We're living on top of each other, so sometimes you haven't got a choice.

One day, me and Lauren are going to kick off and it won't be pretty.

EIGHT

They held the interviews first thing Monday morning in the MDR, calling us in from the dining room one at a time. I think it was probably alphabetical, but I couldn't swear to it, because I don't know everyone's surname. Ilias was in first, I remember that, then a couple of the Informals and then Jamilah. The rest of us sat there, twiddling our thumbs in the dining room, waiting our turn.

I had my headphones on, listening to nothing.

I can't lie, I was like a cat on hot bricks.

There was a copper in there with us – a woman who smiled a bit too much – and she'd made it clear that they didn't want us talking to each other about what had happened two nights earlier, and definitely not talking to anybody who'd already been questioned before we went in. Didn't stop some people talking about other things, obviously. Didn't stop Ilias asking the copper if she wanted to play chess or Jamilah offering to sort her feet out.

It was properly frustrating, though.

I just had to hold it in, tell myself that I'd have plenty of time to find out what the others had said later on.

I understood why, course I did. You don't want information to be tainted or untrustworthy so it can be easily discounted down the line. You'd be amazed how careful you need to be about that ... about everything. We once had a six-month murder inquiry fall apart at the last minute because nobody had thought to offer a suspect – who had been brought in the night before his interview – something to eat. Can you believe that? His solicitor argued that his client had not been in a fit state to be questioned, so the entire statement got thrown out and the case fell apart. That's the way it is, these days.

It got me wondering, sitting there waiting to be called down to the MDR, just how reliable any of our statements might prove to be. I wasn't including myself, obviously, but surely these coppers knew the kind of people they were talking to. Easy enough for a brief with five minutes on the job to pick holes in anything L-Plate had to say, or The Thing. Not very hard to convince a jury these were not what you'd call solid witnesses.

Ladies and gentlemen, you have been told that Witness A can clearly identify the accused, but you should also know that she believes the moon to be a hologram ...

I know, I was probably getting ahead of myself just a little back then, but in the early days of an investigation it always pays to think about what might be down the road, because nothing is ever that easy. You need to prepare for all eventualities.

When the copper told me it was my turn, I was out of my seat and away down that corridor like shit off a shiny shovel.

Marcus and Femi were standing outside the nurses' station and Femi said, 'Nothing to be scared of,' as I walked past them, which was ridiculous because I was the last person who had anything to be frightened about. I smiled, so they could see that. Behind me, Ilias was shouting, 'Don't tell them anything,' and Lauren was singing her Murder on the Fleet Ward song again.

Before I'd reached the MDR, a female officer directed me into one of the treatment rooms and asked very nicely if I would be willing to provide DNA and fingerprint samples for elimination purposes. She explained that she was asking everyone on the ward.

'Some of them will almost certainly say no,' I told her. 'The patients, I mean. Don't waste your time reading anything into it, though. A few of them won't tell you their names or else get off on giving you false ones. One or two of them might well bite you if you go anywhere near them with one of . . . those.' I nodded, watching her as she snapped the seal and removed a swab from its container. 'You need to know who you're dealing with.'

Her smile showed plenty of perfect teeth but was dead as mutton.

'Oh, don't worry, we do,' she said. She began talking me through the process as if I was slightly simple, told me that it was painless and explained how she would need to swab both sides of my mouth.

I held up a hand to stop her. 'I've done this,' I said.

'You've had your DNA taken before?'

'No.' My turn to smile. 'I've done what you're doing.' The look on her face was priceless and, just for once, I didn't give a toss if she believed me or not. 'So you don't need to worry too much. I mean yeah, I'm chock full of drugs right now so I'm a bit all over the place, but I probably won't bite you.'

It was the same detective I'd spoken to outside the men's toilet on the night it happened. Well, the early hours of the following day if you want to be accurate about it. The thug in glasses. He was sitting behind a desk in a suit and tie. The same desk the judge had sat behind when I was in there for my last tribunal.

'I'm Detective Constable Steve Seddon.'

I leaned forward to check out the lanyard around his neck. 'I'm Alice Armitage. Al.'

'I know.' He turned a fresh page on the notepad in front of him and began writing.

He'd been given a list of all the patients, of course, and it was probably just that, but sitting there, I preferred to think that someone had told him about me. A colleague of a colleague. Word gets around and there's always some gobshite in the Met you can count on to beat the jungle drums.

'I'm a DC, too,' I said. I leaned back and turned to look at the rain running down the small window. 'Homicide Command East.'

He didn't look up from his notepad. 'Right.'

You can imagine how much DC Seddon's reaction – his lack of it – pissed me off. It was like I'd told him I was Britney Spears. I might just as well have been L-Plate, wittering about chemtrails. He looked up finally and took a deep breath, the hint of a smile to let me know that he understood, and I could see straight away that he didn't really want to be there. That he thought interviewing a bunch of mentals was a colossal waste of time.

Hard to blame him for that, mind you.

'Miss Armitage ... you understand we're here this morning to gather as much information as we can about what
might have happened on the evening of Mr Connolly's death.
That's Saturday evening, yes? Two evenings ago.'

So Connolly was Kevin's second name.

'You could start by telling me anything you think might
be important, anything you might have seen or heard that
you think could help?'

I said nothing and turned towards the window again. I was
going to make *Steve* work for it a bit, see what he was made of.

'OK, so let me ask you if you saw anyone going towards
Mr Connolly's room—'

'I saw loads of people, obviously,' I said. 'Members of staff,
other patients. All sorts of comings and goings.'

'Let me be more specific then. What about after eight-
thirty? We know Mr Connolly went to bed early, just after
dinner, so ... '

I thought about it, but not about his question. It was blindingly obvious that they had not yet managed to establish
the time of death. 'I didn't see anything suspicious,' I said.

'Nobody hanging around near Mr Connolly's room?'

'No.'

He scribbled something, but I couldn't make it out. 'So,
can you recall what *you* were doing that evening?'

'I was watching TV until about ten o'clock,' I said. 'Plenty
of others in there with me, so easy enough to corroborate.
Casualty and some rubbish with Ant and Dec. After that, I
sat nattering in the dining room with Shaun and Tony. We
were still in there when the body was discovered.'

He wrote some more. 'Thank you.'

'Was it a stabbing?' He looked up, put his pen down. 'Easiest way, I would have thought. Nice and quiet.'

He took off his glasses. 'I'm afraid I'm not at liberty to reveal details at this stage—'

I raised my hands to let him know I got it, although, one copper to another, he shouldn't have been quite so Job-pissed. In his shoes I'd have been happy to bring a colleague up to speed. I sat back and told him why a blade was the obvious weapon and let him know how easy it was to smuggle anything smaller than a baby elephant on to the ward. I told him that if they were looking for the murder weapon – and why wouldn't they be – they should widen the search to include the hospital grounds, because there were several patients on unescorted leave who pretty much had the run of the place.

I waited.

I was wearing a T-shirt and I could see he was looking at the scars on my arms.

'Like I said.' He put his glasses back on and turned a fresh page, ready for the next customer.

'There was a fight,' I said. 'Did anyone tell you that? A big one and Kevin was right in the middle of it. It was me that broke it up, actually.'

'When was this?'

'On the Wednesday. Three days before Kevin was killed.'

He didn't like me putting it like that, I could tell, but he was obviously interested. 'Who was the fight between?'

'Well, there were lots of people involved, but mainly it was Kevin and Tony. I don't know if you've talked to Tony yet.'

Seddon looked at a list. 'Anthony Lewis?'

'Yeah. He can be a bit . . . volatile, you know?'

'So, what was the fight about?'

58

I'd heard several conflicting stories and I wasn't convinced that Lauren didn't have quite a lot to do with what happened, but at least one version of events involved Kevin saying something to upset Tony. Something about the Thing, most likely. So that's what I told Seddon, because I thought he should know.

He thanked me, which was nice. Told me I'd been very helpful.

'Least I can do,' I said. 'I mean, I do know how this goes. Waiting for the PM results, whatever the forensic boys come back with . . . and obviously you've got the cameras.'

'Yes, of course.' He was done with me, I could tell. 'We'll certainly be reviewing the ward's CCTV footage. So . . .'

Bingo. The lack of enthusiasm wasn't just down to the fact that he was having to waste his time questioning a bunch of fruitcakes. There are cameras almost everywhere on the ward and yeah, there's a couple of blind spots, but there's certainly one that gives a perfect view of the men's corridor. So he was sitting there, cocky as you like, thinking he'd have the whole thing wrapped up by the end of the day.

Remember what I said about nothing being easy? About thinking ahead?

'Good luck with that,' I said.

He looked at me. 'What?'

'Well, I'm guessing that nobody's told you about Graham.' I saw him glance at his list again. 'About Graham's . . . issues with being watched all the time.' Another look towards the window, because I was in no rush. I was proper buzzed up and loving it. 'What Graham likes to do with leftovers.'

NINE

With one or two exceptions, the staff on Fleet Ward are pretty decent.

Don't get me wrong, I've had run-ins with all of them at one time or another, but by and large they're not a bad lot. Most of the time they're just doing their jobs, right? It's meds and meetings. It's all about your various tests and whether you're behaving in your classes and if your observation status needs reviewing. Thing is, I've had cracking chats with several of them. We've shared a few secrets, talked about partners and kids or whatever, but I still wouldn't say that any of them are . . . friends. End of the day, they can't ever really be mates, doesn't matter how well you get on with them. It's not easy to form that kind of relationship, however nice they might be, because you never know when one of them is going to be holding you down while another one's jabbing a needle in your arse.

If you might be swinging a punch at one of them.

I think it's high time you were properly introduced to the men and women responsible for my care, but I've decided to mix things up a bit. Nobody needs another list, do they? After the excitement of my interview with DC Seddon, the rest of that Monday was predictably uneventful, so, as I mooched around, I decided to entertain myself by casting the members of staff in rather ... different roles. Dealing with them at the meds hatch or in the dining room or nattering with them in the hallways, it struck me that, compared to what goes through the heads of some people in here every day, imagining the doctors and nurses in a series of no-holds-barred, to-the-death UFC bouts wasn't actually that weird. You do need to understand that when people aren't getting murdered, this place can be seriously boring.

On top of which, I've definitely imagined things a whole lot weirder.

So, picture a crowd baying for blood, a microphone descending from the heavens as the fighters are introduced and me in a sparkly bikini prowling the ring between rounds. On second thoughts, best not imagine that if you want to keep your dinner down ...

FYI, I haven't bothered giving any of this lot nicknames because they have their names on their badges, like I used to have mine on my stab vest. Oh, and as far as job titles go ... well, the doctors are obviously the doctors, but I still don't really know the difference between a nurse and a healthcare assistant. I mean, in theory an assistant would be assisting a nurse, because they're probably a bit less qualified, but most of the time that doesn't seem to matter and everyone just mucks in. I suppose that, when the only thing there's no shortage of is patients, it's all hands to the pump.

OK ... let's get ready to *rumble*!

Dr Bakshi is the consultant psychiatrist, so she's the big cheese around here. Her first name's Asma, or maybe Asha, and I'm guessing she's Indian. She's always been nice to me; reassuring, you know? Says that there's no reason I shouldn't get well again, but that I do need to be careful with the psychosis, because any further drug use could bring it on again. It's like breaking the seal on a bottle, she said, or once the genie's out of the bottle ... something along those lines. All scary stuff, but only if you believe that you were properly *un*well to begin with. I'm not saying I was behaving what you'd call normally through the whole thing, but there are shades of grey, you know? Shades of crackers.

She doesn't use too much medical gobbledegook and she listens a lot – I guess that's just being good at her job – but I certainly wouldn't want to mess with her, because she's the one with the power to send me home, or, if not, to make my life in here a lot harder than it is. She's also the one member of staff I try not to be too much of a smartarse with – even if I can't help myself, sometimes – because she's the only one I know is cleverer than me.

Bakshi's a bit older than the others and she doesn't strike me as much of a scrapper, so to make things a bit fairer when the fighting starts I'm pairing her with someone, two against one. I need to partner her up with one of the nurses and it's a fairly obvious choice.

Debbie's very Scottish and *very* ginger, but more important ... she's big. Not big like Lauren's big, but like she could easily bench-press Bakshi if she had to. Or me, come to that. If something kicks off between any of the female patients, it's likely to be Debbie who'll come steaming in to sort it out. Actually, most of the blokes in here are more scared of Debbie than any of the male members of staff, even Tony, who's still not convinced she isn't the Thing and always gives her a wide berth. She's loud and rude and she's ridiculously sweary.

It's one of the reasons I thought that Kevin's room, after the murder, must have been a proper horror-show. Debbie's scared of bugger all and she was the one that found him, remember. She came bombing out of that corridor like she'd stumbled into the Texas chainsaw massacre.

I mean, I know better now, obviously.

I'm teaming Debbie and Bakshi up to take on George, who's another one of the nurses. He's the ward's gentle giant, and yeah, I'm being just a bit sarcastic. I'm not saying he's rough when he doesn't need to be, but let's just say he's well aware that he's a big lad. Holding himself back, like he'd love nothing more than for Ilias or Tony to have a pop at him. He's got a proper Geordie accent and of course he's a Newcastle fan, which I take every chance to wind him up about. Telling him that clearly means he's madder than anyone in here.

He told me once he always wanted to be a copper, but they wouldn't let him join, and that made me wonder just what George might have got up to when he was younger. I mean, these days they'll let any nutcase in.

So, first up then, it's Bakshi and Debbie versus George. *Result*: even with two against one, and despite the fact that Debbie would probably fight dirty, George is the only winner here, taking the pair of them out inside the first thirty seconds. Quick and ugly.

I reckon a match-up between the ward's two healthcare

assistants would give the crowd a better spectacle and certainly a longer one. Malaika's Indian, same as Dr Bakshi, only with a really thick Brummie accent. Pure *Peaky Blinders*, Malaika is, but with a better haircut (red streaks which look cool) and without the hidden razor blades. Trust me, none of the people who work in here are a soft touch, but she's definitely not the strictest. If you're watching something on TV, she'll maybe let you have another ten minutes after you're supposed to be in bed, and if you were on escorted leave and she took you outside for a cigarette, she wouldn't rush you back in the second you'd stubbed it out. She's a smoker herself, so she's always happy enough to go with you.

Malaika's pretty tight with George, always whispering in corners, and for a while, I thought there was something going on between them. Then I found out she was gay – it was actually George that told me – so I let my overly fertile imagination run riot in other ways. It's fun to make things up about the staff, invent weird and wonderful private lives for them. Like Malaika probably had quite a strict upbringing, maybe an arranged marriage she got herself out of, so now, when she's not at work, she's wild and into all sorts. Death-metal and coke and stuff. I know she's got a temper on her, too, because I heard her arguing about something with Debbie the other day.

I wonder how she'll fare, toe to toe in the arena with the Polish Punisher.

Mia would probably be popular with the crowd. She's got spiky blonde hair and a cute accent and she's pretty, but if I'm honest she's a bit of a black hole, personality-wise. She doesn't socialise much, by which I mean she never 'hangs out' or tells you anything about her life outside Fleet Ward.

She probably thinks she's being smart, because some of her colleagues who have let things slip have paid for it later on. Thing is, that just means we make it up, like I did with Malaika. So, Mia . . . definitely some kind of dominatrix on the side, and that's not as much of a leap as you might think. Sometimes I catch her staring at some of the other patients, when she doesn't know she's being watched, and once or twice I've seen that pretty face looking seriously cruel.

Malaika versus Mia. *Result*: a much trickier one to call, and Mia's a bit of a dark horse, but my gut says Malaika would probably come out on top.

The final bout is another one that's going to be close, even if it's a man against a woman. Marcus is the ward manager, because he's the senior nurse, I suppose. Very tall and wiry, Nigerian, I think, because he told me he was born in Lagos. That's in Nigeria, right? I reckon 'even-tempered' would be the best way to describe him. I've only seen Marcus really lose it once – with Lauren, no surprise there – but he doesn't really smile a lot either. In fact thinking about it, he doesn't seem to have much of a sense of humour at all. I would have thought that was pretty bloody important working in a place like this, some of the stuff that goes on, but he's obviously good at his job or he probably wouldn't be ward manager. The rest of the staff all seem to like him, anyway.

He talks very slowly like he's choosing his words carefully, and in perfect English, like someone reading the news, but every now and again there's a slight stammer which gives certain patients a golden opportunity to take the piss. Some people just enjoy being cruel – naming no names – but a few of the others seem to genuinely find it funny because they don't understand boundaries. You know, 'Look out, here comes M-M-Marcus', all that. Lauren always manages to dig out an appropriate song to try and wind him up. Elton John or David Bowie are particular favourites.

Ch-ch-ch-ch-changes . . .

B-B-B-B-B-B-B-Bennie and the Jets . . .

Ha, ha, ha. Stupid b-b-b-bitch.

I'm not too sure what part of Africa Femi's from, but she's got a thicker accent than Marcus. Small, but stronger than she looks (I think all the nurses are), and she's really good at bringing certain patients out of their shells. The ones who just withdraw in here, you know. She talks about her kids with them or tells terrible jokes and sometimes she even joins in when Lauren's singing, which is probably taking the cheery thing too far.

She's another one who's definitely got a short fuse, though, but I've only ever seen it with other members of the staff. Saying that, I don't think she likes confrontations because one time I caught her crying in the toilets after a bust-up with someone. She doesn't take any shit, I mean she's not a pushover or anything, but Femi's one of those the patients will go to if they need a favour or a word putting in with Dr Bakshi or something.

I said there's nothing of her, right? She's properly tiny, like her clothes would fit a ten-year-old, so I do wonder if maybe she had her own issues with food once upon a time, because she's always picking at something grainy-looking in a Tupperware container. I mean, apparently a lot of people working in mental health used to be patients, so I wouldn't be surprised. Poacher turned gamekeeper sort of thing. It's funny, because the only person she's ever remotely spiky with is Donna, so maybe she's a bit freaked out dealing with someone who's got the same problems she had. Once, she gave Donna a major telling-off about something and ever since then Donna's called her Femi-Nazi, which would be a pretty nifty UFC nickname now I think about it.

Marcus versus Femi. *Result*: controversial, but I'm going with Femi for this one. I'm not sure Marcus has got a lot of fight in him and I think Femi could take care of herself if she had to.

So, a few fight-night facts about the men and women who take care of us and perhaps a bit of creative 'embroidery', but you get the picture. Full disclosure, I should probably mention that one of the members of staff stepping into my imaginary UFC ring almost certainly sexually assaulted me. Right, 'almost certainly' . . . makes it sound a bit vague, but I'm as sure as I can be, taking into account the issues with memory and medication. I'm not going to say who it was because I really don't like to think about it very much, but if they did it to me, you can bet they've done it to others.

L-Plate told me the same thing had happened to her once, at a different hospital. She told me that she'd made a complaint, but that she'd just been called a drama queen.

'Best to keep your head down,' she'd said. Crying in my arms she was at the time. 'Don't make waves.'

Obviously, as a copper, I want to see people who do this kind of thing get what's coming to them, because that's my job, but I also know that, things being the way they are – me being where I am – I need to steer clear of trouble. Believe me, it goes against the grain, but it's a little easier to come to terms with now I'm smack in the middle of a murder case.

67

TEN

Visiting hours in here are pretty relaxed, but there isn't any sort of official visits area. You just have to grab a bit of privacy wherever you can, so just before dinner time on the Tuesday, me and Tim Banks found a couple of chairs in the music room. Jamilah was already in there reading a magazine and she was clearly earwigging, so I just gave her evils for a few minutes until she pissed off. As soon as *she'd* left us alone, Lauren stuck her head round the door and asked Banksy if he wanted to hear her song.

He said that he was busy.

She told him it was a really good one.

He said maybe another time.

She told him he was a cunt and then closed the door.

'Nice.' He looked at me. 'So, how you doing, Al?'

Tim's probably the most regular visitor I've had. Mum and Dad have been down a couple of times, but it usually means a night for them in some hotel and it's never pleasant because they get so upset. Sophie came in once, which was nice, but she was a bit freaked out by Tony (the postcard incident) so I don't think she's in a hurry to come back. We text and talk on WhatsApp, so it's all good. She tells me how boring her new flatmate Camilla is, even though she's apparently a lot tidier than I was.

I was never boring to live with, nobody could ever say that.

Banksy's been great, though. He understands. Yeah, it pisses me off that nobody else from work has been in, all those people I'd thought were mates, but I get it. I'm damaged goods, aren't I?

I told Banksy I was fine. He said I was looking well.

'Relative though, isn't it?' I smiled. I knew I looked like death warmed up.

'Better than last time, anyway,' he said. 'Colour in your cheeks.'

'So, come on then.'

'Give me a bloody chance.' He dug into his pocket and brought out a notebook. He'd made notes, God bless him. Like I said, he's someone I know I can count on.

A bloody good copper, Banksy is.

On top of which, he was Johnno's best mate.

I'd called him two days before, on the Sunday night, after I'd talked to Seddon. I'd brought him up to speed, told him to do some digging and asked him how soon he could get in to see me. Like I said, it wasn't our team working this, but I knew he'd be able to ask around and call in a few favours. I knew he could find out *something*.

'What's the story, then?'

He was flipping through the pages of his notebook. 'Can't remember the last time I saw you this fired up,' he said.

'A murder tends to do that,' I said. 'Plus, I've been a good girl, so they've cut the dose of my mood stabiliser.'

Banksy found the page he was looking for. 'Well, you were right about that much, at any rate. It *is* now a murder investigation.'

'*Yes!*' It was just me and him, so I didn't bother trying to hide my excitement. 'I fucking knew it.'

'Not a stabbing, though. You jumped the gun a bit there.'

I waited.

'Cause of death was asphyxia. Victim was suffocated, basically. Pillow's their best guess.'

I thought about that. Kevin wasn't a weakling, but he wasn't a big lad either and he'd have been half asleep, zonked out on whatever meds he'd been given last thing. Pressing a pillow over his face wouldn't have been difficult and it wouldn't have taken very long. 'What about time of death?'

'That's a bit trickier,' Banksy said. 'The pathologist reckons some time between nine o'clock and ten-thirty.'

'Which pathologist?'

'That weirdo at Hornsey. The one with all the tattoos and piercings.'

'Right.' I'd never met the bloke, but he had a reputation.

'Now, they think they can narrow that down because they already know the victim went to bed early, just after eight-thirty, and they know the nurse who was doing the rounds—'

'Debbie.'

'Yeah ... she checked on him at nine-thirty and he was sleeping, not a problem. They've got her observation charts or whatever, got her on camera going in and out, right? So, now they're thinking, OK ... we're obviously looking at whoever killed him sneaking into his room sometime between then and when Debbie makes her next round just after ten-thirty and discovers the body.'

'Screams the place down.'

'All nice and straightforward, so they reckon, because they'll have their killer on tape, but apparently there's some kind of technical issue with the cameras. So . . .' He stopped when he saw me grinning.

'Not exactly technical,' I said.

I told him the same thing I told Seddon yesterday.

Aside from his pathological fear of being second in line for anything, I explained, Graham – the Waiter – is more than a little twitchy when it comes to being watched. 'He usually does it straight after mealtimes,' I said. 'With whatever food's left over. He stands on a chair and uses anything he's not eaten to screw with the cameras. Porridge or pudding or whatever. Mashed potato is his favourite; he's deadly with that. A nice handful of leftover mash . . . *splat* . . . camera knackered.'

Banksy looked horrified. 'Can't they stop him?'

'Oh yeah, they try to. He always gets a major bollocking and they put him on Within Eyesight or Within Arm's Length or something, but they can only keep it up for so long. After that, they do what they can to keep an eye on him, but he's pretty sneaky about it. Eventually he finds a way to clamber on to a trolley or get on somebody's shoulders and smear something gloppy over as many cameras as he can get to before they catch him. At first it was a big deal, I mean they took it dead seriously and they'd be cleaning the cameras up straight away. Then it just became something they got used to and nobody could really be arsed to get it fixed that quickly. Marcus says it's a health and safety issue, nurses with buckets and cloths climbing up on stuff or whatever, so these days they tend to wait for one of the hospital janitors to come along with a ladder and sort it out. Pain in the arse for them, obviously, but pretty funny.'

'Not if you're running this investigation,' Banksy said. 'According to the log, the camera covering the men's corridor went out just after half-past nine and wasn't . . . cleaned up until just before the body was discovered. So, yeah, they're looking at the murder taking place during that same hour, but it's also an hour when the camera was out.'

'Fucking Graham.' I shook my head.

'Fucking Graham.'

'Just when dinner's finishing,' I said. 'Staff cleaning up, people milling about all over the shop. Always a bit full-on, that time.'

'Something else.' Banksy was looking at his notepad again. It was hard to contain myself. 'They found drugs in the victim's bedroom. Quite a lot of drugs.'

'What kind of drugs?'

'I don't have the details, but . . . pills. Prescription stuff, sound of it.'

'Jesus.'

'That's it.' He closed his notebook. 'Trust me, I had to twist a few arms to get *that* much.'

I told him I appreciated it, said I'd try not to bother him again. 'I can't promise, obviously.'

'Obviously,' he said. Then, when he'd stood up and was hanging about looking awkward: 'Listen, Al, don't bite my head off, but I'm not convinced this is the kind of thing you need right now. That it's good for you.'

'Are you joking me? It's exactly what I need.'

'I mean, shouldn't you just be . . . ?'

'What? Chillin'? Putting my feet up? Catching up on all those good books I should have read?'

'You know what I mean, Al. Come on, I don't want to debate this with you again, but you know you've not been well. I mean, you do admit that much, right?'

'You're a top bloke, Banksy.' I walked to the door, waited for him to follow. 'But you're not my dad.'

A minute later, while we were standing at the airlock waiting for someone to let him out, he said, 'I saw Mags the other night.' Like it had just popped into his head.

'OK.' I could feel something jumping inside and was trying not to let it show in my voice. 'How's she doing?'

Maggie was Johnno's girlfriend.

Five months pregnant when he died.

As pregnant as she was ever going to get, as it turned out.

'Yeah, she's all right,' Banksy said. 'She was asking after you.'

That didn't help things and I was grateful when I saw Mia coming with the keys. 'You all done?' she asked, a little more chipper than usual.

'Yeah, we're done,' I said.

Banksy gave me a big hug before he stepped into the airlock, and when he was inside with Mia, signing out and waiting to go through the second door, I pressed my palm against the window, then kissed the glass, pretending to cry like we were lovers saying a final goodbye or something.

It made him laugh and he stuck two fingers up.

As soon as he was gone, I checked my watch then went back to my room to make a call. That calmed me down a bit, knowing I'd be sorted before very long. Then I went to get my dinner.

ELEVEN

It was just a regular house call, that's all. An everyday ACTION as part of an ongoing sexual assault case that involved talking to everyone on the local sex-offenders register. Run-of-the-mill stuff. Obviously, though, no story like this – no once-in-a-career tragedy – ever starts with 'we were on the trail of a vicious, chainsaw-wielding serial killer', does it, because then you'd know how it was going to turn out.

There'd be no surprise.

You look ahead. I said that earlier, didn't I? You try to prepare for all eventualities, but no amount of preparation or due diligence or just bog-standard keeping your wits about you is going to help when life just turns round, says 'bad luck, mate' and gobs in your face.

Turns the world upside down.

Turns you into somebody else.

The somebody Johnno and I were looking for that morning was not at home, but his flatmate seemed happy enough to let us in and answer a few questions. It was a flat above an electrical shop in Mile End and, from the doorway, it looked nice enough. Nicer than we were expecting, anyway.

Not too much of a shithole and we'd visited plenty of them the previous few days.

Yeah, I could see that the bloke was wired, you learn to recognise it, so straight away Johnno and I exchanged a look. *We good with this?* I seem to remember that I rolled my eyes or raised my eyebrows or something and he knew what that meant. Just a doper or a crackhead who probably won't be able to string a sentence together anyway, so let's get this over with and head to that greasy spoon a few doors up for an early lunch.

I've already said I had a feeling we had nothing to worry about and that everything was going to be fine, but if I'm honest it wasn't quite that. It was more like I didn't have a feeling that it *wasn't*.

I should have had and I didn't.

I asked the bloke, nice and polite, if he'd mind me taking a quick look around, while Johnno sat down with him on the settee to ask a few questions about his absent flatmate. The bloke – stick-thin, a bit weaselly, par for the course – said he didn't have a problem with that, but we'd need to get a shift on because he had to go and meet somebody.

Johnno and I looked at each other again. A dealer, most likely.

I went into the bedroom of the man we were actually looking for and started poking around. I put on some nitrile gloves and opened drawers and looked in the wardrobe and under the bed. Standard stuff, but you never know what you might stumble across, so I was cautious, like I always was.

I could hear Johnno in the front room.

Do you know where your flatmate is now? Do you know when he'll be back? Have you any idea where he was four nights ago . . . ?

It didn't sound hugely productive.

As soon as I'd lifted the mattress I could see the DVDs gaffer-taped to the bed frame, and I was just reaching in to take one out when I heard the bloke shout. I can't remember what he said, and thinking about it, it was probably just a noise. Hoarse and high-pitched, like he was in pain.

When I came back in, I could see the pair of them struggling on the settee, and when Johnno turned his head and shouted at me to call for back-up as I was on my way across to help him, that's when the bloke threw the punch.

What I thought was a punch.

It wasn't until the bloke staggered to his feet and dropped the Stanley knife that I saw what had happened.

The blood on the blade.

The blood that was starting to pulse between Johnno's fingers and splash on the carpet.

That pattern – those hideous blue-green swirls – is still there sometimes when I close my eyes.

The rest of it's all a bit scrambled in my head, if I'm honest, like it was just a few seconds and like it took for ever. The bloke mumbling and strolling out of there like it was nothing and he was pissed off that we'd held him up. Me trying to key the radio and still keep my hands pressed against Johnno's neck. Those stupid gloves, slippery with all the blood, and his shirt changing colour.

Shouting about an ambulance and whispering to Johnno.

Telling him to keep still, to hold on.

Feeling his boots kicking against the carpet underneath us and knowing I was wasting my time.

Knowing that both of us were gone.

There. Not to excuse the fact that I did some stupid things, that I *still* do them now and again, but just so you know . . .

As we've already established, Within Arms' Length is at the shitty end of the obs stats ladder. A status that really means you've got no status at all. But for those privileged few, for the *chosen*, the Holy Grail of stats awaits them in the 1983 Mental Health Act's very own VIP enclosure. I'm talking about the five-star, business-class status that is . . . Unescorted Leave.

Be still my beating heart.

Actually racing most of the time, thanks to the anti-psych meds.

To put it more simply: Fuck yeah!

Fifteen minutes might not sound like much, but trust me, you savour every sodding second of it, because you're *outside*. On. Your. Own. Free to smell air that actually smells like air – as much as it ever does in north-west London – and to enjoy the relatively dogshit-free green space available within the hospital grounds. It's something you have to earn, natu-rally, and you must demonstrate a clear understanding that, if you leave the hospital grounds, the police will be sent to bring you back pronto, and you can kiss goodbye to unes-corted anything for a good while.

Yeah, of course I understand. Police, totally . . . got it.

Like I'd said to Banksy a couple of hours before, I'd been a very well-behaved patient of late. A damn sight better than the few weeks previously, that's for sure. I'd earned a degree of trust, Dr Bakshi had said, and I should do my very best to maintain it.

'I promise,' I said. 'It means a lot.'

George let me out of the airlock just before nine o'clock. He looked at his watch and told me I needed to be back by quarter past.

'To the second,' I said.

'I'll be waiting,' he said.

I smoked a cigarette by the main entrance to the unit, just in case George or anyone else was of a mind to pop down and check, or was watching me from one of the windows.

I thought about the drugs they'd found in Kevin's room.

Had one of his visitors smuggled them in for him? *Quite a lot*, Banksy had said. OK, sneaking in the odd bottle wasn't out of the question, but more than that was hard to imagine. Kevin must have been trying to sell them to someone on the outside, though, however he got hold of them. There'd definitely be a market for it and I had a feeling he'd been involved in stuff like that before he came in.

I couldn't think of any obvious way he'd got hold of the drugs in here, though.

Nicking a pack or two of aripiprazole from an unguarded trolley was not beyond the bounds of possibility, but there's some proper locks on the medical supplies rooms, so a large quantity would definitely have been trickier. No, some things on the ward might not be as shipshape as they should be – the mash-on-the-cameras thing for a kick-off – but they do tend to be quite careful about the meds.

The whole suicide thing.

So, where was Kevin getting the drugs and why was he stockpiling them in his bedroom?

I was still thinking about it while I strolled down to a spot just inside one of the hospital gates. Billy was waiting by the wheelie bins, playing some stupid game on his phone.

'Been a while,' he said.

I handed over the twenty pound note and he handed me the baggie. It would be more than enough. He'd pre-rolled a freebie for me, which was thoughtful.

'Things got a bit messy,' I said.

Billy folded the note into his well-stuffed wallet and began scrolling through his messages. 'Got messy again, have they?'

'In a different way,' I said, as he walked away towards the main road.

At exactly nine-fifteen I rang the bell and watched George sauntering towards the airlock. He nodded, reaching for his keys, so I leaned against the window and said, 'Bang on time, mate,' and hoped I wasn't shouting or grinning like an idiot without knowing it.

I told George I was going to get an early night and winked at Donna as I marched straight down to my room.

'Sleep well, pet,' George shouted.

He'd smelled it on me, though, course he had.

Ten minutes later, him and Marcus were knocking on my bedroom door and there wasn't a fat lot I could do. While they turned my room upside down, I stood outside in the corridor and cried for a few minutes, holding Malaika's hand and listening to her telling me I was 'daft'. I knew they'd find the weed – it was tucked into the toe of one my trainers – but I'd rolled a couple before coming back in and stashed them, so at least there was that.

Think ahead and keep your fingers crossed, right?

Later, after I'd shouted for a while and kicked the door

until my foot hurt, I lay down and tried to sleep. I thought the weed would help, because it usually did, but there was too much rattling around inside my head. Mine would be the first name mentioned at the following morning's staff meeting and my next assessment wasn't likely to go well, but I decided it had been worth it.

A short-term fix, I'm well aware of that, but it was what I needed.

TWELVE

There aren't too many secrets in this place – there are plenty of patients and staff members with big mouths – so I wasn't the least bit surprised that several of my fellow sectionees were keen to join me for breakfast and get the skinny on my escapade the previous evening. They all chipped in or had questions. I told them it was just a bit of weed, that it was no big deal and it's not like I'm the only person in here that's ever tried to smuggle drugs in, but I suppose anything that breaks up the monotony is exciting.

You'd have thought I was Pablo Escobar or whoever.

Lauren was smirking, like I'd made her day. 'Should have come to me and we could have sorted something out together.'

'Sorry.' I raised my arms and mock-bowed like I wasn't worthy. 'I'll know next time.'

'Fuck you,' she said.

'Should have used the old "prison wallet",' Ilias suggested.

'Stuck it up your arse. I don't reckon they'd have looked up there.'

I thanked him and said I'd bear that in mind as well.

'You reckon somebody snitched on you?' L-Plate asked.

'I didn't tell anyone,' I said. 'Because I'm not stupid.' If I had then someone would almost certainly have had a quiet word with Marcus or one of the others. Donna, because she was trying to help me. Ilias, because he thought it was funny. Lauren, because she's a bitch.

'They bump you back to Within Eyesight obs?' The Thing asked.

'If you're lucky,' L-Plate said.

'They haven't told me yet.' But they would, as soon as the morning staff meeting had finished. I wasn't massively worried, because even if they wouldn't be letting me outside again in a hurry, I knew I could be on basic hourly obs again quickly enough. I knew how to behave to get back into Dr Bakshi's good books, besides which there simply weren't enough staff around to keep an eye on everyone all the time.

'Careful who you talk to,' Tony said. 'I still reckon one of the nurses is the Thing. The Scottish one.'

Graham, who hadn't spoken up as yet, patted me on the shoulder. He whispered, 'Nice try, though,' then grabbed a plateful of porridge before setting off to mess with some cameras.

Lauren started singing 'Back on the Chain Gang.'

L-Plate and Ilias both asked if I could let them have my dealer's number.

Ten minutes later at the meds hatch, once Femi had handed my paper cup of pills across, I leaned close to her and asked, 'Have any drugs gone missing lately?'

'I don't understand.'

'From in there.' I nodded behind her. 'Any stuff unaccounted for?'

'Not as far as I know.' She was holding out the cup of water and smiling at the voluntary patient who was waiting in line behind me, but I didn't move.

'So, you would know?' I waited. 'All the staff would be told about it, right?'

'Why are you so interested in this?' Femi was starting to look concerned or uncomfortable, I couldn't be sure which.

'It's part of my investigation into Kevin's death,' I said.

She shook her head, still brandishing the water, then raised a hand, inviting the Informal behind me to step forward.

I turned and smiled at him. 'Almost done.'

'The police have already asked us these questions,' Femi said.

'So, what did you tell them?'

'I'm afraid we are not allowed to discuss such things with patients.'

'Maybe not normally.' I leaned closer. 'But somebody killed Kevin and drugs had something to do with it—'

'You need to step away now, Alice—'

'—and I'm going to find out how he got them.'

Behind me, the Informal muttered something as he stepped back to let Donna walk past. I turned and winked at him as she marched away down the corridor. I said, 'She's working off breakfast.'

'Take your pills and fuck off,' he said.

'There are other patients waiting.' Femi had raised her voice a little. 'Are you going to move?'

I turned back to her. 'That depends.'

'Do you want me to bring Marcus over here?'

For a moment I thought about asking her to do exactly that. I'd wondered all along if Marcus should be the one to question about the drugs in Kevin's room, before deciding I'd be more likely to get a straight answer out of Femi. Now I reckoned there was no point in getting the ward manager involved until I needed to.

I smiled and took the cup of water.

I swallowed my olanzapine then my sodium valproate, watched her tick my chart and said, 'Thanks for your help.'

That afternoon, I was in the music room with Big Gay Bob, chatting about this, that and – as always – the *other*, when it all kicked off in the 136 Suite.

'I shagged a policewoman once,' Bob said.

'Yeah?'

'In the back of a police car.'

'Nice. Did she put the blue light on?'

'I swear, I always thought women in uniform batted for the other team. No offence, but you know what I'm saying. Bang up for it she was though, the dirty mare.'

'Did she take down your particulars?'

As usual, Bob hadn't a clue that I was taking the mickey and he was grinning and saying something about his 'helmet' when our uplifting conversation was interrupted by the row out in the hall.

Screams and shouts from a voice we didn't recognise.

The 136 Suite is where all those brought in by the police (under Section 136 of the Mental Health Act, hence the imaginative name) are taken to be assessed. It's a 'place of safety' to which the police, having removed them from street/

84

pub/wherever, are obliged to take any individual deemed to be in immediate need of care and control.

Right then, it didn't seem like a particularly safe place for anyone.

I found out later on that the kid – he couldn't have been more than seventeen – had been picked up after a member of the public dialled 999, having spotted him dodging cars on the North Circular. God only knows what he was on or what had happened to make him so agitated, but nurses were running around, grim-faced or barking at one another, while the poor bastard was locked inside the suite, shouting and smashing his head against the glass.

Some shit about spiders . . .

For obvious reasons, the staff don't really appreciate having an audience when there's business like this going on, so Big Gay Bob and I had the good grace to hang back a bit. As did Ilias, L-Plate and everyone else who'd come out to have a nosy. Donna even stopped walking for a few minutes, which I'd never seen happen before.

Seriously, 'restrictive intervention' is not a part of the job that any of the staff enjoy, even if some of them are better suited to it than others. Nobody likes doing it, least of all completing the paperwork and taking part in the compulsory 'incident debrief' afterwards, but when the immediate safety of staff or the service-user is threatened and a de-escalation of the situation is required quickly, swift tranquillisation is usually the only option.

Basically, hold the bugger down and jack them full of sedatives.

I watched as Malaika tried to calm the kid down verbally, while George and Marcus discussed how best to approach and restrain him, Femi did the necessary on the computer and Debbie and Mia ran off to prepare the drugs they would need. A poky lorazepam and aripiprazole cocktail.

The rapid-tranq.

It was dead impressive.

They were a seriously well-organised team and, if it hadn't been for the screaming – I had to cover my ears – and the look of terror on that poor lad's face, it would almost have been a pleasure to watch.

It made me start to think, though.

'Come in handy,' Bob said. 'A couple of bottles of that tranquilliser stuff. You know, if you didn't want ladies to put up a fight.'

'What?'

He said something else after that, probably equally revolting, but I wasn't really listening to him. I was listening to the new arrival yelling and watching him smear drool on the glass and thinking that if, just for the sake of argument, it had been some kind of . . . performance, it was as good as I'd ever seen. I was putting it all together and – then, at least – it made perfect sense.

I began walking away just as George and Marcus steamed into the 136 like a two-man Tactical Support Unit, so I didn't see what happened after that. Must have gone OK though, because apparently the kid settled down and was discharged the following morning. I've no idea what happened to him after that. He might be getting therapy somewhere or he might be playing chicken with himself on a motorway somewhere else, but either way, he was the one that put the idea into my head.

Right then, though, while they were pumping a syringe full of benzos into his backside, I needed to get to my room as quickly as possible and make a call while it was still fresh in my mind.

'So, any news?'

'Bloody hell, Al, give me a chance.' Banksy's voice was low, like he didn't want to be overheard. 'I only saw you yesterday.'

'Quick and the dead, mate.'

'Far as I know they're still waiting for forensics.'

'Yeah, I mean there's no rush. It's only one less nutter, after all.'

'To be fair, I think there's a bit of a backlog, all right? Besides which I don't think they're hopeful it's going to be a lot of help.'

I knew what he meant. Like forensicating a hotel room. More prints and DNA than you can shake a swab at. In the case of Kevin's room that would certainly include all the staff and most of the patients.

I started to tell him the real reason for the call, told him what I'd just seen.

'The Informals come in and go out,' I said.

'Right.'

'Same with anyone who gets brought in on a 136.'

'So . . . ?' Banksy did not sound convinced.

'So, let's say Kevin had got himself involved with some nasty drug dealers.'

'They're all nasty,' Banksy said.

'Properly nasty, yeah? Say Kevin's in over his head. Say he's been paid up front for something he doesn't deliver, or maybe he decides he wants to get out of it but he knows too much. It's the perfect way to get rid of him.'

There was silence for a bit. I could hear squad-room noises in the background, phones and chit-chat. I felt like someone who'd lost a child and then seen a woman out with her new baby. OK, that's putting it a bit strong, maybe, but you know what I'm saying.

'Go on then,' Banksy said.

'Someone comes in, pretending to be a voluntary patient, an Informal, yeah? It wouldn't take them long to figure out the situation with the cameras in here, so they wait until Graham shuts the right one down, do what they've come for, then discharge themselves as soon as.'

'That simple?'

'Yeah, that simple. Listen, I bet I could easily find out who left the day Kevin was killed, or the morning after.'

Another silence. Then, 'It's a bit far-fetched, Al.'

'You haven't even thought about it.'

'I *am* thinking about it. You're telling me that some gangsters hired a hit-man to pretend to be mad. They don't normally go for anything that complicated. They'd just threaten his family or burn his house down.'

'Yeah, but doing it this way wouldn't draw attention, would it?'

'Also, aren't the staff in there trained to know if someone's putting it on?'

'They get things wrong sometimes.'

'Did they get it wrong with you?'

Now I was the one saying nothing for a bit. 'They get things wrong.'

I listened to that gorgeous office chatter for another few seconds. I pressed the phone hard to my ear, but I couldn't make out what was being said or hear any voices I recognised.

'It's a bit of a stretch,' Banksy said. 'You must see that, and, like I said the other day, I'm really not sure this is doing you any good, so—'

'If Kevin was getting the drugs from in here, he had to be getting them out somehow. You've got to admit that much, right?'

Banksy sighed. 'Makes sense, I suppose.'

'So I think you should talk to Seddon,' I said. 'Tell him he needs to check out all Kevin's visitors.'

'I'm sure they're already doing that, Al.'

'We should make sure.'

'They're all good officers.'

'*I* was a good officer.'

Banksy said nothing.

'I was *really* good,' I said. 'Point is, everyone thinks they're a good officer until they're washing the blood off.'

THIRTEEN

This Is What I Believed.

Part One ... because frankly there's quite a lot to get through and I can't really bring myself to think about it for too long. I should tell you that some of it might seem a bit all over the place, but that's only because *I* was all over the place, and I can't swear that I've got what happened when exactly right. I've talked to the various witnesses (Mum and Dad, Sophie, Andy, etc.) to corroborate statements where I could and tried to put together a timeline.

Like every case I ever worked on the Job, except that I was the major suspect.

The PTSD didn't kick in straight away. I mean, I didn't walk out of that flat in Mile End barking like a dog. I got cleaned up and gave my statement. I went home and just curled up, then cried on Sophie's shoulder for a couple of days. But I couldn't sleep and then I started having panic attacks. I swear, these days, it's like every Tom, Dick or

Harry has them, needs a nice cup of tea and a biscuit now and again, but I knew pretty bloody quickly that no amount of breathing into a paper bag was going to sort me out.

Chills or nausea or thinking I was going to shit myself.

Pins and needles, *everywhere*.

Sweating like a rapist and feeling like I was going to choke.

My doctor put me on Prozac fast enough (popping my SSRI cherry), and my boss and his boss were both great about it. *You've been through a terrible ordeal, Al. Take some time* – paid sick-leave, yay! – *and let's see if you're ready to come back to work in a few weeks.*

A few weeks became a few more, but I don't think they really understood how bad things had become until I was actually needed again, when the arsehole who'd carved up Johnno was about to go on trial.

See, I didn't *mind* taking the tablets, but it wasn't particularly enjoyable, and pretty quickly I discovered that a bottle of red wine and a few spliffs every night could do the job equally well. So, on top of some prodigious pill-popping, I started bulk-buying at Oddbins and filling daily prescriptions with Billy. Twice-daily, sometimes. And I felt absolutely great, to be honest; no point pretending I didn't. The panic and the piss-myself terror were all but gone, and I was calm for a while, at least. Until I found out what getting out of your head really means.

So, the trial . . .

I was the prosecution's star witness, of course, but that soon changed when a couple of the DCs working the case came round to go through my forthcoming appearance in court. All very straightforward, and not even official because they weren't allowed to 'coach' any witnesses and were just there to talk about a couple of the questions the defence might throw at me. Sod's law – I was midway through a bit of a bender when they turned up, so it only took a few minutes with them before 'forthcoming' became 'not-a-cat-in-hell's-chance'. Never mind take the stand, I was hardly in a fit state *to* stand, so it was quickly decided I would not be giving evidence at all.

I was gutted, because I'd wanted to be there for Johnno.

I knew both those DCs, but the way they stared while I ranted at them, it was like they didn't know *me* at all.

It didn't much matter in the end, which is the only good part, because the toe-rag got was what coming to him anyway. They had my original statement, a Stanley knife with his prints on, and the bloodstained clothes which the moron had not thought to get rid of.

Next thing, there's a lot of official coming and going with Police Federation reps and the like. Everyone was 'shocked and disappointed' but it was not the behaviour expected of a Met officer – whatever said officer had been through – and, being permanently unfit to return to duty, I hadn't left the powers that be with much choice. The extended paid leave became 'medical retirement', and even though they were nice enough not to nick me for possession they made it clear they were actually doing me a favour and maybe I could do them one by not making a fuss about it.

Handing over my warrant card nice and quietly.

Fair enough back then, I suppose, and being 'medically retired' means I get a small pension which comes in useful, but it still pisses me off looking back at it now. The lack of sympathy or understanding. Yeah, I had a problem with drink and was doing way too much skunk on top of all the pills. As if all that wasn't enough – and it was more than enough for most of my so-called friends – it was around this time that I started to believe some of the things that led me, eventually, to the tender mercies of the Fleet Ward, by way of the less-than-tender process of being sectioned.

Maybe we should leave all that fun stuff until next time.

I should mention, though, that I'd also turned into a bit of a slapper. Up to that point – before Johnno died, I mean – I'd had a couple of longish relationships and even been engaged at one time, but afterwards, once the booze and the weed had begun to work their magic, I decided to really let rip and throw casual sex into the mix.

Why not, right?

There were a lot of wild nights spent in clubs and bars and a lot of miserable mornings spent telling myself I would never do it again after waking up with one loser or another. You know what Coyote Syndrome is, right? When you wake up curled around some stranger and you'd rather chew your own arm off than move it and risk waking them up. I was very familiar with that. I think I fell for the 'Hello ladies' line more than once myself back then, though I was usually the one looking for a quick bunk-up.

Worst part is, I can't remember any of the sex.

Not a single moment.

It was probably all terrible, but still . . .

All very sordid and, believe it or not, it's the aspect of my somewhat chequered past I'm least proud of. That's probably because of where one such encounter led. Because of who it led to.

I can't even remember where I met Andy, but the morning after wasn't quite as terrible as usual and he stuck around until the afternoon. I told him a bit about myself, but not all of it. He told me about his boring job in an office and I remember feeling quite jealous. We saw each other a few times after that and suddenly we were going out. Restaurants and the pictures and stupid cards on Valentine's Day.

All fine and dandy.

It's how things are supposed to be, isn't it?

He knew exactly what he was getting into, I want to stress that right now. He knew. How could he not, for God's sake, the state of me back then?

When he suggested that I move into his flat, I wasn't convinced it was a good idea, but Sophie certainly was. I must have been a total nightmare to live with, so I don't blame her for encouraging me.

'New start,' she said.

Looking back now, it's quite funny, because I can see how desperate she was.

'Could be just what you need, Al . . .'

It wasn't, and you already know that things with not-as-nice-as-I-thought-he-was Andy went tits-up very quickly – before I'd taken all my stuff out of the boxes, more or less – but there's all manner of fun and games you don't know about yet, and I think I'll save the more lurid details for the next instalment.

The cutting and the masks and the hospital.

The plot to murder me.

You really don't want to miss that. Watch this space.

FOURTEEN

Half an hour or so after I'd talked to Banksy, Marcus knocked on my door. I shouted 'fuck off', which is my standard reaction, to be fair, but I was angry that Banksy had rubbished my fake voluntary idea. I still thought it was something worth following up.

Marcus knocked again and this time he didn't wait for an answer. The bedroom doors can be locked and we've all got our own keys, but most people don't bother because we're in and out all day and the staff have to come in so often for checks. We've each got a small cupboard inside our room with a padlock. That's useful for any valuables, because sometimes phones or iPods can go walkabout, but the doors themselves tend to stay unlocked.

Marcus walked in and sat down on the end of the bed, like we were best mates. 'Back to WEO,' he said.

Within Eyesight Observation. No big surprise, but it didn't do much for my mood. It's exactly like it sounds and would mean a nurse keeping an eye on me twenty-four hours a day. Watching me eat and following me into the toilet. Even at night, there'd be someone sitting outside my half-open bedroom door.

'Fine,' I said. 'Whatever.'

He didn't seem in any hurry to leave, just sat there fiddling with his ID, dangling from its ever-so-cheerful rainbow-coloured lanyard. 'It's a shame, that's all,' he said, eventually. 'You'd been doing really well.'

'Not well enough to be sent home.'

'*Well*, all the same. Better.'

He was trying to be kind, I can see that now. His voice, as always, was low and dripping with concern. That didn't stop me wanting to upset him and make the rest of his day as awful as mine was going to be. 'Maybe I'm just messing you all about and behaving the way you want me to,' I said. 'Saying all the right things.' I tapped the side of my head. 'Maybe in here I'm still massively fucked.'

'If that is the case, the only one you're making a fool of is you,' he said. 'It's your weekly assessment the day after tomorrow, so let's see what happens.'

'I know exactly what's going to happen,' I said. 'Well, I know what's not going to happen.'

'Do you not think we *want* you to go home?'

He looked like he genuinely meant it but, staring at him, I found myself thinking about what Tony had said about a member of staff being the Thing, and even though the whole idea is just about the maddest thing I've ever heard I sat there for half a minute trying to imagine what it would be like if it was actually true.

'We want all the patients to go home,' he said.

I tried to manufacture a smile. 'Well, whether I'm massively fucked or not, and I'm not saying one way or the other, I mean it's your job to work that out—'

'Not true,' he said quickly. 'Perhaps that is Dr Bakshi's job, or part of it anyway, but the rest of us are here to keep you safe.'

'Either way . . . I might be massively fucked, but you're the one that *looks* like you are.' I leaned close and studied his face. 'You look knackered.'

He laughed, gently. 'Yes, I am very tired. We all are.'

'You need to pace yourself, mate. It's not even Wednesday lunchtime yet.'

'We don't have the luxury of pacing ourselves,' he said. 'On top of which Malaika is off sick today.'

I hadn't noticed she wasn't around.

'The agency have not sent a replacement.'

'Never enough dosh,' I said.

He nodded. 'Governments have short memories.'

'Yeah, I hear what you're saying.' It wasn't very long ago that Marcus and the hundreds of thousands like him were heroes. The saviours of a nation. I'd been one of those standing outside my flat, clapping in the street.

'It was never applause we needed.' Marcus stood up. 'It was money and the proper equipment. Four nurses died on this unit.'

'Yeah,' I said. 'Public funding is one thing that's always been massively fucked. Same in the Met.'

He stopped at the door. 'That's another thing.'

'What?'

'This is what tells me that you still have a fair way to go before you *are* well. You talking about the police.' He was playing with his stupid ID card again. 'Like you are still working for them.'

'OK, now you really *can* fuck off,' I said.

He didn't. 'Why were you asking Femi those questions?'

'I don't know what you're on about.'

'Missing drugs.'

'You've got no idea how crime is actually solved, have you?' I was kneeling up on the bed now, my voice a good deal louder than his and both fists clutching the duvet. 'You probably think it's all about CCTV and mobile phones and all that technical crap, don't you? The truth is, doesn't matter how much of that stuff you've got, crime actually gets solved because human beings like me ask questions.' I took a few deep breaths. 'One of your patients was murdered, I'm not sure if you're aware of that.'

'What happened to Mr Connolly was truly horrible,' he said. 'But I still have patients like you to take care of and keep safe.' He took hold of his badge again, held it up like I'd never seen it before. 'That is my job.'

'Right, and I don't need you to tell me how to do *my* job, fair enough?'

'It's not your job, Alice.'

I was still screaming when he closed the door.

After that I tossed my duvet and pillows around for a while, heaved the mattress on to the floor exactly as George and Marcus had done the night before and turned the bed over. Then once I was out of breath and had put everything back together again, I lay down until I was feeling a little less like putting my fist through a window.

I needed to get my act together, because there was lots to do.

I would start getting into this properly the next day.

There were plenty of people to talk to and I had no shortage of questions to ask.

FIFTEEN

I woke up Thursday feeling jumpy and knowing that if anyone so much as said good morning there was every chance I would do them serious damage. All I wanted was to scratch and kick at something or someone. I don't know if they'd upped my dosages without telling me, but half an hour after I'd taken my morning meds – fighting the urge to fly across the counter at Femi – things had swung much too far the other way and just walking to the toilet and back felt like wading through treacle.

When Donna walked past it was like she was sprinting.

I knew that the morning was a washout. I was no use to anyone, up and down like a yo-yo, so I went back to bed.

All being well, I'd get stuck into the interviews come the afternoon.

That's just the way it goes sometimes.

A bit later, before I had a chance to talk to anyone, Jamilah left.

It's not like there's a fanfare when it happens or anyone

makes an official announcement, so most of the time people just go home or get sent somewhere else without you even knowing. They're just ... not there any more. But a few people were talking about it when I got up again so, when the woman of the moment finally appeared in the corridor with her wheelie suitcase, me and a couple of the others were standing around to watch her go.

It wouldn't be doing my investigation any favours, of course. It was one less person to talk to, one less witness who'd been on the ward when Kevin was killed, but the Foot Woman had never been high up on my list of suspects. I just couldn't see her sneaking into Kevin's room, giving his feet a quick rub then popping a pillow over his face. Like I said, it wouldn't have taken much, but she was just too ... wispy. I doubt she'd have been able to strangle a mouse.

When she was at the airlock, shaking hands with the nurses, we all took our shoes off and waggled our feet at her. It was Lucy's idea. Jamilah smiled and nodded, but I don't think she got the joke.

'I give it two weeks,' Ilias said. 'Two weeks and she'll be back.'

I went to the toilet and had a little cry after Jamilah left.

For me though, not for her.

Yeah, it would have been nice to commandeer the empty MDR and use that as a makeshift interview room like Seddon had done, but with nowhere else even remotely suitable, I had to think on my feet a bit. Use whatever opportunities presented themselves. Also, now the staff were starting to get on my case, I didn't want to make too much of a song and dance about it anyway.

I needed to do things quietly, to be subtle.

Neither of which I'm good at.

After lunch, I saw that The Thing, the Walker and Big Gay Bob were still sitting in the dining room, so I joined them. Obviously one of the nurses – Mia, as it happened – joined me.

I sat and listened for a few minutes. Subtle . . .

'How long's that corridor out there?' Tony asked Donna.

Donna shook her head.

'Whatever it is, I reckon you must walk miles every day, right? You must be dead fit.'

Donna lifted her T-shirt and pinched at her belly, struggling to squeeze as much as a millimetre of fat between her fingers and thumbs. 'Need to get this off,' she said, looking away. 'It's disgusting.'

Tony grabbed a handful of his considerably larger belly. 'Maybe I should join you. I need to start getting in shape. The Thing's coming for me soon, I can feel it.'

While Tony started telling Donna all about his shadowy nemesis for the umpteenth time, I slid across to Bob and leaned close.

'How did it go with the police the other day?' I glanced across, but happily Mia, who was sitting a few tables away, wasn't paying the slightest attention.

Bob nodded slowly. 'The one taking the samples was a little cracker, I know that much. I gave her my phone number.'

'What did you tell them?'

'What do you mean?'

'Like, where were you when it happened?'

'When what happened?'

'When Kevin was killed.' I punched him on the arm. It was meant to be playful, but I saw him wince.

'I can't remember.' He winked at me. 'That's what I told them.'

'Right . . .'

'Because I was having a bad day and I really couldn't.'

'Meaning you can remember now?'

Now the nodding was a little more enthusiastic. 'Yeah, I was watching the telly.'

'OK.' He'd certainly been in there when I'd left to go the dining room. Several of them were – Donna, Lucy and Ilias for starters – and I already knew that's what they were likely to tell me.

'I wanted to change the channel,' Bob said, 'but Lauren wasn't having any of it. There was a film on the other side with Gwyneth Paltrow in it and she's the one who talks about her fanny all the time so I really wanted to watch it. Lauren said I couldn't, though. I remember sitting there, staring at the back of her stupid head and thinking how badly I wanted to punch it.'

'Did you hear anyone saying anything about Kevin? Anything bad, I mean . . . before it happened?'

Bob shrugged. 'There's always somebody falling out with someone, isn't there? I know Lauren didn't like him very much.'

'Did she say why?'

'He just got on her nerves, I think.' He lowered his voice. 'They were arguing by the airlock one time and I heard her call him a two-faced little ponce . . . something like that. Mind you, everyone gets on Lauren's nerves, don't they?'

I saw Tony get up to fetch a glass of water from the jug at the serving hatch. I stood up and went across to get one myself.

'Funny sort of time, isn't it? A strange atmosphere, don't you reckon?'

'Same old, same old,' Tony said.

'Yeah, but now, I mean. After what happened to Kevin.'

He downed half a glassful, then stared at me. 'I suppose.'

'You must be feeling a bit bad, though.'

'Must I?'

'After that fight and everything. I mean, did you and him get the chance to make up before ... '

'That ruck wasn't my fault,' he said. 'The police were giving me grief about this the other day and I told them, it was nothing to do with me.'

'Certainly looked like it from where I was standing.'

'That's bollocks. It had already kicked off when I got there. I was trying to break it up and someone threw a punch ... can't even remember who it was, now ... I was just defending myself.'

He was starting to get a bit worked up, so I checked to see if Mia was watching, but she was deep in some conversation with George.

'I'm not going to stand there and let myself get smacked, am I?'

'Right,' I said. It's hard to take anything seriously, coming from a bloke who believes a demonic entity can disguise itself as a postcard, but it certainly seemed as though Tony was telling the truth. I felt a twinge of guilt because of what I'd told Seddon a few days before. 'So, who did start it?'

'Not really sure.' Tony finished his water and examined the empty glass as though there might be something lurking at the bottom of it. 'Lucy told me she thought maybe Kevin and Shaun were having a row and it got out of hand.'

'Yeah?'

'Lovers' tiff or something.'

I'd check with Lucy. I'd never seen Kevin and Shaun exchange a cross word, so if that was what had started the big fight a few days before the murder it would be interesting to find out what the two of them had been arguing about.

'It was well funny, though.'

'What was?'

He jabbed a finger into my shoulder. '*You*. Standing on that chair and making a big speech.'

Suddenly I didn't feel quite so guilty any more. I had half a mind to get on the phone to Seddon, tell him I had more information and drop Tony even further in it. Tell Seddon he'd confessed or something.

'Laying down the law,' Tony said.

Because I could, couldn't I?

If I felt like it, I could say anything about any of them.

They'd deny it, but that didn't matter. Most people in here are too drugged up to remember what they've told anyone half the time, never mind what they might have done. Most of them don't even think they should *be* here, for Christ's sake.

Now Tony was laughing, a deep *hurr hurr* that was annoying at the best of times, and right then made me want to smash my water glass into his face. He pointed and started to shout, so that everyone else in the room could share the joke. Bob started to laugh, too.

'I am a police officer . . . remember?' Tony was bellowing and trying to do my voice, high-pitched and stupid. 'I am a *police* officer!'

Now I could see that Mia, along with everyone else, *was* looking. I decided that I'd got about as much information out of Tony as I was likely to get and headed quickly to the door. Donna was already on her way out, keen to put in some hard yards, so I followed her out into the corridor, fell into step next to her and began to walk.

SIXTEEN

'What was all that about?' Donna asked.

I still felt angry about it and the speed-walking wasn't helping to ease the tension. 'Just Tony taking the piss,' I said.

'Want me to mess with him a bit? Tell him I'm the Thing?'

'No, you're all right,' I said.

We had already walked the length of the corridor three times as far as the MDR, turned and walked back again.

'I think it's good that you're trying to find out what happened,' Donna said.

'It's important,' I said.

'Police are obviously doing sod all.'

I don't know why I suddenly felt the need to defend a service that had seen fit to kick me out on my arse. Something deep-seated that hadn't gone away in spite of everything, I suppose. I couldn't think of a time when I hadn't wanted to be a police officer. I still can't.

I said, 'I'm sure they're doing everything they can. It takes time to build a case, to put a list of likely suspects together and interview them, to process forensic evidence.'

'Like on *CSI*?'

I bit my tongue. That stupid show is the bane of a detective's life, making shit up and presenting it as gospel. I'd seen any number of trials go down the toilet because jurors thought they knew things once they'd seen them on the TV. Because they were too stupid to know the difference between forensic fact and fiction.

'They'll be able to find out exactly who'd been in Kevin's room, won't they?' Donna nodded.

'Not necessarily.'

'Because these days you just need a sample of the air.'

Like I said . . .

We walked past the examination rooms again, the occupational therapy room and the meds hatch. Again. Mia, who was clearly taking her WEO duties seriously but had drawn the line at following the pair of us up and down like an idiot, had staked out an observation post in the doorway of the nurses' station. We walked past the music room and the 136 Suite, turned right at the dining room and headed for the airlock.

Lauren stuck two fingers up from the toilet doorway.

Ilias said, 'Idiots,' as we marched past him.

'Did you hear anything about Kevin and Shaun having an argument?'

Donna shook her head.

'You know, the big fight?'

She shook her head again, eyes wide and fixed. With these athletes it's all about focus. 'What about drugs?' I asked. 'You know anything about drugs going missing?' She nodded as we turned at the airlock and began another lap. I quickened my pace to keep up with her. 'What?'

'*My* drugs,' she said. 'They go missing all the time.'

'That's not what I—'

'Well, they get taken at any rate. Soon as I get them brought in, they confiscate them. My Hydroxycut and my caffeine pills. That bitch Debbie even took my laxatives, for pity's sake. They take everything I really need off me, then give me anti-depressants and Kwells to stop me drooling, like they know what's best. *I* know what I need, Al, because it's my body.' She glanced at me and shook her head, tears in her eyes. 'My *laxatives* . . .'

As we walked past the nurses' station again, I saw Mia writing something down. Behind her, Marcus pointed at me and something snapped. I felt it, you know? Like a tiny bomb going off inside.

I turned to Donna. 'Why do you *do* this?'

Donna swallowed and began walking even faster.

'Seriously, what is the point? Marching up and down this corridor like a clockwork lunatic, trying to lose the weight you haven't put on because you don't eat anything. Literally, nothing. Staring at yourself in the mirror all the time and thinking you look fat, which is what ordinary idiots like me do because most of us probably are ... while you actually look like a jogger in fucking Auschwitz or something. I mean, seriously. All that rubbish you were coming out with the other night about Kevin killing himself. You don't even see the irony of that, do you ... ?'

I stopped to get my breath back. Donna had moved ahead of me anyway now and I could hear her crying. Ilias was watching me, sitting backwards on a chair outside the 136. He said, 'You tell her. Skinny bitch.'

Suddenly I felt terrible for upsetting Donna and I knew I needed to knock it on the head for a bit.

Have some time to think.

My meds were beginning to wear off. I'd become well used to the sensation, like bathwater draining away, and to tell you the truth I didn't know if that was a good thing or not. Was I better at all this, at doing my job, with or without the anti-psychotics and the Selective Serotonin Reuptake Inhibitors, whatever the hell they are? I wasn't sure what 'clear-headed' even meant any more. I stood in the corridor staring at the sickly-yellow wall, panting like some knackered old dog and wondering what Johnno would think about it.

Knowing exactly what he would say.

Take a fucking break . . .

I could see that, as per usual, Tony was standing at the exit with his bags packed, as I walked across to the meds hatch. There was, equally predictably, one person ahead of me, waiting for his mid-afternoon prescription. That was fine though, because the Waiter was exactly the person I was looking for.

'Sounds like you had fun with those cameras,' I said. 'Last Saturday, after dinner.'

Graham spoke without turning round because he did not want to miss that hatch opening. He was staring at it all the way through our conversation. 'I always have fun.'

'Just random, is it?'

'What's that mean . . . random?'

'Which camera you shut down. Just an accident, was it, that on Saturday night it happened to be the camera covering the men's corridor? Kevin's room.'

'Yeah, an accident,' Graham said.

'You sure nobody suggested it? Nobody asked you if . . . maybe you fancied doing what you do to that particular camera?'

'I just picked that one.' He shuddered and shook his head. 'I didn't like the look of it.'

'Do people ever ask you?'

He took so long to answer that I wasn't sure he'd heard me. 'Sometimes.'

'Like when?'

Another long pause. Graham looked at his watch. He thrust his hands into his pockets, took them out again. 'Once someone asked me to put food on the camera in the music room because someone else had been playing the guitar and she didn't like it, so she wanted to go in there and smash it. Smash the guitar. Don't ask me who it was, though, because I'm never going to tell you her name.'

I didn't bother, because it wasn't important. Lauren, obviously . . .

'Did you tell the police about that?'

'Yes, I had to, didn't I?' He tapped at the hatch window. 'Someone obviously told them that sometimes I mess about with the cameras, because they asked me all sorts of questions about it. It wasn't very nice, actually. It was like they were accusing me of something.'

'That must have been upsetting,' I said.

'Are *you* accusing me of something?'

'Absolutely not,' I said.

He tapped at the hatch again. 'Good, because I wouldn't like that.'

The window opened to reveal George, who said, 'Hello, Graham. Fancy seeing you here.'

Graham laughed and leaned on the counter, so I knew the interview was finished. He took his meds like a child collecting a prize. He said, 'Thank you, George,' and marched away without looking at me.

I stepped forward to take mine, then moved quickly away.

'No, thank *you*,' George said.

L-Plate was next in line, so I lingered while she picked up her pills. Just your basic anti-depressants and stuff to combat the withdrawal. Methadone or whatever. I knew that, because she had an injection once a month for the heebie-jeebies.

I can't stand needles, so I've always opted for the tablets. Sometimes, if I'm lucky, I'll get oral dispersibles, which are basically just these wafer-thin squares that melt on your tongue. Yum!

I collared her as soon as she stepped away from the hatch.

She raised her hands. 'Too close . . .'

'Sorry, L.' I raised my own hands in apology and moved back a little. 'I just wanted to ask you . . . I heard that you know what started the big fight a couple of days before Kevin was killed.'

'Heard from who?'

'It doesn't matter, honestly. Something about a row between Kevin and Shaun?'

'Oh, that, yeah.' Lucy leaned back against a wall and began doing weird stretches, like she was practising some kind of psych-ward t'ai chi. She was wearing a Calvin Klein T-shirt and tracksuit bottoms same as me, only I was damn sure she hadn't bought her trackies at JD Sports. 'Well, to be honest I didn't hear very much, babe. They were shouting at each other after the last occupational therapy session. I was only in there because I wasn't very happy with what I'd painted that day and I was trying to tidy it up a bit.'

'What were they arguing about?'

'I wasn't trying to eavesdrop or anything. I mean I really wasn't, so I just caught snippets of it. There was something Shaun wanted Kevin to do and Kevin wasn't keen. Shaun was telling him he had to, that he was being stupid . . . that was about it.'

'So that was what the fight was all about?'

'Who knows what started *that*,' Lucy said. She stopped the stupid stretching and leaned as close to me as I ever saw her get to anyone. 'You think it had something to do with why Kevin was murdered? A grudge or whatever?'

'I'm trying to piece it together,' I said.

She put her arms up, stretching her fingers towards the ceiling tiles, then cocked her head to whisper, '*I'd* heard it was a drugs thing, and I have to say that wouldn't surprise me. Obviously, you know my history, right? Well, the fact is, one does learn to recognise it in other people.'

I knew what she meant. Like coppers knowing when someone was iffy.

'I suppose it's kind of a junkie gaydar.' Lucy laughed, a silly, high giggle. 'I'm just saying, I always thought drugs were a part of Kevin's life in one way or another.'

I didn't tell her that she was bang on the money. As far as I knew, I was still the only person on the ward – the only patient, at any rate – who knew about the drugs discovered in Kevin's room, and I certainly wasn't going to tell her about it. A detective learns early on that it's not clever to furnish a witness with any information that may prejudice the statement they're about to give you.

Lucy resumed her exercises, tossing back her head and rolling her hips around. 'Is that any help to you, babe?'

I hadn't got the first idea, besides which I'd noticed Mia wandering across from the nurses' station. She stopped a few feet away from us and smiled, just to let me know that she knew exactly what I was up to, had been up to most of the day.

As it happened, at that moment I was perfectly happy to stop for a while.

I'm still not sure if it was some kind of early comedown, but I felt like a sodden blanket had been thrown across me. It wasn't even two o'clock, but I was wiped out suddenly; bone-tired, as though, when I'd been talking to Donna, I'd walked a hundred times further than I did.

I can see *now* that it was mental – isn't everything? – because I was doing it all. Normally, on a job like this one, I'd have been working as part of a good-sized team. Maybe talking to a single witness, collating statements or putting together a report on suspicious mobile activity, while Johnno, Banksy and the rest of the squad were busy doing other stuff. I'd have one thing to concentrate on, one area of the investigation to put all my energy into, but now everything was down to me and I was finding it all a bit stressful to say the least.

I trudged back towards the women's corridor thinking about the three people I still wanted to talk to.

The Grand Master, the Sheep, the Singer.

It would have to wait, though, because right then I was finding it hard enough to put one foot in front of the other.

I all but fell into my room and slept for the best part of eight hours.

SEVENTEEN

You probably won't be amazed to discover that, once dinner and after-dinner meds are out of the way, the most popular recreational activity in this place of an evening is settling down in front of the idiot box, and not just because of the appropriate nickname. Actually, I don't think that anyone in here is an idiot, but you know what I mean. A lot of people are probably quite smart, unlike the TV itself, but even though that's not got the biggest screen in the world or the widest selection of channels, it's where most of the patients end up in the hours before bedtime.

Watching what's on, or arguing about what's on, or ignoring what's on but still there anyway.

Make no mistake, there *is* a variety of other pastimes and pursuits catered for on Fleet Ward. Aside from looking out of the window at the breathtaking views of the A41 there are newspapers every day and, for readers, a decent selection of books in the OT room (if you like thrillers or chick-lit,

116

which I do). There's a few jigsaws (pieces gone missing or been eaten). There's Jenga and Cluedo and Scrabble and of course, if you prefer a solo hobby, there's always frantic masturbation, which, judging by the faces of the housekeeping team when they're changing the beds every day, remains a perennial favourite. Now I think about it, leisure-wise, there's often a degree of multi-tasking, and I say that with confidence, because I once saw someone masturbating *while* they were playing Scrabble.

But it's the telly that tends to unite everyone in here, even if they rarely get a say in what they get to watch, and it strikes me that the makers of *Gogglebox* are seriously missing a trick.

. . . and in a hospital in north London, Ilias, Donna and Bob have settled down to watch Bake Off. *It's pastry week and the contestants are . . . oh God, no . . . Donna is running round and round the sofa and Ilias appears to be taking his pants off . . .*

I woke feeling a damn sight better, but also annoyed at having slept through dinner. I made short work of some crisps and a box of Jaffa Cakes that Banksy had brought in because, aside from being properly ravenous, I didn't fancy taking my last lot of meds on an empty stomach. Having sweet-talked Femi – who had just shut up shop – into handing them over after hours, I wandered into the TV room, well up for it.

Aside from Donna, who someone told me later had gone to bed early because she was upset about something, pretty much everyone was in there, which was helpful.

Most important, Ilias, Lauren and Shaun were in there.

There are two fake leather sofas at the front and a variety of chairs scattered around behind. A few armchairs that almost certainly have things living in them and plenty of the hard blue ones that are knocking around all over the ward. They're usually lined up around the walls in here, but as soon as the TV gets switched on people drag them into the middle of the room to get a better view. There's even a few low tables dotted about so people can keep their tea or nuts or Fanta within easy reach.

It's nice enough, as it goes, long as you don't mind the farting.

Everyone has their spot, of course, and I've seen it kick off more than once if a favourite perching position is snaffled. Ilias likes to sit at the back, from where he can provide a foul-mouthed commentary if he's in the mood, or occasionally throw things. Shaun prefers a chair near the door and Lauren, as always, was in prime position on a sofa at the front, her fat fist wrapped around the remote control as though it were a sceptre. Or a sock full of snooker balls.

I pulled one of the empty chairs across and sat down next to Ilias.

'What's on?'

'It's all shit,' Ilias said. He stared at me, suspicious. 'You weren't there for dinner.'

'I was asleep.'

He grunted, then cupped his hands round his mouth, like nobody would hear him shouting otherwise. 'Turn it over!'

Lauren stuck up a finger.

'Why do you care, if it's all shit?'

'It's the what-do-you-call-it . . . the principle,' Ilias said. 'Why should that cow decide which shit we have to watch?'

We sat and watched for a couple of minutes. Some chefs on a road trip. It wasn't unenjoyable, as it happens.

'You've been here about as long as me,' I said.

'Longer.' He sounded proud of the fact, and said it again, keen to make sure I knew. 'I was here the night they brought you in.' He let out a low, phlegmy chuckle. 'Shouting about lights in the garden and funny music and all that.'

I ignored that, took a few seconds, and nodded. 'Makes sense, because you always know what's going on around this place. Who's getting off with who, who's got the hump about something, all that. You keep your ear to the ground.' I looked at his ear as I said it. Huge, and sprouting long black hairs like he was a hobbit.

Ilias sat back, smiling and humming with pleasure, delighted that someone had finally noticed his contribution. I took the chance to glance over at Malaika, who was running WEO/WAL interference for the evening. She was sitting in a corner, next to one of the less-than-realistic plastic ferns that are dotted around all over the place so that we don't lose our connection with the natural world.

She looked content enough, slowly turning the pages of *Take A Break*.

'So, bearing all that in mind, what's your take on what happened to Kevin?'

He folded his arms and thought about it. 'Kevin wasn't very happy.'

As insights went, considering where we were, it was hardly Hercule Poirot. I said, 'I don't think anyone's exactly thrilled, stuck in here.'

'I'm perfectly happy,' Ilias said. 'You have to have a positive attitude.'

'So why wasn't Kevin happy?'

'I think he felt trapped.'

'Did he say that?'

'He said . . . something. He couldn't get out because people would be upset. I can't really remember.'

'Was this anything to do with Shaun?' I was thinking about the argument the two of them were supposed to have had. Was Shaun the one Kevin felt trapped by?

'Shaun is also unhappy. Now, because of what happened to Kevin, but he was not happy before.'

'Why not?'

Ilias looked at me like I was an idiot. 'You need to ask Shaun.'

I intended to, but I was saving him until last. I told Ilias that maybe the two of us should play chess some time, then stood up and walked to the front of the room.

'Turn it over!' he shouted again.

There was an Informal I'd never spoken to sitting on the sofa next to Lauren, so I turned on the menace and told him to move, told him he was in my *fucking* spot. He swore at me a bit – ignoring the angry shushing from Lauren – then stood up, and from the corner of my eye I saw Malaika doing the same thing. 'It's fine.' I turned and smiled innocently at her. 'Thing is, I can't really see from back there . . .'

Malaika sat down and so did I.

Without taking her eyes off the screen, Lauren moved the remote control to the hand that was furthest away from me. She said, 'Don't even think about it.'

Getting anything at all out of Lauren was going to be a tough one, I'd always known that, but I'd thought about it. About the best way to come at her. I leaned across and started singing, quietly.

'It's so funny . . . that we don't talk any more.' I smiled, but she didn't react. 'Cliff Richard,' I said. 'His best one, if you ask me.'

She turned to me. 'Are you serious? What about "Congratulations"? What about "Wired for Sound"?' She shook her head, disgusted. 'You're a moron.'

'It's true though.' I turned back to the screen, like I didn't care one way or the other. 'We did use to talk.' It was certainly the case that, once upon a time, me and Lauren had exchanged words rather more often than we did now, even if most of the words had four letters in them.

I waited. The three chefs – one of them was Gordon Ramsay – were somewhere in the American south, arguing about the best way to roast a pig.

'What do you want to talk about?' Lauren asked.

I didn't see a lot of point in going round the houses. 'Why didn't you like Kevin?'

'Who says I didn't?'

'A "two-faced little ponce". That's what I heard you called him.'

'So?' She shrugged. 'Doesn't mean I killed him, does it?' She looked at me. 'That's what you're going round trying to find out, isn't it? Miss fucking Marple.'

Ugly as it was, Lauren had a decent head on her shoulders. She was the only one who'd really sussed out what I was up to. Or who let me know she'd sussed it, at any rate. It was my turn to shrug.

'Got any suspects, have you?'

'Bit early for that,' I said. 'It's just a question of gathering information at this stage.'

She said, 'Ooh,' like she was impressed. It might have been at one of the chefs, but I'm pretty sure she was taking the piss.

'So, why was he a two-faced ponce?'

'Because he always tried to come across as such an inno-cent . . . like he was a victim. Him and his boyfriend.' She flicked her head towards the door, where Shaun was sitting on his own. 'Love's young dream, over there. Well, we're all victims of something or other, mate, that's why we're here. So I for one wasn't having any of it.' She sniffed, hacked some-thing into her mouth and swallowed it. 'He was into all sorts.'

'Like what?'

She smiled and it wasn't a good look. 'They found stuff in his room.'

'What stuff?'

She smiled again. 'You think you're the only one in here that knows anything?'

'Who told you?'

'One of the nurses told me. I've been in here a while and they know I don't go around shooting my gob off like some. Can't say I was surprised, mind you. About the drugs, I mean.'

I said nothing.

'Dangerous game to get into, that one.'

I had every right to be annoyed that I wasn't the only one who knew about the drugs, who had inside information, but I'm still angry at myself for letting it show. Clenching my teeth, I said, 'Where were *you* when it happened, then? Did you go into the men's corridor that night?'

'Jesus, love, you're getting a bit desperate now, aren't you?'

'You're not going to answer, then?'

'No comment.' She was enjoying herself now. Like she was the one in the box seat. 'How's that suit you?'

I couldn't think of any other way to get the upper hand again, and before I knew it I was on my feet and moving to stand – very deliberately – between her and the TV screen. There were one or two jeers and the odd shout of complaint from fans of the three chefs, but I could see straight away that I'd got the reaction I wanted from Lauren.

'Move,' she said.

'Make me,' I said.

Malaika laid her magazine to one side and stood up. Debbie appeared in the doorway.

Lauren didn't hesitate. She heaved herself to her feet, and as soon as she'd begun lumbering towards me I ducked quickly past her, grabbed the remote that she'd left behind on the sofa and changed the channel.

'You're dead,' she said.

I made full use of the few seconds I had before Malaika or Lauren could get to me, acknowledging the cheers and the standing ovation from Ilias. It was lovely. I raised both my arms like I'd won something, then lobbed the remote at Lauren before pushing my way through the chairs and settling down nice and quietly next to Shaun.

I waited ten minutes or so, until it had all died down.

Until Debbie had gone back to the nurses' station and Malaika was sure things were calm again. Until the programme with the chefs had finished and Lauren had made a show of changing the channel, so that we could all enjoy *Celebrity Botched-up Bodies*.

'How you doing, mate?' I asked.

'OK, I suppose.' Shaun looked at the floor and began scratching furiously at his head, as though his hair was full of ants. He grunted with the effort. He was never the easiest person to talk to, but he'd gone even further into himself in the days since Kevin had died.

123

Grief, I presumed, but it could easily have been something else. I was still thinking about what Ilias had told me about a big argument, about Kevin feeling trapped. 'Come on, I know how you must be feeling. It's better if you let some of it out though, mate. What Dr Bakshi always says, right?'

Shaun nodded and scratched.

A woman on TV was showing off her horrendous pair of fake tits.

'The thing is, Shaun, the police have asked me to help them with their investigation. Like, an extra person on the inside kind of thing.'

'Yeah?' He gave me a thumbs-up. 'That's pretty cool, Al.'

'Yes, but it means I do need to ask you a few questions, if that's OK.'

He mumbled something that sounded to me like it was.

'Was everything good with you and Kevin?'

'Good?'

'Before what happened to him, I mean?'

'It was OK.' He was mumbling and the looking at the floor wasn't helping, so I had to lean in to hear what he was saying.

'Only I heard you'd had a row . . .'

Now he looked up, like he'd been tasered or something.

'It's fine,' I said. 'Nobody ever gets to say the things to someone who's died that they wish they'd said. Sometimes the last things you say to a loved one aren't . . . kind, but that's how it goes. Don't beat yourself up about it.' I blinked, remembering a voluntary who'd been here for a couple of days and had spent most of the time doing exactly that. Daft bastard had knocked himself unconscious several times.

Shaun was nodding again and his eyes were all over the place.

'Take your time,' I said.

'We were arguing about the drugs,' he said eventually. It was still quiet, but suddenly he was talking nineteen to the dozen. 'Fighting all the time. He was getting these drugs, a lot of them, and I told him it was stupid. I begged him and begged him ... I told him that he'd end up going to prison and he wouldn't be able to get well and I'd be stuck in here and we wouldn't see each other again—' He stopped suddenly and the hand that wasn't scratching went to his mouth.

'Where did he get the drugs from, Shaun?' I waited then leaned across to lay a hand on his arm and began to rub. 'Come on, you're doing ever so well. You're being dead brave, mate.' Rub, rub, rub. 'Where did he get them, Shaun?' Keep saying the subject's name to get their confidence. 'Was there someone bringing them in for him?'

Then I saw his eyes widen suddenly, shift and fix, and I turned to see what he was looking at.

'No, not Malaika ... it's not ... are you saying he got them from someone in here? Is that what you mean, Shaun? Did someone in here—'

I stopped because I saw what was coming. He looked terrified and that bloody finger was pressed to his chin.

'Am I going to die? Am I going to die? Am I going to die?'

I tried to shush him, but the volume just built and built until he knocked the chair over as he scrambled upright.

'Am I going to die? *Am* I?'

Malaika was on her way across and I was trying to hold on to him.

'No, of course you're not going—'

'AmIgoingtodieAmIgoingtodieAmIgoingtodie*AmIGoingToDie?*'

He was screaming it by now and other people in the room

were already on their feet, some of them getting visibly upset and moving away, pressing themselves back against the wall.

Above the cacophony I could hear Lauren yelling, 'Will someone shut that little twat up?'

Having asked me to step away, Malaika was already doing her best, but for once her soft words of reassurance seemed only to be making it worse. I could see the genuine fear on her face, then the relief as Debbie came steaming in to take over.

'What's the matter, Shaun?' Debbie stood there, the spittle flying on to her face and neck as he asked and asked, screeched and pleaded. She closed her eyes and sighed. 'Yes,' she said, finally. 'Yes, I think you are. In fact I very much doubt you'll make it to bedtime.'

Shaun stopped immediately, froze as though he'd been slapped.

Then he dropped to the floor like he'd taken a bullet to the back of the head and began to convulse, thrashing and squealing as Malaika pressed her alarm and Marcus and George rushed in to clear the room.

EIGHTEEN

This Is What I Believed.

Part Two . . . and I'm not going to waste my time or yours, so I can tell you straight off that it began with the lights at the end of the garden. Dim lights I could see pulsing through the trees from my bedroom window. I'd spotted them a few times when I was living with Sophie and she said it was just passing cars or lamps in the houses opposite us. She laughed and said maybe I should think about how much money I was putting in Billy's pocket every week but I wasn't convinced. I could sense it was something more than that, something bigger. I heard music, too, but not anything I could ever place; never a song I recognised or an instrument I could really identify. Just a funny kind of music I hadn't heard before.

I knew I was meant to hear it.

It felt like someone was watching me.

At Andy's place it got worse very quickly, late at night usually, and he said much the same thing as Sophie had said.

So, in the end, I stopped telling him and he probably thought I'd forgotten all about it, besides which everything got sort of taken over by the cutting for a while.

I'd come across it on the job a time or two before. Young girls, usually, with scars on their arms and legs like rungs on a ladder and because I didn't know any better then, I'd always asked myself why.

Stupid fucking question.

It was a . . . numbness, I suppose, an inability to feel much of anything. It was the agony of being ignored. I could always feel that blade against my arm, though (a Stanley knife quite often, oh the irony), and there was no way that even a dolt like Andy could ignore the bloodstained tissues on the bathroom floor. So, yeah, we spent a ton of time in A&E and there were lots of tears and plenty of shouting, but I thought my scars looked pretty cool, and however many days went by when I would say nothing or not leave the house, I never stopped being vigilant. I was always aware that there were people waiting out there in the dark that I couldn't see, keeping an eye on me.

Then I *did* start seeing them and that's when the whole business with the masks started.

In a nutshell (I might as well say it before you do – nut*case* more like), I'd see these people in the back of shot on television shows. In crowds or walking through a scene. They were all people I'd helped put away at one time or another. A bloke who'd killed his wife with a hammer, a woman who drowned both her kids in the bath, a rapist who attacked women outside underground stations. I'd just be sitting there on the sofa with Andy eating crisps and I'd spot them in the background, pretending to be extras or whatever they're called. Thing is,

I knew it wasn't actually *them*. It was people I didn't know wearing masks – people connected to the lights and the music and the watching – *disguised* as these criminals from my past.

Standing at the end of the bar in the Queen Vic.

Or in a restaurant in *MasterChef.*

Or on *Made in Chelsea*, sitting at a table in some coffee shop.

I spent a lot of time on the Internet, back then – OK, I still spend a lot of time on the Internet – but it was exactly what I needed, because I realised I was not alone and believe me, that was massive. There were plenty of other people in plenty of chat rooms, plenty of people in YouTube videos all saying *this is some scary shit* and talking about the anonymous organisations that orchestrated this kind of stuff. They were speaking out about ruthless and powerful groups that were capable of anything and were seriously well connected. Secret societies that watched and waited, then moved against anyone they perceived to be a threat.

That was the only thing I never really understood. The thing I spent every day trying to crack. I couldn't figure out *how* I was a threat to anyone, but I knew as surely as I've ever known anything that I *was*, and that one day soon they would come for me.

I could feel them getting closer.

The people behind those masks were looking straight at me, not remotely concerned that I saw them for what they were. Enjoying it, like: *This is a warning you can do nothing about.*

I was not going to be a pushover, though. I was not going to let myself become anyone's victim, because that was not what I'd been trained to do.

But . . . you have to know your enemy, right?

I suppose I should say that this is when things got . . . cranked up a bit.

One day I just got out of bed and had a smoke and realised that there had to be people in my life who were part of this. It became blindingly obvious and I felt very stupid that I hadn't worked it out before. How could these people who wanted to hurt me do it without recruiting those I was close to?

The ones who always looked so worried and told me to cut down on *this* and stop smoking *that* and, you know, maybe I should think about upping my meds.

Them.

I'd been such an idiot.

A few people laughed when I finally confronted them, which only made me angry and confirmed my suspicions. Sophie looked really sad, but I knew that was simply because I'd rumbled her. Because I'd seen through all of them. My mum just refused to engage however much I told her that I knew who she really was, and I remember the sound of my dad crying down the phone when I asked him how he could betray his child and how it had felt to sell his soul.

I was on it. I was one step ahead of the game.

I can still remember the look on Andy's face, the night it all kicked off. He was just sitting there watching football when I walked in and told him that we had to leave. He wasn't in a great mood anyway because Arsenal were a goal down, but he paused the TV and followed me into the kitchen, stood staring at me like an idiot as I gathered up all the knives.

Asked me what I was doing.

Told me to put the knives back and calm down.

'They're coming,' I told him. Why didn't he look bothered?

Why was he still standing there? 'They're coming to kill us right now and we have to get out.'

It only got physical when he tried to take the knives off me and the next thing we were scrabbling about on the kitchen floor with him talking about the police and me shouting that he was being stupid because we needed to protect ourselves.

I was trying to protect *him*, which was exceedingly fucking noble of me because I knew that he was involved in it, too.

I think I'm stronger than Andy is anyway and I was certainly feeling stronger than normal right then. The whole fight or flight thing, I suppose, and I was determined to do both. It was easy enough to push him away, and when he tried to take the knives off me again – pretty bloody carefully, mind you – I just reached for the half-empty wine bottle on the worktop because he hadn't left me a lot of choice.

I wasn't trying to hurt him.

But if I'd needed to, I wouldn't have thought twice.

There was a lot of red wine everywhere and a fair deal of blood, but I couldn't really think about it too much because obviously I had to search the rest of the house to try and find more weapons. I'd wrapped the knives in a tea towel so I could carry them, but while I was still rooting through the toolbox, Andy had managed to crawl back into the lounge, pick up his phone and ring for an ambulance. The ambulance came with a police car in tow, and after Andy had told the police that he didn't want to press charges – I should be grateful to him for that much, I suppose – we both got taken to the hospital.

One of the nurses in A&E recognised us.

Made some joke about a loyalty card.

So anyway, while Andy was being X-rayed and stitched

up, I was in another room being assessed by a couple of psychiatrists and junior something-or-others from the mental
health team. I wasn't remotely taken in by them, of course,
because I'd learned to recognise people who were part of
the plot to kill me. I told them that all that business with the
knives was just because I hadn't slept for two days, but of
course they didn't listen, because they didn't want to. They
just looked shifty and refused to answer my questions about
the organisation I knew damn well they were involved with,
but either way, several tedious hours later – with my dad on
the phone crying (again) as next of kin – forms were being
filled in, calls were being made, and several hours after that,
I was in the back of another ambulance and I was on my way.

Here.

Home Fleet home.

As I've tried to explain, a few things may have got jumbled up, the odd detail or whatever, but no names have been
changed to protect those who may or may not have been
innocent. That's a fair account of how it all went down, and
even if I can't always remember exactly *what* happened and
when, I will never forget the way I was feeling at the time.

This is what I believed.

Believed. Past tense.

For the most part.

NINETEEN

There aren't too many reasons why I would ever be looking forward to my weekly assessment. I've sat through half
a dozen of the bloody things already and the chat never
changes much and the outcome's always the same. Basically,
I shouldn't start packing just yet. That Friday though, after
the conversations I'd been having over the previous couple of
days, I was moderately excited by the prospect of sitting in a
room with several people who could at least string a sentence
together, none of whom was as mad as a box of frogs.

Whom. Listen to *me.*

All I'm saying, sometimes you miss just talking.

It was the usual suspects gathered in the MDR, though
they'd moved aside the big desk that was used for staff meetings and tribunals. Or police interviews. Assessments were a
bit more informal, a chat as much as anything, so that meant
the tried-and-trusted circle of chairs, so beloved of junkies,
alcoholics and other group therapy lovers everywhere.

Of people who need to *share*.

As always, once I'd sat down, they wasted a few minutes by formally introducing themselves for the record. There's a camera mounted up in the corner, of course – it's not one Graham's been able to get at yet, far as I know – so I'm guessing the sessions are actually filmed. Maybe, when I finally get out, they'll send me away with a copy of my greatest freak-out moments as a souvenir, like leaving Chessington World of Adventures with a picture of yourself screaming on a roller-coaster. A memory of a happy time you can treasure for ever. Anyway . . . Bakshi was present and correct, obviously, and Marcus and Debbie, and a trainee psychiatrist who said her name was Sasha, then didn't speak again for the rest of the time I was in there. As always, I'd been told that I could have a friend or family member with me, but I decided against it. Aside from the fact that Mum and Dad were coming to visit later that day anyway, the last time they'd been there for an assessment, it hadn't gone well.

I'd told Marcus that I didn't need any help fucking things up.

When the staff had finished saying their names and telling people who already knew what they did . . . *what they did . . .* Bakshi looked at me expectantly.

'Oh, I'm Alice,' I said. 'I'm the basket case.'

Nobody who knew me reacted at all, but I did get a smile from *Sasha*.

Marcus kicked things off by running through the current dosages of the assorted medications I was on and confirming that said medications had been taken and appeared to be effective.

'That's all very good,' Bakshi said. She wrote something

down then looked at me across the top of some rather snazzy glasses. 'So, how are you feeling, Alice?'

'Tip-top,' I said. 'Ticking along nicely, ta.'

'I'm glad to hear it. I have to say I'm not quite so pleased at hearing about some of the things you've been discussing with the other patients.' She glanced at Marcus. 'With some of the staff, too.' She waited, but I just stared at her. 'Asking questions about this and that ... the tragic events of last Saturday evening ... as though you were still working for the police.'

I was getting seriously cheesed off with hearing the same thing and I really didn't want to talk about it. I told Bakshi as much. 'I will say this, though.' I sat forward. 'Aren't we always being encouraged to hang on to who we are? Stuff like that. How important it is to remember the people we were before we became ill? Just seems like you're saying one thing one day and then you're moving the goalposts or whatever.'

I noticed Sasha making a note, which pleased me enormously.

'Normally, that would be the case,' Bakshi said. 'But it can be dangerous if the thing you were doing before was what led to your illness in the first place. One of the earliest things you said to me was that it was what happened when you were working with the Met that started all this. The death of Detective Constable Johnston.' She was looking down at her notes. *My* notes. 'The PTSD and so on.'

I had no smart comeback.

I was thinking about Johnno and all that blood coming through my fingers.

It was time for Marcus to chime up. 'Alice, what Dr Bakshi is saying is that it's fine to think like someone who

135

works with the police ... that's understandable, because you did so for many years ... but you need to stop acting like you still are.'

Bakshi nodded. Debbie nodded. Sasha nodded.

'People who retire from the Job are used for all sorts these days,' I said. 'Cold cases, all that.'

'Not when they have been *medically* retired.' Bakshi looked at her notes again. 'Not when they are deemed unfit to ever return to work.'

I was just about ready to smash something, but I didn't want them to know that. I wrapped my fingers around the edge of the chair and took a few long breaths until I felt calmer.

'Then there's the unfortunate incident with the cannabis.'

I smiled, because I couldn't help myself.

Cannabis, like she was saying *phonograph* or *wireless*.

'If we're going to move forward at all, I need your assurance that you will not try to use again. It's my professional opinion that the use of these drugs has been negatively impacting your mental health for a long time and will continue to do so.'

I tried to look shamefaced. I'm good at it, because I've had plenty of practice.

'Obviously while you're denied unescorted leave that can't happen, but if such restrictions were to be lifted ...'

'I won't do it again,' I said. *You won't* catch *me doing it again*. 'I promise.'

'Well, I'm going to have to take you at your word,' Bakshi said.

'I'm sure she means it,' Marcus said.

'But what is more problematic is yet another email from

Andrew Flanagan.' She raised a printed sheet. 'Another message left on his voicemail two nights ago.'

'Not by me it wasn't.'

She began to read the email out, but I had no intention of listening, so I closed my eyes and tried to think of something else. A happy place, or a babbling brook or whatever it is that shrinks and therapists are always wanking on about. I couldn't think of anything suitable quickly, so I just made the loudest noise I could inside my head and thought about Andy being on fire.

'Well?' Bakshi said, when she'd finished.

I kept my eyes closed. 'It's not true, obviously. It's . . . *fake news*. He's gaslighting me again, same as the last time. He hates me because I "attacked" him.' I used my fingers to put quotes around the word. 'Talking about *me* being violent when you should hear some of the things *he* liked to get up to in the bedroom. I can tell you all about it if you want. He's obviously still angry and he's vindictive and he's obsessed with doing anything he can to make sure I don't get out of here.' I thought about hitting him with that bottle; the *clunk* of it and the lovely vibration that ran up my arm. 'He's probably got brain damage.'

'His email is very reasonable,' Debbie said. 'He sounds concerned.'

Now I opened my eyes and stared hard at her. 'How's Shaun today?'

Debbie smiled, like she'd been expecting the question.

'Only I heard he's still not speaking.'

'You know very well that we're not allowed to discuss the health and welfare of other patients.'

'Alice . . .' Bakshi waited until she had my attention again.

'I'm sure you understand that in light of this, and the incident with the cannabis, I won't be approving any lifting of your section today.'

'Oh, really?' I stood up. 'I'm all packed and everything.'

'But I think we can put you back on to basic fifteen-minute observation and we'll see how things go from there.'

I said, 'Cheers,' but I was already on my way to the door. I opened it then turned to look at Sasha, the trainee. 'What does any of this actually train you for? No, really, I'd love to know.'

She opened her mouth and closed it again, looked to Bakshi for help.

I walked out, slamming the door behind me and shouting as I walked away down the corridor.

'Sitting in on a water-boarding session next week, are you?'

TWENTY

I was still in a fairly arsey mood after lunch and post-lunch meds. Trudging towards the music room, I noticed Tony sitting patiently by the airlock with his bags, as likely to be leaving any time soon – courtesy of his non-existent American relatives – as I was. He waved but I couldn't be bothered waving back.

Ilias was already in there playing Connect Four with himself and ignored me when I took off my headphones and asked if he wouldn't mind buggering off. I tried asking a bit more politely, but that didn't work either. Even five minutes of me bashing the living shit out of the bongos didn't shift him, but at least he wasn't showing too much inclination to chat, so I gave up and sat there.

Alone, thankfully, or as good as.

It was all stupidly unfair, because so much of what I'd told Bakshi and the rest of them about Andy was true. He *was* still angry, I knew he was, and he *is* obsessed with me. Oh, and I certainly wasn't making it up when I said he sometimes liked to get a bit rough in bed; the fact that I didn't actually mind is neither here nor there.

The sad truth is that, right then – six and a bit weeks without so much as a snog – I'd have settled for action of any sort. Rough or smooth, kinky or vanilla. There probably wasn't a bloke *in* there I hadn't thought about that way at some point. Tony, Marcus . . . even the hairy little bastard who was playing games with himself in the corner, God help me.

A cuddle would have been nicest of all, though.

Andy had been good at that, once upon a time.

There was a knock, and when I looked up my dad was standing with Femi outside the door. He smiled and started waving at me through the glass like I hadn't seen him (which I obviously had) or might not remember who he was (which had happened the first time he'd visited).

Femi opened the door and my dad came in.

I stood up when he was halfway to me, that big lolloping walk, and he pulled me into his chest as soon as I was within range.

Yeah, a cuddle was good.

'Hello, you,' he said.

As he was taking off his coat, I saw him clock Ilias in the corner before he looked at me and grimaced. I shook my head to let him know it wasn't a problem, that this was as private as we were likely to get.

'So, how you feeling, love?' He sat down.

He asked the question with a little more sincerity than Dr Bakshi had done a few hours earlier, which was nice.

'Where's Mum?'

'Oh . . . she's back at the hotel,' he said. 'She wasn't feeling too clever.'

'You don't need to make things up,' I said.

He nodded. 'Yeah, well she gets upset coming in here, that's all.' He looked at his feet for a few seconds, smiled when he looked up again. 'You sleeping OK?'

I told him that I was probably sleeping too much. The drugs I was on.

'Well, that might be a good thing,' he said.

'I suppose.'

He looked around and pulled a face. 'Bloody Nora, do you ever get used to the smell in here?'

I think I've mentioned Fleet Ward's distinctive aroma already, but in case I'm misremembering, just assume that it's there all the time, and even though I didn't bother answering my old man's question, *no*, you never get used to it.

There's that . . . bleachy hospital smell, obviously, but that's just what's always around, lurking underneath. On top of that, you've also got – in various pungent combinations, depending on the time of day and the 'condition' of certain patients – all manner of other special stinks.

What do wine ponces call it? Top notes . . .

Blood, shit, sick, sweat, piss, jism.

Sometimes you just catch a niff, if a *niff* feels like you've been punched in the face, and other times it's something that lingers and you can't shift, that you can smell on yourself in bed at night however hard you've scrubbed in the shower. Oh, and you smell fresh paint quite a lot, because even though bedclothes and curtains get cleaned regularly, removing any of the above from the walls is going to involve a fair bit of redecoration. There's usually someone in here slapping emulsion around once a week, and even though too much of that can make you feel like throwing up, given the choice I'd take the smell of paint any day.

Dulux Lemon Zest, if you want to be accurate about it.

'Oh ...' Dad grinned and held aloft the plastic bag he'd brought in with him. He set it down on his lap and rummaged inside, to remind himself of the things my mum had put in there so he could list them correctly. 'There's some of those biscuits you like ... a bit of fruit and a few little boxes of juice.' He leaned forward and winked. 'And several *Twixes*, obviously.' He said it like he'd smuggled in a kilo of heroin, or a cake with a file inside, even though the bag might have been checked while he was signing the visitors' book in the airlock. The truth was that, unless you were visiting someone whose diet needed to be carefully monitored, you could bring in more or less whatever you fancied.

I'd actually gone off Twixes a bit, but I didn't say anything.

'So.' He sat back. 'How did it go this morning?' My dad knew what Friday morning meant as well as I did.

I held out my arms. 'Good news,' I said. 'Well, good news for you at least, because the section is still in place.'

'Listen, love—'

'I'm not going anywhere ... and don't tell me you're planning to sit there looking like a wet weekend, as if you're disappointed for me. Can you honestly tell me that isn't what you want?'

'You're not being very fair.'

'Best place for me, right?' I nodded towards Ilias. 'Stuck in here with the likes of him.'

Dad puffed out his cheeks and shook his head. 'Come on, Alice. Even if I do think that now ... how does that mean your mum and me don't want you home and don't want you better?'

I looked away and stared at the wall for a bit, done with a conversation we had in some form or another every time he or my mother visited. It was never going to go anywhere.

'Oh . . . Jeff and Diane from next door. They wanted me to say hello. Pass on their best.'

I turned back to him. 'You told them I was in here?'

'No, but they were over and they asked how you were doing and your mum was getting a bit flustered. I told them you were having your appendix out.'

I laughed a little bit and so did he.

'So, come on then.' He leaned forward and he actually rubbed his hands together, silly old sod. 'What's been happening, then? That funny woman still trying to do things to your feet?'

'She's gone.'

'What about the one who's always waiting? Or that woman who sings?'

I just stared at him. I suddenly realised that my dad hadn't got any idea what had happened since the last time he was here. About Kevin's death and my investigation. It seemed amazing to me because it was so massive, but he didn't know a thing about the murder, the drugs, any of it.

So I told him.

He looked appropriately shocked to begin with and he was nodding like he was interested, but slowly I saw his face change, saw it . . . crease a little, like it always did when he was worried. So even before I'd finished I knew what was coming and knew exactly what that tone of voice would be. I'd heard it when I was fifteen and started going out with a lad who was three years older. I'd heard it the first time I told him I was thinking of joining the police.

'Listen, love . . .'

I tuned out straight away. Some variation on the same tedious *is this* really *a good idea?* toss they'd trotted out in the MDR. Same warnings I'd had from Marcus and Bakshi and even from sodding Banksy.

How come I was the one least qualified to know what was good for me?

I was vaguely aware of Ilias grunting on the other side of the room, so I turned my head still further to see what he was doing. I watched him drop a counter into the Connect Four board, then stand up and move to sit in the chair opposite to plan an opposing move. He clapped a hand to either side of his head, evidently stumped by his own brilliance.

'Alice? Are you listening?'

I slowly turned back to look at my dad. 'I'm really tired,' I said.

He looked like I'd punched him. 'You want me to go?'

'Might be best,' I said. 'Thanks for the Twixes, though.'

'Right then.'

It was only when my dad got slowly to his feet that Ilias decided it was high time he joined in. I watched him march purposefully across to my father and stand close to him. My dad didn't look thrilled about it.

Ilias jerked his head in my direction. 'You her dad, then?'

'That's right.'

Ilias nodded and stepped even closer to my father. 'Listen, if you *procreate* with your daughter . . .' He stopped, seeing the look of disgust on my dad's face. 'Yeah, I know, horrible word, right? But if you *do* . . . you can live for ever.'

I had no idea what to say and could only watch as Ilias, having passed on his pearl of wisdom, strolled from the room. Struggling a bit, I turned back to look up at my dad.

'This place,' he said. He picked up his coat and started to cry.

TWENTY-ONE

Saturday morning, after a fried breakfast and the usual assortment of meds, I prowled about looking for Shaun, but every member of staff I asked was a bit cagey and none of the patients I spoke to knew where he was. Nobody could remember seeing him since he'd lost it in the TV room on Thursday night. There was no shortage of expert opinions, of course.

'I don't think he's been around all day,' Lucy told me. 'Like they spirited him away or something. I heard that he's not speaking to anybody.'

'They're feeding him in his room,' Donna said, as we walked.

'They've moved him to another ward.' Ilias whispered and nodded, the fount of all knowledge. 'Downstairs with the real head cases.'

'The Thing got him,' Tony said.

Shaun finally appeared at lunchtime. Mia led him into the

dining room, fetched his meal, then sat with him at a table well apart from the rest of us. It didn't feel like she was sticking that close because Shaun was on Within Arm's Length obs – though that might well have been the case after such a major wobble – but more that she was there to keep the rest of us away and make sure he had space.

It seemed to me she was being . . . protective, you know?

Like he was vulnerable as opposed to dangerous.

We all stared, obviously, didn't even pretend not to and why would we? Shaun didn't look at anything except the plate in front of him. He didn't say a dicky bird, not to Mia even, and once he'd finished she escorted him out; her hand hovering a few inches away from his back, like she was afraid to touch him.

After he'd gone – back to his room, I guessed – a few people hung around and drifted across to congregate at the same table. They slurped tea or pushed apple crumble around their dishes, many of them only too keen to share their freshly revised opinions of the situation.

'He looks bad,' Donna said.

Ilias grinned at her. 'You think *you* look so fantastic?'

'I reckon it's some kind of post-trauma thing.' Bob looked at me. 'Isn't that what you had?'

I ignored Lauren's bark of laughter and stared at him.

'It's what we've all had.' Lucy laid a hand on my arm. 'We've all been through something, to one degree or other. There's trauma and there's trauma, that's all.'

'Has he spoken at all?' Graham asked. 'Since the other night, I mean.'

Heads were shaken. Ilias let out a loud burp then shook his.

'That's fairly serious, then.'

'It wasn't like he said much before,' Donna said. 'I mean, he was always quiet.'

'If he's actually . . . silent, though.' Graham let out a whistle. 'Just saying, that's not nothing, is it?'

'Yeah, it's bollocks,' Lauren said.

Graham turned to look at her and pointed. 'You were the one shouting at him the other night.'

Bob nodded enthusiastically. 'Yeah, you *shouted*.'

'Shouting because he was being too loud.' Graham was suddenly getting as worked up as I'd ever seen him. 'Because you couldn't hear your precious programme.'

Lauren jabbed a spoon hard towards Graham's face and smirked when he recoiled like it was something a bit sharper. 'Shouldn't you be standing by the meds hatch already like a tit in a trance?' She looked at the watch she wasn't wearing. 'Best hurry up, mate, it'll be open in twenty minutes.' She watched as Graham scuttled from the room, panic-stricken, then went back to her pudding and quickly shovelled a spoonful into her mouth. 'Shaun's putting it on if you ask me. Poor baby's looking for attention.'

I tried not to sound too sarcastic. 'You think?'

'Course he is.'

'It's possible,' Ilias said. 'Maybe he's playing a game or something.'

Lauren nodded, chewing. 'I did something like that myself once. What I did though was just keep repeating the same word over and over, to mess with the nurses a bit. That's all I said, that one word, whatever anyone asked me. Kept it up for two weeks.'

'That's really clever,' I said.

'I know,' she said.

'Shaun's probably feeling bad enough as it is, today. It's been a week since Kevin was killed, remember?'

'So?'

'So you should think about that, and maybe doing all that shouting the other night, when he was already so upset, might not have been the most sensitive thing you could have done.'

Lucy nudged me. 'You're wasting your breath, babe.'

Like I didn't know.

'I couldn't give a toss,' Lauren said.

I turned away, remembering, feeling like it was important. That freaky woman on the TV, showing off her messed-up fake tits. Shaun with his finger glued to some invisible scab or pimple on his chin, asking the same question as he always did, only this time looking like he was genuinely terrified it was really going to happen. Malaika doing her best to calm him down, but getting nowhere. Then Lauren up on her feet, outraged and shouting her big mouth off, demanding that somebody shut him up.

Well, somebody certainly had.

'What was the word?' Bob leaned towards Lauren. 'The word you said over and over again.'

Lauren licked her spoon clean then dropped it into the bowl.

'Cunt,' she said.

Later on I was mooching around, while those who weren't already in bed or otherwise too zombified to watch claimed their pitches in the TV room, when I spotted Malaika heading into the toilets. I stood outside and waited for her to emerge, turned on the tears when I heard the hand-dryer going.

'Hey, Alice. What's the matter?'

I shook my head as though I was far too upset to speak

and let her lead me into an empty treatment room next to the 136. She handed me tissues and gave me some water until I'd calmed down. She shuffled her chair closer until our knees were kissing and asked what was upsetting me.

'I ... saw ... *Shaun.*' One word at a time, breathy and ragged like it was being dragged out of me. I swallowed some more water. 'It's horrible.'

'I know, my love.'

'What's happened to him?'

'I shouldn't really discuss other patients, Alice. I can't—'

'He's my *friend.*' Verging on the hysterical now. 'It's *important.*'

Malaika shook her head. 'I didn't know the two of you were that close.'

'After what happened to Kevin, you know?' I glanced up and saw Ilias peering in through the window. He stuck his tongue out, then, thankfully, moved on. 'We bonded.'

Malaika sighed and took the empty water glass from me. 'You're right, of course,' she said. 'This latest episode *is* horrible.'

'What kind of episode is it, though? What's going on?'

'Well, the good news is that Dr Bakshi is fairly certain that it's only temporary.'

'Oh, that's great,' I said.

'Something has clearly traumatised him.'

'Not what happened to Kevin, though. I mean, this happened after Kevin was killed, so ...'

'Yes. We can only assume it's a direct result of what happened in the television room the night before last.'

'Really?' Fucking ... *really*? Like that wasn't blindingly obvious.

'When a patient becomes extremely disturbed, something . . . shuts down and they just switch off. They retreat into themselves, into their shells. It's a defence mechanism.'

'Defence against what?'

'Everything,' Malaika said.

I nodded, as if I was thinking it all through, which I was. Shaun had been trying to tell me something, but had been so scared that the whole dying thing had kicked in. That's what had started it and I remembered only too well what it was that had finished him off.

'I suppose you had some sort of meeting afterwards,' I said. 'You always do, right? After an alarm or whatever.'

'A debrief, yes.'

'So, what did everyone think had happened?'

'Well . . .' Malaika seemed a little uncomfortable and looked back over her shoulder. To check that nobody was watching through the window? To make sure the door was shut? 'It's always very difficult to diagnose these things on the spot. What's important is that we follow correct clinical procedure, which, of course, we did.'

'What did Debbie think? She was right there when it happened.'

'Debbie was extremely upset.'

'Yeah, I bet. I mean, she'd obviously been trying to help.'

'Of course. When someone is as manic as Shaun was . . . stuck in a loop almost . . . often the best option is to shock them. To do whatever you can to snap them out of it.'

'Snap' was the right word for it.

'Dr Bakshi assured Debbie that it had certainly been something worth trying.'

'You heard Dr Bakshi say that?'

'That's what Debbie told me she'd said.' She shifted her chair back. 'I shouldn't really be telling you any of this, Alice. It's a bit naughty of me, and it's only because I can see how distressed you are.'

'I won't tell anyone,' I said.

Malaika stood up. 'So, are you feeling a little better, now?'

'Yeah, yeah . . . I'm good.' I got to my feet and wandered out through the door she was holding open for me. I didn't look at her or even say thank you, but that's only because I was suddenly struck as dumb as poor old Shaun had been.

There were so many things rattling around in my head. Kevin and the cameras and Seddon and the drugs and the nurses and Shaun. I was struggling to process the information or make sense of any of it. I knew the answer was in there, fighting to get out, but it was all so jumbled.

The drugs, maybe. *My* drugs, I mean.

When it came to seeing the wood for the trees, which was always going to be important if I wanted to break the case, I was seriously starting to wonder if the meds were doing me any favours. If these 'inhibitors' they fed me three times a day weren't inhibiting the very bits of my brain I needed to be working at full tilt.

Names and faces, bits of things people had said.

All racing around my brain and I couldn't put the brakes on.

Stuck in a loop.

TWENTY-TWO

I've worked a couple of murders where attending the victim's funeral was as much about hoping the murderer might show up as it was paying respects to the victim. Sounds a bit far-fetched, I know, and yeah you see it on cop shows, sometimes – *Keep your eye on the mourners, Lewis . . . our killer's in this church somewhere* – but I'm telling you from experience that once in a blue moon it pays off. Maybe it's one of those where the murderer might not be able to resist showing up to gloat or they're a bit weird and need to make doubly sure the person they've done in is actually dead. Sometimes it's a bit simpler than that and you just suspect that the killer is one of the victim's family or friends.

Either way, all I'm saying is that, every now and again, it's worth a detective's while to dig out their black suit and dip into the petty cash for some flowers.

I wish I could say that when I'd woken up Sunday things were any clearer. I was still all over the shop, I'm not pretending I wasn't, but at least I'd woken with an idea. A pretty decent one too, I reckoned, despite all the things I didn't know or couldn't work out. Because I knew my killer *was* in the church somewhere.

In the church, on the ward, you get the point.

I talked to Marcus about it after breakfast – not about the killers going to funerals thing, obviously – and he wasn't against the idea.

'It might be nice.' He didn't seem in the least bit suspicious. 'It's very thoughtful, Alice . . . let me know if we can help.'

'Least we can do,' I said.

It wouldn't really *be* a funeral, of course.

I did briefly consider a kind of *mock*-funeral, knocking up a cardboard coffin or whatever, but in the end it got way too complicated – I couldn't figure out how to replicate the burial or cremation and I didn't even know which of those Kevin would have preferred – so I ditched that plan. Decided to stick with something simpler. The actual funeral might already have happened for all we knew, and even if it hadn't, I didn't think any of us were likely to get invitations, so I spent the rest of the day making arrangements for what I had told Marcus would be a memorial.

First off, I told everyone, including the Informals, what I was planning and did my best to persuade them that they ought to be there.

'He was one of us,' I said. 'It'll be good for everyone to . . . let their feelings out, to express themselves a bit.' And, 'It'll be fun.'

Some were predictably keener than others, but by mid-morning I was pretty sure a fair few would rock up when it came to it. It was something to do, after all, something different. A welcome change of routine.

L-Plate helped me out a bit – Donna couldn't take time off from her packed walking schedule and Ilias said he had a chess match – but putting it all together still took most of the day. Once I'd blagged a suitable space, there was a ton of stuff to move and set up. We had to get the chairs arranged in rows and we needed to get everything looking nice. I wanted pictures, if we could get them, and some suitable decorations, and I wanted music.

I wanted it to be proper.

It would probably end up detracting a little from the dignity of the proceedings, I was well aware of that, but I decided to do it while afternoon meds were wearing off as opposed to when the evening ones were kicking in. It would make things a bit more interesting, I thought, and, with luck, more *useful*. So at six o'clock I was ready and waiting and, half an hour later, I watched – trying my best not to look too excited – as they trooped into the occupational therapy room in dribs and drabs.

All the sectionees, which was perfect.

A few of the Informals, which couldn't hurt.

Most of the nurses.

I guided people to their seats and did my best to calm them down where it was necessary. The music was helping, I think. I'd connected my phone up to a portable speaker Lucy had lent me. I'd wanted something to suit the occasion, maybe a bit of classical, but I don't have a lot to choose from, so in the end I'd settled for Michael Bublé. You can't go far wrong with a bit of Bublé and I have to admit it seemed to be doing the trick.

I wouldn't say the atmosphere was ideal because frankly it was like trying to herd cats, but when things were as settled as they were ever going to get, I turned the music off and walked slowly back to my spot at the front of the room to say my piece.

I'd spent half an hour writing it that afternoon.

'Thanks to everyone for coming.' Ilias shouted 'Get off' but I ignored him. 'I really appreciate you all making the effort and I know Kevin would have appreciated it, if he wasn't dead.'

I nodded towards the picture of Kevin that Marcus had been kind enough to print out for me, which I'd taped to a clipboard and propped up on a table against a plant pot. Not to brag, but I reckon I'd done a tip-top job with the whole room, considering. Me and L-Plate had carted in a bunch of the plastic ferns from other rooms and arranged them on either side at the front, and I'd laid out a bunch of candles on a tray. Smelly ones, like people use in toilets or whatever, but they were all I could lay my hands on.

'This doesn't have to be sad,' I said. 'Because it's all about remembering Kevin when he was still with us. The laughs we had with him, the stupid things that happened. All the same, we should not forget why he isn't with us any more.' A pause for maximum effect. 'Nobody in this room should ever forget that a crime was committed. The very worst crime of all.'

I stopped for a couple of seconds and I have to admit I was a bit flustered because I'd heard a couple more arseholes shouting things from the back. I could guess who they were and what kind of comments they were making, but I needed to press on. I certainly didn't want to look up and risk catching the eye of one of the nurses. Marcus, having sussed what I was up to, glaring at me from the doorway.

'Someone took Kevin from us, and if anyone has anything

they'd like to say about that, I'm sure we'd all like to hear it.' Now I looked up. 'So if any of you has something they'd like to contribute ... maybe something they remember and would like to share, now's the time.' I pointed to Kevin's picture again. 'Come to the front and maybe light a candle for him, and please say whatever's on your mind.'

I stepped to one side and waited. I wasn't sure whether to turn Michael Bublé back on or not, how long I should give it, so I just stood there shifting from one foot to another, and I probably looked a bit awkward, thinking back.

Ilias – why did it have to be Ilias? – saved my bacon.

'He was a cocky little wanker sometimes.' Ilias sniffed and jabbed a finger towards the picture, in case anyone wasn't clear who he was talking about. 'Still out of order, though. What happened to him.' He picked up one of the candles and started walking back to his seat. When I stepped across and tried to take it off him, he got a bit stroppy and said, 'I thought they were free,' so I decided to let him keep it.

Donna came up next, a bit trembly. She said, 'Kevin was really sweet and he never said anything nasty to me, so God bless him.' She took the lighter that I'd set on the tray, lit a candle and went back to her seat.

Several others followed in quick and remarkably orderly succession.

'I didn't know him very well,' Bob said.

'Kevin was good at Scrabble.' Graham nodded sadly. 'Good at doing the rude words.'

L-Plate had written a poem, bless her, and read it very loudly, like a princess in a school play. Something about a seagull flying home that went on too long, then some other bit where 'sadness' rhymed with 'madness'. A couple of the

Informals came forward after that. While they were lighting their vanilla cupcake candles and saying nothing, I looked over to where Shaun was sitting with Femi at the back of the room. He hadn't stopped weeping since he came in.

Then it was the Singer's turn.

I'd been dreading madam's contribution, of course, but even though nothing so far had told me anything I didn't already know, *she* at least genuinely surprised me. She stood there staring at everyone for half a minute or more and there was genuine tension in that room, like she might rip all her clothes off, or just run screaming at someone. Instead, she took a deep breath and started to sing a half-decent version of that 'Hallelujah' song off *X-Factor*, and I swear it was nearly in tune. When she'd finished, almost everyone clapped, and it's the only time I've ever seen Lauren look genuinely happy about anything that didn't involve upsetting someone.

I almost forgot what I was doing this for.

Just when it looked like nobody else was going to do anything and I was getting ready to put the music back on, the nurses and the healthcare assistants started coming forward one at a time. They weren't all in the room at one time, of course, a couple had to be manning the nurses' station, but three or four of them took a turn.

Marcus lit a candle, then George and Malaika.

I looked across at Shaun again, hoping against hope, but his head was on Femi's shoulder and his eyes were closed. Stupid of me really, because what was I actually expecting? I knew what I *wanted*. I wanted him to miraculously recover the power of speech, to stand up and run to the front. I wanted him to say, 'Kevin was being held to ransom by such and such a drug gang and he did . . . something they didn't like and in the end he had to die, so he was killed by . . .'

I wanted that witness who blows the case wide open.

I wanted him to tell everyone what he'd been so afraid to tell me.

Debbie was the last nurse to come up. I saw that she had tears in her eyes as she lit the final candle. I swear I heard a sob before she gently touched a finger to Kevin's picture, then crossed herself.

Quite touching, I suppose, if you give a stuff about any of that.

Everyone drifted away pretty quickly after that. Places to go, people to see. I offered to tidy the room up, but Marcus said the staff would do it later on.

'So, were you pleased with how that went?' he asked.

I told him I was, that I thought it had all gone really well.

'Pleased to hear it,' he said, as I walked past him. He wasn't really trying to hide the sarcasm and it was obvious he was pissed off because I'd shafted him, but I was beyond caring.

My brain was still racing when I got back to my room and more than ever I felt the urgent need to talk everything through with someone. I couldn't get hold of Banksy, so I called Sophie. Maybe I was gabbling or just not making any sense, but either way she didn't seem very interested, so in the end I gave up and let her ramble on about her job for a while.

Her fantastic new flatmate, again.

Her new boyfriend.

After that I decided to just chill in my room for a while until dinner. I'd been working on the memorial all the way

159

through lunch, so I was bloody starving. More important, I was keen to know what people had made of it all and to find out if grief – or what passed for it in a place like this – had shaken anything loose.

TWENTY-THREE

Johnno and I worked this fatal stabbing in Dollis Hill one time.

It was a bad one; not like any of them are ever good, but this one was really nasty. A teacher named Gordon Evans, carved up in his front room in the middle of the day. Point is, we knew very well who'd done it and why – were talking about making an arrest within twenty-four hours of catching the case – but the problem was we were struggling to prove it.

Even with (almost) all the evidence anybody could want.

It was a dispute between neighbours, something simple and stupid. A lawnmower that never got returned or someone complaining about a noisy party. I can't remember the details of why they fell out, but several other neighbours told us they were aware of tensions, so we knew damn well they had. Our only suspect – a charmer of a long-distance lorry driver named Ralph Cox – lived in a house with a garden that backed on to the teacher's. After one conversation with Mr

Cox, despite him claiming that he'd been indoors all day, we were convinced that he'd marched round to Evans's place to have it out and things had got out of hand.

Forty-two separate stab wounds out of hand.

Yeah, so this evidence . . .

Cell-site data meant we were able to place Cox's mobile at the scene, but it was quickly pointed out that living within fifty yards of the victim's property meant his phone would have been pinging off the same mast if he was at home. Marvellous. We had our suspect's prints inside Evans's house, but Cox's claim that he had been there before to discuss the dispute – which to be fair he'd never denied – could not be disproved. We never found the murder weapon, but we had a knife-block from Cox's kitchen that just happened to be missing a knife whose blade was the size and shape of the one that had sliced up Gordon Evans.

We had an eye witness, another neighbour, who said he saw Cox leaving Evans's house on the afternoon in question. By the time we came to take a statement, though, that had become *thought he saw*, then *I'm not actually sure it* was *him* and eventually he made it clear that whatever he might or might not have seen, he wasn't willing to talk about it in court. Yeah, Cox was a scary-looking sod and this witness only lived a few doors away, but still it was a pain in the arse.

Then there was the camera.

There was no CCTV on the street, but the neighbour opposite had a security camera that happened to cover Evans's front door. You can see where this is going, right? A DVR that was full, so nothing recorded.

That just about put the tin lid on it.

All this, on top of which, Johnno and me were getting it in

the neck from a useless DI who was desperate for a result and couldn't understand why we weren't delivering one.

So one night I went round to Johnno and Maggie's place to talk about this case that was doing our heads in. We got Chinese and ate off our laps, the three of us just sitting round moaning about it.

What were we doing wrong? What *weren't* we doing?

'Sometimes you're just going to get jobs like this,' Maggie said. 'Doesn't matter how much you know you've got the right person, it won't go your way.' She leaned against her boyfriend. 'Maybe you should just chalk it up and let it go.'

I was starting to agree with her, but Johnno wasn't having it.

'We're making it too complicated,' he said. 'Coming at it from too many angles and getting . . . bogged down.'

'Bogged down and buggered up,' I said.

'Letting all this evidence we've got get in the way.'

'Not to mention the evidence we haven't got.' I remember I had a gobful of spring roll or ribs or whatever. 'That bastard camera.'

'Sod the camera.' Johnno tossed his fork down and sat forward. 'We don't need the camera . . . we go after *him*. The cocky prick thinks he's laughing, because he knows very well he can dance round everything we've got. So we forget all that and start again. We find something else. We do what we do and we come up with a way to nail him.'

I remember how worked up Johnno was that night, and I'll never forget how excited he was five months later. That was the day we walked out of court having seen Ralph Cox get sent down. Life, with a minimum tariff of twenty-one years.

Six months for every one of those stab wounds.

Long story short, we started digging and found a report filed nine months previously, when Cox had lived south of the river. A woman who lived upstairs from him whose complaint of violent harassment had never been passed on. We brought Cox in for a friendly chat and Johnno broke the scumbag in the interview room.

Wood for the trees, right?

I woke up in the middle of the night and someone was having a shouting match with themselves a few doors along. A proper ding-dong. It sounded like Lucy, but it wasn't a big deal because I was well used to it, and anyway I didn't think that was what had woken me.

I was wide awake and sitting up because I *knew*.

The police had got it all arse about face. I mean, up to that point so had I to a degree, but now I knew exactly where I'd been going wrong. Why I'd been bogged down and buggered up.

You're a star, Johnno.

I'd been wasting valuable time trying to get to the bottom of this or that argument, wondering how drugs had got in and pissing about with daft ideas about hitmen. Newbie mistakes, so bloody stupid. Most important of all, me and DC Seddon both had been casting the net too wide, thanks to Graham and the fun he liked having with mashed potato and the like.

Screw the camera . . .

It was no great surprise that the official investigation had stalled – and it certainly felt that way – because they were still looking for a motive and, biggest mistake of all, they were focusing on a time-frame that left them with two dozen suspects.

Well, for once I was ahead of the game.

Now, I had just the one.

See, it didn't make the slightest bit of difference when that camera had gone off, because Kevin Connolly had been murdered in plain sight.

TWENTY-FOUR

I'd thought it was definitely worth a punt, because they could only say no, but I can't say I was overly confident that Banksy would be able to pull it off. That man is a marvel though, I'm telling you. A right hard bastard if he needs to be, but he can charm the pants off someone when he wants to.

As soon as we'd both lit cigarettes, I pulled him into a hug.

'Thanks for sorting this,' I said.

Banksy said that I was welcome, but I'm not sure I really was, and bear in mind this was before I'd told him what I'd actually brought him in to hear. We sat down on a bench opposite the main entrance and I said nothing for a while. I wanted to spend just a couple of minutes enjoying my fag and feeling sunshine on my pale face before I got into it.

The break in the case . . .

Even before Banksy had turned up – he'd told me on the phone he'd be in sometime late afternoon – I'd decided we should at least give it a bash. The obs stats are the obs stats for good reason, but I knew that every now and again, if such and such a nurse was in a good mood, they might do someone a favour or look the other way. Ilias goes out for a smoke with Malaika sometimes and I'm damn sure he's not supposed to. A month or so before, Donna's sister had been allowed to take her outside for an hour because it was her birthday. Outside as in *away from the hospital and down to the shops*. Obviously with the usual provisos about trust and not absconding and sending the police after her and all that.

So, I definitely thought me and Banksy should at least ask.

I mean, we *were* the police.

Banksy said that Marcus was a bit dubious to begin with – yeah, I thought, I bet he bloody was – but apparently, once Banksy had flashed a pukka warrant card and explained that we really needed privacy because there was a sensitive police matter to discuss, he'd softened a bit.

Bansky had thanked him for his cooperation, he told me, and promised that we wouldn't go far.

I stubbed out my fag and turned to look at him.

'Let's hear it then,' he said.

I won't lie, I've seen him look keener. So I tried to stay calm as I laid it all out and not let on how fired up I was. I told him about the drugs that had been smuggled out of the ward after being given to Kevin by an insider (with a healthy percentage presumably coming back to that same insider once they'd been sold). I told him about the irrelevance of the camera on Kevin's corridor, the time when it was on and when it wasn't. Finally, I told him what had happened to Shaun – or, to be accurate, what had been done to him to ensure that he couldn't tell anyone what he knew.

I asked Banksy for another cigarette when I'd finished. I lit up and waited.

'So, why kill Kevin?' he asked, finally. 'You know, if there's this cushy little drug thing going which presumably everyone's doing very nicely out of. Why scupper it?'

'I don't think Kevin wanted to do it any more.'

'You're just guessing though, right?'

'Look, I know him and Shaun had been arguing and I think that's because Shaun wanted him to stop. In the end Shaun got his way, so Kevin told everyone involved that he wanted out. That's why all those drugs were found in his room, because he wasn't passing them on to his connections any more. He'd had enough.'

'So they decided to kill him, that's what you're saying?'

'Yeah, maybe they did . . . his connections on the outside.' I held up a finger. 'Or maybe it was just one person's decision.' Banksy nodded. He already knew who I was talking about of course, because I hadn't wasted any time in telling him who had killed Kevin. 'What about if Kevin had been stockpiling those drugs? Holding on to them as some kind of insurance policy or something?' Then another idea struck me which suddenly made perfect sense. 'Maybe he was using those drugs to blackmail her.'

'Seriously?'

'Why not? Or at least planning to down the road.' I was a bit annoyed with myself for not working this out before, but I wasn't going to blame myself for not being match-fit after everything that had happened. 'Sounds like a pretty decent motive to me.'

'How come she didn't take the drugs, then? When she killed him?'

I shrugged. 'Couldn't find them.' I still didn't know exactly where in Kevin's room the drugs had been hidden. 'She certainly wouldn't have had much time to go looking for them, turn his room over, whatever. A couple of minutes, that's all she would have been in there for. In, pillow over his face, and out again.'

Bitch, I thought. Stone cold bitch.

I flicked my fag-end away and watched Banksy nodding like he was thinking about it. Course, he was actually trying to decide the best way to tell me what he really thought, but I didn't know that at the time, did I? Right then, I was still buzzing because I'd broken the case wide open, sitting there like a twat waiting for him to tell me how we should work it.

'I still don't quite get this business with Kevin's boyfriend.'

'Shaun,' I said. 'I've said his name like a hundred times.'

'Yeah, with Shaun.'

I told him again what had happened that night in the TV room when Shaun had gone up the pole, what had been said to him and how he'd been ever since.

'So, she knew that's what would happen, did she?'

I nodded, remembering her exact words. Stone cold . . .

'She knew he wouldn't be able to speak afterwards?'

'That's her *job*, isn't it?' I chose not to tell him what Malaika had said to me on Saturday. All that bull about an attempt to 'shock' Shaun out of his mania and Dr Bakshi *allegedly* saying it had been something worth trying. I didn't bother telling him because it was blindingly obvious that Malaika had been every bit as alarmed by what had happened in the TV room as me. That she only said what she did afterwards because the nurses look after one another and she was trying to stick up for her colleague. As a copper I'd done similar things myself and so had Banksy.

So it wasn't relevant.

I said, 'Look, Shaun had been trying to tell me everything that night. He was desperate to let me know it was one of the staff ... right? That was what set him off, because he was terrified. Because he knew what the woman who'd killed Kevin was capable of.' I didn't want to talk to Tim like he was daft or wet behind the ears, but I couldn't understand why he wasn't *getting* it. 'She needed to shut him up.'

'Yeah, I hear what you're saying,' he said.

We watched a well-dressed, middle-aged couple walking hand in hand towards the entrance. Lucy's parents. I waved and Lucy's father conjured a frosty smile.

'I tell you something else,' I said. 'The woman who killed Shaun also sexually assaulted me.'

'*What?*'

'When I first came in.'

Banksy looked properly confused. 'Why are you only telling me this now?'

'I just want you to know the kind of person we're dealing with.'

'What did she do?'

'I don't want to talk about it.'

'Fair enough, but you know ... make a complaint, Al. I mean that's something we *can* arrest her for.'

I shook my head.

He sighed and sat back. Muttered, 'Fucking hell ...'

I clocked him checking his watch and guessed that we didn't have much time left. 'So, are you going to talk to Seddon, or what?'

Another sigh. 'This isn't my case, Al. You know that.'

'You're still a copper, though. It's your duty to bring new information to his attention, at least.'

'I don't think there is any new information.' He turned and looked at me, the expression of a doctor about to deliver bad news. 'I just don't think it hangs together.'

'Come on.' I felt like I might lose it at any second and I was clutching on to the edge of that bench for dear life. 'How long have we worked together, Banksy? You knew Johnno, for God's sake . . . you know *me*.'

He couldn't look at me. 'I used to,' he said. 'But, you know . . . *this*?'

By the time he did look up, I was on my feet and away. 'Nice to have a natter and a fag,' I shouted back to him. 'Don't worry, mate, I can see myself back up.'

When I stomped into the lobby, I saw that Lucy's mother and father were standing inside the lift, waiting for it to close. I shouted, 'Hold the doors,' and ran to join them. I pretended not to notice them inching towards the back wall as the doors began to shut.

But it didn't help.

I'm not using the fact that I was angry and looking to lash out as an excuse for what I said. I don't remember the last time I needed an excuse for anything, but it's an explanation, fair enough? Obviously I knew who they were, so I get that it was bad. I knew who they were visiting and I knew exactly why she was there.

As the lift juddered slowly up, I turned round and grinned at them.

I said, 'I've just been shooting up outside.' I moaned a bit and rubbed at my arm. 'Smack is just *fabulous*, don't you reckon?'

TWENTY-FIVE

Tuesday morning I was determined to get stuck in, so after breakfast and meds I worked through some old contacts on my phone and made a few calls trying to find the number for Seddon's incident room. The direct line, I mean. I'd wanted to do it the day before once Banksy had left, but I knew that, by then, most of the people I needed to speak to would probably have gone home already. It didn't much matter in the end, because when I got back on to the ward there were too many distractions – George was trying to dissuade Graham from making a fresh dent in the wall with his head and Lauren was shouting at Femi about someone coming into her room and going through her stuff – so I was finding it hard to focus on anything approaching work.

That's been the big problem up to now.

Life in this place, getting in the way . . .

I was never the type to cut corners. Never one to take the easy route, or 'delegate', when most of the time that really

172

means skiving off. No, really, if I was working a case I was like a fucking *laser* ... I was dead focused. In here, though, it's hard to concentrate on anything for more than five minutes without something kicking off. I can sit in my room and do stuff on my laptop if I have to, but like I tried to explain to Marcus, that's not what being a detective is about.

You need to get out there and engage with people.

Nine times out of ten, engaging with someone on the ward means arguing with them or just keeping them out of your face. Watching them nod off or just amble away while you're talking. Listening to a blow-by-blow account of some sexual encounter that didn't happen or else some half-arsed cobblers about how radio waves are reacting with metal in the vaccinations we were given as kids and turning us into aliens.

Then there's all the other stuff you have to do, the routines that eat into your day. I know, I'm normally the first one to moan about how boring it is in here – at least it was, before bodies started piling up – but there's still the meals and the one-to-ones and the tests and the groups and the community meetings and the washing and the visits and the meds.

Mustn't forget the meds.

Like I said before, I'm still struggling with the best way to manage them as far as making headway in my case goes. It's hard to get anywhere when the drugs are wearing off because I can get a bit jittery, and when they're kicking in I'm every bit as likely to zone out completely. So taking all this shit three times a day means I've only got a small – what do you call it? – window of opportunity, which isn't ideal.

Like I'm going after a suspect with one arm tied behind my back.

It is what it is, though, and anyone who knows me will tell

you I've never backed away from a challenge. They'd definitely say that. Not that I trust many of them now and it's not like they'll even talk to you, but you get what I'm on about.

I got the number I was after in the end, though it took a while and one or two of the conversations were a bit awkward, but I didn't really have a lot of choice.

'Bloody hell, Alice!' DS Trevor Lambert, who I'd worked with a hundred years before. On a team somewhere in south London now. 'Blast from the past or what?'

'Been too long, Trev.'

'What are you up to?'

'Oh, the usual, you know.'

'You still working up west?'

'For my sins, yeah. Listen, there's a murder case and it's kicking everyone's arse, if I'm honest, mate. I wondered if you could do me a favour.'

'What do you need?'

Trevor clearly hadn't heard about my misadventures and I wasn't going to put him straight, was I? It was him that found me the number I needed, as it goes. Called me back with it, good as gold.

'We should have a pint and catch up.'

'Let's do that,' I said.

'Fair warning though, I'm a bit fatter and a bit greyer than the last time I saw you. That's the kids, I reckon.'

'Yeah, we should definitely get together ... I'll give you a bell when this thing eases off a bit. Up to my tits at the moment ...'

Then, once I'd called the Incident Room: 'DC Seddon isn't available at the moment.'

'I'd like to leave a message, then.'

'What's it concerning?'

'Just tell him it's about the Kevin Connolly murder.'

'Can I take your name, madam?'

'I don't think you understand. I'm actually here. Where the murder happened. I'm on the spot.'

'OK, but I'll still need your details.'

I gave the woman my name then I gave her my rank. She took my mobile number and assured me that a member of the team would call me back.

I stayed in my room for a couple of hours after that, trying to decide the best way forward while I was waiting for Seddon to ring. It was hard, though, because after a while I began to think about Johnno then about Andy and those two-faced psychiatrists at A&E and everyone else who'd betrayed me. I started to wonder if Seddon could even be trusted at all.

I opened my laptop and did some Googling.

How much does a nurse earn?

British nurse average wage.

Steven Seddon Met Police Record.

Just before lunch, L-Plate knocked on my door and strolled in. There was going to be an occupational therapy session in the afternoon, she announced, and was I going to come. I told her that I didn't know they'd found the money to get the OT woman back and Lucy said they hadn't, that one of the staff was going to run the session.

'Probably won't be as good,' she said. 'But it'll be nice to do some drawing again.'

'I've got things to do,' I said.

'Come on, Al, it'll be fun.'

'Will it?'

Lucy giggled and leaned close, whispering, like it wasn't

just the two of us in the room. 'I'm going to imagine her with no clothes on . . . stark bollock naked . . . and draw that. It'll be hysterical. Or repulsive, I don't know yet.'

'Imagine *who* with no clothes on?'

'Debbie. She's the one who's organising it.'

It didn't take me long. 'OK, sounds like a plan,' I said.

TWENTY-SIX

The occupational therapy room had been put back to the way it normally was. The way it had been before Kevin's memorial, I mean. The orange curtains open, a scattering of tables and chairs, the locked materials cupboard at the end of the room.

There were maybe six of us in there.

Me and Lucy sitting together. Ilias, Bob and I think Graham . . . or it might have been Donna. Doesn't matter.

I sat and watched as Debbie opened the cupboard then cheerfully distributed paper and felt-tip pens along with boxes of crayons for the less ambitious and some large pads and watercolours for those who wanted to try something a bit more advanced. She said we could paint or draw anything we wanted to, but lifted one of the ferns on to a table in the centre of the room in case anyone fancied a bash at a still life. One time someone had suggested we should have a life model, but even though Ilias had immediately volunteered the suggestion was quickly given the thumbs-down by the staff. The following week, Ilias had waited until none of the nurses was looking and whipped all his clothes off, which, trust me, is something I cannot ever un-see.

All that hair.

Lucy says that sometimes she still wakes up screaming, though to be fair she does that a lot anyway.

'We've got a couple of hours,' Debbie said. 'So there's no need to rush anything. Let's see what we can come up with.' She took a pad and a few pens for herself and went to sit at a table on her own.

Back when there was still some money so they could do things properly, we used to get up to all sorts in OT sessions. We had a few afternoons messing about with an ancient Wii which was a right laugh. Tennis and *Mario Kart* and stuff. We did drama a couple of times, which I quite enjoyed, but it always ended up a bit lively because Bob tried to turn everything into a sex scene. One week the woman who used to run things even got a friend of hers to bring a potter's wheel in. Again, that didn't go well. Graham immediately used his clay to disable the nearest camera while most of the other blokes just made cocks (their own, all predictably huge), and when the therapist suggested they might want to go in a different direction everyone just started chucking stuff about. I was finding bits of dried clay in all my cracks and creases for days afterwards and there are still a few blobs of it stuck to the ceiling.

Paper and pens was fine for today, though.

I wasn't there because I think I'm Picasso anyway.

'How come you got to go outside yesterday?' Lucy asked.

It was unusually quiet as everyone laboured over their masterpieces, so I took care to keep my voice down, hoping that Lucy would take the hint and do the same. 'It was a police thing,' I said.

'About Kevin?'

'It's not something I can really talk about.'

'Oh, OK then.' She went back to her picture.

'But, yeah.'

Lucy nodded, slashing her pen from side to side on the paper, which she told me later was how you shaded things in. 'Are you going to be working on the case, then?'

'I *am* working on it.' I looked down at what I'd managed so far. It was going pretty well. 'I'm working on it *now*.'

I knew I had plenty of time, so I spent as much of it watching our substitute therapist as I did putting my felt-tips to good use. Mostly she kept busy with whatever she was drawing, but she was watching *us* too, because it wasn't like we were art students or anything and a pencil can do a lot of damage in the wrong hands.

In here, almost anything can.

A plastic fork, a broken guitar, a pillow . . .

At the table in front of us, Ilias suddenly screwed up the piece of paper he'd been working on and threw it away angrily. He put his hand up like a schoolboy and waited for Debbie to look up and see him.

'Can I draw a vagina?'

'If that's what you want,' Debbie said.

'Can I have it when you've finished?' Bob asked.

The sun was streaming through the windows and that pissed me off quite a lot, because I'd really enjoyed that half an hour outside with Banksy the day before. The being outside part of it, anyway.

It was hot, so it was hard to concentrate.

I knew that I had to, though; that I needed to make a good job of this. I tried not to spend every second willing the mobile in my pocket to ring and then, when I *did* finally feel it buzzing against my leg, I tried not to kick the table over when it turned out to be fucking Sophie.

Lovely 2 talk to u the other day. Miss u so much.

A sad-faced emoji.

The time went really quickly in the end, and when Debbie announced that we only had a few minutes left I looked across to see what Lucy had come up with. She'd done exactly what she told me she'd do, even if it was a bit cartoonish. I studied the pair of saggy tits with bright red nipples as if I was some expert on *Antiques Roadshow*. I stroked my chin and told her the tits were 'strikingly hideous' and that the curly orange bush that covered most of the subject's bottom half was 'especially disgusting'.

She looked across at Debbie and stroked her own chin and laughed until I thought she might wet herself.

'Right then . . .' Debbie said.

Despite the two hours everyone had put in, they all buggered off fairly sharpish when the time was up – Lucy included – without apparently being bothered about what they'd drawn or painted or daubed and certainly not giving a toss what anyone else might think about it.

I hung around though, obviously, and helped Debbie collect all the work up, except mine which I wanted to keep back until the moment was right. Once the materials had been locked back in the cupboard, she wandered back over to me and rubbed her hands together.

'Shall we have a look at our wee exhibition?'

Mostly it was the predictable scrawls, except for Ilias's vagina, which was remarkably detailed and really quite disturbing. 'Holy fuck,' Debbie said, laughing.

She stopped at Lucy's picture and stared.

'I think it's supposed to be you,' I said.

'Not bad.' She laughed again and pointed at the orange bush. 'Though I don't usually let things get *that* wild downstairs.' Then she held a hand out towards the sheet of paper I was holding. 'Come on, let's have a look at yours then.'

I didn't even try pretending to be reluctant and handed it over.

I'd done much the same thing quite a few times, done it with Johnno and with Banksy. When you've decided it's the right time to casually slide a photograph across an interview room table. A close-up of injuries, a victim's battered face, blood-spattered flesh or clothing. That moment when you show the most shocking picture you can get hold of to the animal you know very well is responsible for it, because you're looking for a reaction or, if you're lucky, an admittance of guilt.

At the very least, you're trying to get a read.

Like I said, I'm not much of an artist, but I reckon I'd managed to get what I was going for. A single bed with guess who lying on it. There was no face, obviously, just the pillow where the face should have been, although I don't think I'd been able to make it look that much like a pillow, so it was more sort of a blurry rectangle. I was pleased with the collection of little bottles, though. Dozens of them scattered about under the bed, with a few of them lying on their side. Best of all was the figure on one side of the picture, shadowy, kind of, like someone was creeping out of the room, with a few tiny dots of red and yellow and blue and green, right at the edge. The flash of a rainbow-coloured lanyard.

I stood and watched Debbie looking at my picture.

I wanted to get that read.

'That's fucking excellent,' she said, pointing. 'Honestly. The way you've done the shadow and everything. You going to keep it?'

I shook my head.

'You could put it up in your room if you want.'

'I don't think so.'

She looked at me. 'You all right, Alice?'

'I saw you at Kevin's memorial.' I waited, just a beat or two. 'You looked upset.'

'Because I was,' she said. 'I still am.'

'I saw you ...' I crossed myself, though after the up and down part I wasn't sure which shoulder you were supposed to touch first.

She nodded and smiled. 'Glasgow Catholic girl,' she said. 'Not a very good one, mind.'

'Confessing your sins and all that?'

'Not for a very long time.'

I gathered all the pictures together in front of her and straightened them. I made sure mine was on the top.

I said, 'Maybe you should think about starting again.'

TWENTY-SEVEN

Wednesday lunchtime, more than twenty-four hours after phoning the incident room and I was climbing the walls – staring at them, bouncing off them – because I was still waiting for Detective *Cunt*stable Seddon to call me back. Actually I'd just about given up waiting, because by then it was blindingly obvious he wasn't going to. I'd half expected to be ignored anyway and you didn't need to be a genius to work out why that might have been.

Who called? That mad woman who's in there, the one who got thrown off the Job? Yeah, well, I think I've got better things to do than waste my time listening to her crackpot theories . . .

I was damn sure *Steve* had no end of better things to do. Like having a wank or refilling his stapler or sticking needles in his eyes.

Part of me had always suspected I'd end up working this case on my own.

I'm not going to lie, it was a bit scary . . . out of my comfort zone and everything. I'd always worked as part of a team and within that I'd always been partnered up, which was how I liked it. The banter and the piss-takes to kill those endless hours in the car together. Someone always there to celebrate with you when things were going well or help you drown your sorrows at the end of a bad day.

Someone to watch your back as well, let's not forget that.

Even if it didn't work out particularly well for my partner.

Well, if the only way I could get a result on this case was to do it on my own then that was how it would have to be. I'd managed pretty well so far. I wasn't just going to work it, though, I was going to *crack* it ... I mean I'd cracked it already, because my crackpot theory wasn't just a theory, but I was going to make damn sure the guilty party got what was coming to her.

I'd do it for Kevin and I'd do it for Johnno.

I'd do it to show Seddon and all those officially involved that they'd been wrong to ignore me and stupid to refuse my help.

I'd do it so all those jumped-up arseholes with pips on their shoulders who decided I should be 'medically retired' would see that I was a copper to my toenails.

I'd do it because it was the right thing to do.

I'd do it for the buzz and the rush of the blood pumping and because for the first time in forever it made me feel like a person again.

I'd do it because so many people had told me not to.

I'd do it because it would be a big fat *fuck you* to everyone who'd conspired to put me in here. To that crackhead with a Stanley knife in his pocket and the pair of Job-pissed pricks who decided I wasn't fit to testify and those doctors who didn't listen when I told them I'd only freaked out because

I'd been awake for forty-eight hours. To Andy ... for sure, and to Sophie and to Mum and Dad and the rest of them. To good Catholic Debbie, obviously, who hadn't got a clue that I'd worked it all out or that I was coming for her and who'd live to regret the day they'd found me a bed on her ward.

I'd do it because I *loved* it.

I'd been keeping a close eye on the time, just so I could be at the meds hatch when it opened. It took some serious self-restraint not to elbow Graham out of the way when it came to it, but in the end I decided that a few more minutes weren't going to kill me. I didn't want to wait much longer than that, though, because I knew I wouldn't be able to do anything – least of all pick up the phone and call in a massive favour – while I was feeling frazzled and fidgety and likely to do something daft. Not a chance. I couldn't do things properly while a whispering voice inside my head was telling me to march straight up to Debbie and pin her against the wall.

The voice nobody but me could hear telling the one that came out of my mouth just what to say.

I know exactly what you did and I know why you did it.

Tempting, course it was, but that was not the way I was planning to go.

Mia opened up the hatch and once Graham had shuffled up and taken his pills I stepped cheerfully forward to collect mine. I smiled and said, 'Thank you,' like a good girl.

A good officer.

Lucky for me that I caught DI David Dinham on his way to work. He was obviously doing a late turn, which was never anyone's favourite, but it had been a while since shift patterns meant anything to me. One day I might get up good and early and the next I won't bother to get up at all. Some days I get dressed and some days I can't be arsed, meaning I'll slob around in the pyjamas I was issued with or, if I feel like making an effort, I might push the boat out and parade around the place in my own trackies and T-shirt, but the point is that it doesn't much matter.

The days are measured out in meals and meds, simple as that.

Lucky, though, because coppers have flappy ears and Dinham wouldn't be free to have the conversation that I was planning while he was sitting in the office. Last thing I'd heard, that office was in Brighton or some other seaside place, which was convenient for me, because him working outside the Met meant there was no reason the Kevin Connolly case would be on his radar. Unlike Trevor Lambert, though, Dinham was aware that I'd been ... in the wars as far as the Job was concerned, but that was fine.

'Oh ... hey, Al.' Yeah, he was well aware. 'Listen, I'm in the car, so ...'

'I do hope you're hands-free,' I said.

'Course I am.'

'Glad to hear it. So, how's tricks, mate?'

'Tricks are ... good. What about you?'

I don't think he knew the details – where I was and why – but I didn't see any reason he needed to know. 'Well, I've been better, Dave, I'm not going to lie ... but I've been worse an' all, so no point belly-aching about it, is there?'

'No, I suppose—'

'I need a favour.'

'Right.' I could hear the panic in his voice. 'What sort of favour?'

'I need intel on a suspect.'

'A *suspect*?' He clearly knew enough.

'On an *individual*, all right? Less you know about it the better ... but I need financials, yeah? What has this woman got in the bank? Savings, mortgage, credit report, all that. Basically I need to know if she's got more money than she should have.'

'Right, and how exactly are you expecting me to find all this out?'

'Oh, come on, Dave.' If I still had access to the Police National Computer I could easily have got the information I needed myself. But that avenue of inquiry had been taken away along with everything else, which is precisely why I was asking Dinham. Why was he making it so difficult? 'Five minutes on the PNC.'

'Are you serious?'

'Five minutes.'

'Look, I don't know how long you've been ... I mean have you forgotten all this stuff?'

'I haven't forgotten anything,' I said.

'In which case you know that the minute I log on I've left a digital fingerprint. Everything I search for is a matter of record and I'd need to provide a very good reason why I was searching for it. I couldn't even run a number plate for you, and unless this individual gives their consent I'd need a court order to access their bank details.'

I could hear that he was breathing quite heavily. I imagined him sweating a bit, knuckles white around the steering wheel. I almost felt sorry for him. I said, 'I need this.'

'For Christ's sake, Alice, it's a sackable offence.'

'How long have we known each other, Dave?'

'Are you not listening—'

'I *need* this.'

For almost a minute all I could hear was the rasp of his breathing again and the growl of traffic. Finally, *finally*, he said, 'Look, there might be another way.'

I waited.

I ran my finger down the crack in the wall next to my wardrobe.

I pushed a fingernail in and began to dig at it . . .

'There's a bloke I know,' he said. 'Ex-Job, running a private investigation and intelligence firm.'

'Really?' I knew what that meant. Some boozed-up old saddo sitting in a car spying on unfaithful husbands and wives.

'Actually, he's got a decent set-up. I think he can find out pretty much anything. I don't know exactly how he does it and I don't really want to know . . . but I reckon he could get what you're after.'

I scraped harder at the paint around the crack. I picked at it until my fingernail split and rubbed the blood into the dirty yellow paint.

'You'd need to pay him, obviously.'

'That's fine,' I said. 'What's his name?'

'Look . . . give me five minutes. I need to pull over. I'll send you a link to his website.'

'He's got a *website*?'

'Like I said, he does all sorts. Some of it's kosher, but I'm fairly sure that some of it . . . isn't.'

Ten minutes later, he texted me a link and I got straight online.

The Pindown Investigations (stupid name) website was

fairly impressive, no denying it. Some tasty pictures of fast cars and binoculars and computers. All manner of stuff banging on about the wide range of services on offer and the excellent value for money they were able to provide.

Covert surveillance, employee vetting, mystery shopping (whatever that was). These activities were – so they promised – tailored to a client's requirements and 'guaranteed to exceed expectation'. It was handy that I couldn't find the word *ethical* anywhere, but *unorthodox* popped up quite a few times which was nice to see. The fact that it didn't say that they were members of the Association of British Investigators was another good sign, and after a few minutes' digging I found the bit that said they would be more than happy to discuss my particular requirements and provide a bespoke service.

Bespoke was good. I loved the sound of bespoke.

Get in touch, they said. Tell us what you need. We can assure you of absolute confidentiality.

Confidentiality was nice, obviously – like a bonus – but I didn't think it was going to matter much in the end. Once I'd got the intel I needed and you-know-who was being pulled apart in an interview room, all bets would be off anyway, and by the time charges were being pressed nobody would care one way or the other how I'd got the information.

It was all about the result.

I sucked the blood from my finger and fired off an email.

Then I went to get my dinner.

TWENTY-EIGHT

It was one of the best nights ever in the TV room, though for the life of me I couldn't tell you what everyone was watching, because I wasn't really paying attention. Not to the TV, anyway. I'd got in early to bag a VIP seat next to Lady Lauren up the front and sat there, happy as Larry, while she got more and more pissed off because I was wearing my headphones. I wasn't listening to anything, obviously, so I could hear the TV perfectly well, but I just sat nodding my head like I was well into my tunes and really enjoying myself because I knew it was winding her up.

You've got to have a hobby, right?

When Lauren couldn't control herself any more and started waving her arms around and having a go at me, I made out like I couldn't hear. I just shook my head and pointed at my headphones until eventually she started shouting.

'What are you playing at?'

'I can't *hear* you.' I deliberately said it too loudly, you know, like people do when they've got headphones on. I pointed at them again and said, 'I've got *headphones* on.'

'Take them off then.'

It was hard to keep a straight face because by now I could hear other people shouting 'Quiet' and 'Shut the fuck up' from the back. I thought Lauren was going to have a stroke or start frothing at the mouth or something, so in the end I slid the headphones off and looked at her, all innocent. 'What?'

'Why the hell are you watching the telly with those things on?'

'I just like the company,' I said.

The company was no better than it ever was and I was actually there on surveillance, keeping an eye on one particular nurse who was sitting in the corner like butter wouldn't melt. I watched her get up and move between patients, trying to keep a lid on things, because quite a few people were on their feet and shouting by now. That's how it works in here. One patient kicks off a bit and the rest of them tend to join in, like that Russian bloke and his dogs. Chekhov?

I watched her speak calmly to each of them in turn, a hand laid on an arm where it was needed, until some semblance of normality had returned. As normal as it can ever get when a woman is walking from wall to wall and a slightly camp bald bloke keeps pointing at the TV and announcing, 'I've shagged her.'

It was funny, I thought, that the nurse never said anything to Shaun.

I watched her go back to her seat and sit there staring at me. I'm sure anyone else who clocked it thought it was because I was the one who'd started the trouble, but I knew it was because she'd seen me looking at her and that was fine, because I wasn't trying to hide the fact.

I knew she was worried.

I knew she should be.

I stared right back and smiled until she looked away.

Once everything had settled down again, I put my headphones back on, loving how Lauren was still bristling next to me like a fat fucking cat with its fur up. I took out my phone like I was changing the track or whatever, but I was really checking my emails. It wasn't like I was expecting Pindown to get back to me that quickly and certainly not this late, but it couldn't hurt to have a look.

Just spam, and some funny video from my dad which I'd look at later, and a message from Dr Bakshi reminding me that I had my next assessment the day after tomorrow.

I texted a reply to confirm my attendance: Is there a dress code?

Just after half-eleven, Marcus, Malaika and Femi came in. A few extra staff always turned up around this time to make sure the TV got turned off without a row – Lauren once smashed a window when she wasn't allowed to watch the end of QVC – and that everyone was gearing up for bedtime and given extra meds or painkillers where necessary.

I was still watching Debbie, of course, so I was well aware that when I headed out and started drifting towards my room she was following me.

It wasn't obvious, she was far too canny for that, making out like she was gently shepherding several of us towards the women's corridor, just doing her job same as normal, but I could feel her eyes on my back.

So I slowed down, like I was distracted or something.

I let Donna and Lucy go past me, and waited for Debbie to catch up.

She had that concerned face on, the same one I'd seen just before she'd done what she did to Shaun. Someone else who thought they could fool me by wearing a mask.

'Is everything OK?'

'Absolutely,' I said. 'Is everything OK with you?'

'It's not me we're talking about.'

'Maybe it should be.'

She sighed and that mask of concern thickened a little. 'What's the matter, Alice?'

I said, 'Nothing's the matter, everything's great,' and for the first time in a while, I meant it.

'Is there anything you want to talk to me about?'

I knew there would be soon enough, but right then I was happy to enjoy myself. 'I'm fine, Debbie,' I said. 'But thanks for asking.'

'You sure?'

I'd looked on Google, so I knew the right way to cross myself. Forehead, chest, left shoulder, right shoulder. 'I swear to God.'

TWENTY-NINE

I was chatting with one of the janitors who was trying to clean sticky toffee pudding off the camera outside the nurses' station when Lauren came bounding – well, waddling at speed – towards me. Having wound her up so successfully the night before, I was all set for argy-bargy, but I could see immediately that there was nothing to be worried about.

She looked like she'd won the lottery.

She winked at me, rubbing her hands together then pointing towards the closed door of one of the examination rooms at the end of the corridor. She hissed, 'Fresh meat.'

That explained it. 'Serious?'

She nodded and beamed, excited as a kid on Christmas morning. 'Got here a couple of hours ago, Ilias reckons.'

'Yeah?' I was surprised it had taken this long for someone to fill the bed that had been unoccupied since Jamilah had left. It was usually one out, one in, like straight away. I wasn't complaining though. 'Man? Woman?'

'Some woman, apparently . . . fifty-odd, he reckons.'

Donna was passing by on her morning route march and had clearly overheard. 'I've already seen her,' she said. 'Seems nice enough.'

Lauren and I both wheeled round immediately, desperate for more details, but Donna had gone, heading quickly away towards the airlock. It wasn't a big deal because we knew she'd be back again soon enough and there was no way Lauren would let her go next time without pumping her for every bit of info she had.

She'd already begun to sing, throwing her own, horrific idea of twerking into the mix, as she mangled the words of a Bob Marley song.

'New woman, new blood, *new* woman new *blood* . . .'

That should give you some idea of just how giddy the patients in here can turn when a newbie gets brought in. I'm not talking about an Informal because they're rarely worth getting the flags out for. I'm talking about a brand spanking new section-monkey.

Same as I was, a couple of months ago.

It's easy to tell which is which, because it's a whole different process.

The ones being sectioned don't go to the 136 for a kick-off and they usually rock up in an ambulance, fresh from A&E. The Informals are on their own if they're asking to be admitted, or with coppers hanging off them like that poor bastard who'd been dodging traffic. The unfortunates who are likely to be here for at least twenty-eight days tend to arrive with one or two distressed rellies in tow, a doctor or two and maybe a social worker to make an outing of it. They're all over the place most of the time. They're still confused about what had happened to them back at the hospital or why the hell people had turned up at their house with legal documents. They're angry because they think they've been conned and some of them (yours truly, very much included) scratch and spit their way through the admittance procedure like they're being dragged towards a firing squad.

Ah, the procedure . . .

You know when you check in to a nice hotel?

Well it's bugger-all like that.

You know when you check into a shit hotel?

No, not like that either.

There's some basic medical stuff to begin with, which if you ask me is just them going through the motions, really. I mean it *is* a hospital, in case you need reminding. *Oh, your blood pressure's up a bit.* Well, *that's* a real surprise. There's your meds to sort out. The ones you might well be on already – for a dodgy heart, gut problems, diabetes, whatever – and the variety pack of new ones you'll be taking from now on. There's loads more paperwork to be completed and of course you have to be issued with a handful of faded printouts telling you where you are, why you're being detained and who's who on the ward. Your care plan, your daily routine, your right to privacy and dignity . . .

Then, talking of which, you take your clothes off and they dole out the jim-jams.

Then they take your stuff away (remember my potentially lethal bra?).

Then, finally, several hours after stepping into then out of that airlock, you're escorted to your lavish sleeping quarters, where a smiling nurse will show you your bed like you've never seen one before and ask if there's anything else you need. I remember that all I wanted was the Wi-Fi code and for the smiling nurse to fuck the fuck off.

No prizes for guessing who that particular angel was.

So, to take a step back, you can understand why we get so worked up when someone new arrives. Why it's such a big deal. Yeah, it's always nice to see a fresh face, maybe make a new friend, but mostly it's about the pecking order.

A new patient means everyone else moves up one.

Lauren, who already reckoned she was in pole position, was dancing with Graham and Lucy by now. It was like a party. I was all set to stick around, every bit as eager to catch my first glimpse of the gang's latest member as anyone else, but when my phone buzzed and I saw who the email was from, I knew that it would have to wait.

It wasn't like the new girl was going anywhere.

Half an hour later I was back, hanging around near the entrance to the women's corridor with the rest of the welcoming committee – Lauren, Donna, Lucy, Graham, Ilias and Bob – and waiting for the newbie's coming-out parade. Shaun was watching from the doorway of the music room. Tony was sitting by the airlock with his bags packed, but he was watching, too, in case our newest arrival was the Thing.

Everyone was in high spirits, yakking and smiling, so *I* must have looked like I'd just been shagged silly by Tom Hardy or something.

'What *you* so happy about?' Ilias asked.

My grin got even bigger. 'Just … this, you know. A new face.'

Ilias nodded, peering anxiously towards the examination room. Same as the rest of us, he knew how long the induction process usually took and that, any time now, the latest admission would emerge and be escorted to her bedroom. 'You want to play chess after?'

'Yeah,' I said. 'Sounds good.'

I *was* excited to meet my new wardmate, but the real reason for my good mood was the phone conversation I'd just had with the man from Pindown Investigations, which could not have gone better.

'Howard' was extremely friendly and didn't ask too many questions. He told me how much his 'investigation' would cost and asked if I could transfer half the money straight away. I told him that wasn't a problem (three cheers for that police pension) and asked how long he thought it might take.

'It's all pretty standard stuff,' he said. 'Should have everything you need sometime tomorrow.'

Some deep-seated, law-abiding part of me was gagging to ask *how* he was going to get hold of all this 'pretty standard stuff' but it was just a low, muffled voice, you know? There was something far stronger screaming inside me, desperate to get this information and to *use* it. I didn't want him to know that though. I didn't want anyone to know just yet.

I said, 'Hopefully talk to you tomorrow then.'

When the woman came out of the examination room, me and Lauren and the rest of them surged forward, like groupies outside a stage door. Marcus and George stepped out from the nurses' station to make sure we didn't go any closer and George shook his head, like we were all being a bit sad.

'Come on, give her some room.' He lowered his voice. 'Remember how it was for you.'

I'm damn sure the woman wasn't fifty ... closer to forty if anything ... but I could see why Ilias had told Lauren she was older. I don't think he'd had a proper look. You know how they reckon TV cameras make people look fatter? Well this place can put ten years on you, easy. Sometimes I look in the mirror and see my mum staring back at me.

My mum, if she wasn't well.

The new girl was white and tall and skinny – not *Donna* skinny, but a bit on the scrawny side – with dark hair tied up in a scrunchy. Her head was down, but I saw her glance up at us all, just for a second, and I could see the bruising under one of her eyes. She was moving well enough though, certainly not the usual Fleet Ward shuffle, and I remember thinking that, in spite of everything, she looked ... determined.

'Just make some space and let Clare come through,' Marcus said.

So now we had a name. I nodded at Lucy and Lucy nodded back.

There was a nurse escorting her, of course, a hand on her arm, and it could not have been more perfect. That same mask of concern she'd worn for me the day before. I stared at her, rushing like I'd had a double dose of something, because I knew she was on borrowed time.

As they came alongside us, Lauren reached out a hand and Debbie ushered Clare quickly past. Graham waved and Donna murmured, 'Nice to meet you.'

'I'm Ilias,' shouted Ilias. 'And you're not.'

I watched her being led away towards her bedroom and I had to fight the urge to chase her down and tell her to watch herself. Tell her that this place wasn't safe, whatever it said on her bits of paper. I wanted to point at Debbie and say, 'I hope for your sake that she wasn't the one that examined you.'

'All right,' George said. 'Show's over.'

Lucy and Donna walked away, arms linked, giggling like schoolgirls. Graham took his place at the meds hatch and Lauren wandered over to torment Tony for a while. I stood with Ilias and Bob watching as Debbie opened a bedroom door at the end of the corridor.

'We going to play chess then?' Ilias asked.

I told him to get lost and watched Debbie invite Clare to enter.

Bob sidled up and nodded. 'I did her in a flat in Peckham one time ... the new bird. She went like a bat in a biscuit tin ...'

I was thinking about that mask, about how good it would feel to watch it slip, as I saw Debbie follow the new arrival into the room and close the door behind her.

THIRTY

Dr Bakshi said, 'You look happy, Alice.'

'Because I am,' I said. Because I was.

'That's very nice to hear.' She began slowly turning the pages in front of her. 'And I enjoyed your response to my text message, though I see you haven't dressed up.'

'These are my best trackies,' I said.

It was certainly the most upbeat I'd felt at my Friday-morning assessment session in a dog's age. I could sense something good was coming. Good for me, at any rate. I'd been hoping that Debbie would be sitting there in the circle, like she had been the week before, but they do these things on rotation, so Malaika was keeping Marcus company today. That tight-lipped trainee from last time wasn't anywhere to be seen either. Maybe I'd frightened her off.

So, just the four of us. It was cosy.

Marcus made the official introductions and Malaika did the meds report. I was still 'responding well' to the regime apparently, which was always nice to hear, even though most of the time their idea of *well* and mine were very different.

'By all accounts, you've had a productive week.' Bakshi looked at Marcus, then at me. 'Would you agree?'

'Yeah, I've had a cracking week,' I said.

Malaika nodded, like she was on my side.

'Though I gather there was a minor incident in the television lounge on Wednesday evening.' Bakshi glanced at Marcus. 'Some disagreement with Lauren?'

I laughed and shook my head. 'Just a spot of handbags, that's all. Nothing to get excited about. Lauren didn't think I was giving *Grand Designs*, or whatever the hell she was watching, enough respect. Yeah, it was daft, but I shouldn't have reacted.'

'It's good that you can understand that.' Bakshi turned another page. 'I gather it was an interesting occupational therapy session on Tuesday.'

'You heard that, did you?'

'The nurse who was overseeing the session submitted a written report.'

'Did you see any of the pictures?'

'Unfortunately, I didn't.'

'Oh you should,' I said. 'Lucy's one especially. I swear, she's like the Leonardo da Vinci of pubes.' I stared at Bakshi, straight-faced. I might have been imagining the hint of a smile in return.

'Well, that's all very positive, and I'm delighted that you're making progress. All that said, however, I'm sorry to say that I won't be lifting the section this week.'

'OK,' I said.

I could see that they were all a little taken aback at the calmness of my response, the absence of histrionics, and I have to admit I was pretty surprised myself. No, I probably wouldn't have argued if they'd told me I could trot off home that afternoon, but for the first time in two months I had a reason to be there. A reason to stay, at least until I had the proof I knew was coming, and a chance to act on it.

'Can you guess why that might be, Alice?'

'Why what might be?'

'Why your detention under section three of the Mental Health Act needs to stay in place, for the time being at least.'

'I haven't got a clue,' I said. 'I didn't freak out and show Marcus my tits, did I?'

'No,' Marcus said. 'You did not.'

When I saw Bakshi lift up the sheet of paper, I knew what was coming, but I was genuinely confused.

'At least there was only one late night phone call to Mr Flanagan this week.'

'No way,' I said. 'I never called Andy.' For once I wasn't lying, either, not intentionally.

'Quite a memorable one, though.'

Not for me it wasn't.

'I'm not going to read out what you said, but suffice it to say it was just the one word.' She looked at me, waiting for the penny to drop. 'A very offensive word, repeated over and over again.'

I nodded. Like I'd taken a leaf out of Lauren's book. But I could not remember doing it.

'Oh, right. *That* call.' Malaika shifted in her seat and I swear I saw her trying to stifle a smile. 'Yeah, sorry. I meant to call him again to apologise, but I must have forgotten. It was a moment, that's all, though ... of being really angry and doing something stupid. Just one moment, in the whole week.'

Bakshi looked at Marcus. Marcus shrugged.

'Well, I'm taking it as a very good sign that you're not disputing that what you did was wrong.'

'Oh, I know it was.' I wasn't going to tell her that I thought it was piss-funny and I certainly wasn't letting on that I couldn't remember making the call in the first place. 'It was dead wrong.'

Bakshi nodded and began to tidy her papers. 'In which case, on Marcus's recommendation, and in the hope that this progress continues, I'm happy to move you back on to escorted leave.'

That was it. Short and seriously sweet.

I smiled, nice and humble. A day that I already knew would be one to remember had got off to a blinding start.

'Cool,' I said. 'Thank you.'

Clare was sitting with Shaun and Femi at lunch while the rest of us sat together and watched her. Shaun was still keeping up the whole Marcel Marceau thing, but the two women were talking quietly as they ate. I don't think Femi was sitting as close to Clare as she was because of a Within Arm's Length obs stat or anything so I presumed it was part of the normal process of easing the new arrival in gently.

Not wanting to leave her alone with the rabble just yet.

She hadn't shown up for dinner the previous evening and I hadn't been there for breakfast, so for all I knew this might have been her first group mealtime. I asked the others and they all thought it was.

'Has anyone actually spoken to her yet?'

Heads were shaken.

'Not really had a chance,' Ilias said. 'She was with George at the meds hatch first thing and now Femi's stuck to her like shit on a blanket.'

Heads were nodded.

'Femi-Nazi,' Donna said.

'I reckon she's a bit up herself.' Lauren sat back, ready to give her full appraisal of the newcomer, and looked horrified when I stood up. 'Fuck d'you think you're going?'

'Say hello . . .'

I wandered across to their table, told Shaun to budge up and squeezed in between him and Clare. Femi gave me a hard stare, so I smiled to let her know that my intentions were wholly friendly. 'No worries,' I said. 'Just being matey.'

If anything, I was in an even better mood than I had been an hour or so before when I'd sauntered out of the MDR. It wasn't just what they'd said in the assessment meeting, it was what they hadn't said. Not one of them had mentioned the interesting drawing I'd done in the occupational therapy session. Nobody had said a word about any of the conversations I'd had with Debbie over the previous few days.

Like they'd never happened.

That meant that *she* hadn't said anything, and there could only be one reason for that, right?

Guilty as sin and she knew I knew it.

'I'm Alice,' I said. I stuck out a hand. 'Al . . . whatever.' Clare proffered her own, limp hand and I squeezed.

'Clare.'

'With an I or without?'

'Like the county in Ireland.'

'Oh, you Irish, then?' I didn't think I could hear an accent, but she hadn't said much, to be fair.

'My mum is.'

I leaned close to her. Said, 'Listen, why don't we grab a cup of tea and go somewhere a bit quieter for a good old natter?'

'I'm not sure that's a good idea,' Femi said.

'All I'm saying . . .' I looked at the nurse, 'I wish someone had talked to me when I first came in and yeah, I know she's had the official spiel and all that, but she's going to get a much better idea of how things really work in here from someone like me than from one of you lot.' I smiled. 'With all due respect.'

'Sounds OK,' Clare said. A London accent, I decided. Somewhere south of Watford Gap, anyway.

'You make a fair point,' Femi said. 'I should run it past Marcus though.'

'No sweat.' I stood up and reached out a hand towards Clare. 'We'll just be in the music room, so if he's got any problem with it, he knows where we are.'

We'd barely got our arses into chairs in the music room when Ilias came barging in. I asked if he wouldn't mind buggering off and giving us a bit of privacy, but before he'd had a chance to open his mouth Clare burst into tears.

Ilias pointed, looking thrilled. 'What have you done to upset *her*?'

I was searching around for tissues, then saw her pull one from her sleeve and bury her face in it. 'It's not me, you twat, it's *you*.' I walked over to him and whispered, 'I think you just scared her a bit, that's all. Just do me a favour and give us a bit of time on our own?'

Astonishingly, Ilias turned and walked out without saying a word, and by the time I sat down again, Clare had stopped crying.

'You OK?'

She tucked the tissue back into her sleeve. 'I'm fine,' she said.

For the next ten minutes we drank our tea and I gave her the lowdown on Ilias, Lucy and the rest of the gang. I told her their nicknames – well aware that I'd need to come up with one for her – and as many of their strange habits as I could remember. I told her not to let Lauren use her bathroom under any circumstances. I told her about Graham and the waiting, Donna and the constant walking, and when I got to Tony's preoccupation with the Thing, she just stared at me like she'd never heard anything like it.

'I've barely even started, love. Proper madhouse in here.'

She thought that was funny.

I'd just started to dish the dirt on the staff when Clare looked up, noticed Shaun peering in at us through the window and immediately burst into tears again.

'Jesus . . .' I got up to shoo him away and yet again, by the time I'd sat down with her again the crying had stopped and the soggy tissue was being nudged out of sight. 'Is it *blokes*?' I asked. 'You got a problem with blokes?'

She shook her head.

'Thing is, there's quite a few in here, so you might need to have a word with someone about that.'

'I'm fine,' she said.

'You can talk to me,' I said. 'I've had some training—'

'Carry on with what you were saying before.'

I immediately decided that she must have had some kind

of breakdown after being raped. It made perfect sense, and I don't know why I hadn't clocked it earlier. I know they normally try to put patients like her on a single sex ward, but that it isn't always possible. There'd been a woman like that in here when I arrived, and I'd talked to any number of victims who'd been through much the same thing when I was on the Job.

'Tell me about the nurses,' she said.

I moved my chair a little closer to hers. 'Well, I'm not sure if anyone mentioned it to you . . . I mean they almost certainly didn't . . . but we had a murder in here a couple of weeks ago. One of the—'

And just like that, she was blubbing again.

So, not blokes then.

I'll be honest, the on-off waterworks were doing my head in by now, so I got up and opened the door, keen to find someone else to deal with her. I saw Mia outside the 136, so I shouted and waved, and while I was waiting for her to stroll over I decided that – pain in the arse as Clare 'like the county in Ireland' was – I did, at least, have a nickname for her.

Clare, aka Tiny Tears.

It was even funnier, because she was tall, yeah?

While Mia was still on her way across, I felt my mobile buzz in my pocket. I took it out and checked the message.

> I think I've got everything you need. Call me for
> details. Howard.

Now I *seriously* couldn't care less about the sobbing behind me as I marched quickly past Mia and away towards my bedroom. Funny, isn't it, how the stars align at moments like that – or you think they do – because who do you reckon was the last nurse I saw before I turned on to the women's corridor?

Debbie looked up from the window of the nurses' station as I passed.

'Someone's happy.'

I didn't stop walking. 'Delirious,' I said.

THIRTY-ONE

The man from Pindown Investigations sounded every bit as upbeat about things as I was.

'Like I thought, it was pretty run-of-the-mill stuff. Nothing a bit of know-how and the right computer program couldn't handle. Didn't take me very long if I'm honest, and I'm telling you, Alice, so you know I'm not one of those people who string an investigation out for no good reason except to charge a client more for the job.'

'I appreciate that, Howard.'

'So you'll know where to come if you ever need this kind of service again, right?'

I was running out of patience. About-ready-to-punch-a-hole-in-the-wall running out of it. I needed to *know*. 'What have you got for me then, Howard?'

'So ...' I could hear pages being shuffled. 'The subject lives alone in a two-bedroom flat in Edgware. She runs a small car and, as far as holidays go, last year she managed two weeks in the Scottish Highlands. Went with her sister, I think—'

'What about the money?'

'Well, I'm just giving you the what-do-you-call-it . . . context. But if you want details . . .' More pages being turned. 'She's currently running a small overdraft of £112.75 on an HSBC current account. It's within her agreed limit, but an overdraft none the less. She's missed two mortgage payments on her flat in the last six months . . . there *are* a couple of outstanding credit card debts, but nothing massive and she's got a credit rating of 375 which is about the national average . . . well, a little below if we're being picky.'

'Right.'

'So, whoever she is, your subject isn't exactly minted. I'd say she's just about getting by.'

'What about deposit accounts, savings, whatever?'

'Well, there's a small sum in a deposit account that's tied into her current account, but it's just where any interest gets put. We're talking about a couple of quid, that's all.'

I could feel acid rising up from my stomach, imagined the filthy bubble of it emerging slowly from my mouth and wrapping itself around me. I'd been lying on my bed, but when I tried to sit up, I thought I was going to be sick. 'There must be something else.'

'Not that I could see,' he said.

'What about offshore accounts, overseas banks, trusts or whatever?'

'Sorry, what? You're talking very fast.'

I took a deep breath and said it again.

'Well, I suppose it's a possibility, but that would involve widening the investigation significantly, and—'

'You've missed something. You *must* have done. I mean it's obvious that she's hiding the money, isn't it? Why don't you *get* that?'

He said, 'Do you mind me asking what this individual does for a living? If that's information you're happy to share.'

'She's a mental health nurse.'

He laughed. The useless twat actually chuckled. 'Well, there you go then.'

'What are you on about?'

'Have you any idea how little they get paid? Nurses.'

'She's a *nurse* who's dealing drugs to patients, fair enough?' I knew I was shouting. I could hear my own voice bouncing back off the walls, but sometimes it's the only way to make people see sense. 'She's obviously making a lot of money from selling drugs but for some reason you can't find it. She also happens, *by the way*, to have murdered someone who was threatening to expose her and I know this for a fact, so don't try and tell me I don't know what I'm talking about. Because she's got motive and she had opportunity and I've spoken to witnesses and taken *statements* for God's sake and you were the one who told me that you could get the proof. You *promised* me you'd get the proof and now I don't know what the hell I'm going to do. Do you want her to get away with it? Seriously, is that what you want?'

For a few seconds, all I could hear was the two of us breathing and the noise of Lucy moaning in the room next door. Then Howard said, 'I think I should probably . . . step away from this.'

'Kevin Connolly couldn't step away, could he?'

'I should also remind you that you need to pay the remaining half of my fee—'

'Johnno couldn't fucking step away.'

I was on the floor now, though I still don't remember falling off the bed, and by the time I'd finished swearing at him, my so-called investigator had already hung up.

I remember thinking that the floor was the ceiling and clinging on to the end of my bed for dear life to stop myself falling.

I remember doing a lot of shouting, and even if I can't remember what the words were – I mean there probably weren't any words – I know I *did*, because it felt like I'd swallowed glass for a couple of days afterwards.

I remember someone knocking, asking if I was all right.

I remember ringing Howard back, but he obviously saw it was me calling and didn't answer, so I just did the same thing as when I'd left that message for Andy and said the C-word over and over again for ages. I knew it would be OK, though, because there wasn't any chance Howard would be writing Bakshi a letter.

Mostly, though, I remember my conversation with Johnno, because it was only when he started talking some sense into me that things became clearer and I began to feel they were a bit less hopeless. To see another option.

'It's like with the Evans case,' Johnno said. 'Like with Ralph Cox.'

'Is it?'

'You just need to find a different way, that's all. Something a bit more direct.'

He was sitting next to me on the floor, in that brown suede jacket I always liked. I told him that he should probably be holding on to something if he didn't want to crash into the ceiling, but he told me he could look after himself. He smiled a bit when he said that, like he knew very well how ironic it was.

'I'm sorry, Johnno.'

'About what?'

'About everything, mate. You and Maggie and the baby. Letting you down, I mean.'

'You didn't let me down, you soft sod.'

'You know that when I try to picture your face it's always got blood on it? Just ... spatter. Did I ever tell you that? Sometimes I see it on my fingers, too, and my clothes ... like when you and me were on the Job and they spray stuff with luminol to show up the blood.'

'You didn't let anyone down, Al.'

'I'm a walking fucking crime scene, Johnno.'

'You're not going to let Kevin down, either. I know you're not ...'

And then I was properly calm. Getting there, anyway. I wasn't thinking about the money any more, or gathering evidence; none of it.

I knew exactly what I needed to do.

THIRTY-TWO

I collared her outside the nurses' station after dinner.

'Debbie, can I have a word?'

'Course you can, darlin'.'

'In private, I mean.'

She glanced at her watch then pointed towards one of the examination rooms. 'Let's go in there.'

When I'd sat down, I nodded towards the door she'd left open. 'You might want to shut that,' I said.

She shrugged then pushed the door until it was almost closed. 'I'll leave it open just a little bit,' she said.

Like she thought I was dangerous.

'It's fine,' I said. Because I *was*.

She pulled a chair across and sat down. 'So, what can I do for you, Alice?'

Before I knew what I was doing, I had reached into my pocket for my mobile, pressed a few buttons and was holding it out towards her. 'Look at this,' I said.

She watched, started to smile.

To this day I can't quite explain what I was doing for that minute or so. It wasn't like I'd changed my mind or chickened out or anything, it wasn't any kind of clever delaying tactic. It was a switch that tripped for no good reason. I just forgot myself and . . . went somewhere else.

'That's funny,' she said.

I was showing her the video my dad had sent me a few days earlier. A monkey being shown a magic trick, for fuck's sake. I was smiling *myself*, even though my hand was shaking as I held the screen up. Christ alone knows what happened or where my head was at right then, but looking back now I was like a hitman who pulls out a gun then gets distracted by the colour of the curtains. 'Look at the monkey's face when he sees it . . .'

She laughed at the monkey's double-take. 'Ah . . . that stuff's brilliant,' she said. 'I love all those cat ones.'

Then, just like that, the switch flipped back again. I slipped my phone back in my pocket and looked up to see her staring at me.

'I know what you did,' I said.

'OK, Alice.' She shook her head. 'What did I do?'

'I know that you murdered Kevin and I know you did it because of the drugs.' She looked at me like I was mad and I know that sounds like a strange observation bearing in mind where we were, but trust me, it's a look they try very hard *not* to give anyone in here. They're trained to do precisely the opposite. That's why it made such an impression. 'Kevin didn't want any more to do with the whole thing and he was almost certainly threatening to blackmail you with the drugs you'd already given him and which he'd hidden. The drugs you couldn't find when you went into his room that night.'

'OK,' she said.

It was just pouring out. I couldn't remember the last time I'd felt so confident or in control, so the person I wanted to *be*.

I felt like I was fucking invincible.

'You killed him on your first round of checks . . . or maybe your second, it doesn't really matter. But you'd certainly already done it by the time you went in that third time and "discovered" the body and started screaming the place down. That was pretty clever, I'll give you that much. I'm not sure if you knew Graham had already put the camera out of action or not, but either way he really did you a favour, didn't he? It made everything so much more com-plicated for the police than it actually needed to be.'

'OK,' she said.

'Then you got scared, because the person who was closest to Kevin knew exactly what you were up to. Maybe Shaun said something to you, told you he knew you'd murdered Kevin, but even if he didn't, you decided it would be best to shut him up anyway. To be on the safe side.'

'You're talking about what happened when Shaun had that episode in the TV room?'

'I'm talking about you silencing a key witness, yeah.'

Debbie nodded, thought for a few seconds. 'So, it was Kevin's room in that picture you did the other day?'

'Right, like you didn't know.'

'And it was me in the room.'

'Who else did you think it was—'

I stopped when I saw George poke his head around the door. I'm not sure if it was the look on my face or Debbie's that he'd clocked. 'Is everything OK in here?'

I sat back and pointed a finger. 'You should ask *her.*'

By the time Debbie turned to look at him, she had a very different mask on. Up to then her face had been sort of dry and pinched, but now she was smiling. She said, 'We're fine, thanks, George. It's all good. Alice is just telling me a story.'

THIRTY-THREE

This Is What I Believe.

Believe. Present tense . . .

The Earth is definitely not flat.

5G is not going to turn us all into zombies.

There are people in this world with too much wealth and power who will do anything they have to, including murder where necessary, to mould society into whatever shape suits them, while making sure the rest of us don't know who they are. I'm not talking about spooky shit with robes and candles and human sacrifice. Not secret satanists or people who are really lizards. I just mean rich and powerful people doing bad things to hold on to what they've got and protecting their equally rich and powerful friends. You only have to look at what's going on in the world and that makes perfect sense, doesn't it?

My mum and dad are obviously not part of anything like this and are genuinely good people.

My ex-boyfriend Andy isn't either. He's just a dick.

You have to go slightly mad to become properly sane.

The Beatles obviously existed and they were great, apart from the weird Indian stuff and that stupid song about an octopus.

There were no criminals wearing masks on my television.

Drink and drugs were partly, but not wholly, responsible for everything that led up to me being 'retired', and everything that's happened since.

Johnno died because I was not a good enough copper.

I did not hurt anyone, except when I was trying to protect them and myself, and I would do so again.

Being banged up with mad people is not great for your mental health.

Almost all the people working here do an amazing job, clinging on by their fingernails, and there's rarely a day goes by when I don't think that being a copper was a doddle by comparison.

I was sexually assaulted. I *was*.

If they sent me home tomorrow – to a recovery house for a few weeks probably, then to Mum and Dad's – I would be absolutely fine.

I will meet someone, get married and have a family like everyone else.

At some point, I will work as a police officer again.

Kevin Connolly was murdered just over two weeks ago on this ward by Deborah Anne McClure (FRCN). You already know the hows and whys so I don't need to repeat them. You probably want to know how our conversation in the examination room ended, but there really wasn't much more to it after George interrupted us. All you need to know is that her mask stayed firmly in place until Debbie announced that she needed to be on duty at the meds hatch and left.

She had nothing to say. Nothing.

Yeah, a straight-up confession would have been nice, but that was as close to one as you can get. Her coming clean there and then would certainly have been a good result for me and, bearing in mind what was around the corner, would definitely have done her a major favour.

So, here we are. That's us bang up to date.

Well, aside from the blood-soaked elephant in the room, which is the fact that, two days later – yesterday to be precise – I was the one who found Debbie's body.

PART TWO

FIGHT OR FLIGHT

THIRTY-FOUR

As you can imagine, it's been all fun and games around this place the last twenty-four hours. A right old palaver. The police have packed up and gone, for the time being at least, but everything's still all over the shop.

Everything and everyone.

Right now, we're all gearing up for this afternoon's 'community meeting' which should be interesting to say the least. It's safe to say we won't be talking about how bad the food is, or the need for a private visiting area, or Ilias's constant farting, or any of the other fascinating topics that normally crop up at these things.

Probably just the one item on the agenda this time.

Yesterday . . .

I gave the police an initial statement when they first arrived, an hour or so after I'd found the body, and I reckon I did pretty well, considering I was probably still in shock. This was after they'd bagged up my bloodstained trackies and T-shirt and trainers, and sat me down in an exam room with a mug of tea and a nice friendly DC called Pauline.

Is there anyone you'd like us to call, love?

I hadn't even had a chance to shower, but I know how it works. I told them as much, made sure the officers at the scene knew they were dealing with someone who understood the procedure. Who fully grasped the importance of getting a witness's statement, *my* statement, while everything was still . . . fresh. As I pointed out to Pauline, I hadn't so much as washed my hands yet, so things could hardly have been any fresher.

I think I'll be all right. I've had blood on my hands before.

Pauline and her older male colleague were just the first detectives on the scene, but the MIT that ended up catching the case would probably be a different team from the one that was dealing – or *not* dealing – with Kevin's murder. I guessed the two teams would be putting their heads together at the very least, once the left hand of Homicide and Serious Crime became aware of what the right hand was doing. That's not something you can ever take for granted in the Met, but even allowing for the usual administrative bullshit and basic incompetence, two murders – in the same place in the space of a fortnight – were pretty likely to raise a red flag.

I mean, you would have thought.

'So, you found Miss McClure's body when you visited the women's toilets, is that correct?' Pauline seemed a bit . . . mousy for my liking, then I remembered that she was talking to someone she'd presume was almost certainly traumatised.

I nodded. 'Saw it as soon as I opened the door. Well, you could hardly miss it.'

'What time would this have been? Approximately.'

'It was ... what, an hour ago? So about half-past three.'

'You could see straight away that it was Miss McClure?'

'Yeah, I saw the ginger hair. I mean I noticed the blood first, obviously. There was a lot of blood.'

'So, what did you do?'

'Well, I had first-aid and life support training when I was on the Job, so I got down on the floor with her to see if there was anything I could do. I mean it was pretty obvious there wasn't ... I could see how many stab wounds there were ... but it just kicked in, I suppose. I did CPR for ... I don't know, half a minute or so? That's why ...' I held up my hands so she could see the blood dried between my fingers, gathered in the lines on my palm and at the base of my nails.

'What about the knife?'

'That was lying on the floor a few feet away, under one of the sinks.'

'So you didn't touch it?'

I looked at her to make sure she knew what a daft question it was. 'Of course I didn't touch it. Obviously I was aware that me giving first aid might compromise evidence on the body itself. That couldn't be helped, but I certainly know better than to go anywhere near the murder weapon.'

She was writing all this down, ready to pass it on to the full-time investigators, once they were assigned. 'So, when did you shout for help?'

'While I was doing CPR,' I said. 'Then I ran out and I was still shouting and Marcus came in, then Malaika, and they took over. Or maybe Malaika got in there first, I can't remember. It was all a bit panicky.'

'What about before you went in? You didn't see anyone coming out?'

I told her I hadn't.

'You didn't see anyone going in before you?'

I was getting a bit irritated by now and told her that I didn't make a habit of logging activity in and around the women's toilet.

'I have to ask,' she said.

'Course,' I said. 'Sorry for being snappy.'

'It's understandable,' she said. 'This can't be easy for you.'

She asked for my details, so I told her that I was likely to be staying exactly where I was for the foreseeable future, but gave my mum and dad's address as a back-up. When she asked for my phone number, I said, 'Steve Seddon's already got my number.' I could see that she recognised the name. 'Not that you'd know it.'

'It's best that I have it, too,' she said.

Once she'd thanked me for my help and given me a number to call should I be in need of counselling, Pauline wandered out into the corridor to join her colleague, who'd been taking a statement from Marcus.

Marcus came in and sat with me.

'You OK?' He was staring down at the blood that had dried on his own hands. His friend's blood.

'I'm fine.' We said nothing for a while, just stared into space, then I nodded down at his hands. 'You get used to that.'

Marcus took a few deep breaths then looked at me and shook his head. He said, 'What the fu-fu-fuck is going on?'

I'd heard him stammer plenty of times, but it was the first time I'd ever heard him swear.

Now, L-Plate comes running up to me outside the dining room like the world is coming to an end. She looks like she's been crying, though to be fair, she looks like that more often than looking like she hasn't been.

'What's the matter, L?'

'This meeting.'

'I know,' I say. 'Yeah, it's bound to be a bit upsetting, but I think that's what it's for, so—'

'No, not that—'

'So people can let their feelings out a bit—'

'I don't know what to *wear*.'

'*What?*' I watch her shaking her head, clutching at the material of a glittery Dolce & Gabbana sweatshirt like it's some old rag she's pulled on, and I quite fancy punching her in the tits. Instead, I ask, 'Who gives a toss what you wear?'

'*I* do,' she says.

'Are you on the *pull*?' I see a hint of a smile. 'You think Ilias is even going to bother changing his pants? You think Donna won't have the same sweaty tracksuit on she has every bloody day?' Her smile widens. 'Look, I know what's happened is freaking us all out a bit, but this meeting isn't anything to worry about, I swear. It's certainly not something you need to get tarted up for.'

'You promise?' she asks.

I nod, and find myself trying to remember the last time I'd got tarted up for anything.

Mists of bloody time.

It was some stupid office thing I went to with Andy. One of those where they dole out crap awards, and I remember I'd borrowed a dress off Sophie because I didn't have any-thing nice with long sleeves. All night I was letting Andy know, a bit too loudly, that his HR manager was looking at me funny, like he knew something or was trying to send me a bad message. Andy told me to keep it down because I was showing him up, so I just smoked a couple of spliffs in the car park, drank a gallon of prosecco and was sick on the way home.

I never even had Sophie's dress cleaned before I gave it her back.

Now, L-Plate nods and says, 'Sorry, Al . . . having a bad day.' She looks about seven years old, standing there chewing her fat bottom lip like she's trying to be brave, and I feel bad for wanting to punch her.

'No need to be sorry,' I say.

George and Mia wander out of the dining room. They've been setting the chairs up for the meeting. I say, 'All set?' but they just carry on walking towards the nurses' station. They both still look a bit shell-shocked.

I reach out, without thinking, to touch L-Plate's arm, then tell myself off for being an idiot when she flinches. 'Listen, forget what I said. You can dress up if you want. You can wear anything you bloody well fancy.' I nod towards the women's corridor. 'Come on, let's go and get your outfit sorted.'

THIRTY-FIVE

Marcus stands up and says, 'Thank you for all for coming, especially at this very difficult time.' This is no bog-standard community meeting and it's clear he's prepared something when he glances down at what he's written on a small piece of card. 'Obviously, we are all deeply shocked by what's happened. To lose a friend and colleague this way is terrible, but our main concern has to be for all of you. How you are feeling, how we cope with what has happened and how we move on from this, together.'

Graham puts his hand up. When Marcus looks at him and nods, Graham squirms in his seat for a few seconds, like he's embarrassed to find himself in the spotlight.

He asks, 'Has something bad happened?'

Marcus mumbles a few words to Mia who immediately stands up and walks across to where Graham is sitting. She politely asks Donna to move up one, then sits down next to Graham and takes his hand.

I'm thinking that's sweet of her.

I'm thinking that Graham is a bit further gone than I thought he was.

I'm thinking, *deeply shocked* is a bloody understatement and that what happened on Sunday is only the second most shocking thing I can think of. I would have thought the most *holy fuck this is properly bonkers* shocking thing is . . . Marcus standing there, saying all this while he knows damn well that whoever stabbed his 'friend and colleague' to death is sitting right there with him in the same room.

How can he *not* know that?

I can only assume the police have come to the same conclusion. I'm not sure who the Met's hiring these days, but even a bunch of sixteen-year-old work-experience detectives should have figured that much out by now. Yes, there were a couple of visitors on the ward at the time of the murder, but it's hard to imagine that Donna's mum or Ilias's idiot younger brother had much of a motive for killing Debbie. That's if *anyone* had what an ordinary punter might think of as a conventional motive. Rage, revenge, love, sex, money, all the old favourites.

By now you should be well aware it doesn't take much in here.

There were several Informals around at the time as well, of course, but those who were able to provide the police with permanent addresses got the hell out of there as soon as they could. I mean, wouldn't you?

Aside from a couple of voluntary patients of no fixed abode, that just leaves those of us on section plus the members of staff who are still breathing and, like Marcus said, they've all shown up for the meeting.

Looks like it, anyway.

There's maybe twenty people in the dining room.

A big circle of chairs.

Marcus says, 'Before I open the meeting up to the floor, I want to introduce someone who's going to say a few words about the position of the ward moving forward.' He points towards the only person in the room I don't recognise.

Ilias leaps to his feet, looking a bit panicky. 'Where's the ward going?'

'Well, this man will tell you,' Marcus says.

Ilias sits down again, but he still looks worried.

The man – middle-aged with grey hair – stands up and introduces himself as a member of the hospital's Foundation Trust Board. 'I wanted to let you know that there have been . . . discussions about closing the ward.' He sounds like someone off the radio. 'At least temporarily, in light of the recent tragic events. It was suggested that it might be better for the mental well-being of all patients if they were moved elsewhere.'

Several members of staff nod. I'm thinking we should probably be more concerned about our *physical* well-being.

'In the end, however, we have decided to keep the ward open and functioning as normal.' He glances at Marcus. 'As normally as we can, at any rate.'

I think that *normal* is not a word he would be using if he'd ever set foot in this place before today.

'Firstly, I must be honest and acknowledge the sad fact that we would simply not be able to find enough alternative beds for everyone, certainly not in London. Secondly, the board was of the opinion that everyone would benefit from as little disruption as possible and that patients would probably be in favour of leaving things as they are.' He looks out at us all. 'That you would prefer to stay together.'

I can see the sense in what the bloke's saying, but I consider asking if maybe we can just get rid of Lauren.

It strikes me that keeping the ward open might be what the police would prefer as well. It's always better if a detective can keep all their suspects in one place. As the posh bloke sits down and Marcus stands up to say a bit more, I'm finding it hard not to imagine the whole thing as some warped, psych-ward version of Cluedo.

Mr or Mrs Mental, in the toilets, with a dagger.

Or an air-locked room mystery. Ha!

Now, various patients have begun standing up and shouting out questions, making observations or just shar-ing random thoughts, while Marcus tries to maintain some semblance of order.

'Can we use the bogs again?' Lauren asks.

'Yes, you can,' Marcus says.

'Good, because the men's bogs stink.'

'*You* stink,' Bob says. 'You stink of fish.'

'Was there a lot of blood?' Ilias asks.

'I don't think it's helpful to talk about that,' Marcus says.

'Where's Debbie?' Graham asks.

Now, it's my turn. I'm sitting next to Shaun and he starts, nervous as a kitten, when I stand up suddenly. 'What about some security?'

Marcus looks at me.

'That's a good idea,' Tony says. 'Stop the Thing coming in.'

'Yeah, but what if the Thing *is* the security?' Lauren asks.

'Oh, Jesus,' Tony says.

Marcus is still looking at me. 'What do you mean, Alice?'

'Well, this place obviously isn't safe, is it?' I look around for some support and I'm pleased to see Lucy and Ilias nodding. 'You have a duty of care and you're supposed to keep us safe. I mean, that's basically why we're here, right? When you're more likely to get killed on a closed national health ward than you are in the arse-end of Hackney on a Friday night, I think something needs to be done about it. I reckon we deserve to have some decent protection.'

Marcus looks at the bloke from the Trust.

The bloke from the Trust seems a little uncomfortable, but says, 'It's certainly something we can discuss.'

'There we are,' Marcus says.

'A couple of big bastards with tasers,' I say. 'Or even better—'

Marcus holds up a hand. He says, 'I think you've had your answer, Alice,' and looks around for another question.

I sit down again and put my earphones in and spend most of the rest of the meeting wondering why Marcus is being so off with me. I also spend a few minutes asking myself why Lauren felt the need to be such a bitch to Tony and thinking how much I'll enjoy telling Ilias *exactly* how much blood there was. The look on the hairy little sod's face.

We all enjoy passing on the details of a proper drama, don't we?

A quarter of an hour later, when the meeting's breaking up, I amble across to Malaika and ask if she fancies escorting me outside for a cigarette. She immediately feels for her own pack and lowers her voice.

'God, I've been desperate for one of you to ask.'

It's drizzling a bit, so we stand close together beneath the overhang at the entrance to the unit. Malaika has crashed me one of her fags to save me the hassle of rolling my own, which is dead nice of her.

Like I said before, she's one of the good ones, and the Brummie accent always cheers me up.

'Police are coming back tomorrow,' she says.

I nod and hiss out a stream of smoke. 'They'll be making an arrest probably.'

'You reckon?'

'Yeah, they'll know who did it by now.'

'I wouldn't bank on it.' She gives me a knowing look.

'You're fucking kidding me,' I say. '*Again?*'

'Graham put three different cameras out of action on Sunday.' She holds up the requisite number of fingers. 'The dining room one, the one outside the 136 and the one in the corridor that covers the women's toilets.'

'Unbelievable.'

'You were talking about making things safer?' she says. 'Back in there? First thing we should do is get Graham moved to another ward.' She hunches her shoulders. It's getting nippy out here. 'The coppers who were here gave Marcus a real bollocking about it. Lecturing him about "serious lapses in security", like it was all his fault.'

'Yeah, well that's because it's made their job a lot harder.'

I stand there saying nothing for a while and thinking about two murder investigations, both with massive spanners in the works thanks to the security cameras covering the scenes being buggered. Yeah, Graham pulls this shit a lot, but even so. Once is seriously unlucky, but for that to happen twice is a hell of a coincidence.

I wonder if the police are thinking the same thing.

236

'You weren't very fond of Debbie, were you?' Malaika says from nowhere.

'Who told you that?'

'Well, Debbie said something.'

'What?'

'No ... nothing specific. Just that the two of you hadn't really bonded.'

I stare at her. 'What does that even mean? Have you *bonded* with Lauren or with Bob? I'd be amazed if you had. You just hit it off better with some people than you do with others, right?'

'I suppose,' Malaika says.

'To be honest, there's times when I don't know how you stop yourself giving most of the arseholes in here a bloody good slapping.'

She smiles. 'It's a struggle,' she says.

I'm not sure Malaika's being completely upfront about what Debbie said or didn't say to her about me. Still, if she doesn't already know about it, I don't see much point in telling her what *I'd* said to *Debbie* a couple of days before she was killed. What I'd accused her of.

I can't change that, can I?

Even now she's dead, I certainly don't take it back.

We stub our cigarettes out on the wall behind us and Malaika says, 'Come on then ...'

I don't move, because suddenly all I can think about is meeting Billy out here a couple of weeks ago. Those spare joints I stashed inside a pipe, just a few feet away from where we're standing.

A quick hit would be lovely, and there's never any harm in trying, is there? I don't *think* she'd dob me in just for asking.

Truth is, the evil bastards aren't the only ones that can wear masks, and these past few months I've mastered quite a few useful expressions that I can plaster on pretty quick when the situation calls for it.

Shame-faced, aggrieved, dangerous, sad, desperate, untroubled . . .

Now, I do my best to look . . . winsome.

'I don't suppose you fancy taking a walk for five minutes?'

Malaika grins and lays a hand in my arm. She says, 'Don't push your luck.'

THIRTY-SIX

It's quarter-past three in the morning, I'm wide awake and there's blood everywhere.

Or there *was* . . .

I lie in bed and wait for my heart rate to slow a little, then try to regulate my breathing, the way I was taught after this happened the first time. Long breath in through the nose, count to three, then slowly out through pursed lips. It's hard to focus because someone's shouting along the corridor.

I take another long breath in . . .

Early on, I said that I didn't believe the recreational drugs I'd been taking before I got sectioned were the only thing responsible for me ending up here, and I stand by that. Equally, now that I'm clean-and-sober-ish, I don't think the drugs I'm being fed by doctors four times a day – the *good* drugs – are the only reason for what's happening right this minute. What's been happening, on and off, ever since I got here.

Something's messing with my head, though.

Awake or asleep, there's something directing this horror show.

I let the breath slowly out again.

That's one of the problems. Whenever this happens, I'm never sure if it's a dream or not. I mean, I know it's not *real* ... but when it ends, I don't know if I've woken up or if I was awake the whole time and it's only stopped because my brain's decided it wants to go somewhere a bit less scary for a while. Like a circuit breaker tripping when the current gets unsafe.

Three-two-one ... you're back in the room.

There was blood, like I said. There's always plenty of blood. Thinking about it rationally – just for a minute – it's all hugely predictable. Wherever I am – and that part's always a bit fuzzy and vague – I can't stop crying and thrashing around in a massive panic, and there's no way I can get the blood off because there's so much of it and when I do manage to wipe just enough of it away to remind myself what my skin actually looks like more comes bubbling up through my pores. Blood that isn't mine, I mean. Like I'm living and breathing and ... *being* the stuff.

It wasn't my fault. It wasn't my fault. It wasn't my fault ...

It's Johnno's blood, obviously ... a fountain of it gushing from the wound in his neck. I don't need Bakshi or anyone else to work that much out.

Or at least, it used to be.

Now, there's even more to wade through, to wash off, to drown in, because Debbie's blood is sloshing about in the mix as well; drenching everything in the dream or the hallucination or whatever the hell it is.

There's a difference, though.

Before, it was all about guilt, of course. When it was over, I would lie awake, breathing like I'm doing now and feel it eating me alive, no matter how many times I told myself that I hadn't been to blame for what happened to Johnno.

I'm not guilty, I'm not guilty.

Not. Guilty.

Now though, I'm feeling something else and it paralyses me far more than guilt has ever done. It's knocking on for half-past three and, if I've had any sleep at all, I know there's no chance of me getting any more.

I stare at the door. I look for a shadow moving beneath it. I listen for the noise of someone outside.

I'm absolutely fucking terrified.

THIRTY-SEVEN

I told you how rubbish I am with names – back when I was on the Job, I had to write them down in my notebook – and, sitting there in the MDR, I forget what the two coppers are called almost as soon as they've introduced themselves. In my head and gone again. So, rather than sit there squinting at their IDs, I decide to go down my normal route and make something up.

It . . . lightens things, which is good. For me at least.

One of the women is shorter than the other and a bit on the dumpy side, while her mate strikes me as slightly posher, so it doesn't take long to give them celebrity alter-egos. A different kind of double act. I just need to get that theme tune out of my head and stop imagining them both with fags on and enormous latex bellies, pretending to be blokes and trying to shag inanimate objects.

Like a pair of fat sleazy Bobs.

DC French looks up and says, 'I understand you were the one who found Miss McClure's body on Sunday afternoon.'

242

I tell her that she's spot on.

'That can't have been a particularly pleasant experience.'

'I've had worse,' I say.

'Really?'

I look at her, then watch as DC Saunders – who's obviously done a bit more in the way of preparation – leans across and whispers something, then begins turning her colleague's pages for her and pointing something out. I'm assuming it's all there. The flat in Mile End. What happened to Johnno.

'Oh yes.' French looks up and nods sympathetically.

When asked, I tell them exactly what I'd told the detective a couple of days ago. The body and the blood, the CPR until Marcus and Malaika arrived, the knife on the floor underneath the sink. Predictably, they ask me the same daft questions about anyone I might have seen going in or coming out of the toilets before me. I say much the same thing I said on Sunday, though I'm a bit less sarky about it.

'It's a shame you even need to ask,' I say. 'I mean, you'd know exactly who'd been in and out of the toilet if that camera hadn't been buggered about with.'

French's chair squeaks as her arse shifts in it.

'You'd be making an arrest by now, am I right?'

Saunders clears her throat and says, 'No, it's not ideal.'

She looks away, all set to move on. She doesn't change her face, doesn't elaborate, doesn't give any indication that they think a camera being put out of action again could be even the slightest bit suspicious. *Not ideal?* I tell you this for nothing: any faith I might have that this second investigation will be handled any better than the first is already being seriously tested.

'There's something we wanted to clear up,' French says.

'Oh yeah?'

'We've been told by the ward manager that, a short time before Miss McClure was killed, you had accused her of being involved in the murder of a patient here just over a fortnight ago. Kevin Connolly?'

So, that's why Marcus was being weird with me at that meeting yesterday. Debbie had obviously gone running to him as soon as I'd confronted her, probably moaning about unacceptable verbal abuse or some such. Bleating to her boss about me having another one of my delusions or the need for stronger meds to control my fantasies about still being a police officer.

'Well, I'd known she was involved in that murder for a while,' I say. 'I only told her to her face on the Friday. About forty-eight hours before she was killed.'

'I see.'

'And "involved" is putting it mildly, by the way. She was the one doing the murdering.' I sit back and fold my arms. 'I'm relieved that you've finally brought it up, as it goes.'

'Why's that?

'Because it means that you've connected the two murders. I mean, they *are* connected. You know that, right?' I wait. 'Come on, how can they not be?'

French and Saunders look at one another.

'You working with the other lot, then? With Seddon's team?'

'The two investigations have been ... merged,' Saunders says.

'Who's running it?'

They exchange another look. Finally, Saunders says, 'Detective Chief Inspector Brigstocke.'

I recognise the name but I don't know him. 'Is he any

good?' I wait some more, but neither of them seems awfully keen to discuss the capabilities of their SIO. The room's getting seriously warm and I think about asking one of them to open a window.

'You seem tense, Alice,' French says.

'Do I?'

'A bit on edge.'

'Well, of *course* I'm on edge. I'm shitting myself.'

'Why would that be?'

It obviously needs spelling out for them. 'I thought Debbie was running the whole drugs thing on her own, OK . . . but I was obviously wrong. She was clearly working with someone else on the inside and whoever that person is decided that Debbie couldn't be trusted to keep her mouth shut. Look, I didn't make a huge secret of the fact that I thought Debbie was the one who'd killed Kevin, all right? Or that I had my suspicions, at least. So, maybe her accomplice reckoned it wouldn't be too long before Debbie was arrested, and that when she was, she'd spill her guts about exactly who else was involved. So best to get rid of her. I suppose looking at it that way, I'm partly to blame for what happened.'

Saunders is scribbling. 'Right . . .'

'I wasn't the one with the knife though, was I?'

'No,' French says.

'That's something else . . .'

'What?'

'I told Seddon two weeks ago about how easy it would be to get hold of a knife in here and he didn't listen. Wouldn't even return my calls when I had crucial information. If I'd been taken seriously a bit sooner, Debbie might have been nicked long before whoever she was working with had the chance to shut her up for good. That's what I'd call dropping the ball, big time. So yeah, I'm not exactly relaxed right now ... because chances are whoever carved Debbie up in the bogs knows that I've put the whole thing together. Which means they might decide to come after me next.'

Saunders puts her pen down. 'Are you worried for your safety?'

To be fair to the woman, she looks genuinely concerned. She might not give a monkey's, of course, but it's been a long time since I've been able to tell the difference.

'Always,' I say.

Hang out the flags, Shaun the Silent has begun communicating again.

Notice I don't say 'speaking', because apparently that would be asking a bit much, but he's ... making himself known.

Something, I suppose.

So, quarter of an hour ago, I sit down next to him to have my lunch and, without looking at me, he scribbles something on a serviette, scrunches it up into a tiny ball and presses it into my hand. A special secret message, just for me. He doesn't seem massively bothered when I open it up there and then, but that's probably because of what it says.

this mince tastes like dog-shit.

No, it's not exactly the Gettysburg Address, but it's a start, right? So I immediately rush off to grab some paper, then come back to see if Shaun has any other words of wisdom to impart. It's got to be worth a try, because if he knew about

Debbie killing Kevin, then chances are he knows who her accomplice is.

Who killed Debbie.

So far, bugger all, but let's wait and see?

There's the usual noisy chatter, because by now quite a few others have been interviewed, same as I was, and are mad keen to tell everyone how it went. L-Plate's twittering about her interview like she's just been given the third degree.

'I didn't think those two women were very nice,' she says. 'The ones on Sunday were much nicer. Mind you, they took some of my clothes away with them.'

'Mine too,' Lauren says. 'My best T-shirt and joggers. I'd better get them back or I'll be kicking off big time.'

I pointed out that clothing samples had been taken from everyone, staff included. Without stating the blindingly obvious and telling them it was because they were all suspects, I reassured them that it was standard practice.

'Really though, they were a bit . . . fierce,' L-Plate says.

'Probably lesbians,' Ilias says. The voice of reason as always, spraying the table with gobbets of shepherd's pie.

I didn't think French and Saunders were fierce at all, but I suppose it's daunting if you're not used to it. Or if you haven't been on the other side of the table yourself, like I have. I need to keep reminding myself that this lot are civilians, that they don't know the game. When Donna asks when they'll be taking our fingerprints and DNA, I gently remind her that it's already on record, because the last lot did all that and your DNA doesn't change from week to week, whatever she might have seen on CSI.

Lauren tells me I'm a smartarse.

I tell Lauren she's an idiot.

Big Gay Bob loudly tells *everyone* that DC French could probably do with losing a few pounds, which immediately sends Donna out into the corridor to start walking off the spoonful of peas she's eaten. 'Mind you, I quite like a chubby bird,' Bob says. 'They're always grateful.'

It doesn't look like Shaun has anything else he wants to share, and Tiny Tears has nothing to say for herself either. She just sits there pushing her food around and watching me from the other end of the table, which makes me uncomfortable to say the least. I start to lose interest in the conversation when Tony says he had a feeling that the other copper might have been *you-know-who* and I finally zone out completely when Lauren starts singing 'I Fought the Law'.

Oh, the other big news is that Graham, the Waiter, has gone.

Spirited away while I was being interviewed, just like that. Off to bang his head against a different wall, wait at a new meds hatch and chuck his dinner at the cameras on some other ward. Maybe Malaika said something after the chat we had about security yesterday, or Marcus took the roasting he got off those coppers to heart and decided he had no other option.

Either way, we're a body down.

Three, obviously, if you count Debbie and Kevin.

At least Graham can be thankful he wasn't taken out of here in a bag.

THIRTY-EIGHT

It's been pretty full on since breakfast so, once I've gobbled down the last meds of the day, I decide to retire to my sump-tuous boudoir a bit earlier than usual. Getting an extra hour or two of sleep feels like a top idea, plus I fancy some time on my own. Tempting as it might be to veg out in the TV room like I normally do and wind Lauren up if I get bored, I need to chill for a bit, so I sit on my bed working my way through a packet of Hobnobs and dicking around on the internet for a while.

I start to feel more relaxed straight away. Just me, with my finger on a trackpad that can take me anywhere. I laugh out loud when it strikes me that this is the happy place I couldn't get to a couple of weeks back, in that hideous assess-ment session.

But what is more problematic is yet another email from Andrew Flanagan . . .

I watch a few stupid videos for a laugh and catch up on

some celeb gossip until I've finished the biscuits. Then I spend half an hour cruising some of the newsgroups and private chat rooms where, once upon a time I try not to think about too much, I wasted half my life.

Now, though, it isn't about convincing myself I'm not paranoid. It isn't a question of finding like-minded mentalists, so I don't feel like I'm the only one going through ... whatever it *was* I was going through. These days, it's just curiosity.

I swear ...

I watch the vlogs and read the bat-shit comments.

I think, *get a life.*

I only stop when I start to suspect there's someone standing outside my door. Then I'm convinced there is. I know it's not one of the nurses because Mia was round, doing the half-hour checks, ten minutes ago.

I tell myself to calm down, that I've got sod all to be scared of.

I creep to the door and press my ear against it. There's definitely someone there, I can hear them breathing. It's probably the gentlest of knocks, but I step back like someone's let off an air-horn.

'Who is it?'

'It's Clare ...'

Oh, so now Tiny Tears is talking to me. I open the door and hold out my hands like, *What d'you want?* and watch her standing there looking awkward.

'Were you asleep?'

'Well, if I was, I'm not now, am I?' She looks like she's going to cry and I'm buggered if I'm putting up with any more of that. 'It's fine,' I say. 'I wasn't.'

'Is it OK if I come in?' she asks.

I sigh, and step back to let her in, and she lowers her gangly self down until she's perching on the edge of my bed. She clutches at one hand with the other and shakes her head and says how awful it is, what happened to that nurse. She looks at me and I realise she's waiting for me to agree with her.

'Yeah,' I say.

The look on her face tells me that I haven't quite managed to conjure the pity or sympathy she was expecting and it shocks me a bit, because I was really trying. Debbie is the first murder victim that I've been anywhere near since I left the police. Do I sound uncaring ... do I *feel* uncaring because I didn't much like Debbie and know what she was guilty of? Or is it because the empathy that was there on the Job is something I've lost? Would I be as destroyed as I used to be at the murder of a neglected toddler, or a pensioner who's been battered to death, or *anyone*? I want to know the answer, but at the same time I really don't want to be in a position where I get it.

'So, come on then,' I say. 'How did you end up in here?'

She shakes her head.

'It's OK, you don't have to keep it secret. It's not like prison.' I smile, because I really want to know. 'Well, it's a *bit* like prison.'

'I don't want to talk about it.'

'No probs,' I say.

I reckon her reluctance is a bit strange, though. Most people in here tend to fall into one of two camps. Either they're desperate to tell you everything or they don't believe they should have been sectioned at all and that there's been some horrible mistake. Graham, for all his tricks and tics, was one of the latter, forever waiting for someone to acknowledge their administrative error and tell him he could go home. Kevin and Shaun only ever really confided in each other, but others are a bit more forthcoming about their episodes and misdemeanours.

Ilias kept taking his clothes off in shops.

Bob had a breakdown after his wife left him – what a shocker!

Lucy freaked out after taking too much heroin. Or maybe it was because she hadn't taken enough. Doesn't make much odds.

Actually ... thinking about it, I kind of fall somewhere between the two extremes. Yeah, I'm happy enough to admit that I went a bit bonkers, to talk about the knives and the people on my TV, but I still don't think I should be here. So maybe it isn't quite as clear-cut as I think it is.

Still none the wiser about Tiny Tears, though.

She says, 'I think we could be friends.'

'Do you?'

'Best friends, maybe.'

She looks at me and I shrug like, *Why not?* but something about her is telling me to keep my distance.

'You were so nice, the day I came in.'

'I was being nosy,' I say.

'Nobody else really bothered. I mean obviously they wanted to gawp a bit, but none of them offered to help, like you did.'

'Well, let's see,' I say.

She seems happy enough with that. 'Tell me more about the nurses,' she says. 'You were going to tell me, remember?'

Right. The afternoon she arrived. Before she started blubbing for the umpteenth time in like ten minutes and I lost the will to live. 'What do you want to know?'

252

She shuffles her arse back on my bed a little, makes herself more comfortable. 'Everything,' she says.

There doesn't seem much point in telling her about Debbie, but for the next half an hour or so I give her the skinny on the rest of them. I tell her Malaika's probably the best bet if she needs a fag and that Femi-Nazi's got a temper on her. I tell her that George is a failed copper and that Marcus can be pretty strict sometimes and that she shouldn't hold out too much hope for any deep and meaningful conversation with Mia.

She seems to be enjoying herself. She laughs at my jokes and my daft attempts at some of the accents and looks suitably shocked when she's meant to. I'm actually quite enjoying myself, but then she stands up, just like that, and announces that she's tired. She tells me she wants to go to bed, says it like it's the most important thing I've heard all day.

I say, 'Oh, fair enough,' and watch her walk to the door.

After she's gone, I wait until I'm fairly sure everyone else is in their room and pay a quick visit to all the other women on the corridor. I knock on doors and put my head round. Sorry to disturb you, just a quick question.

I want to know if any of the others have had a visit. If anyone else has been asked if they want to be Clare's best friend.

Nope. Just me.

THIRTY-NINE

Banksy says, 'I'm amazed it took you this long to call.'

'You're happy that I have though, yeah?' I'm trying to be funny, but I'm genuinely chuffed that he's even speaking to me. I think I'd been a bit off with him last time he was here. 'You're happy, I can tell.'

'I'm ecstatic,' he says.

I'm back in my room, watching rain battering at the window and it's almost like I can *hear* the grease from the bacon at breakfast cranking up the cholesterol and turning my arteries to Twiglets. 'You heard the latest news from the Ward of Death, then?'

'Yeah. Like I said, I was expecting you to call Sunday night.'

'I was a bit busy,' I say.

'What the hell's going *on* in that place?'

'You know it was me that found her, right?'

'No.' There's a pause. 'I did not know that.' He sounds concerned and it's lovely. I suppose it's fair enough, because

254

we're close, plus he knows that the last time I was any-where near a blood-soaked body, things didn't turn out so well. 'You OK?'

'Yeah.'

'Straight up?'

'Why wouldn't I be?' Stupid question, bearing in mind what I just said, but Banksy knows better than anyone that, when I was on the Job, I dealt with far worse things than a single murder victim on a bathroom floor. I tell him I'm good, or as good as I'm ever going to be surrounded by nut-ters, at least one of who's homicidal. I tell him not to worry. I tell him he's a top mate.

'So, come on then . . . what are you hearing?'

'What am I hearing *where*?' he asks.

'From the MIT. Their plan of action or whatever. It's a DCI called Brigstocke who's running things, apparently, but I don't know if—'

'Al . . . we went through all this before. I don't have any information, because it's not my team.'

'You said you knew.'

'About what happened, yeah. It's not like there's *that* many murders, is there?'

'I know how many murders there are,' I say.

'That's all, though. Look, if any stuff . . . filters through or if I happen to hear something, I'll let you know, but right now you're asking the wrong person.'

'Has someone told you not to say anything?'

'What?'

'Have you been told not to talk to me about the case?'

His sigh rattles a bit. 'I haven't got time for this, Al.'

The rain's getting heavier. Tin tacks falling on a drum.

Above the noise I can hear Lauren singing in the distance, which is definitely the best place for her to be.

'Remember when you were here last time?' I ask. 'When we talked about the drugs gang and how maybe they'd sent someone in pretending to be a patient to kill Kevin?'

'Yeah, and I thought it was stupid,' he says.

'Yeah, and so did I eventually ... and then I *knew* it was because I found out who really killed Kevin, but maybe this time it isn't. A new patient arrived just before Debbie was murdered.'

I let that sink in, then tell him all about Tiny Tears. How she was weird when she came in, and yeah, I know everyone's weird when they come in, but there was definitely something off about this one. I tell him about her coming to my room last night.

'What's wrong with wanting a friend?' he asks. 'Wouldn't you have wanted that when you got there?'

'It was like she had an agenda.'

'Doesn't make her a killer, Al.'

'Like ... commit the murder, then make sure you get matey with the one person on the ward who can solve it, because she's an ex-cop. Same as she solved the last one. Got to be worth thinking about, at least?' I keep at him for a while and I know he's probably not listening, but eventually he promises me that yes, he will think about it.

Then he says, 'Shall I come in to visit next week?'

Before, Tim's always said *I'll be in tomorrow* or *See you on Wednesday* or something, but now he's made it a question, and I suspect that's because he wants me to say no.

I say, 'Only if you've got time.'

*

My dad rocks up in the afternoon. I say *rocks*, but my dad's never actually *rocked* anywhere in his life. He's more of a lolloper, a marcher on a good day, but anyway ... he arrives.

Femi comes to find me and takes me to meet him.

I stretch out a hand for his plastic bag of goodies before I've even said hello.

Of course I'm happy to see him, but I wish he'd let me know he was coming, or at least give me some notice so we could arrange the best time. He still hasn't got his head round the timings of my meds so, depending on where I am in the cycle, he could turn up and find me bouncing off the walls and yapping like an excited dog, or I might be Mogadon Mary. Today, he's drawn the short straw and gets a daughter who's not exactly at her sharpest and talks like she's coming round after an operation. Several times he has to ask me to repeat myself or I just ignore what he's saying completely.

It's not sparkling, all I'm saying.

We're sitting at one end of the music room and Clare's reading a book in the opposite corner. I know she's earwigging and I wonder if she's expecting me to bring her over, maybe introduce her to my dad as my new bestie. After a few minutes she gets up and wanders out, which is a relief, because she's starting to give me the willies.

Once we've got the chit-chat out of the way – *Mum's fine and Jeff and Diane send their best and hope the operation went well* – I catch him up with my news. The latest murder. It takes a while for me to pass on all the grisly details, droning like a recording on half-speed.

It's a few seconds before Dad says anything. He just opens

his mouth and closes it again. Then he says, 'This isn't bloody acceptable.'

He's got a point. I mean, catching MRSA would be bad enough, but nobody expects to be taken into a hospital where patients are getting bumped off every couple of weeks. 'No, it isn't.'

'Do you feel safe?'

'Well, not . . . particularly.' It's quite an effort to get such a difficult word out. 'But what can I do?'

'It's ridiculous,' he says. 'Somebody should go to the papers.'

'It's already in the papers, Dad.' They'd run a story in the *Evening Standard* the day before about the murder, though they hadn't named the victim or linked it to Kevin's death. The paper was being passed around the ward like a cheap prostitute.

'To complain, I mean.'

'What's the point of complaining?'

'I can't hear you, love.'

I ask him again. 'You going to go on Tripadvisor? Give it a one-star review?'

He swallows hard and looks upset. 'No need to be nasty,' he says. 'I'm only concerned about you. Alice . . .'

I focus a bit and smile at him. 'Yeah, I know. Thanks.'

'So, apart from . . . all that. You feeling any better?'

I smile again. Sometimes, straight after a dose of benzos, you can't help smiling even when you've got sweet FA to smile about. 'I feel different,' I say.

'A *good* different?'

I nod. Slowly. 'Most of the time.'

My dad's face lights up. Same way it did when I won the

400 metres in the house athletics or when I played a comedy servant girl in that stupid play in the fourth form. 'That's fantastic,' he says. 'Your mum's going to be really happy when I tell her that.'

'Mum hasn't called me for ages,' I say.

'I know she hasn't, love.' He stares down at his brown brogues for a few seconds. 'Thing is . . .'

'She gets upset,' I say. 'Yeah, I know.'

Twenty treacly minutes later, Dad says he'd best be getting off and I really like having his arm around me as we're walking slowly towards the airlock. He says a cheery hello to Donna, like she's some nice girl he chats to in the post office once in a while, and he even manages a thumbs-up for Ilias who's repeatedly tossing a tennis ball six inches in the air and shouting *Yes!* every time he catches it.

Dad stops when he sees Tony at the airlock with his suitcase. Tony waves and my father raises an arm in return. It's a bit awkward, though, and looks more like a Nazi salute.

'Why does he *do* that?'

I tell him about Tony's non-existent family.

'Well, at least you've got me and Mum,' he says.

'Yeah, but you can't get me out of here any more than Tony's made-up rellies.'

He gets a bit upset again. He's looking at me and, fuzzy-headed as I am, I know he's thinking about that girl who could run really fast and do funny voices in daft plays. He's thinking that he's lost her.

'It isn't your fault,' I say. 'Everything that's happened.'

He blinks slowly and shrugs. 'How can it not be, love?'

'It was Grandad Jim's fault.' I shake my head, sadly. 'Him touching me like that when I was little.'

259

Dad stares at me.

'Joke,' I say.

Tony is waving again, but now my dad is too stunned to wave back, so I just stand there with him for a bit and I know I'm the worst daughter in the world.

FORTY

I'm mooching around before dinner, bored and not quite sure what to do with myself, when my mobile rings. It's the investigator bloke from Pindown, so I drop the call. I don't really want to speak to him but I'm not going to turn my phone off – I would never do that – so when he calls back again almost immediately, I decide to answer.

It's something to do, isn't it?

He says, 'First off, Miss Armitage, I'm not at all happy about the offensive language on the voicemail you left.'

That makes me smile. A cuntathon I *could* remember. 'It's just a word,' I say. 'Get over yourself.'

'It was abuse, plain and simple.'

I laugh out loud. I'm glad I took the call, now.

'I was in half a mind to report it to the police.'

'Well, we both know you're not going to do *that*.'

That gives him some serious pause for thought. He might be an ex-cop, but he doesn't know *I'm* one or that I'm well

261

aware how dodgy his business practices are. His silence tells me he knows that he's not dealing with an idiot, though.

'Secondly, I'm still waiting for the second half of the payment.'

I'd completely forgotten about it, but I'm not going to tell him that. I'd rather have a bit of fun. 'Well I still haven't decided if I'm going to pay it,' I say. 'I mean I wasn't that pleased with the service. "Guaranteed to exceed expectations", that's what it says on your website, and that would only be the case if I'd had no expectations at all. I had very high hopes, I really did, but frankly, Howard, it was piss-poor.'

There's another pause before he says, 'I'm very sorry to hear that, but I'm still expecting to be paid in full.'

'What if I don't?'

'Then I might have to consider taking legal proceedings.'

It's so tempting to tell him he can whistle for his money. To say, 'So fill your boots', or 'See you in court'. I'm seriously thinking about it.

'So?' he says. 'Are you going to pay, or what?'

I assume that if I was involved in legal proceedings of some kind then they'd have to let me out of here to do whatever's necessary. That would be my right, surely. I mean, what if you get called up for jury service? Do people in places like this ever get called up for jury service? Yeah, I'm thinking it might be fun, taking Howard on, because it's been a long time since I stood up in court, and don't forget, the last occasion when I *should* have been there, I wasn't deemed to be a fit enough witness. I always gave a good account of myself in front of a judge, everyone said that. I prepared well and made sure I did a good job. So if it comes to any kind of legal battle now, I'm damn sure I'll win, and even though I know it won't be the Old Bailey or anything, I decide that I might even be able to get a few other things off my mind while I have the chance.

Bring it on.

Then I see L-Plate walking towards me, and she's usually up for a laugh, and suddenly I can't even be bothered to talk to this bloke any more.

I say, 'Yeah, I'll send it,' and hang up.

L-Plate's about to walk right past me, but I put out a hand. She steps back a bit, obviously. 'Hey, L . . . you want to do something?'

She stares at me and her face looks a bit odd, like she's trying to work something out.

'I'm always up for thrashing you at Jenga if you fancy it.' She doesn't look keen. 'Or we can play cards or something—'

'You are joking, right?' She shakes her head. 'You're un-believable, do you know that?'

'What?'

'After the way you treated me at lunchtime? The way you spoke to me?'

'Eh?'

'I don't even want to talk to you right now.'

'You're going to have to help me out here, L . . .'

I'm sure she's about to storm off, but she's clearly decided to stand her ground and let me have a piece of her mind. Not that she's got an awful lot to spare. 'Well, you certainly didn't need any help at lunchtime,' she says. 'Not when you were calling me a "vacuous posh bitch" or leaning across to steal my food and saying it didn't matter because smackheads don't have a big appetite anyway. Flicking bits of it back in my face, then pissing yourself and telling me to grow up when I started to cry.'

Now she tries to move past me and I put out an arm to stop her.

She screams.

George steps towards us from the nurses' station and I hold up my arms to let him know everything's all right. I keep my voice low and steady. I say, 'Honestly, L, I haven't got a clue what you're on about. Why the hell would I do any of that? We're mates.'

'I have no idea,' she says. 'Because I'm just a pathetic junkie and you're a full-on mental case?'

I close my eyes and try to think. 'I don't believe you,' I say. I'm not sure there's anything else I *can* say.

'Why don't you ask Donna or Bob? They were both there.'

I can't do anything but watch her turn and walk the other way. Then I stand there, with George watching me, and desperately try to recall even a moment of what L-Plate's just described. What I'm supposed to have said to her is bad enough, but I'm way more alarmed by the fact that I can't remember saying anything at all.

I can't even remember having lunch.

When my mobile goes off again, I snatch at it, desperate to let fly at that arsehole Howard with some *properly* abusive language, but it's not him phoning.

There's no caller ID.

I answer and grunt a hello.

There's a few seconds of crackle, half a breath, then the line goes dead.

FORTY-ONE

I try to talk to Lucy while we're queuing up for dinner, but she ignores me and carries her tray across to a table as far away from mine as possible. Ilias wants to chat, but I don't let him. I can't bring myself to eat much anyway so I leave pretty quickly.

I'm all over the place.

I go to be given my final meds of the day, then drift into the music room while everyone else is still eating and grab a paperback. I'm hoping it might distract me a bit. Shaun is the only other person in there but I'm not expecting *him* to disturb me, and he doesn't. I keep an eye on him though, just in case he's got any other messages he wants to send, so with that and the whole Lucy business ... I find myself reading the same page of the stupid book over and over again.

Lauren saunters in, drops down into the chair next to mine and belches.

'Reading's a waste of time,' she says.

265

I'm in no mood to rise to her bait. 'You reckon? And here's me with you pegged as a bit of a bookworm yourself. You know, knocking out a few songs then relaxing with a bit of Charles Dickens or whatever.'

She doesn't rise to *my* bait. She just belches again and calmly gives me the finger. Says, 'Twat.'

I make a show of going back to my book, but I only manage half of that same bloody page before she leans across.

'Anyway, I thought you'd be far too busy for reading.'

I put the book down. 'Yeah?'

'Yeah ... you've got another case to crack now, haven't you, Columbo?'

'Have I?'

She leans even closer, heaving her fat tits across the arm of her chair. 'I'm guessing your bedroom wall is like one of those ... boards they always have in the police shows. You know, so the detective can keep track of the murder investigation.' She's on a roll now, enjoying herself. I glance across at Shaun, but he doesn't seem to be paying much attention. 'So there's probably a picture of poor old Debbie taped up right in the middle, with her name underneath, and loads of lines and arrows, all drawn in felt-tip on the wall, leading to the people she knew or whatever. To the suspects.'

'Yeah,' I say. 'It's exactly like that.'

She shows me a few brown or yellow teeth. 'Unless ...'

I look at her. Stupid thing to do, I know, but I can't help myself.

'Well, we all know you thought Debbie was the one who killed Kevin, don't we?'

I don't know about *all*, but I'm not surprised that Lauren knows. Marcus would have discussed it with the other nurses and one of them was bound to let it slip at some point. Or found themselves unable to resist sharing a bit of gossip about one patient with another. George, maybe, or Malaika.

'So?'

'So . . . it must have been doing your head in that she'd got away with it. I mean the police obviously hadn't worked it out or she'd have been arrested, right? I'm not as experienced as you with this stuff, but I think that's how it's supposed to work. So she's just swanning around, free as a bird and all the time you know what she's done. You're the only one who knows that she's guilty.' She shakes her head. 'I'm just saying . . . if that was me I don't think I could have handled it. I don't think I could have coped, seeing that murdering cow every day, laughing and joking after what she'd done to poor old Kevin.'

I glance over at Shaun again. He's hanging on every word.

'Is there a point to any of this?' I ask.

'Only that maybe, seeing as nothing was happening to her and that, you know, justice wasn't being done . . .' She shrugs as if she doesn't really need to say any more.

'Just spit it out,' I say. 'You can sing it, if it helps.'

She slowly brings a finger to her lips like a naughty school-girl, stares at me for a few seconds, then hauls herself up and wanders out. Almost as soon as the door closes behind her I hear scratching and look over to see Shaun scribbling on a scrap of paper. Whatever he's writing doesn't take long and he scrunches the paper into a ball, then steps over to press it into my hand before hurrying from the room.

I open it up and read the message.

thank you

FORTY-TWO

French and Saunders are back for more interviews this morning, and according to Ilias they've brought a friend along, but before I'm called in to see them, I get a chance to say sorry to L-Plate. I know now that all the stuff she accused me of yesterday actually happened, because Marcus made a point of catching up with me before bedtime and asked me about the 'bullying' incident in the dining room at lunchtime. He was not happy. For obvious reasons – like not remembering *any* of it – there wasn't a fat lot I could tell him, but he made it clear we'd need to address my unacceptable behaviour at Friday's assessment meeting.

Looking forward to *that*.

A few of us are in the music room waiting our turn, so I go and sit by L-Plate. She doesn't immediately get up and move, which I take as a good sign. I've had the odd falling-out with her before and I know this is a bit more serious than arguing about a game of snakes and ladders, but she doesn't normally stay angry for very long.

If people bore grudges every time there was a cross word in here, none of us would be talking to anybody.

'Listen . . . about yesterday,' I say.

She says nothing. She's going to make me work for it, which is fair enough.

'I'm really sorry about what I said. The food and everything.'

'OK,' she says.

'I don't think you're posh and vacuous.' Obviously I *do*, but you know, not in a bad way.

'So, why did you do it?' she asks. 'Why did you say all those horrible things?'

'I've got no idea, L. Just a wobble.'

'Then you denied it, which made it much worse.'

'I know.'

L-Plate's still waiting for me to explain, but I don't want to tell her that I simply don't remember. I don't want anyone to know that. It's not like I haven't forgotten stuff in the past, going places and meeting people, whole evenings sometimes, but it's always been booze- or weed-related. Just a woozy blank after a heavy session, where the memories should have been. This is different though, and I don't have any explanation and it's scaring the hell out of me. I have no way of knowing *when* I forgot it or if I was forgetting it even while it was happening. It's not even like it was anything deeply unpleasant or traumatic. I've done far worse things about which I can remember every sordid second.

I should probably talk to Bakshi about it, but if there's something going seriously pear-shaped in my brain, I'm not sure I really want to know.

It's all a bit bloody scary.

'I was ashamed,' I say.

L-Plate nods slowly, then beams, then claps to celebrate the moment. Like I said earlier, not a bad bone in her body. Not as many as some of us, anyway.

She starts rattling on about something or other, but before she can get into her stride George comes in and says the detectives are ready for me. I tell L-Plate we'll catch up later and follow him out.

I'm about to knock on the door of the MDR when it opens and a woman steps out. I'm guessing she's the 'friend' that Ilias was talking about and she's certainly a bit more glamorous than French or Saunders. She looks a bit . . . Malaysian, or something? Long dark hair tied back with a red band and a snazzy skirt. I'm still wondering why three police officers have been deemed necessary when the woman holds out a hand and introduces herself.

'I'm Dr Perera,' she says. 'Why don't we talk outside?'

I shake her hand. 'Oh . . .'

'Don't worry, I've already spoken to the ward manager.' She smiles and gently turns me round. 'Come on, it's a nice day.'

We walk up towards the main hospital buildings and find a bench. The weather *is* pretty nice and there's a few more people milling around in this part of the grounds than there are down where the unit is hidden away. We can see the entrance to A&E and, as you'd expect, there's an old dear standing just outside the doors with an oxygen tank and a fag on. I think it's compulsory.

Makes me wish I'd brought some tobacco and Rizlas out with me.

'What kind of doctor are you?' I ask.

'I'm a forensic psychiatrist.' Her voice is quiet, but she's very well spoken. 'I work with the police now and again.'

'Oh, *well*.' I nod back towards the unit. 'This must be tailor-made for you.'

She smiles and she's got perfect teeth. 'You would think, right? Actually this is the first time I've been involved with a case like this. It's normally crimes that are a little more ... outside the normal range, shall we say?'

'What, serial killers, that kind of thing?'

'That kind of thing,' she says.

I'm instantly jealous. 'I *so* wanted to catch a decent serial killer case,' I say. 'Never had a sniff. Oh ... I'm ex-Job.'

'I know,' she says.

I like that she's done her homework and it makes me feel like we're colleagues, so I can't resist asking if she was involved in any of the big cases in London that I can remember. The killer couple from a year or so ago. The case with the cats from before that. I try to make it matter-of-fact so as not to sound like too much of a fan-girl.

'Yes, I advised on both those investigations,' she says.

'Nice,' I say.

'Well, not particularly.'

I look back towards A&E. I'm hoping there might be something exciting to see, someone rushing in with half their face missing maybe, just so I've got some stories to tell when I get back to the ward. The best I can do is a crying child and a woman with her arm in a sling. I watch the old woman stub her fag out and wheel her tank back through the doors.

'I've read your notes, Alice,' Perera says.

271

'Al,' I say.

She nods. 'But it's always better to hear these things first hand. Can you tell me what happened just before you were sectioned?'

I shrug. 'I smacked my boyfriend over the head with a wine bottle.'

'Right. When you had all the knives.'

'Yeah, to protect him. Have *you* got a boyfriend?'

She says that she has.

'So you'd do whatever you had to if he was in danger, wouldn't you?'

'We haven't been together very long,' she says. 'I met him during one of those cases you mentioned, actually.'

'So he's a serial killer?'

She laughs and her eyes widen, and I think, whoever her boyfriend is, unless he's also a part-time male model, he's definitely punching above his weight. I purse my lips and suck in a noisy breath. 'Going out with a copper is asking for trouble,' I say.

'Well, I know it can be,' she says, 'which is why we don't live together.'

I say, 'Smart,' and yes, I'm well aware she's only giving me snippets of personal information to build up a rapport or whatever. I know how it works. It's fine with me though, because I like hearing it. Bakshi's been treating me for months and I know bugger all about her.

As it is, the softening-up period doesn't last long.

'Would it be fair to say you didn't like Debbie McClure very much?'

I give it some thought, because I think I should. 'We never really got on,' I say. 'Couldn't tell you why.'

272

'But you thought she was responsible for the death of Mr Connolly?'

'I *know* she was and no, I certainly didn't like her much after that. Just saying, we weren't exactly best mates to begin with.'

She nods. She isn't writing anything down and I wonder if she has some kind of recorder in her bag. 'And you thought you were being ignored by the police who were conducting that investigation, yes?'

'I didn't *think* I was being ignored,' I say. 'I *was* being ignored.'

'So, how did that make you feel?'

'Ignored.'

'Were you irritated? Angry? Were you running out of patience?'

'Yes, with the police. Too effing right I was. I was pissed off at the incompetence of that idiot Seddon and the rest of his team. I mean, it was on a *plate*. It was on a sodding plate.'

She says, 'Right,' then leans her head back like she's just enjoying the sunshine for a moment or two, but I can see the cogs turning. 'After what happened to Detective Constable Johnston, you felt you were denied the chance to give evidence against the man who murdered him. That's right, isn't it?'

'I was a bit all over the place back then,' I say.

'You never got to play your part in getting justice for a murdered colleague.'

'The bloke was put away. That's what counts.'

'How did that make you feel?'

Here we go. Feelings again. 'Look, I know this is what you do, but I've got to tell you that I never worked on a single murder case where how someone *felt* about this, that or the other thing counted for anything. You just have to catch them, right?'

'You're correct, Al,' she says. 'How someone is feeling at a particular time *is* a ... large part of what I do. I believe it can be hugely important, and so do the senior officers who have brought me in to help with this case.' She smiles again, but there aren't quite so many perfect teeth on display this time. 'So I'd be very grateful if you could tell me.'

I sigh and stare across at the entrance to A&E again. Still nothing to get excited about. 'I wasn't very happy about it,' I say.

'OK, good. Thank you, Al. Now, do you think it's possible that you had similar feelings, or that those old feelings resurfaced, when you saw that the investigation into Mr Connolly's murder had stalled? When, despite you putting it on a plate for the police, Miss McClure was getting away with it. Did you perhaps feel ... thwarted?'

There it was, though I'd known it was coming for several minutes. The shrink was laying it all out a bit more politely than Lauren had done last night, but she was saying much the same thing. Asking much the same question.

It makes complete sense, after all. Sitting out here, the pair of us all pally in the sunshine, I don't know if she's going to be talking to Ilias or Bob or the rest of them, but right this minute I'm a suspect. Of course. How could I not be?

When you think about it, I'm the *obvious* suspect.

I understand, but it doesn't mean I have to like it.

'Can we go back inside now?' She's not actually a copper, so I'm guessing she can't really refuse.

'If that's what you want,' she says.

I stand up and start walking back and, once she's managed to catch me up, I say, 'This boyfriend of yours. Is he the kind of copper that gives a stuff about feelings?'

She doesn't answer, so I'm guessing we're about done.

FORTY-THREE

Detectives French and Saunders and their tame trick-cyclist have left and suddenly there's a weird atmosphere on the ward. Weirder than normal, I mean. Usually, at any time of the day or night, there's one or two people plodding around in a bit of a daze, but now it's like *everyone* is . . . subdued. Nobody seems very keen to discuss what's been happening, to talk about anything come to that, and I start to wonder if the staff have got together and decided to up the dosage on everyone's sleepy-pills.

If it's something they do whenever it's necessary.

When things get a bit stressful or if they're understaffed.

So make that . . . all the time.

I remember reading somewhere that prison officers are quite happy that their prisons are in the grip of a Spice epidemic, because zombified inmates are that much easier to handle. The prisoners are happy being off their tits because it helps them forget they're, you know, *in prison*, and it gives the screws a bit more time to put their feet up and do sudokus. It's a win-win. It's hardly a big leap to imagine Marcus and his team doing whatever it takes to make *their* working lives a bit more peaceful, is it?

I might ask Marcus when I get the chance, but I doubt he'll admit it.

For now, it's just me, Big Gay Bob and Tiny Tears chilling out in the dining room. I'm actually quite glad that there hasn't been a lot of chat about this latest round of interviews, because if it was to start now, I can guess the kind of thing Bob would have to say about the hot psychiatrist.

[*Puts hand on cock*] *I told her to analyse* this!

Instead he says, 'I miss Debbie.'

'Why's that?' I ask.

I'm still thinking he's cueing himself up for a crack about his history of rumpy-pumpy with Scottish women, but he just looks sad. 'Because she was nice.'

'Was she, though?'

'Well, not to everyone, I suppose. Her and Femi didn't like each other very much and she had that big row with George.'

'What big row?' I ask.

'A couple of days before she was killed, in one of the exam rooms. I don't know what they'd fallen out about, but I could hear them shouting.'

I know Debbie and Femi had clashed a few times, but this is the first I've heard about her and George. I should try and ask George about it when I get the chance.

'She was nice to *me*, though,' Bob says.

'Why wouldn't she be? *You're* nice.'

'Thanks, Al,' he says. Then he shakes his head. 'Not nice enough to stop Sandra leaving.'

The wife who walked out on him. Because Bob was constantly shagging other women. Or because he was constantly talking about shagging other women. Or because it wasn't actually women he wanted to shag.

I'm not even sure Bob knows.

The best I can manage right now is, 'Shit happens sometimes, mate.'

'Why would someone kill her?' Clare asks, from nowhere.

Bob looks horrified. 'Someone killed *Sandra*?'

I put my hand on his arm and tell him that nobody's killed his ex-wife and that everything's OK. Then I turn and give Clare a good, hard look. She's been sitting watching me for twenty minutes, keeping shtum even though she looks like she's got plenty to say. Like she's trying to psych me out, you know what I mean?

I can hear Perera's voice: *How does that make you feel?*

Properly uncomfortable, if I'm honest.

What is her fucking game?

'You tell me,' I say.

'I haven't got the foggiest,' she says. 'How could I?'

Why would someone kill her?

All whispery and wide-eyed, she is. Above it all. As if what's happened is just incomprehensible and she's asking the most difficult question in the world. Like it's something *she* can't possibly know anything about, while she's conveniently ignoring the fact that if I'm the obvious suspect – because I thought Debbie killed Kevin *and* I found the body – then the fact that Debbie was murdered five minutes after she arrived on the ward makes Tiny Tears a pretty close second.

'Oh, come on, don't be shy,' I say. 'If you've got a theory

then let's hear it. Obviously you'll have shared it with the police by now, but don't keep the rest of us in suspense.'

It probably came out a little more spiteful than I intended and her eyes start to brim with tears as per bloody usual. I don't feel bad, though. I'm perfectly happy to sit here and watch her weeping herself to soggy pieces.

'I was just making conversation,' she says.

'Yeah?'

'I'm interested, that's all.' Her head drops but, by sheer force of will she heroically holds the tears at bay. When she looks up again, there's a hint of mischief, which I do not like one bit. 'You know who killed her though, don't you?'

'Who told you that?'

Even if she intends to tell me, she can't get the words out through the volley of racking sobs that she simply can't fight off a moment longer. She splutters and gulps. She presses her hands to her face to staunch the tsunami of convenient waterworks.

Doesn't much matter. I'm guessing gobby Lauren said something.

George appears in the doorway to see what the matter is. Jesus H Christ . . .

I'm certainly not going to tell Clare why Debbie was murdered. I was very happy to pass on what I knew to the police and alert them to the fact that Debbie had a drug-smuggling accomplice with a very good reason to want her silenced, but I don't see any reason to tell any of these numpties.

'I think it's because she was ginger,' I say. 'Homicidal ginger-phobia.'

Clare's still sobbing, but I know she can hear me and she's got one eye on George approaching with tissues.

'I bloody love ginger girls,' Bob says. 'Minges like copper wire.'

It's great to have him back.

There's half an hour before lunch, so with nothing more exciting on offer, I nip back to my room for a spot of casual Googling. I've just typed in *memory blackout* when my mobile rings. There's no caller ID showing and whoever's calling hangs up after I answer, same as last time. A wrong number probably or scammers of some sort, but still, I'd like to know if someone's pissing me about. Time was, I might have been able to call in a favour from the Forensic Telephone Unit, but those days are long gone. I think about maybe getting Banksy to do it for me, but that would mean asking *him* a favour and I reckon I've used up all my credit.

Back to Google . . .

The first page is full of articles that refer to excessive alcohol consumption and a couple mention Valium and Rohypnol. I don't think anyone's been slipping either of *those* into my dinner, so I try again and add *not drug or alcohol related* into the search. Predictably, this gives me a bunch of pages about memory loss that are specifically about those things but, after scrolling for a while, I find *Other Causes of Memory Blackouts*.

I wish I hadn't bothered.

Low blood pressure seems to be the most common one and there was nothing wrong with my BP when it was checked yesterday, same as it is every bloody day. So . . .

Epilepsy, lack of oxygen, psychogenic seizures. WTF?

I'm fairly sure I'd know if I'd had a psychogenic seizure and, once I've looked it up, I'm positive I haven't. Got to say, though, it sounds exactly like what Shaun had that night in the TV room, and now I'm even more convinced – not that I need to be – that poor dead Debbie would have known just which buttons to press to bring it on.

She'd managed to shut him up, but imagine how perfect it would have been for her if she'd managed to wipe out Shaun's memory as well.

I'm still thinking about the 'thank you' note he passed me last night.

It seems like *he* thinks I killed Debbie, too.

It only takes a few more minutes' rooting through the search results before I come across pages full of articles about memory loss as a symptom of PTSD. I was expecting as much. I skim-read a few, but I'm not convinced that's what's going on. They're all about memory loss as the brain's coping mechanism, which would mean that, in my case, I would be blanking out the 'traumatic incident' because it's simply too painful to remember. I'm not saying it's a ridiculous idea, but it's been a year and a half since Johnno was killed, so could it really be delayed that much? More important, it's not like that's what being blanked out, is it? I've got no memory at all of flicking bits of fish finger at L-Plate, while I can remember every hideous moment of what happened in that crack-head's flat.

The pattern on that carpet. Blue and green and blood-red.

It doesn't make any sense at all.

I close my laptop and decide that Google is brilliant if you want to know which film you've seen some actor in, or how old someone is, but that using it to try and work out what might be wrong with you never goes well.

I leave my room and prowl around a bit, not sure what to do with myself.

Like a fart in a colander, my mum always says.

They'll have started dishing up lunch by now, but I don't much fancy sitting there chit-chatting with the rest of them. I'm not really up to it. I can usually sweet-talk Eileen into giving me a sandwich or something once the service has finished and they've all buggered off, so I decide to leave it a while.

I walk past George and Femi without saying anything.

I ignore Tony, who's drumming on his suitcase by the airlock.

One of the Informals – who might be called Trevor – is sitting on his own in the music room doing a jigsaw, so I wander in. He's fifty-ish and wears a suit – without a tie, obviously – like he's just arrived from an office somewhere. He's a bit red-faced, like he might be a drinker, but beyond that I've no idea what his story is. I've seen him around the last few days, but we've never really spoken, which is my bad, probably. Normally I prefer to stick with my own crowd, because there are fewer surprises, but right now I'm uneasy about it.

I want to talk to someone I don't know at all.

I sit down and say, 'All right?'

His jigsaw's nearly finished, but he immediately starts breaking it up, not angry or anything, just nice and calm like that's what he has to do because he's been interrupted. He needs to start all over again, simple as that. As soon as he's finished and all the pieces are laid out in front of him again, he looks up and smiles at me.

'All right?'

FORTY-FOUR

'Sorry about your jigsaw,' I say.

'Doesn't matter,' he says.

'Do you always start again? If you're interrupted?'

'Those are the rules.'

'It must happen a lot.'

'Yeah, I've never finished it.'

'Why don't you just take it to your room and do it in there?'

He looks at me like that's just about the stupidest idea he's ever heard, so I decide not to labour the point.

'You got nowhere to live then?' I can only presume, because the police had not allowed him to leave after what happened to Debbie, that his abode is ... unfixed.

He shakes his head. 'Only for a couple of nights at a time.' He looks around. 'This isn't too bad, though.'

I can't imagine how bad the place where he was staying before must have been. A freezing, rat-infested hovel. Or a Travelodge.

'Don't you think things are a bit strange in here right now?' I ask.

'Well, I'm not sure I've been here long enough to tell.'

'I've been here quite a while,' I say. 'And it feels to me like something bad is coming.'

He laughs. A high-pitched, girlish giggle.

'Why is that funny?'

'I think something bad has already come, don't you?' He laughs again and mimes a frenzied stabbing, like the killer in *Psycho*.

'Something else,' I say. 'Something bad for *me*.'

'Oh, right,' he says. 'Like what?'

I fight the urge to say, *well if I knew what it was I might be able to do something about it*. Instead I just shrug and say, 'Some people in here think I killed Debbie.' I realise that he might not even have been here long enough to know her name. 'The nurse.' Now I'm the one miming the stabbing. 'In the toilets.'

He nods. 'Did you?'

I stare at him and ... *bingo*! All this time I've been banging on to Banksy about killers coming in here and pretending to be patients and it suddenly strikes me that an undercover police officer would make a damn sight more sense. I'm annoyed I didn't think of it before. He comes in a few days after Kevin is killed, because Seddon and his useless team are running out of ideas, then after the second murder there's all the more reason for him to stay where he is. Get to know the suspects a bit better.

Fuck, why not?

It's definitely what *I* would have done, back in the day.

He's holding a hand up now and shaking his head. 'No, don't tell me. I don't want to know.'

If I'm right, he's certainly convincing, but the best UCs are seriously good at this. Problem is, some of them can immerse themselves in their roles a bit *too* much. I knew an officer one time who was undercover for Serious and Organised and, a month after he'd helped bring down one of the biggest gangs in West London, he was done for armed robbery himself.

'I'm not sorry she's dead,' I say.

'Fair enough,' he says.

I move my chair a little closer to his and lower my voice. 'But somebody in here thinks I did it, and the reason *why* I'm supposed to have done it makes me a target.'

'Yeah, you're right,' he says.

'What have you heard?'

'No, I mean you're right . . . that's bad.'

'I don't know what to do,' I say. 'I don't know who to trust.'

'You shouldn't trust anybody.'

'No . . .'

'Or . . . you could trust everybody. That might work as well.'

I watch him smile and give me the thumbs-up. He seems very happy with his plan. He's either a copper who's ridiculously good at his job or he's as mad as a hatter.

'I'm scared,' I say.

'Oh yes, so am I,' he says. 'All the time.'

'I don't like it. I've only ever been really scared once before and I didn't like it then, either.'

'What did you do?'

'I fought back,' I say. 'I got weapons.'

'Right.' That fires him up and he turns his head and starts to look around the room, searching for something suitable. I'm quite excited, so I do the same.

Bongos, the broken guitar, a collection of board games. Nothing that's going to do anyone a great deal of damage.

He slaps his hand on the table in frustration, then shrugs, as though it was well worth a try. He says, 'Do you want to have dinner?'

It's sweet, like he's asking me on a date, and I find myself grinning.

'Could do,' I say. 'But *just* dinner, yeah? I'm not a slag.'

He giggles again. Mutters, '*Slag.*'

'Then maybe afterwards we can come back here and I'll help you finish your jigsaw.'

His face darkens immediately and he leans forward, wrapping his arms protectively around the scattered pieces. He sniffs and looks sideways at me.

'Oh no you *fucking* won't.'

FORTY-FIVE

Mr Jigsaw – who isn't called Trevor at all, but turns out to be a Colin – is sitting as far away from me as possible without actually being in a different room, and I find myself dining next to Lauren. This is, of course, a major treat. She eats with her mouth open, humming tunelessly through her nose and leaning into me when she reaches for salt and pepper and ketchup. Then ketchup again.

She says, 'That psychiatrist the coppers brought along was nice.'

'Was she?' It's a relief to hear that I wasn't the only patient Perera talked to. But then Lauren spoils it, like she was always intending to. 'Yeah, we had a cracking natter. Talked about all sorts of things.'

I can't help thinking that she means all sorts of people and that what people really means is *me*. Her fat gob twists into that punchable smile, the one she slaps on if she's enjoying herself and whenever she wants me to think she knows something.

What's really annoying is that it works.

'Pretty as well, don't you think?' she says.

'I suppose.'

'Proper lez-bait.' Lauren nods and ladles more stew into her mouth. 'I saw Malaika eyeing her up.'

Talking of which, I'm all too aware that Clare is watching me from the table opposite. She's sitting with Donna and Ilias, but doesn't seem interested in whatever those two are talking about. It wouldn't surprise me if Tiny Tears had cosied up to Lauren as well and is patiently waiting for her to report back on *our* conversation once we've all finished eating.

'She must have had a field day with you,' Lauren says. 'That psychiatrist.'

'Must she?'

'Course. Your thing about who killed Kevin, you thinking it was Debbie and all that.' She leans so close that her greasy hair is like some massive spider on my shoulder and she whispers as if she's making a dramatic announcement in a scary film. 'Murder most *foul*.'

'Oh, fuck off,' I say.

She snorts so some stew comes out, then goes back to her dinner.

I see Tony walk up to the serving hatch and decide it might be nice to join him for a spot of pudding. I tell Lauren to fuck off again for good measure, and when I get up to leave, she picks up one of the plastic knives and jabs it aggressively at nobody in particular.

I can tell that she wants me to notice.

Once we've both collected bowls of runny trifle, I ask Tony if I can have a word. He doesn't look thrilled about it, but I tell him it's all right and guide him gently towards the empty end of one of the long tables. For a big bloke, he's fairly ... biddable. Mia and Femi are sitting at the far end, but they're gassing away anyway and I know that if I talk quietly enough they won't hear us.

'I think you're right,' I say to Tony.

'What about?'

'*You* know ...'

Just like that he goes from being wary to proper crapping himself. He starts looking around the dining room frantically, but I reach across and grab hold of his arm. 'It's fine,' I say. 'I swear.'

He looks at me and gradually starts to calm down a little. His chest is still heaving, mind you, and it feels like he could bolt any moment.

'Where is it?' he asks.

'I'm not sure, but you really don't need to worry, because it's not ... your Thing. It's *mine*.'

His eyes widen. Now he's not going anywhere.

'I reckon I've got a Thing too,' I say. 'But it's different from yours, because I know it's a *person*. I know it's living and breathing and it's walking about in here.'

He looks around again, but more slowly this time and a lot more sneakily, because suddenly we're in this together. He reaches across the table and takes hold of *my* arm. 'I'm so sorry, mate.'

'Thanks.' I shrug. 'At least I know.'

'It *will* kill you, you know that, right? That's the reason it exists. So you need to be careful.'

'Oh, I'm being very careful, and the best part is, I don't think it knows that I'm on to it or that I'm watching out. Does yours?'

'I'm not sure.' Tony screws his eyes up and shakes his head. 'It's so bloody clever, though. Like one step ahead all the time.'

'How did you find out about it?'

He pushes trifle around his dish. 'When I was eleven or twelve. First I thought it was, you know ... like an imaginary friend? He turned up in my bedroom one night after my dad left, so we'd sit up there and talk about when Dad was coming back and things would be OK again and that was nice.' He smiles, just for a second or two. 'Then, after Mum passed, he came with me to the care home, and once the bad stuff started happening in there he wasn't quite so friendly, you know? One day he just wasn't around, but I always knew he was coming back and that when he did, I wouldn't recognise him. That now it was an *it* and not a *he* any more, yeah? I knew that eventually it was going to hurt me, but the worst thing is, I never understood why.' He lifts up a spoonful of trifle but just stares past me and lets it run off the spoon. 'To this day, I don't know what I did to make the Thing so angry with me.'

We sit there for a while saying nothing.

Over Tony's shoulder I can see people starting to leave. I watch Lauren get up and notice Clare follow her out half a minute later. I glance over at Colin, but any UC worth his salt is way too smart to make surveillance of me obvious.

'Do *you* know, Al?' Tony asks. 'Why *your* Thing wants to hurt you?'

I nod, because I know that telling him will make me feel better. 'Because it thinks I killed someone.'

'OK.'

'And it wants to punish me for it.'

Tony grunts, like that's all perfectly reasonable. He points the V of two fingers towards his eyes. 'Want me to keep an eye out for you?'

I'm not going to walk round the table and hug him, but it's the most I've wanted to hug anyone for quite a while. I thank him, though. 'I'll be fine, Tone,' I say, and I reckon I almost sound convincing. 'You watch out for *yourself* . . .'

For the third night in a row, once I've taken my meds, I decide to duck out of a night in the TV room and head to bed early. Well, to my bedroom at least. I'm not sure I'll be getting a lot of sleep.

As soon as I'm there, though, I wonder if I've made the right decision. I can't settle and it's a constant struggle to hold the scary ideas at bay. With the others around to annoy me or make me laugh or just be their ordinary bizarre selves, at least I'd be distracted and there'd be less time for me to upset myself and dwell on things.

On what people are thinking about me, saying about me.

On what Perera took away from our little natter.

On badness and blood.

On *forgetting* . . .

It's Malaika doing the half-hourly checks on this corridor tonight and, when she knocks on the door which I've taken to locking all the time, I don't want to unlock it. I just stand close to it and tell her that everything's fine.

'Come on, Alice, you know the rules. I have to *see*.'

I open the door a few inches, muster a smile then close it again.

291

I think I doze off for a while eventually, it's hard to be certain. Asleep or not, it's the usual gory fun-fest, and however much later it is when Clare knocks, I refuse to answer. I just lie here and listen to her knocking until she finally gives up, her mouth close to my door whispering about how she thought we were friends.

It will *kill you, you know that, right?*

FORTY-SIX

I'm like a child that's overtired. I'm fractious and weepy and it's hard to think very straight. Even though I'm physically wiped out and it felt like the walk to the MDR was going to kill me, my brain is still firing off signals so fast that by the time my body chooses to act on one, the instructions have changed. I'm not ... in sync with myself. It's like I keep deciding to go on a journey, but as soon as I've taken the first few steps, thick fog comes in from nowhere and I get lost straight away.

Does that make any sense? Probably not.

I'm starting to lose track of the days. Easy to do in here at the best of times. It must be Friday because of what I'm doing this morning, so ... five days since Debbie was killed?

Marcus and Bakshi are both watching me while Marcus makes the pointless introductions then launches into the usual blah-blah-blah about meds and statuses and care plans.

I straighten out my legs and immediately pull them back again.

I fold my arms, then put my hands behind my head, then slide them beneath my thighs.

I hunch my shoulders. I relax them again. Hunch and relax . . .

When Marcus has finished, I can see they're all still looking at me, so I try to concentrate and tell him that I prefer these slightly more intimate Friday-morning get-togethers. It's just Marcus, Bakshi and George today. No trainee-this or Junior-that.

'Every bed on the ward is occupied,' Marcus says. 'And sadly, we are still a nurse down.'

'Nurse down . . . nurse down!' I say it without thinking, like an emergency alert. A tasteless joke. The same way I said *officer down* a year and a half before, in that flat in Mile End, when I was trying to key the radio with those stupid slippery gloves.

'Are you all right, Alice?' Bakshi asks.

Perfectly on cue, I stifle a yawn. 'I'm not sleeping very well.'

She looks at Marcus and says, 'Well, let's see if we can help you with that.'

Marcus scribbles something down, a reminder that I need more pills probably, but I'm thinking that anything short of an elephant tranquilliser isn't going to make a great deal of difference right now.

'The sleeping issue aside,' Bakshi says, 'are things OK generally?'

I nod and say, 'Absolutely.' I'm probably nodding a bit too much.

Things are a long way from OK, but whatever I've said

to other patients, I don't really want to say it to this lot. Nobody here is squeaky-clean all the time, but despite a couple of recent . . . transgressions – the call to Andy and the home-delivery weed affair – they've still been talking about progress, like I'm actually making some. Barring disaster, I'll be out of here in four months anyway, but I certainly don't want to do or say anything to scupper my chances of the section getting lifted sooner.

'Yeah, things are good.'

Bakshi gets down to it. 'I gather Marcus has already told you that we need to discuss the incident with Lucy on Wednesday.'

I'm ready for it. 'Look, I know what I did was totally unacceptable and I've already apologised to Lucy and she's cool about it. It was a blip, that's all.' A smile, a shrug, a *no big deal*. 'Me and L are mates again, so no worries on that score.'

'Well, not on that score perhaps, but my understanding is that you didn't actually remember doing it *at all*.' She gives a little hum, and there's a question mark at the end. 'That has to be a cause for concern.'

Alarm bells are starting to ring a little. I'm sure Lucy wasn't telling tales, but she must have let something slip. 'Well, what I did was a bit . . . vague, that's all. Fuzzy, yeah? It's not like I couldn't remember—'

'OK. That's fine. So, do you remember verbally attacking George yesterday, in the dining room?'

I blink and, just for a few seconds, I consider bluffing it out. I could say 'Yeah, course I do, it was only yesterday', but they'd only ask me to talk about what happened – whatever the hell it was – so I know I'll be found out. All I can do is look at George.

'When you were sitting with Bob and Clare?' he says.

Right, got it. When Bob was talking about how much he misses Debbie and Clare started crying. Yes, I can remember that, but I don't think that's what they're on about.

George is looking at me and I can see he is on my side, willing me to remember. Eventually he sighs and says, 'When I came over to the table, you were verbally abusive, Alice. *Very* abusive.' He's not happy at having to tell the story, that's obvious. 'You kicked a chair, as well.'

Bakshi is waiting.

What the hell can I say? My stomach's jumping and my head is screaming for help and I've got . . . *nothing*. I can only really say sorry to George, so that's what I do.

He nods and sits back. 'No worries, pet.'

'Are you forgetting things a lot, Alice?' Bakshi asks.

Now I'm panic-stricken, fidgeting like I've got fleas and seeing any prospect of early release drifting away up the Swanee. God knows where the idea suddenly came from that I should be honest with them, because, sitting where I am now, I almost never tell the truth.

'It's just those two times,' I say. 'That I know of, anyway. I mean, there might be other things . . . bits of conversation or whatever. It's like . . . the opposite of a flash, you know? Like it's stuff that happens when the lights have suddenly gone off. Just . . . a gap.'

I wonder if they're thinking about transferring me somewhere else, one of the wards downstairs even. If they want to extend the section three and detain me for more than six months, I'm not even sure what number section that is. Then I notice that Bakshi actually looks pleased.

'It's understandable, Alice,' she says. 'These kinds of

blackouts are a well-documented symptom of PTSD. It's just the brain's way of taking care of itself. When it gets ... overloaded, it shuts down for a while.'

'I was reading about that,' I say.

'Well, good. Now ... the PTSD you suffered after the events of eighteen months ago resulted in quite a different set of symptoms, but again this variation is perfectly normal. These things affect people in diverse ways every time. What happened to Detective Constable Johnston led to you having a serious, potentially dangerous breakdown and this time, after the trauma of discovering Nurse McClure's body, the PTSD is taking a different form altogether. The odd ... blip as you call it, and some sporadic episodes of memory loss. It's a rather more benign form, thankfully.'

'Right.' It doesn't feel very benign. It certainly didn't last night when I was lying awake, listening for noises outside and sweating through my sheets, but I see what she's getting at. 'So, what do we do?'

'There is medication that can help,' she says. Marcus scribbles again. 'So we'd like to start you on that straight away. It's actually the same thing used to treat the cognitive symptoms of Alzheimer's.' She smiles at the look on my face. 'Don't worry, you certainly do not have that.'

'That's a relief,' I say. 'Oh, by the way, are you sure I haven't got Alzheimer's?'

George smiles at the stupid joke and I instantly forgive him for ratting me out.

'The tablets won't eradicate these blackouts overnight,' Bakshi says. 'But the symptoms *will* ease and, as you know better than most people, PTSD in whatever form can be resolved with professional help.'

297

'Thank you,' I say. I'm not sure I've ever said it to her before.

Not meant it, at any rate.

'This is all very positive,' Marcus says.

'Bang on,' George says.

'It's always positive when you can identify a problem early and start dealing with it. If it makes you feel any better, Alice, you should also know that you are far from being the only patient who is ... struggling a little after what happened to Nurse McClure. Some members of staff, too. In many respects, the whole of the ward is suffering with PTSD right now.'

'That's really nice to know,' I say. Things might be looking up, but I still don't think it's a good time to remind him that somebody on his ward is a killer. Or tell him that whoever that is wants to see me dead. 'Safety in numbers, right?'

As soon as I walk out of the MDR, I'm waylaid by Femi who tells me that I have a visitor. Before I have a chance to ask any questions, she's opening the door to one of the small consultation rooms.

'Everywhere else is busy,' she says. 'So I've put your friend in here.'

My visitor is standing up as I step into the room.

'Hey, Al,' Andy says.

FORTY-SEVEN

It only takes a few seconds of me standing there and staring at him, before Andy looks away. I smile, because it's such an unexpected treat to see how nervous he is. He says, 'Oh . . .' then reaches down to a paper bag on the table and lifts out the gift he's brought with him.

Now I stare at that instead.

'I didn't really know what to bring,' he says. 'I was thinking maybe a book or something, but I couldn't decide what to get . . . and you know, people *always* bring fruit, right? I guessed you wouldn't be short of fruit.'

It's a cactus. A fucking *cactus*.

'I thought it would be nice in your room,' he says.

'Cheers,' I say. 'I'm grateful, obviously, but just saying I can think of a few other things that might have been more useful. I mean . . . a vibrator would definitely come in handy.' I sit down then lean forward to study the spiky monstrosity on the table. 'It's the right shape, but I don't think I'm quite that desperate yet.'

There's a dry, perfunctory laugh before he sits down again. Our chairs are uncomfortably close together. 'It's hard enough to know what to bring when it's . . . you know, a *normal* hospital.'

'This *is* a normal hospital. Didn't you see the big sign at the entrance?'

'You know what I mean,' he says.

His hair is a bit longer than it usually is and he hasn't shaved for a few days. I think he's lost a bit of weight, too. He certainly looks different from the last time I saw him; two months ago, when he came in a couple of days after I'd been sectioned. Remember what I said about people going to funerals just to make sure someone was actually dead? He was a bit pale and puffy back then, sweating through his cheap work suit and wearing those shoes I always hated. The ones that look like Cornish pasties. Oh, and he had a huge bandage on his head, mustn't forget that.

Now, I've got to be honest, he looks pretty damn fit.

He's still a massive cunt, though.

'So, how's things going?' he asks. 'I read in the paper about that nurse being killed.'

'Did you?'

He shakes his head. 'Pretty bloody mental.'

'Yeah, it was nice of you to call,' I say. 'You know, to check I was all right.'

'Come on, Al. I knew you were all right. It wasn't like it was a patient, was it?'

'Actually, a patient was killed two weeks before that, but let's not split hairs.'

'You serious?'

'Out of sight, out of mind though, yeah?'

'It's not like that—'

I sit forward suddenly and enjoy the fact that he recoils slightly. 'You *haven't* been calling me, have you? Calling from a different phone then hanging up?'

'Why would I do that?'

'I don't know, why would you do a lot of things? Why would you call the police on me? Why would you put me in here?'

'That's not fair,' he says. 'You know why.'

'Why would you tell the doctors that I've been calling you all the time and leaving messages?'

He blinks. 'Because you *have*, Al.' He sighs and reaches into a pocket for his phone. 'Do you want me to play one of them to you?'

I shake my head and tell him not to bother.

He says, 'No, I really think you should hear this.' He dabs at the screen then holds the phone towards me.

'Hey, fuckface ... guess who? Yeah, it's Crazy Alice with the word from the ward. Anyway ... you'll be horrified to know that I'm doing much better, no thanks to you, and that I'll be out of here soon ... very soon with a bit of luck. I just wanted you to know that. Hope your poorly broken head's a bit better ... fucking Humpty Dumpty with your broken head ... but I'm not sorry I did it. I had to, because I knew what you were up to and I still know, but there's no point you or your friends trying to watch me when I'm around again, because I'll be watching you. OK? Hope you feel big and clever for putting me in here, but all I'm saying, it's going to come back and bite you in the arse ... because I've had a lot of time to think and now I've decided what I'm going to do and you aren't going to like it one bit. Anyway,

just wanted to let you know all that. So . . . sleep well and sweet dreams, Humpty.'

'I'm sorry,' I say, once he's turned it off. 'It's the meds.'

Andy doesn't look convinced. I watch him put his phone away and try to scramble my way back up on to my sliver of moral high ground. 'Those emails you've been helpfully sending haven't done me any favours, by the way. But I'm guessing that was the point.'

'I was worried about you,' he says.

'Course you were.'

'I'm still worried about you. That's why I'm sitting here, with a stupid cactus in a bag.'

Through the small window in the door, I see L-Plate walk past, then step back and move to stare in. I presume she doesn't know it's Andy I'm talking to, even though I've told her all about him, but either way she clearly likes the look of what she's seeing. She nods approvingly, then raises her hand to her ear to make a comedy *call me* gesture.

Andy sees me looking, but by the time he does the same, L-Plate's gone.

'So when do you think you'll be getting out?' he asks.

'Depends on how many more of those emails you send to my psychiatrist,' I say. 'How *worried* you are.'

'Come on . . .'

'Four more months, all being well.' *If I survive that long. If I can work out who the enemy is. If my head doesn't get any more messed up than it already is, so I can manage to avoid them or take them on.* 'Why? You worried I might just turn up on the doorstep one day?'

'No.'

'Don't worry, I'll be sure to bring a bottle.'

He's probably trying to smile, but his mouth just . . . twists. 'I think it's only fair that I know,' he says. 'That's all. There's still all your stuff in the flat, obviously.'

'You didn't chuck it out? That's really sweet.'

'Seriously, Al—'

'No, it *is*.'

'Where are you going to go?'

'Is that an invitation to move back in?'

For the first time, there's the tiniest twinge of guilt at seeing him look so uncomfortable. My head must be even more messed up than I realise. 'It'll probably be a halfway house kind of place,' I say. 'Just for a bit, then hopefully the council can find space for me somewhere. There's no way I'm going to live with my mum and dad.'

'That all sounds . . . OK,' he says.

'And, you know, I'm still hoping to get my job back. So . . .'

Lucy must be spreading the word, because now Donna is taking time out from pounding the corridor to peer in. It's like a skull looming at the window. I wave her away.

'Listen, Al,' Andy says. So I do, because he says it in such a way that I know it's going to be good. 'When everything happened . . . you said some weird stuff to me, you know? Accusing me of all sorts. Saying I was involved in what was going on or what you *thought* was going on . . . that I was doing things to try and hurt you. Like I was part of some big plot or something. And I wasn't. I promise that all I was ever trying to do was help you.' He leans towards me and he's *actually* wringing his hands. 'You do know that, don't you, Al? I mean . . . you know that now, right?'

I say nothing. I just stare at him until he looks away again. He really wants an answer. He wants the answer that will make him happy, at any rate. I'm certainly not going to give him *that*, but I don't particularly feel like telling him what I *do* think, either.

I reckon I've told more than enough truth for one day.

'Trust me, Andy,' I say, eventually. 'I've got far better things to worry about at the moment. Fair enough?' Blimey, I couldn't help myself. I told him the truth anyway.

He seems OK with that, or at least he accepts it's the best he's going to get, so for the next fifteen minutes or so it's just chit-chat. He asks how my mum and dad are, and how Sophie is. What the food's like in here and if I've made any friends. He talks a bit about his job and how he's been finding it hard, but all I can think is *boo-hoo* and it doesn't sound like it's got any less tedious.

I wait until he does a funny shift in his chair and clears his throat. Until he thinks he's done an ex-boyfriend's duty. Until he's about to say, 'Well, I'd best be off' or 'OK, I'll leave you to it'.

'So, you been seeing anyone else?'

'What?'

'Getting any action, now I'm safely out of the way?'

He *ums* and shakes his head. I can't tell if he means *no* or if he's just finding it hard to believe I'm really asking. It doesn't make a lot of difference.

'Don't panic, Andrew,' I say. 'I'm only making conversation.' I'm *not*.

'OK.'

'I don't really give a shit.' I *do*.

There's that shift again. 'Listen, I think I should probably—'

'No,' I say. 'I'm the one who decides when it's time for you to go.' I manage a pretty decent impression of the woman who saw impostors on *EastEnders* and enjoyed slicing up her arms. I roll up the sleeves of my shirt to make the poor sod's predicament even clearer. The woman who fought him over possession of the kitchen knives and smashed his head open with a bottle.

'Yeah, that's . . . no problem.' He looks at his watch. 'I'm not in a rush.'

'Great,' I say.

I see him glance at the door, like he's praying a nurse might come in and give him the chance to make a dash for it. They don't, so I sit there and say nothing, watching him squirm and hoping that, if these stupid blackouts do carry on, this doesn't turn out to be a moment I forget.

FORTY-EIGHT

At lunchtime, I eat crisps in my room and think about my conversation with Andy. I can still remember every wonderful moment, thank God. It's obvious that I'm not the only one thinking about it, because by dinner time the Fleet Ward bitches are all a-twitter.

They want details and they want dirt.

It's like we're back at school and they've just found out I was fingered behind the bike sheds by the captain of the football team.

Which I was, obviously . . .

'You didn't tell me he was that good-looking,' L-Plate says.

I try to look offended. 'So what, you think I'd be shacked up with some munter?'

'No, but he's still a bit out of your league,' Donna says.

Big Gay Bob is the token bloke at the table. 'With birds, I always prefer it if I'm the one who's out of *their* league,' he says. 'There's way more chance of getting your leg over.'

Everyone ignores him, though I can't be alone in trying to picture the unfortunate woman who thinks that Bob is a step up. A blind pensioner with low self-esteem, at a push.

'This the ex, is it? The one whose head you smashed in with a wine bottle?' Lauren asks the question nice and casually while she mops up gravy with a slice of bread.

'Yeah, that's him,' Donna says. She helpfully picks up the plastic ketchup bottle to demonstrate. 'She brained the bastard.'

'I hope it wasn't something expensive,' L-Plate says. 'Such a waste.'

I reassure her that the wine in question wasn't one she'd think was expensive, which seems to mollify her. 'Doesn't matter if it's Château Ponce or Château Lidl, does it? The bottle still weighs the same.'

'Why did you hit him?' Clare asks.

Tiny Tears gave me a nod at breakfast, but this is the first time she's actually spoken to me all day. Not a word about her knocking on my door last night and my refusal to let her in. It feels like she's got a game plan of some sort that I can't figure out yet. Same with Colin, aka Jigsaw Man, who's conspicuously ignoring me, which is exactly what I'd expect an undercover officer to do.

'None of your business,' I tell Clare.

Lauren nods slowly. Mutters, 'History of violence.'

'Yeah, and you should probably remember that,' I say.

She laughs. 'I don't care what you've done, love,' she says. 'I'm not *scared* of you.' She says the word like the very idea of it is ridiculous. 'I'm not scared of anybody.'

'What does that mean, anyway?' I turn to stare at her. 'What I've done?'

307

She shrugs, because she doesn't need to spell it out, then she definitely gives Clare a sly look and I'm pretty sure I see Donna and L-Plate exchange a glance, too. I look across at Colin, who's making out like there's nothing more interesting than his dinner, then over to Mia and Femi who are apparently deep in conversation on a table at the far end of the room. I catch Tony's eye and he winks, as if to let me know he's still watching out for my Thing, that he's still got my back. After our conversation yesterday, I'd decided that he was more or less the only person I could trust. Now I'm not even sure about that.

Lauren's already moved on, they all have, and now there's some aimless chat about people's first pets.

But I'm not really listening.

There was a time not so long ago when I'd strut round this place like I still had handcuffs in my pocket and a taser on my belt. I wasn't looking for trouble, I'm not stupid, but I wouldn't back away from it. Lauren never put the wind up me like she did a lot of people, because I'd dealt with plenty like her on the Job. Women who hate themselves so much that they have to take out their frustrations on other people. On their kids, more often than not. The likes of Lauren in a place like this didn't bother me at all.

I'm not the same person any more.

It's been a long time since I recognised myself. The Alice I was two years ago, I mean. Now I don't even recognise the person I was two weeks ago.

Suddenly, I'm scared of *everybody*.

'Not going in to watch TV?' Marcus asks.

I've taken my meds and now I'm sitting in the main

corridor, my back to the wall outside the nurses' station. It's brightly lit and I've got the widest field of view I can think of anywhere on the ward. I can see people coming from any direction and, if it's someone I don't like the look of, I've got enough time to make myself scarce or get a nurse to sound the alarm. Truth is, I don't much fancy sitting in front of the TV with everyone else, but I don't particularly want to go back to my room, either. Not until I have to, anyway. It's started to feel even smaller than usual, like it's shrinking night by night and if for some reason I let the wrong person through the door, I've got nowhere to go.

'Can't be arsed,' I say.

'There's usually something good on a Friday night, isn't there?'

I don't answer, so Marcus sits down next to me.

'It was a good session this morning,' he says. 'Your assessment.' He waits, but I don't say anything. 'Didn't you think so?'

'I suppose.' I watch Ilias come out of the dining room and start walking in our direction.

'You're actually very lucky, Alice,' Marcus says. 'It might not feel like that now, but it's always so much better when you know what the problem is. These issues you're having are clearly PTSD-related, so now we can deal with them properly. With some patients you never know. *They* never know. Months go by, years even, and there is no explanation for why they're the way they are.'

Ilias walks past without even looking at me and turns on to the men's corridor, presumably heading for his room.

'Is there anything else bothering you?' Marcus asks. 'Aside from the blackouts?'

Malaika comes out of the nurses' station carrying a cardboard box. She takes it into one of the examination rooms. The corridor's empty, so I glance at Marcus.

'Just the not sleeping,' I say.

'OK . . .'

I can tell Marcus isn't quite buying it. He's too good at his job and he can smell bullshit a mile away. I'm wondering how much I can tell him. I mean, normally I'd say sweet FA about what's *actually* going on, because the minute I open my mouth about anything like this they just presume all my craziness from before has dropped in for a visit and I end up rattling with all the extra anti-psych pills. Now, though, *they've* given me an . . . explanation. It's like this new diagnosis they're all so pleased with themselves about has given me a get-out-of-jail-free card.

It can't hurt to test the water a little.

'You quite sure about the PTSD?' I ask. 'What's causing it?'

His grunt is emphatic. 'Your symptoms are very common.'

'I do know about PTSD,' I say. 'It's why I'm in here, remember?'

'Perhaps it isn't as severe as last time, but as Dr Bakshi explained—'

'It's not *enough* though. I found a body. So what?'

'I think for most people that would be traumatic enough. So soon after Kevin's death, too. Let's not forget that.'

'Yeah, but I'm not most people, am I? I saw far worse things than that when I was a copper. Plenty of bodies . . . kids and whatever, and none of that stuff screwed my memory up and all the rest of it. Just saying, it feels a bit . . . convenient.'

Marcus says nothing for maybe half a minute, lets his head drop back like he's happy with a few moments of relative peace and calm. Then he turns to look at me. 'What's . . . *all the rest of it?*'

Malaika comes out of the examination room and walks back into the nurses' station. Ilias emerges from the men's corridor and turns towards the TV room. He gives me a strange look as he passes and I watch him until he disappears.

'I think I'm in danger,' I say.

'What kind of danger?'

In for a penny, right? 'Someone wants to hurt me. Wants to *kill* me.' I see the obvious question on his face. 'The same person who killed Debbie.'

'Why would they want to kill you, Alice?'

I'm not an idiot, so I know that Marcus could be the very person we're now talking about. I don't think it makes much odds. Except for the coppers and that psychiatrist they brought with them, I've thought the same thing, at one time or another, about every person I've spoken to since it happened.

OK, so not *all* of them. Maybe not Lucy.

'Because he or she was working with Debbie,' I say. 'Debbie was using Kevin to smuggle drugs out of here, which was why she killed him and why she was killed. The fact I know that makes me a target.'

It feels a bit odd, saying all this to Marcus, being so upfront and matter-of-fact about what's going on, but it's not like he doesn't know, is it? Debbie had told him exactly what I'd said to her before she was killed. He was the one who passed that information on to French and Saunders.

'I don't feel safe,' I say. 'Locked up in here, I'm a sitting duck.'

I look around. A few more people are coming out of the dining room now and walking in different directions. Patients and staff. Heading to their rooms for a quick lie down before watching telly, outside for a smoke, to the toilets or the meds hatch.

Colin is talking to Tony.

Femi is talking to Donna and Lucy.

Clare is talking to Lauren, the two of them thick as thieves all of a sudden.

'I don't think it's very nice,' Marcus says.

I turn to look at him, thinking that's a strange way of putting it. A massive fucking understatement, considering what I've just told him.

'You talking about Debbie like that.'

'*What?*'

'People I have worked with have died before,' he says. 'You know that. But not like this. Never like this.' He looks at me. 'I went to visit Debbie's sister last night, to pass on my condolences. To see how she was coping. She has been *destroyed* by what has happened . . . the whole family has been destroyed.' He shakes his head. 'So no, what you are saying is not acceptable. Debbie was my colleague, but she was also my friend.'

'Yeah, and Kevin was mine.'

'I'm aware of that, Alice, but the fact remains that it is wrong to attack a person's reputation when they are not here to defend themselves.' He stands up, because he doesn't want to continue the conversation or he's got meds to administer. Either way.

'Well, she's dead so she probably doesn't give a shit!' I shout after him as he walks away. 'Anyway, she's not the one who needs defending.'

FORTY-NINE

Suddenly I'm wide awake and I don't have a clue what time it is, but it's pitch black and I'm tangled in wet sheets and, far more important, I know there's someone in my room.

I know there can't possibly be, because the door is locked.

I know there can't be, because I'd have heard them coming in.

But I know that there is.

The staff all have keys so they can make round-the-clock checks when they need to, and even if it's not a member of the staff, someone might have found a way to get hold of a key. Someone managed to get hold of a knife easily enough, didn't they?

I *told* them. I told almost *everyone*, but they wouldn't listen.

I lie perfectly still and wait for my eyes to adjust to the darkness.

I can't make out a shape and I can't hear anyone breathing but me. I'm not really surprised, though, because whoever's

314

in here with me, they're good at this. I'm struggling to suck up enough spit to swallow, never mind scream, and even if I could, there's always someone screaming about something, so it's not like I could count on anyone rushing down here to help.

Christ, it's going to be so easy, because I've got nothing to fight back with, and now a voice inside my head is telling me, *Who cares? There's not a fat lot worth fighting for anyway, so what's the fucking point?*

I'm not worth fighting for.

So I relax, just a little, because there's not much else I can do, and I think, *This is you, then, you silly, soft cow.* Lying here, giving Tiny Tears a run for her money and waiting for the Thing to do what it's come for.

FIFTY

I'm having breakfast sitting on my own. I say having, I couldn't eat a thing if you paid me, but I'm in here with everyone else because I was desperate to get out of my room first chance I got and now I want to be somewhere I can keep an eye on them all. See who's matey with who all of a sudden and who's giving me evils. Tune in to the chatter. Check out the alliances.

I'm still shaking this morning, but more importantly I'm still *here*.

Obviously . . .

If I was being paranoid, I'd say there *was* someone in my room last night and that it was a warning from a person who's clearly enjoying scaring the crap out of me. Someone there to deliver a simple message: *Best stay on your toes, because I can get to you any time I want.*

If I was being paranoid.

I think it was actually a warning to myself. Early notice that the threat level was being ramped up, the way the government does sometimes with terrorists or whatever. My subconscious mind, having processed all the evidence and read all the signs, laying out a possibility, a probability even, and showing me exactly what could happen if I wasn't careful. Telling me, in no uncertain terms, while I still had a chance to do something about it.

Either way, the message was the same and I received it loud and clear.

Wherever he is, Graham would be proud of me, because the moment the breakfast service is done with and the meds hatch opens, I'm out of the dining room and first in line to get drugged up. I take the three different doses that Femi hands over and signs off on – three, because I'm assuming the new Alzheimer's pills are among them – and go looking for Malaika.

Ten minutes later, I still haven't managed to find her, so I collar George on his way from the nurses' station to the MDR and ask him where she is.

'Malaika's not come in this morning,' he tells me.

'Really?' Malaika was my best bet, same as always. I'll need to find someone else fast.

'Bit bloody short-handed, tell you the truth,' George says. 'I think Marcus is on his way in, and he won't be best pleased having to give up his Saturday—'

'Can you take me outside?'

George rolls his eyes. 'Morning gasper, is it, pet?'

'Yeah, but . . . I just need some air.'

'Well, you'll have to give me ten minutes. Something I have to finish, then I'm all yours. Just one fag, mind.'

'You're a star,' I say.

George carries on towards the MDR and I nip back to my room to grab my tobacco. I'm in and out as quickly as I can, but I still make sure the door's locked while I'm in there. I lock it again when I leave, because the last thing I want when I come back is to find someone in there waiting for me, then hurry out to wait for George at the airlock.

I've only just got there when Tony arrives carrying his suitcase. He sits down next to me.

'They're coming early . . . flown in from Detroit.' He grins and pats his case. 'So I packed as soon as I woke up.'

'I saw the Thing last night,' I say.

'*Where?*'

'In my room. Well, I didn't *see* it exactly, but I saw what it would be like if the Thing was there. The shape and everything.'

'That happens to me all the time.' Tony lifts his case on to his lap, holds it against his chest and whispers, 'What I'm hoping is . . . that when I go, the Thing might stay behind.'

'I thought it always followed you.'

'Yeah, so far. But I was thinking . . . maybe it's getting tired of always changing into different things, or it's stopped being angry with me. I mean it could have killed me by now, if it really wanted to.' He looks at me. 'Yours might give up, too.'

'I'm not going to let it have the chance,' I say.

Why do I keep saying *it*? I know *my* Thing is walking around in here somewhere on two legs. Easier than saying *he or she* all the time, I suppose.

Tony puts out a hand and says, 'Good luck, Al,' like we

318

won't be seeing each other again. I know he's not going anywhere, but I shake his hand anyway.

'Cheers, Tone.'

Besides which, having seen all those stab wounds in
Debbie McClure, he or she is definitely an *it*.

When George comes ambling round the corner, I jump to
my feet ready to go. He puts on a comical burst of speed and
by the time he gets to me he's pretending to be out of breath.
He's already got the keys in his hand.

'Honestly.' He looks at Tony and shakes his head, then
mimes puffing on a cigarette. 'Bloody addicts, eh?'

I never smoked roll-ups before I came here. Didn't smoke
much of anything come to that. I was one of those annoying
part-time smokers who just scrounged fags off other people
at parties, but now I'm every bit the addict George was talking about, and it's always roll-ups, because it's cheaper and
that's what everyone else in here smokes. These days, I can
roll a fag blindfolded and with one hand, but you wouldn't
know it. Not now, seeing me spill tobacco and tear *two* Rizlas
while I struggle to stop my hands shaking.

'Here,' George says. 'Let me.'

'I didn't think you smoked,' I say.

'I don't, but I reckon I can make a better job of that than
the pig's ear *you're* making . . .'

I hand over the tobacco and the papers and lift my face to
the sun until he hands me back the cigarette.

'Thanks.'

He lights it for me, steps from shade into sunlight himself.
'Those new meds'll kick in pretty quick,' he says. 'Sort these
memory issues out.'

'Hope so,' I say.

'Those *blips*.' George looks at me. 'That's all they are, right, pet?'

I'm trying to decide whether to tell him the truth when I remember what Bob told me on Thursday and decide it would be much more useful to ask George about his row with Debbie instead. I'm just working my way round to it when I spot a bloke walking quickly down the hill from the main entrance towards us.

I stop and stare at him.

'What?' George asks, turning to look.

'Who's that?'

He's not a doctor, because he's already close enough for me to see that there's no lanyard flapping around against his chest, but he's not a visitor, either. Anyone visiting this place is ... tentative. Doesn't matter if it's their first time or if they're old hands, nobody ever sets foot in the Shackleton Unit without a degree of apprehension or, more often than not, plain reluctance. It's never going to be a picnic, is all I'm saying.

You certainly don't walk towards it ... purposefully, like it's something you're looking forward to. Not the way this bloke is bowling down that hill, only a few seconds away now, like there's nowhere else he'd rather be

'Who *is* he?'

'No idea,' George says.

'Can you go and find out?' George looks at me like I'm starting to take the piss and he's done more than enough already. '*Please* ...'

He mutters something under his breath then sighs and starts to trudge up the hill.

I'm still watching the mystery bloke, because there's something far too easy and confident about him. A shape that's familiar. So, as soon as George has taken enough steps towards him, just enough steps *away*, I turn.

And I run.

I'm wearing trainers and I'm fast. George isn't and he's a big bloke, so by the time I turn to look he's already fifty yards behind me.

He's waving and shouting.

I run . . . past humming generators and overflowing skips, then across a car park and now it's all downhill towards the side gate. Two people are walking towards me, but they step quickly out of my way. They both look a little alarmed and a glance tells me they're hospital staff who know it's never a good sign when someone comes running hell-for-leather from the direction of the Shackleton.

I run . . . and I can see my dad's face light up when I come round that last bend and he's jumping up and down and urging me on and, even though I'm knackered, I find a final burst of speed and sprint towards the finishing line where a couple of the other parents are holding up a tape.

I dip at the last minute, like you're supposed to . . .

. . . out through the gate and then I stop. I'm bent double, panting on a quiet road that I don't recognise, so I look both ways but I've not got the first idea which way I should go. It's been a long time since I've run that fast and it feels like I'm going to be sick, but I know I need to keep running, one way or another, before George catches up to me.

Left or right. Shit . . . I need to pick a direction, but I can't, because I haven't got a clue where I'm going.

Just ... away.

For fuck's sake, Al ...

Me and Johnno in Greggs, one lunchtime. Pushing the boat out. There's a woman tutting in the queue behind us and Johnno's getting tetchy because I can't decide between a pasty and a sausage roll.

Just pick *one,* Johnno says.

So I do.

FIFTY-ONE

I really don't want anyone to think that I was planning to do this when I talked George into taking me out for a fag. I swear I just wanted to get off the ward for a few minutes and get my head straight. It was only when I saw that suspicious-looking bloke that I knew I needed to get away. It wasn't like I was regretting not having any breakfast and was suddenly desperate for the tea and toast that's sitting in front of me right now.

The café was the first place I came to, that's all. I couldn't run any further, and I wanted to be with people.

With normal people.

There was a reasonable crowd in here when I came in. There still is, but now they're all eating, which I suppose is why the woman behind the counter can take a few minutes off. Anyway, that's what I'm thinking when she waltzes round the counter and walks across to sit down at my table.

She was friendly enough ten minutes ago, when I ordered.

and whatever else has happened to me, I think I've always been a pretty good judge of people. So, when I finally find the courage to look her in the eye, I say, 'I'm really sorry, but I can't pay for this.'

'I guessed that,' she says.

'I mean I *can* . . . but I haven't got any money on me.'

'It's a mug of tea and a slice of toast,' she says. 'I think I'll survive.'

She watches me eat for a while, then turns to wave when one of the other customers leaves. They all seem to know her, so the place has obviously been here a while, and I wonder if she runs it on her own. There's no sign of anyone else, even though there must be someone back there in the kitchen knocking out all the bacon and sausages or whatever. She's wearing a wedding ring . . . so maybe her husband? I'm trying to work out her set-up, trying to work *her* out. I reckon I can still do that. I try to do it with newbies on the ward, same way I did it back before things fell apart, with other coppers, and with suspects, obviously.

I sip my tea and take another bite of soggy toast. I sneak looks at her. I'm not scared any more and I've got my breath back and I'm suddenly enjoying myself, putting flesh on this woman's bones.

She's at least sixty, but she's dyed her hair very blonde like she still gives a shit what people make of her. Or maybe she's done it precisely because she doesn't. Either way, it's good. She sounds local, so I wonder if she's opened a place in the area where she grew up. Or maybe there's been a greasy spoon here for ever, like a family business, and she took it over from her parents. I wonder if that was what she wanted, what she'd imagined for herself when she was younger.

I'm making suggestions to myself, trying to guess what her name might be, when she saves me the trouble.

'I'm Sylvia,' she says.

I would never have guessed that. I'd been leaning towards Veronica or Madge. 'Alice . . .'

'So, what's the story, Alice?'

I look at her and she's sitting there like she's just asked me what the time is. She says she knows I've *got* a story, I mean *hasn't everyone*, so the rest of the toast goes uneaten and my tea goes cold while I tell her. Everything. When I've finished, she doesn't look as if she's wishing she'd never asked, but maybe she's just got a naturally kind face.

She nods towards the door. 'That place up the road?'

'Hendon Community Hospital,' I say.

'Yeah.' She gets up and walks across to a tall fridge against the wall, comes back with a can of Coke and sits down again. 'I had a cousin went through the same thing as you. Years ago now. They didn't really call it what it was back then, though. Didn't give it a name. Everyone in the family just said she was *suffering with her nerves*. You know?'

'Is she OK now?'

Sylvia shakes her head. 'She's not with us any more, bless her. Well out of it if you ask me.' She opens her can. 'The suffering bit's right, though.' She looks at me. 'I can *see* it, love.'

I don't know what to say, so I just stare down at the scratched red tabletop.

'I can't even imagine what it's like . . .'

I finally look up and I swear she really wants to know. An old bloke comes in and she asks him if he wants his usual. When he says he does, she tells him to sit down and says she'll be with him in five minutes.

Then she turns back to me.

'Sounds stupid, but a lot of the time you're just ... *irri-tated*,' I say. 'It's so bloody infuriating when people don't believe you.'

'I know that's how it must feel,' she says. 'But most people just don't know how to react to that kind of thing, do they? I'm not sure *I* do, tell you the truth. You tell someone you're ... I don't know, getting messages from God through the patterns on your wallpaper ... I don't mean *you're* saying anything like that, love ... but what are people supposed to make of it? It's hard to go, "Oh, all right then", because that's only ... reinforcing it, don't you think?'

'Yeah, but it's *also* like me telling someone my name's Alice and them telling me that it's not.'

She nods slowly. 'Oh, righto ... I'm with you.'

'That's how sure you are. You don't just *think* these things, you *know* them.'

She nods again. 'Got it, love.'

'So it's like everyone's basically saying you're stupid or calling you a liar.'

'Or telling you you're mad.'

I laugh, and it's nice. 'Right, but even if you *are* being a bit mad you don't think you are.' Now *I* nod towards the street. 'Nobody over there thinks they're mad. Not properly. Yeah, they might have gone off the rails for whatever reason, but—'

'Everyone goes off the rails now and again,' Sylvia says.

'I know.'

'What use is bleedin' rails, anyway? Just keep you going in the same direction and that's no fun, is it?'

'No ...' She's trying to make me feel better, so I don't tell

326

her that I'd give anything to be back on those boring rails again. Facing the direction of travel. Moving forward ...

'So, what about you?' she asks.

'What *about* me?'

'Never mind that lot over the road. How are *you* feeling? Now, this minute.'

I look at her and it makes me think about my mum, so I start to cry a bit.

'Come on, now.' She pulls one serviette after another from a metal dispenser and hands them over. I snivel and splutter into them.

'I'm in so much trouble,' I say.

She tells me everything's going to be OK and puts one of her hands on mine. It's warmer and softer than I expect. I don't know if she's forgotten about the old bloke and his 'usual', but after that we just sit there for a while saying nothing, while she glugs her Coke and makes shushing noises.

And for a few minutes, it *is* OK. I forget about Kevin and Debbie and whoever's after me. I forget about Johnno and all the blood that came out of him, because the woman I'm sitting here with is quiet and kind. Because she doesn't make any assumptions. Because she doesn't want anything, or think anything bad, and best of all, I know she isn't judging me.

And then it's over, because I see George jog past the window with a policeman in tow. George glances in and a few seconds later they're both coming through the door.

'Oh,' Sylvia says.

For a moment or two, while everyone in here is turning to see what's happening, I wonder if she's called them. Could she have done it when I wasn't paying attention or when she went to fetch her drink? Maybe she signalled to whoever's in the kitchen.

George walks over to the table, and even though he doesn't look angry, I'm sure he is.

He says, 'Come on, Alice.'

Sylvia stands up, so I do the same.

Then I decide that Sylvia probably didn't call anyone, because when the policeman – who looks about sixteen – puts a hand on my arm, she shakes her head and says, 'There's no need for that, son.'

I promise her that I'll come back to pay for the toast and she shouts after me as they're leading me towards the door. 'You can have a proper fry-up next time. You take care … OK, love … ?'

FIFTY-TWO

'I'm really sorry you had to come in on a Saturday.'

'I didn't come in just because of you,' Marcus says.

'Oh yeah,' I say. 'Malaika . . .'

'Good job I did, though.'

We're sitting close together in one of the exam rooms. It's warm in here and it stinks of bleach and puke and I remember the two of us sitting in exactly the same place almost a week before. Then, Marcus was the one who needed comforting; stammering out his shock and disbelief at what had happened just across the corridor to a woman whose body was still warm.

Both of us with blood on our hands.

I say comforting, but at a guess – bearing in mind the whole absconding and being brought back by the police thing – that's probably not Marcus's primary concern at this particular moment. Aside from a physical assault, legging it is about as serious as it gets in terms of patient behaviour. I know there's going to be consequences, but I don't have a problem with that and I'm not expecting to get anything you'd describe as a proper bollocking. It's not like I took anyone hostage or went over the wall at Belmarsh or anything.

To be fair to Marcus and the rest of them, even when they're reading you the Riot Act in here, they tend to do it very gently.

'So, why did you run away, Alice?'

'You know why.' He says nothing, like he's forgotten or maybe he doesn't think it's much of an excuse. Either way, it's annoying. 'What I told you yesterday.'

He nods. 'You not feeling safe, you mean?'

'Me not *being* safe,' I say.

'I understand,' he says. 'George says that you saw someone. Outside.'

'Yeah. He looked *well* dodgy, and the way things are right now, I'm not taking any chances.'

'So you ran.'

'I would have come back.' I can see he's got that bullshit detector turned up nice and high. 'OK, so I probably wouldn't. Not straight away.'

'Where would you have gone?'

'I wasn't thinking that far ahead.'

If I'd had the chance to walk out of that café in my own sweet time, I honestly don't know where I would have headed. I'd probably have called Banksy in the end, maybe asked if I could crash at his place. Thinking about it, though, he might well have made the phone call I'd suspected the woman in the café had made, and I probably wouldn't have held that against him.

'It was nice,' I say. 'Just being away for a bit.'

'Alice, listen to me.' Marcus puts down his clipboard, the notes for a report he'll have to write on the 'incident'. 'If you continue to take your medication and make an effort to stay calm, so that we can help you ... you can be away for a lot longer than a *bit*. You can go home.'

'Not sure that's going to happen now,' I say.

'What do you mean?'

'I don't know ... things are coming to a head. I'm not saying that's what I want, but I don't think I've got a lot of say in it.' I was thinking about this all the way back from the café and I'm almost certain of it now. The scary stuff's getting really close and I can't stop it because, actually, I'm not sure I'm supposed to. 'After Kevin was killed and I started running round trying to find out who'd done it ...' I see his expression darken. He doesn't want to listen to me bad-mouthing his 'friend and colleague' again. So I don't. 'It's as if I started something, you know? Set a ball rolling. I'm not going anywhere until it hits and even though I'm not thrilled about what's coming, it feels like I need it to happen.'

I take a few seconds then look at him. 'Does that make sense?'

He picks up his clipboard again.

So, clearly not.

'I've spoken to Dr Bakshi,' he says. 'Of course, she was not happy to hear what happened, but she agrees with me that, in all probability, this was just another ... blip. The panic is all part of the same PTSD, and if you continue to take your new medication, we should see some improvement reasonably fast.' He glances down, scribbles a word or two. 'Of course, we can't allow any more time outside, for the time being at least.' He smiles, trying to lighten things. 'George tells me you were really fast ...'

I smile back. I *was*. I *am* ...

'And for the next few days we will need to put you back on Within Eyesight Observations.'

WEO is fair enough and it's what I was expecting. I mean, it's a hospital ... what else were they going to do? Make me wash my own pyjamas? Take away my Scrabble privileges?

'Yeah, so about that,' I say. 'As far as which member of staff is keeping an eye on me all the time, is there any chance I can choose?' Even as I'm asking, I'm trying to decide which of the nurses I trust the most. Or which one I distrust the least.

'I'm afraid that's not possible,' Marcus says. 'It wouldn't even be possible under normal circumstances, and you already know that staffing is a major issue at the moment.'

'So, when's Malaika coming back?' If Marcus had agreed, she would probably have been my first choice.

'I don't know,' he says. 'Unfortunately, she isn't answering her phone at the moment.'

The tiniest of alarm bells rings at the back of my brain, but it's drowned out by the clattering of a trolley outside as Marcus gets to his feet.

'Remember what I said, Alice.'

I walk to the door, and for a few seconds before opening it I just stand there and do the deep-breathing thing. Because I have to and because this is the way it's going to be from now on. I hate it because they're my friends, but I'm scared to death about stepping outside and having to greet whichever member of the crazy gang I run into first.

'You said a lot of things.'

*

I curl up in the corner of the music room wearing my head-phones and a *Do Not Disturb* expression and, thankfully, there aren't too many comings and goings. The Jigsaw Man wanders in but just mooches for a few minutes, pretending he's not looking at me, and then wanders out again. L-Plate spots me through the window and comes bursting through the door like we haven't seen each other in weeks. It looks, for a moment, like she might overcome her phobia and actually hug me. Nice as that would be, I tell her I'm a bit down in the dumps and ask if she'd mind sodding off and giving me a bit of space. L-Plate says *no sweat, babe, no sweat,* but makes me promise that we'll see each other later, because, you know, she *really* needs to catch up with me.

I watch her scamper away and think *she's not the only one.*

I stare at my phone for a while, then find myself firing off a text to Sophie: Wassup byatch?

She doesn't reply straight away like she normally does, so I sit there and wonder where she is and what she's doing on a fine Saturday afternoon. In the flat, probably, watching one of those old black and white films she loves, or doing a massive clean which she loves almost as much, or out buying overpriced tat in Camden Market. Sitting in the pub, maybe. *Not* looking at the other drinkers like they're aliens or boring her mates rigid trying to describe the funny music she keeps hearing. Lying in bed with her boyfriend, and not staring out of the window at the lights she can see at the end of the garden. Not telling him she knows he's 'in on it', while he pats the mattress next to him and tells her not to be so daft.

The phone pings.

Sophie Mob: hey you! how's the madhouse??

Same as usual.

Sophie Mob: what you up to?

Not much. I've been a bit up and down.

Sophie Mob: 🙁 want me to come and see you?? i can bring chocolate!! 👍 😊

It's fine, don't worry. I was thinking about you
that's all.

Sophie Mob: thinking about you too. LOTS xx

There's nothing for a minute or so. I think that's probably it, then the phone pings again.

Sophie Mob: just so you know, camilla is WAY cleaner than you but not as much fun 🍾 🖤

She knows all about what had happened with Andy, but I can't decide if the bottle of wine emoji is a joke or not. Nice, either way.

I am Queen of Fun!

Sophie Mob: US when you get out!! 🍾 🍰

I hope it's a bigger cake than that!

Sophie Mob: seriously though. cannot wait. not the same out here without you. 💔

It was stupid, I suppose, to think that Sophie was going to make me feel better. She almost always does, like she's got a gift for it, but all I'm feeling is sad, until the switch goes and suddenly I'm raging. Because none of this is fair and what's happening is not my fault and now I'm scrolling down to the emojis myself and I'm getting busy.

I send the message and immediately feel guilty, so I quickly shoot a smiley face off, but the damage is done.

Sophie Mob: WTF AI??

I sit back, then remember what I forgot, and now I feel terrible because I never got around to saying 'sorry' like I'd meant to. It was why I texted her in the first place, because I should have said it a long time ago. I look up to the camera in the corner of the room and give everyone a big, smiley wave. I've got no idea who's watching, or if they'll appreciate just how *hilarious* I'm being, but it doesn't much matter.

I'm not going anywhere until it hits . . .

The damage is done.

FIFTY-THREE

Forever ago, just after Kevin was killed, but before everything got properly dark, I walked into this room and was greeted like some conquering hero or whatever because I'd scored a bit of weed and been rumbled. Today, though, I don't want to sit and make nice with them all. I don't want to pretend everything's fine and listen to them talking at me, but what I want doesn't seem to count for much any more. I'm not given any choice in the matter. As soon as I set foot in the dining room, Lucy jumps up and I'm all but dragged across to sit down and eat with everyone else, just because I did a bunk and got escorted back a few hours later by a constable with acne.

Jesus, they want to know *everything*. What I did and how it felt. They want me to relive every moment of my great adventure.

You'd think I'd tunnelled out of fucking Colditz.

'Did you put up a fight?' Bob asks.

I tell him that there wouldn't have been much point.

'Didn't you even struggle a *bit*?'

Ilias seems outraged, as though I've somehow let the side down. 'You should have given that copper a good hard kick in the nuts,' he says. 'Got a few decent punches in, at least. They wouldn't do anything because this is a hospital, right?'

'*Special* hospital,' Donna says.

'Because *we're* special,' Bob says.

Ilias is nodding. 'Yeah, of course, so what are they going to do?'

'They could take away my Scrabble privileges,' I say.

Tony laughs, *hurr hurr hurr,* and Ilias laughs, eventually. Even Lauren seems to think it's pretty funny and I wish I was in the frame of mind to enjoy the moment a bit more. Or at all.

'George says you were in some café.' Lauren waits, stabbing at chips.

'Is that right?' I don't much like the idea of George saying anything to anyone. 'What else did he say?'

'You were eating toast.' She senses my unease and pounces on it. 'That a big secret, is it? Another one?'

'What other one?' Lucy asks.

I pretend I didn't hear Lauren's last comment and that it's all a bit of banter. 'Did he tell you what I *had* on my toast?'

'Like I give a toss.' Lauren is furious, suddenly. 'Dogshit?'

You ask me, there's been a bit too much *telling people things* in this place and I should know, because back when I was still trying to solve the first murder, I was the one doing most of it. Now, though, every conversation makes me tense and jumpy. The ones I'm part of, or the ones I overhear, and most especially the ones I'm not around for but know damn well are happening. The whispers and the knowing remarks and the double meanings. *Why did you run?*, Marcus asked. Now I'm asking myself, why I didn't *keep* running. If I had my way, everyone here would be made to shut up right now. Let them pop their pills and do their puzzles and scoff their burgers and chips with their traps firmly shut.

Same as Shaun.

Shaun. Even though he's got more reasons than most to want Debbie dead, he's actually the only one I really trust. Yeah, I considered him as a suspect, but only for like ... five seconds. Shaun wouldn't hurt a fly.

Lucy says something, but I don't take it in. I'm watching Colin, the Informal, who's sitting on an adjacent table with Clare. I'm wondering what the two of them have suddenly found to talk about.

'Al?'

I'm just a link in the chain of it. This ... watching. I'm watching them while Mia sits at a different table and watches me and we're all being watched by the camera in the corner. Up to now it's not something I've really thought about too much, but suddenly I understand what poor old Graham used to get so worked up about. Why he chucked mash at the cameras and banged his head against the wall.

I suppose there's a difference because I'm only really worried about one person, while Graham didn't like *anyone* watching. Trouble is, that one person could *be* anyone.

'Alice ... ?'

I look at Lucy, who stares at me and says, 'You're miles away, babe.'

'She's remembering the sweet taste of freedom,' Tony says.

'It tastes like toast, apparently,' Lauren says.

338

Bob punches the air and shouts, 'Freedom!' like he's Mel Gibson in *Braveheart*. Donna and Lucy do the same and Lauren starts singing that old George Michael song.

Not freedom, I think. *Safety*. Then it strikes me that, much as a certain person must be chuffed to bits that I've come back – my *anyone*, my *Thing* – they're probably loving the fact that I ran away in the first place. I remember what it felt like in my room the night before. As much as anything, I'm sure that whoever killed Debbie and now wants to kill me is getting off on the fact that I was scared enough to try and escape.

So, I might be back here again, exactly where they want me, but I'll be fucked if I'm going to show them I'm afraid.

'It was good, actually,' I say. 'Getting out for a bit.'

'How was it good?' Donna asks.

She seems desperate to know and I think it's bonkers how quickly people in here have become institutionalized. Most of them are on a 28-day section, which means less time on the ward than me, but they talk like they're lifers. As if going to a café or having a job or even walking about outside in proper clothes is something they can only ever dream about.

'Yeah, *do* tell,' Lauren says.

Then I remember that, for some of them, this is their umpteenth time in this place or another one like it. That they've probably spent more time in those faded pale-blue pyjamas than they have in their own.

Lifers . . .

'Well, just spending a bit of time with normal people.' I nod towards Ilias. 'You know, talking to someone and not thinking they might suddenly take their trousers off.'

Ilias grins and salutes.

'Or just talking to someone who's actually standing still.' Donna blushes.

'Someone who isn't singing all the time or talking about all the women they've shagged.' I look across to the other table. 'Someone who doesn't burst into tears if you say the wrong word and someone who can finish a jigsaw when there's another human being within a hundred bloody yards of him.' I show them all a smile. 'You know, *normal* people.'

Lucy grins and lifts her paper cup like she's toasting us all.

I touch my own cup to hers. 'Don't get me wrong though, I missed you all like mad.'

There are the predictable jeers and groans. Ilias says, 'Balls' and Lauren lobs a chip at me.

'Right, it's ridiculous I know, but I actually did. Look, I would have come back anyway ... I was happy to come back. Happier than I was before I came here, anyway. I know being stuck in this place was never on anyone's to-do list or anything, but it's not that bad, is it?'

'It's awful,' Bob says. 'If you don't think it's awful you probably deserve to be here.'

'OK, sometimes it is ... but the best thing about Fleet Ward is, nine times out of ten, there's something happening. Yeah, it's seriously weird a lot of the time, but you've got to admit, there's always stuff going on. Stuff to look at and talk about and get involved in.' I nod towards the windows. 'We all think everyone out there is living it up, having the time of their lives, but the truth is, most of the time it's pretty dull.' *What use is bleedin' rails, anyway?* 'Well, not in here, it isn't. One thing this place isn't *ever* ... is boring.'

'I'm bored right now,' Lauren says. 'Listening to this.'

'I'm just saying, that's why I'm OK with coming back.

Because there's going to be things happening.' I look at everyone around the table, then up to give that camera lens a good hard stare. 'And whatever happens, I'm ready for it.' I sit back. 'OK, speech over . . .'

Tony smiles at me and winks while Lucy and Donna nod enthusiastically. Ilias actually claps and I want to kiss him for it.

The legs on Lauren's chair scream against the floor as she pushes it back and stands up. 'Right, that's enough shits and giggles for one day. I'm going to get a few pills down my neck, then it's *Pointless Celebrities*, *Casualty* and *Mrs Brown's Boys*.'

Lauren's announcement of the evening's scheduled viewing, as carefully selected by Lauren, is like a starting gun going off. *If* it was a race that involved standing up and sitting down again, pissing about in the doorway and, in Ilias's case, polishing off everyone's leftovers.

I wander out into the corridor.

Marcus and George are talking outside the nurses' station. Marcus catches my eye and nods.

I smile at him and take my place in the queue for meds.

Once I've swallowed the three different lots of capsules and tablets, I stand around trying to decide what to do and where to go. I'm glad I said my piece back in there. I feel stronger, *readier*, but it certainly doesn't mean I want to spend the evening bunched up with everyone in front of the box.

I can sense someone standing close behind me and I presume it's Mia, taking her WEO duties a bit too seriously. When I feel a hand clutching at mine I turn round and discover it's Shaun.

'All good, mate?'

He starts to pull me towards the TV room.

I say *no* and tell him I'm not up to it, that I'm ready to turn in.

He grunts and keeps on pulling.

Shaun clearly wants company, so in the end I stop fighting him and follow the herd. I'm remembering the safety in numbers thing and asking myself what's the worst that can happen. Then I remember that *Mrs Brown's Boys* is on, and decide that's probably it.

FIFTY-FOUR

I don't recognise any of the celebrities on *Pointless Celebrities*, but to be fair, I'm not paying too much attention to what's happening onscreen. I'm watching the watchers. Tony's gone to bed, but the rest of them are settled in good and proper.

Clare and Colin are still sitting together, just behind Lauren who's in pole position as usual, remote in hand. Donna and Lucy are next to one another, with Bob sunk into an orange beanbag I've never seen before on one side of them, and Ilias sprawled in an armchair on the other. Mia and Femi are keeping an eye on things from opposite corners of the room.

I'm up at the back with Shaun, our chairs so close that you'd struggle to slip a fag-paper between us.

He's still holding my hand.

Twice I've asked him if everything's all right, twice he's nodded and twice I haven't believed him.

There's nothing much to report until Jigsaw Man – who's

clearly never been in the TV room before – speaks up and asks if there's any chance Lauren could change channels. 'Because *Through the Keyhole*'s on in a minute.'

'There's no fucking chance,' Lauren says.

Mia says, 'Come on now, Lauren.'

Lauren turns round and looks at Colin, making it clear that if he pipes up again, she'll stick one of his jigsaws where the sun doesn't shine, piece by piece.

I look at Shaun. 'Why is she always such a bitch?'

Shaun has moved on from the screwed-up scraps of paper routine. These days, he carries a pen and a block of Post-it notes around. Puts what he has to say on paper, then tears off the note and passes it across. Now, he lets go of my hand and does exactly that.

i know why she sings all the time.

'OK,' I say.

do you want to know why?

There doesn't seem much point telling him I don't really care, because he's already writing again. This time, it's several Post-its' worth, so I turn back to the TV until he's finished. On *Casualty*, someone has fallen off a ladder. Shaun taps me on the arm and passes me the torn-off notes one by one.

her dad killed her mum when she was a teenager. not sure how . . . (more)

I look at Shaun, then I look at Lauren, then I read the next note.

> she's been in and out of hospital ever since. she reckons there's a voice singing in her head all the time. sometimes she sings to drown out the singing in her head ... (more)
> sometimes she sings along with it if it's a song she knows. now it's just her thing.
> i think her <u>mum</u> was some kind of singer. in pubs or whatever.

I stare at the back of Lauren's head for a minute or so. I screw up the Post-its and put them in my pocket. 'She's still a bitch, though.'

Shaun shrugs.

'To *you*, especially. Remember that time in here, when she was screaming at you? Just before Debbie came in and ...' I stop because I can see that he's starting to get agitated. It was stupid of me to mention it, but before I can say sorry, Shaun's scribbling again.

> did you like the note i gave you on wednesday?

I'm not sure which note he means, then I see him put a hand over his heart and mouth *thank you*. The message he'd passed to me in the music room, after Lauren had as good as accused me of stabbing Debbie to death.

'It was nice.' I lean so close that my lips brush his ear as I'm whispering into it. 'I know what you think I did ... what lots of people seem to think I did ... but you're wrong.'

He leans away and stares at me like I'm talking nonsense, then starts writing again.

serious??

'Serious.'

Shaun thinks about this for a while. Now the man who fell off the ladder has had some kind of heart attack. Bob is asleep on his beanbag and Clare and Colin are talking quietly.

Shaun passes me another note.

i'm glad she's dead anyway.

I nod and squeeze his arm. It's understandable, I think, as Shaun continues to write. Considering that she'd turned the man Shaun loved into a drug smuggler, then suffocated him when he didn't want to play along any more. If I was Shaun, I wouldn't just be glad, I'd be *delighted*.

doesn't matter <u>who</u> killed her.
 doesn't matter <u>why</u>.
 she was <u>horrible</u>.

I stare down at the pink square of paper and something about what's written starts to nag at me. It's ... the middle bit. Not knowing *who* is fair enough, but how can Shaun not at least have a basic understanding of *why* Debbie McClure was murdered? He knows that she was passing drugs to Kevin to sell. He knows that she killed him.

I point at that underlined *why* and start to ask Shaun what he means, but he shushes me and shakes his head. He's

346

agitated again. He's poised to write something else, but he seems uncertain. No, he's *scared*, just like he was that night in this same room, right before the am-I-going-to-die business kicked in and he stopped talking.

I watch him write something, then cross it out. He tears off the note and screws it up. He glances at me, then at others in the room – I can't be sure who – then starts again.

He finally tears off the note and passes it to me, low down, like he really doesn't want anyone else to see. It's an odd feeling, being frightened for someone else suddenly, but the look on Shaun's face makes me think that whatever the note says, writing it might be the bravest or the stupidest thing he's ever done.

there's something i need to tell you.

I start to say that we should probably go somewhere else to talk, but then my phone rings, and when I see who's calling I say, 'Later' and stand up fast because I need to answer it. Shaun looks bereft as he watches me leave with the phone still ringing. I'm aware of some sarcastic tutting and catch the look of naked hatred from Lauren at having her peaceful enjoyment of Saturday night TV so rudely interrupted.

It's still ringing as I try to find somewhere quiet to take the call. Or at least somewhere I can't be overheard. I settle for the chair next to the airlock.

'Hey, Banksy . . .'

'I'll have to be quick,' he says. 'I've only got a minute.'

He sounds very serious. 'OK . . .'

'I've just found out. They're going to make an arrest in the morning.'

It's a few seconds before I can say anything or even breathe again. 'Who is? Which—'

'It's only the one team now. An arrest in connection with the McClure murder.'

I stare through the airlock towards the lift. The doors open and I watch a young couple step out and move towards the door of the ward opposite mine. They look nervous. 'Do you know who it is?'

'That's literally all I've heard. The forensic results are in and everything's apparently lined up, so they'll be coming to the hospital first thing tomorrow.'

'Right . . .'

'Just thought you'd want to know. Listen, I've really got to—'

'No worries. Listen, thanks, Banksy . . .' I wait, but he's gone.

I put my phone away, walk back into the main corridor and turn towards my room. This is exactly what I've wanted since the moment Debbie came screaming out of Kevin's room. Since I started coming back to life and feeling like a copper again. This is validation, isn't it?

So I wonder why I barely register that George is talking to me as I pass him, why my heart is dancing so hard that I can see my T-shirt move against my chest and why it feels like I might be sick.

What have I got to be frightened about now?

I open my bedroom door thinking that I don't want to know the answer, but by the time I've locked it behind me, I know full well that I don't have a lot of choice.

FIFTY-FIVE

I haven't slept. I know I haven't. How could I?

It doesn't matter though, because there's still blood.

The bedroom light is on because I didn't want to lie here in the dark and it's about as quiet as it ever gets in here. Just the rise and fall of an indistinct voice which I presume is coming from the nurses' station and the distant hum of those generators I ran past yesterday.

It's almost three in the morning and I've been awake the whole time.

But there's still blood.

'It's not just mine,' Johnno says. 'You know that already though, right?'

I nod. To Johnno, to myself, to the mirror on the wall that's opposite my bed. 'Not even sure you had that much *in* you.'

'It's *hers*.'

'Well, course it is, why wouldn't it be? I was covered in the stuff. Down on that toilet floor.'

Johnno sighs and says, 'Come on, Al . . .'

'Come on *what*?' He says nothing. 'Listen, if you're just trying to put the wind up me, Phil Johnston, you're doing a bloody good job.'

'Look at the evidence,' he says. 'It's what we *do*.'

I'm shaking, but it's all right, because I don't think he can actually see me. Mind you, I was shaking last time he did see me. Last time he saw anything. 'Come on then, smartarse, help me out.'

'You found the body.'

'Nobody's denying that.'

'Just a fact that's worth bearing in mind,' he says. 'A supporting fact.'

'Supporting *what*? Where's this so-called evidence?'

'*They've* got evidence, Al, and that's all that matters.'

'This is getting on my tits now, Johnno.'

'You had a motive,' he says. 'Several motives actually, if we're really going to get into it. You thought she'd killed Kevin who was a friend of yours and you thought she was going to get away with it. You felt ignored, and I mean, why wouldn't you? You felt like your opinion was worth nothing. That *you* were worth nothing. I'm not saying all this just to be horrible . . .'

Fuck it, I'm crying now. 'I know you're not.'

'Oh, and we shouldn't forget that the camera covering the crime scene had been conveniently disabled.' He smiles. 'You and me have got a history with cameras, haven't we, Al?'

'Graham did that,' I say. 'Graham *always* did that.'

'And talking about forgetting . . .'

'Right.' I'm very cold, suddenly. 'I was wondering when we'd get to this.'

'What did Bakshi say, and Marcus? That these blackouts are all perfectly normal. What did Dr Perera say?'

'I know what they all said, but you're going to tell me anyway.'

'It's understandable,' he says. 'When something like this happens. Just because you're not the victim of a crime or even a witness to it, doesn't mean you wouldn't want to wipe it out. Or that the crime wouldn't wipe *itself* out.'

My head aches and my guts are churning and I just want to see that smile again and hear him tell me that everything's going to be all right. I want to *make* him smile. I screw up my eyes and sniff back the snot. 'Isn't this the point where you produce the gruesome photograph?'

'Some things are just too terrible to remember,' he says.

'I remember *you!*' I think I'm probably shouting now. 'I remember every second of what happened that day.'

'Yeah, but that wasn't your fault, was it, Al?'

'It feels like it was.'

'You don't understand,' he says. 'Back then, *you* hadn't done anything ...'

Johnno's clearly said his piece, because he starts to fade and I know that when he's gone, all I'm going to be left with is his blood. Sloshing around in my head. His blood and hers. I'm crying and shivering and I still can't remember, but whatever's locked up in some part of my brain which I've lost the combination to, there's one thing I've never forgotten.

I lean towards the shadow of him that's still left.

'You were always a better detective than me,' I say.

I don't know long it is – probably just long enough for me to stop being quite so bloody hysterical – before I pick up the phone and dial my parents' number.

'Alice . . . ?'

'Hey, Mum.'

'It's . . .' She's reaching to turn the lamp on and looking at the clock-radio on the bedside table. 'Nearly four o'clock in the morning.'

'I know. Sorry . . .'

I hear my dad mumble something. He'll be heaving himself over in bed about now and asking my mum who's calling, even though at this time of night there really aren't that many candidates. She mouths my name. Now he sits up and mouths something back. Something like *is everything OK?* She shakes her head, *I don't know,* and takes a deep breath.

'So, how are you, love?'

'I'm good,' I say. 'Not sleeping too well, which is why I, you know . . . why it's so late.'

'Only Sophie called us yesterday and she sounded a bit worried.'

'Yeah?'

'Some conversation you'd had with her. I don't know.'

All those knives and coffins and things. 'Oh, she's just being daft,' I say.

'Are you sure?'

'How's Grandma?'

My mum clears her throat. She's probably plumping up the pillow behind her. 'Well, I called her the day before yesterday and she's . . . much the same. She asked how you were doing.'

I doubt that. Last time I saw my grandmother, she hadn't got the foggiest who I was. Probably best, I reckon.

'What did you tell her?'

'I don't remember,' Mum says. 'I think I just said something . . . vague.'

'Well, next time she asks . . .' she won't, '. . . tell her I've been promoted to sergeant, will you? That'll perk her up. Or you could always just rattle out the appendix story, like you did with Jeff and Diane.'

'Yes, sorry, love . . . that just came out.'

'Unlike my appendix.'

'We didn't know what else to say.'

'I'm kidding, Mum . . . it's fine. Just hope they never ask to see the scar.'

My mum laughs. It's a bit nervous, but still, it's not something I've heard for a while. 'We were thinking we might come down again and see you one day next week. Well, *I* was.'

What am I supposed to say? 'You don't have to.'

'I want to.'

'It's fine, honest. I know it's no fun for you.'

'I'm not coming because it's *fun*,' she says. 'I'm coming because that's where . . . you are.'

I don't say anything, because I can't, and I know that Dad is looking at her again, wanting to know what's going on. What I'm talking about. My mum's probably shaking her head at him again or, if she's in the mood, mouthing *shut up, Brian* . . .

'Is there any particular day that's best for you?'

'Not really,' I say.

'What about a time, then? Dad says that when he came in on Wednesday you were a bit . . . I don't know.'

'Yeah, I wasn't at my sharpest. Look, it doesn't make any difference what time you come.' I'm being honest about that much, at least.

353

'Oh, that's good,' she says. 'Well, I'll call beforehand, anyway. See if there's anything particular you want me to bring . . .'

We talk for quite a while after that, twenty minutes, maybe. About if the biscuits my dad brought in last time were the right ones, and the problems he's having with his back, and the day when Jeff and Diane's grandchildren came round for tea.

'I made a Victoria sponge,' she says.

My mum's always had that kind of soft voice. The sort that makes you feel things will get a bit better, even when there's no chance of that happening. I find myself getting sleepy, which is good, because I'll need to be on the ball come the morning.

'Listen, Mum, I'll let you get back to sleep.'

'I'm wide awake now, love. Anyway, you still haven't said why you're ringing at half past stupid?'

That's my mum for you. Always the one to ask the awkward questions.

'I was just ringing for a natter,' I say. 'That's all.'

How can I tell her that I'm calling to say goodbye?

FIFTY-SIX

It's the second day running that I haven't eaten any breakfast, but this time I don't even bother going to the dining
room to not eat, because I want to be ready and I'm guessing
they'll come good and early. It's what I would do. I have a
conversation which I've already forgotten with Femi at the
meds hatch, then another with Donna as I take the bottle of
water and step away to swallow the multicoloured contents
of the paper cup.

The anti-psychotics, the mood-stabilisers and whatever
the new ones are.

Then I wait.

It feels strange around here this morning, though I'm well
aware that could just be me. Projecting, I think it's called.
The members of staff I've run into since I got up definitely
seem a bit tense, though, and I can't help wondering if
they've been pre-warned. It would make perfect sense and
again, it's what me or Banksy or any detective with a bit of

355

nous would have done. So the arrest team have the ward set up just the way they want, before they come steaming in.

Two, possibly three of them.

An extra person in handcuffs with them when they leave.

Marcus is still around. I've never seen him here on a Saturday *and* a Sunday and although I'm guessing they're still short-handed, because it doesn't look like Malaika's back yet, it might just as easily be because he knows what's going to be happening.

I step in front of him when he emerges from the toilet.

'When are they coming?'

'When's *who* coming?'

It seems convincing, so I decide to give him the benefit of the doubt, and, of course, there's one very good reason why the members of staff might not know anything about it. Why the last thing the police would do is pre-warn them. Because perhaps the person they're coming here to arrest is a member of staff.

Fuck's sake, Al. Keep it together . . .

My voice or Johnno's. It's hard to be sure any more.

It's only fifteen minutes since I took them, but it looks like the drugs are muddying up my thinking already, because I know exactly who the police are coming for.

I take up my position on a chair at the airlock and I'm relieved to see that Tony hasn't decided on an early-morning vigil today. I really don't need any company. I look out through the two doors towards the lift, same as I did yesterday when I was here talking to Banksy, and I think about the couple I saw on their way to the ward opposite this one.

A journey they did *not* want to make.

They were late thirties, tops, so who were they going to

see? It might have been a sibling or maybe a parent, but they looked so bloody nervous that I can't help but imagine they were visiting their own child. A teenager, if I'm right. Even if I don't always behave like an adult, does the fact that I'm so much older make things any easier for my mum and dad? It doesn't take long before I decide it's probably the exact opposite. That teenager might recover, with his whole life still ahead of him, while *my* best years – such as they were – are only visible in a rear-view mirror.

I stare at those lift doors and wait for them to open.

How the hell are my mum and dad going to cope with . . . *this*?

They will, of course, because back when I was having those good years, I saw it too many times to count. Parents standing by their children, no matter what. Bravely, stupidly. I was always kind of . . . impressed, even if I couldn't quite understand it. Some of the things their kids had done that they were happy to overlook. You *can't* understand it, that's what Johnno said, not until you're a parent yourself.

This was back when he was all set to become one . . .

I'm guessing that particular ship has sailed for me now, but there *was* a drunken evening when Andy and I talked about what it might be like and, for about five minutes, I even thought about doing it in here, if you can believe that. Maybe asking one of the ward's many eligible gentlemen to do me a favour, donation-wise, then borrowing a turkey-baster from the kitchen. I think I was well off my tits at the time—

The lift doors open and out they come.

Three of them, I was right. Two uniforms – a man and a woman – and a second bloke I'm guessing is the DI. Fifty-something, with a brown leather jacket over his shirt and tie like he's ten years younger and fitter. As they walk towards the door, I watch him put on a lanyard that's definitely not rainbow-coloured, turn his ID card the right way round and exchange a few words with his colleagues.

Words of caution, probably. A request for those less experienced than him to stay calm, no matter what they might have to deal with.

Bear in mind what this place is . . .

I stand up when the detective rings the bell and our eyes meet through the glass, but then Marcus appears, moving quickly towards the airlock with his keys at the ready. Yeah, he definitely knew to expect visitors.

He asks me if I'd mind moving away from the door a little.

So, I do, but not far.

Once the doors are locked again and the officers are inside, there are handshakes and mumbled introductions. Marcus holds out an arm as if to guide them to a pre-arranged room, which is when I step forward.

'Alice, please—'

I ignore Marcus and step close to the man in the leather jacket. 'Can I have a quick word?'

'That's a bit tricky at the moment,' he says.

He takes half a step past me and I go with him. 'I'm ex-Job,' I say.

Marcus is ready to intervene, but the DI stops and looks at me. 'OK. I know who you are.'

Of course he does.

'It won't take long,' I say. 'It's important.'

The detective nods at his uniformed colleagues to let them know I'm not dangerous – at least not right this minute – then at Marcus. He says, 'It's fine,' and while the two uniforms stay by the door, me and the detective follow Marcus towards the MDR.

It feels like a long walk, suddenly.

Donna is already on the march and stares as she passes. Clare and Colin stand together and watch from the dining room doorway. Bob is gawping outside the nurses' station and, from wherever he's lurking, Ilias gleefully shouts, 'Someone's in trouble.'

For once, he's spot on.

Marcus shows the detective into the MDR, allows me to follow, then before he steps out and closes the door, gives me a look that would normally shit me up for the rest of the day. A warning look, that tells me he's got my number and that I should really think carefully before I do something stupid.

Right now, though, I don't even blink.

The desk is in position, so I'm thinking there must have been a tribunal in here recently, or maybe there's one arranged for later in the day. I stand and watch the DI walk behind the desk, take off his leather jacket and toss it across the chair. He sits down and invites me to do the same.

'I think you spoke to my . . . partner,' he says. 'Dr Perera?'

'Right.' So he's the one. I look at him and I think, yeah, *definitely* punching above his weight.

He introduces himself, but like a few times recently, the name doesn't stick. It's simple enough, but it's . . . gone as soon as it's arrived. It doesn't matter, because I know that by the time this is all over, it'll be a name I'll probably never be able to forget.

'What can I do for you?' he asks.

'Well, I know why you're here,' I say. 'I know how these things work, so I thought I'd save you some time.'

'That's always good.' He waits.

So, here we are, then ... and suddenly all those things that once mattered so much seem very far away and utterly unimportant. Like minor bits of mischief and silliness. Masks and the scars on my arm and the clunk of a wine bottle against a skull.

Oh, just bloody say *it, Al* ...

My voice or Johnno's. It really doesn't matter. There's no accent, otherwise it could just as easily be a woman bleeding out on a toilet floor.

'My name's Alice Armitage,' I say. 'And I murdered Debbie McClure.'

FIFTY-SEVEN

The detective says nothing.

I stare at him. It's not a hard face, but it looks . . . lived in. There's a thin, straight scar running across the bottom of his chin which, for some reason, makes me trust him a bit more than I might otherwise, and his hair is greyer on one side than the other. I can sense that he's definitely not stupid and, unlike his girlfriend, I'm guessing he's rather more interested in facts than feelings.

When it comes to what he makes of my confession, though, I can't read him at all.

Is he waiting for me to carry on? Surely it's his turn.

I can hear muffled voices whispering outside, then Marcus very much *not* whispering as he tells whoever's eavesdropping to move away from the door. Ilias and Lucy is my guess. I wonder what the two uniforms are doing. If they're clever they'll be drinking tea in the nurses' station or, if they're not, they'll be learning a few lessons I never got taught at the training college just a mile up the road. I almost feel sorry for them, backed into a corner somewhere by a small but well-practised mob, to be mercilessly eyed up, sworn at, sung to . . .

'Why are you telling me that?' the detective asks, eventually.

I'm a bit thrown by the question, you want to know the truth. I've sat where he is now – not the MDR, but you get the idea – and listened to a fair few suspects spill their guts over the years, and *why are you telling me that?* was certainly never *my* first thought. I was always too busy thinking of the work me and everyone else on the team had been saved. My modest shrug at the heartfelt congrats from senior officers, even if the confession was freely offered and I just happened to be the lucky cow in the interview room at the time. The smiles in the office and the pats on the back and all the lovely drinks I wouldn't have to pay for that night.

I'm confused, because I've slapped it on a plate for him, but maybe he's just one of those awkward bastards. Every team's got one.

'Sorry . . . what do you mean, *why?*'

He sighs, like he's just figured out this might take a bit longer than the few minutes I'd promised. 'OK, a different question, then. How about starting with why you murdered Miss McClure?'

This isn't how it's supposed to go. I'm damn sure he knows all of this, but I get it because these days the job is all about ducks in a row, making everything watertight before you take your case to the CPS. A pain in the arse, but you know . . . fine.

So I tell him all those things that his girlfriend had gently suggested as we sat in the sunshine just three days before. Things she would subsequently have passed on to him and that I'd heard from others several times since.

I didn't want Debbie to get away with killing Kevin.

I wanted to see some kind of justice done.

I couldn't stand feeling ignored.

I feel a few warning stabs of panic as I'm running through my motives for murder *again*, so I tell him not to worry if I have to stop for a bit and do some funny breathing. He tells me it's fine and to take as long as I need, but in the end I just about keep it together. Actually, considering where we are and what I'm telling him, I'm amazed that I'm managing to stay as relatively calm as I am about all this. As matter-of-fact.

I suppose because that's what it is.

When I'm done, he asks if I'm all right to carry on.

I tell him that I am.

'So ... can you take me through exactly what happened last Sunday? I presume you followed Miss McClure into the toilets ... or maybe you were in there waiting for her, I don't know. Tell me what happened once the pair of you were in there together.' He sits back and folds his arms. 'Tell me about killing her.'

For the half a minute or so it takes me to say anything, I'm hoping for some kind of medical miracle, perfectly on cue. For the fog to lift suddenly, like it would if this was a TV thriller, *CSI* or some shit. Obviously, it doesn't.

'I'm not sure I can tell you *exactly*,' I say.

'Well, maybe not every detail then, but ... did you come at the victim from behind?'

He waits and I say nothing.

'Did you stab her in the neck first or in the stomach?'

He waits and I say nothing.

'Did you carry on stabbing her once she was on the floor?'

'I can't *remember*.' I hadn't wanted to raise my voice, but it happens anyway. 'Fair enough?'

He nods, like this is exactly what he was suspecting and isn't he just the best detective in the fucking world, but it's ridiculous, because this is surely something else his girlfriend would have told him. Work-related pillow-talk, whatever. Because I was a suspect ... the *obvious* suspect ... Perera would definitely have been in regular touch with Bakshi and Bakshi would have told her all about the memory blips, the PTSD, all of it.

'I've been having these blackouts,' I say. 'You can check because it's all in my notes and it's all perfectly normal. I can't remember exactly *how* I did what I did ... it's like I just woke up suddenly and I was in there and she was on the floor with blood everywhere. But I know I did it, isn't that enough? I *must* have done it, any idiot can see that. *I* discovered the body, *I* knew what she'd done, *I* had a motive.' I'm tired, suddenly. 'I'm not sure how much more you need.'

I don't know what the hell's happening now, because when he looks at me he's calm, like he doesn't need anything.

'Everything you've said may be true,' he says. 'But it doesn't change one very important fact.' He sits forward slowly and rubs a finger along that scar on his chin. 'You didn't kill anyone, Miss Armitage.'

The look on my face is definitely not one I've practised. Christ knows *what* it is, but I see him clock it and suddenly it's like he's my best mate.

'Alice—'

'I don't understand.'

'Bearing in mind everything you've told me, I can see why you might—'

'Why are you *here*?'

He sits forward. 'Nobody's disputing that you discovered the body, and because of that, you already know that we were able to recover a knife from the crime scene. Under one of the sinks, just like you said it was. The post-mortem confirmed that this was the murder weapon and forensic tests carried out on the knife since then have provided us with all the fingerprint and DNA evidence we could have asked for.' He waits, to be sure I'm taking it all in. '*That's* why I'm here. Because we have solid evidence pointing us towards an individual on this ward.' Now, he actually smiles. 'It's not *you* though, Alice. OK? It's not you.'

Once the shock has worn off a little, he can obviously see the question on my face, and if he hesitates, it's not for long. I'm probably looking a bit desperate and pathetic by this point, like a dog that doesn't know why it's spent the last week being kicked.

So he does me the favour I'm asking, copper to copper. He tells me who he's come to arrest for the murder of Debbie McClure.

'No way.'

He nods. 'It's their prints on that knife and their DNA. Goes without saying I'd like you to keep this information to yourself . . . for the next twenty minutes or so, at least.'

'Why the hell would they want to kill Debbie?'

'That I can't tell you,' he says. 'Because I haven't got the first idea. I intend to find out though, obviously.'

I'm too stunned to say anything else. Sort of . . . looking down at myself while I'm trying to process what he's told me.

It's not until I see him reaching round for the box of tissues on the shelf behind him that I even realise I'm crying.

'Something else you were wrong about.' He slides the box across the desk. 'Debbie McClure wasn't the one passing drugs to Kevin Connolly, and she wasn't the one who killed him.'

'*What?*'

'They got prints off a few of the bottles that were found in his room. We brought someone in for questioning and arrested them for murder yesterday afternoon. Thought you should probably know.'

I stare at him, struggling to think straight. To think at all.

He stands up and pulls on his jacket. He comes round the table and stands over me, a little awkward. 'Maybe you should give yourself five minutes before you go back out there.'

I can't do much other than nod and blub.

The detective moves towards the door, then stops. He says, 'You've got nothing to feel bad about, you know. You shouldn't blame yourself. I mean, I say that, but you probably will. Because that's what the likes of you and me do, isn't it?'

FIFTY-EIGHT

Obviously I was joking before and I don't really think Marcus and his team ever whack up the dosages to make their lives a bit easier, but you certainly couldn't blame them today. I mean, if ever there was a time that might have called for some creative medication . . .

Everyone does seem strangely subdued, though, and you don't usually get that with all the patients at the same time.

All the patients and all the staff.

Nothing's been arranged, there were no announcements or whatever, but while the arrest is being made the rest of us find ourselves hanging about like statues in the TV room. For once, the telly's just a big dusty box in the corner and nobody seems to care very much. Nobody seems to know what to do or say or why we're here at all.

It's like everyone's just . . . gathered. Cows in a field.

I'm happy enough to sit there and enjoy the stillness and the quiet, and it's lovely to be ignored even if it's only for a few minutes. To vanish. True to form, none of it lasts very long and it's obvious that most of the people I'd stupidly thought were quietly contemplating the morning's events were actually gagging to sound off about them.

As soon as the first one pipes up, the dam well and truly bursts.

'You ask me, it was always on the cards.'

'Yeah, course it was. There was always something very iffy about that one.'

'Not just iffy. *Dangerous* . . .'

'Dangerous, right. I always knew that.'

'No, you did not,' I say. 'None of you knew anything.' Heads turn and, just like that, I'm not invisible any more, but that's all right because I no longer want to be.

It's what always happens, isn't it? As soon as a killer is discovered, they come pouring out of the woodwork: the ordinary gobshites who waste no time in letting everyone know – especially the papers who are usually paying for it – that they always knew there was something 'off' about their neighbour or workmate or acquaintance. I've never been able to abide that sort of cobblers, especially when I was one of those whose job it was to catch the killers in the first place.

To pick up the pieces afterwards.

'If any of you really knew anything, why didn't you tell the people who might have been able to do something about it?' Suddenly, they're all a bit less keen to share their opinions. 'Don't you think that might have been helpful? I mean, if you had, then maybe Debbie might still be alive. If you actually *knew* and you've kept quiet about it until now, then some people might say you're partly to blame for her being killed.'

Now there's some nodding, a few grunts of agreement.

It's nice.

'Yeah, that's fair enough, I suppose.'

'Sorry, Al. Yeah, sounds a bit stupid when you put it like that.'

'Right. I mean, you're the one who understands all this stuff, being a copper and everything . . .'

There are more nods and a couple of them ask me what I think will happen now. I tell them that no two cases are ever the same, then talk them through the basic stages of the process, from arrest to prosecution. I talk and it's the best I've felt in a while, because everyone in that room is hanging on every bloody word . . .

It would be lovely if that was what had *actually* happened after I'd made my big speech about responsibility. It would have been the high point of a very strange day, but life isn't like that, is it? Not on Fleet Ward, anyway.

Instead, there's some cat-calling and a stifled giggle. One of them asks me who the fuck I think I am and someone else tells me to piss off.

They don't even know about who killed Kevin yet – well, the patients certainly don't – and I'm sure that when they do, when they find out how wrong I was, I'll be in for some serious stick.

I can live with that.

I've grown used to being doubted and threatened and scared.

Being laughed at feels like nothing any more.

I'm aware of movement in the corridor outside and someone stands up to announce that the police are leaving. That's the cue for the rest of us to jump to our feet and crowd into the doorway. Nobody says anything, but we crane our heads, elbow and jostle to get a better view.

I briefly catch the detective's eye as he and the uniforms guide their suspect, none too gently, towards the airlock.

We stand and watch as Lauren is led away in handcuffs.

PART THREE

HEADS OR TAILS

FIFTY-NINE

Ilias just called to say Lucy's going to meet us in the pub and he'll be round to pick me up in ten minutes. I told him that was fine. The truth is, though, I'm actually in a bit of a state, because I don't want to keep him waiting, but I'm not ready and I still can't decide which top to wear.

I stand in front of the mirror and hold the two tops I'm trying to choose between up against myself.

Black or red, black or red, black or red?

Why is this so difficult?

I might just toss a coin, like I do a lot these days. I use a heads-or-tails app on my phone and actually it's been working out pretty well. Not just for stupid stuff like which outfit to put on, but for all the important decisions, too. I'm still not finding it very easy to trust my own judgement, but I reckon that's understandable, all things considered.

Just a question of time, really.

I've been out of hospital a couple of months now and I'm

doing all right. To start with, I was transferred to a halfway house type place for a couple of weeks which wasn't brilliant, but then the council came up trumps and found this place. It was here or going back to Huddersfield and even though Mum and Dad said they'd be happy to have me home, I wasn't sure they really meant it. Plus, you know . . . *Huddersfield.* This place is handy, because it's just across the bridge from Brent Cross, on the top floor of a house that's been converted into flats. I've got a decent-sized room and access to a small garden. I can't say I've exactly bonded with the other tenants but that's probably no bad thing. The bloke on the ground floor with one ear and a scary dog is definitely dealing crack. For some reason his cooker's out in the hall, so sometimes I come back late and find him frying sausages just inside the front door. There's a woman below me with a baby and I'm not sure which of them wails the loudest, and there's some other bloke I've never seen, but I smell him on the stairs sometimes and I can hear him swearing in the middle of the night.

I think it's best if I keep myself to myself.

That's not to say I don't have a social life, because I get out and about as much as I can. There's no Wi-Fi here, so I walk over the bridge to the shopping centre every day. I sit in Costa for a couple of hours, have a coffee or a sandwich and get online. I try to keep in touch with people. Banksy seems to have gone AWOL, but I talk to Sophie and one or two others.

And I see a fair bit of Ilias and Lucy. They both got out of hospital before me, but we talked on the phone, and as soon as my section was done and dusted and I was finally out of there myself, we started meeting up. If we go out, Lucy tends to pay for most of the meals and drinks, but I think that's fair enough. Even though her parents live in a house that's probably got a gift shop she still gets benefits, if you can believe that, so she can afford to put her hand in her pocket. Lucy's still ... Lucy, but I don't think she's back on the smack and she actually high-fived me the other day, so she's way better than she was.

Me and Ilias have actually become dead close. We talk all the time and he's got some fantastic stories and even though he's still not great with ... *boundaries*, I'm not expecting him to whip his cock out at any moment. Like, he told me all about his older brother teaching him to drive and about this horrible car crash just after Ilias had passed his test. He told me how he walked away without a scratch, while his brother's been in a wheelchair ever since. He told me that his brother was the good-looking one and the clever one and, as it turned out, the unlucky one. It was his brother who'd taught Ilias to play chess, too, and he's actually really good.

Well, he thrashes *me* every time we play, but I'm slowly getting better.

Most of the time, when we're together, we end up talking about what happened on the ward. Why wouldn't we? I don't think we'll be sending Christmas cards or anything, but we gossip about what the others are doing and about all the stupid things that happened and we usually end up laughing.

As to what *did* happen on the ward, it would be fair to say I wasn't surprised that Lauren never got charged, or when she came marching back into the TV room on her first night back, every bit as chopsy as always. More so, after being held in a cell for a couple of days. I wasn't surprised when Ilias

375

started pointing and chanting *you're not singing any more* and Lauren slapped him hard enough to knock him off his chair.

If you want to know what I think, the detective's heart had never really been in it. I'd seen it, that moment when I caught his eye as they were leaving with their prime suspect. Of course, he had to arrest Lauren because of the DNA and the prints on the knife. He had evidence. The only problem was the evidence he *should* have had but *didn't*.

Rusty as I was, even I'd worked that much out.

Why hadn't Lauren been covered in blood? I'd seen how much of it there was, I'd seen the stab wounds, so I knew, same as the detective knew, that by rights she'd have been covered in it. They'd taken everyone's clothing away for forensic testing and they hadn't found so much as a drop of Debbie's blood on Lauren's precious T-shirt.

Now, it seems obvious why the detective wasn't particularly worried. He was simply going through the motions by arresting Lauren, when he probably knew all along that he already had Debbie's killer in custody, because it was the same person who'd murdered Kevin.

Poor old Shaun's still in hospital, and so is Donna and Tony got moved to the ward downstairs. Bob's section got extended, although all anybody's been able to find out is that he made 'inappropriate advances' to one of the nurses. I think it was probably Mia, but Lucy says she heard it was Marcus, so who knows? I'm not sure what happened to Tiny Tears or the Jigsaw Man and I don't much care.

We're all doing OK, though, me and Ilias and Lucy. We talk and we share things and we look after each other. Last time we were out, Ilias raised his pint glass and we toasted.

'To the three mental musketeers . . .'

So, this place isn't a palace and I'm not exactly minted and I've all but given up on ever working with the Met again, but I still think I'm doing pretty well. Most important, my head's together for the first time in a long while. I've worked everything out. I know now that what's important when you're dealing with a bastard like PTSD is that you face it head on.

Then, you can *own* it.

If you don't, you're just playing some part you think makes other people comfortable, and that's when you end up with a mask you can't ever take off.

Whatever that Alzheimer's drug was must have done the trick, because the blackouts stopped happening pretty quickly and all those things I'd forgotten started to come back. Just flashes at first, but then longer and longer stretches until there weren't any holes any more.

Now, I can even remember the song that was going through my head just before walking into that toilet and finding Debbie's body. I remember the blood, the shape of it pooling around her like wings and I remember turning and seeing the knife. I can recall every moment of it with perfect clarity. *Too* perfect, sometimes.

I can remember exactly how I felt, too. The desperate need to do something, that instinct to preserve life kicking in, and then the panic and the horror when I realised that I couldn't. The memory of those few desperate minutes in that toilet has returned, complete and terrible.

Only now, of course, I know there was someone in there with me.

SIXTY

I open up the app, press the button and watch the virtual coin spin.

There's a nice, satisfying *clink* as it lands.

I start to put the black top on . . .

Back in the MDR that day, when the detective told me I'd been wrong about who had killed Kevin, I'd felt like a mistreated dog that had been given one final, hard kick for good measure. Sitting there and sobbing, I remembered being with Shaun in the TV room, the night he collapsed and stopped talking. His eyes shifting and fixing on the nurse who was sitting in the corner and me, like the smartarse I am, thinking I knew what he was trying to let me know.

No, not just *a* nurse, you idiot. *That* nurse . . .

I remembered the same terror on his face when he was writing me those messages, when I didn't give him time to explain the very last one.

There's something i need to tell you.

Now I know what that was and I can finally understand what I'd thought was his confusion about why Debbie had been killed. During the course of my so-called investigation into Debbie's death, I'd asked myself a few times if I was being stupid in never suspecting Shaun. Well, I was and I wasn't. The fact is, though he was not unhappy that a woman he hated was dead, Shaun never had a motive for killing Debbie, because he knew she wasn't the one who'd killed Kevin.

He'd known who that was all along.

Malaika.

Now I can't decide which colour lippy to go with, so I quickly reopen the heads-or-tails app and that decides for me.

Electric Orchid, if you're interested.

As to *why* Malaika killed Debbie, the best guess is because Debbie found out about what she'd done and was threatening to expose her. Poor Debbie, who had been trying to do the right thing, but could not have known just what the person she was dealing with was capable of.

The clearer everything becomes in my mind, the worse I feel every day about what happened to Debbie and guiltier about the things I believed she'd done. Not just Kevin's murder, but the whole . . . sexual abuse thing. I *did* believe it, for a while at any rate, but now it seems obvious that it was all about convincing myself (and Banksy) that I was after the right suspect. Maybe I just resented Debbie being a bit . . . offhand when she examined me that first day. Or it could just be that I got what actually went on mixed up with what Lucy told me had happened to her.

To be fair, I was mixing a lot of things up back then.

I say best guess, by the way, because Malaika still hasn't

379

come clean about a great deal. I only know this because the detective told me a couple of weeks ago, but he didn't tell me too much I hadn't already worked out. The truth is, I put most of it together myself.

I can still do that.

So, here's the thing. You have to walk through *two* doors to get into that toilet. Two doors. There's a pointless little space when you step through the first door before you open another to go into the actual toilet, and those few seconds between the first and second door opening were crucial.

Malaika had stabbed Debbie to death only moments before I went in, and when she heard that outer door opening, it gave her just enough time to duck into one of the cubicles. That's where she was all the time I was on my hands and knees doing CPR and it wasn't until I ran out screaming that she was able to step out of the cubicle and start playing the hero herself. Remember how confused I was about whether it was Marcus or Malaika who'd come in to help first? Well, she'd been in there all the time, and the fact that she'd been covered in blood afterwards, same as me and Marcus, wasn't suspicious because she'd been pumping the dead woman's chest like we had.

Christ, talk about thinking on your feet.

As to whether Debbie's murder was premeditated, they won't really know unless Malaika tells them. When the detective came round, which was nice of him, I was able to help a bit with that, because I remembered Lauren complaining that someone had been going through her room and that was three or four days before Debbie had been killed. The detective told me that was very helpful information, which definitely put a spring in my step. Lauren freely admitted that it was her knife and told the police that before it was stolen it had been hidden in the webbing under her mattress. Just like those DVDs, that day Johnno had been killed. Weird, eh?

There's some suggestion that it might have been Malaika's plan all along to put Lauren in the frame for Debbie's murder, but I'm not sure I buy that. The DNA and prints on the knife alone were never going to be enough to send anyone with a half-decent defence team down. I reckon she just discovered Lauren had a knife, so knew exactly where to get it when the time was right. The detective told me Malaika hadn't said a fat lot, certainly not admitted to anything, but he isn't bothered because they've got enough evidence anyway. The clincher was getting Graham to admit that Malaika had been the one who'd asked him to put the camera out of action that day. Good old Graham. When the case comes to trial, I bet he'll be hanging around by that witness box a good hour before he's due to give evidence.

And when it's my turn?

I swear to tell the truth, the whole truth and nothing but the truth. Well, I'm finally getting my chance, so why wouldn't I?

I jump a little when a handful of grit crackles against my window and, when I stand up to look, I can see Ilias beaming up at me from the pavement. I hold up a finger to say *one minute* and the cheeky bugger holds up a finger that means something entirely different.

I grab my bag, phone, keys . . . check I've got everything.

I hope it's not a stupidly late one, that him and Lucy aren't set on making a big night of it or anything. We've already had several of *them*. Don't get me wrong, I'm bang up for a few drinks and I know we'll have a laugh, same as always, but I don't really fancy being out that long.

These days, I like spending time on my own, too.

I double-lock the door to my flat, then breathe through my mouth as I start down the stairs. I can't hear the woman or the baby or the dog, so a clean getaway looks like it's on the cards.

Ilias has his face pressed against the glass in the front door.

I'm good and ready for a night out, but the truth is I'm already looking forward to getting back. To standing at my bathroom window in the dark and staring out at those milky-white lights, pulsing through the trees at me from the far end of the garden.

EPILOGUE

From: Timothy Banks Banksy1961@hotmail.com

To: Alice Armitage GoAskAlice@btinternet.com

Subject: SORRY

Hey, Al. Sorry it's been so long and that I haven't been to see you in your new place. Sorry I haven't called or returned your messages. I'm sorry if you think I haven't been a good friend, but trust me, I really have. That's what all this is about really and the big SORRY is for what I need to say, what I haven't been brave enough to say until now.

God this is hard to write.

I've been waiting until I was sure that you were doing better and it certainly sounds like you're getting back on track. I couldn't be happier about that, I swear, and I want you to remember that when you get to the end of this. If you're feeling like you never want to see or hear from me again.

The truth is I should never have come to see you in the hospital. I mean, I wanted to see you as a friend, but I shouldn't have helped you. I shouldn't have let myself get involved in it all. I should never have got sucked in.

I need to say straight away that civilian support staff do an important and incredible job for the Met. You did an incredible job and you should be proud of everything you did to help coppers like me. But it's not the same, Al, it's really not and this is the bit I've been most scared about writing, but I just need to say it, nice and simple.

You aren't a police officer. You were never a police officer.

I'm sorry, mate, but there it is. I know that while you were in hospital, a lot of people in there played along with the fantasy. Maybe they didn't know it was a fantasy, I mean you're an adult so why shouldn't they believe what you tell them? Did they ever actually check? The police officers who came to the ward knew the truth, I'm fairly sure of that. The shrink working with them and the DI who made the arrest certainly did, but at any rate nobody ever seemed to contradict you or try to tell you that you were . . . Christ, I don't know how to describe it. I don't really want to say deluded, because that makes it sound like you weren't suffering and I know you were. But it was a delusion and that's all there is to it.

This next bit is difficult, too . . .

It feels like I'm ripping off a sticking plaster or something, but I need to do it.

Johnno was my partner and not yours. My partner, Al. I was the one who went with him to that flat in Mile End and I was the one who watched him bleed to death. I was the one who fucked up.

Yeah, I know Johnno was your friend too, and what happened to him obviously hit you very hard. Every bit as hard as it hit me, harder even, I know that now. I suppose that's when all your problems started, the drink and the drugs, and that's one of the reasons I feel bad telling you all this now, because it could so easily have been me that lost it and ended up the same as you.

Maybe that's why I came to the hospital as often as I did. There but for the grace of God, all that.

I've been talking to the therapist I went to see after what happened to Johnno and she said this was a good idea. Me finally telling you everything, I mean. She told me that it might be painful, but that being honest would be better in the long run. For both of us, she said.

I do feel like I was responsible in some way for what you went through. I should never have told you everything that happened in that flat, because I know now that it's what you came to believe had happened to you. I feel like I planted the idea or something. I know you did believe it, too. I never felt like you were stealing my life, anything like that. I know you couldn't help it, Al. But I also know that I can't carry on pretending it's just this weird thing that happened. We both need to be honest with ourselves.

I said something before about being brave enough to finally send this, but I know I'm actually being a coward because I'm just pressing a button and not sitting down and talking this through with you in person. I just couldn't face that, so I'm sorry again. More sorry.

I don't know if this is the right thing to do medically or whatever, but I've looked this stuff up online and nobody seems to know what the right thing is or when the right time might be. It's the right thing for me though, I know that. There have been far too many lies already and my sanity matters every bit as much as yours.

I really hope you've already started coming out the other side of all this. I hope you're better and getting on with a normal life. You deserve to be happy.

I want the best for you, Al, I promise you that.

Take care, mate.

Banksy x

Detective Sergeant Tim Banks read through the email he'd agonised over long into a great many nights and rewritten so often that he'd forgotten what it had said to begin with. He closed the email and dragged it into the drafts folder. He finished what was left in his wineglass, then opened the email again.

He moved the cursor until it was hovering over the send button.